F·I·R·E
BENEATH·THE·CAULDRON

F·I·R·E

BENEATH·THE·CAULDRON

EDITED BY GEOFF HANCOCK

Thistledown Press

Canadian Cataloguing in Publication Data
Main entry under title:

Fire beneath the cauldron
ISBN 0-920633-77-3

I. Short stories, Canadian (English).* I. Hancock, Geoff, 1946-

PS 8321.F57 1991   C813'.54   C90-097147-9
PR9197.32.F57 1991

Book design by A.M. Forrie
Cover illustration by Jerry Didur; slide photography by Terry Cuddington

Typeset by Thistledown Press Ltd.
Printed and bound in Canada by
Gagné Printing
80, ave St. Martin
Louiseville (Québec)   J5V 1B4

Thistledown Press Ltd.
668 East Place
Saskatoon, Saskatchewan
S7J 2Z5

Acknowledgements:

Thanks to Cheryl Sutherland, Caroline Walker, Paddy O'Rourke, Glen Sorestad and Sue Stewart for their ongoing support in a complex project. I must also thank Gay Allison for her excessive patience and editing skills, and my lovely daughter Meagan for letting me use my word processor from time to time. I must also thank Stephan Islas, Mantak Chia, James Hillman, Robert Bly, Michael Meade, Fedor Zelina, and my men's group for clearing the path to profound and mysterious happenings. Without their love and support, I would not have had the courage, as the alchemical dictum puts it, to dissolve myself in my own water.

This book has been published with the assistance of The Canada Council and the Saskatchewan Arts Board.

"The Celtic Moon Goddess was associated with a magic cauldron which the goddess brewed for a year and a day. At the end of that time, there flew out three drops of the Grace of Inspiration. The goddess, Cerridwen, gives the gifts of poetry, inspiration, and wisdom to her devotees: the ancient Druids' Mistress of Art. The three legs of the cauldron refer to the three phases of the moon, and the three aspects of the Goddess—Maiden, Mother, and Crone. Added to which, as a hollow vessel it is a feminine symbol."

Patricia Crowther,
The Lid Off the Cauldron:
A Wicca Handbook

CONTENTS

INTRODUCTION

Geoff Hancock

Notes Towards an
Understanding of the Canadian Imagination

"The work of the artist meets the psychological needs of the society in which he lives, and therefore means more than his personal fate, whether he is aware of it or not. . ."

Carl Jung, "Psychology and Literature",
The Spirit in Man, Art, and Literature

Some of the finest work in Canadian literature is being done in short fiction form. Short fiction has a place of special importance which is only now beginning to get serious critical acceptance. A new generation of writers present great vitality in their challenge to form and content. A confidence comes through these stories: call it a self-portrait, a cross-section of the Canadian imagination.

The Canadian short fiction is the most contemporary of narrative forms, the most exotic, the most exceptional. Because it is the most exceptional, it is also the most problematic. Short fiction is an unbounded genre, not constrained by the conventions of longer fiction. Fiction has all manner of techniques, of literary devices, of prose styles, of contents.

Fictions in *Fire Beneath the Cauldron* include homes crawling with worms, parodies of famous stories, a woman who becomes a goddess, a barmaid who murdered her husband, a trick played on a man in a maternity class, dreamscapes, and fictions that doubt they can be written. Short fiction is an unwieldy genre.

But in these bizarre images, our human needs are met. These images are a product of inner projection, illuminations from the deepest dark of the human psyche. As Jung puts it in *Psychology and Alchemy*, "[The alchemist] experienced his projection as a property of matter, but what he was in reality experiencing was his own unconscious."

What is clear in these fictions is that the Canadian personality is no longer fixed, solid, sure, righteous. Canadian fiction is alive and open to new development. The rigid aspects of our personality are less static, more dynamic. Fiction's urge for transformation meets our psychological needs.

Short narratives are problematic within the context of contemporary Canadian literature. Most theories of short fiction are narrow and inadequate, though they do provide some sense of orientation. Part of the problem is that stories explore many levels of reality; sometimes directly, sometimes in vague evocations. A "realistic" writer like Alice Munro is seen as mythical and magic in some readings, such as Beverly Rasporich's interpretation of the mythical pagan world of female deities, Earth Mothers, and Alice the author as Mother-Goddess behind the Text in *Dance of the Sexes: Art and Gender in the Work of Alice Munro*.

More complex are the many methods of text-centred criticism. These include rhetorical and syntactical analyses. Literary philosophers argue that narrative is a rhetorical system, whose meaning arises from metaphor, motif and syntax.

Other critics have written extensively on the subject of the text as body and gender-based readings. In the "body as text" argument of Roland Barthes, presented in *The Pleasure of the Text*, there is a sexual definition of writing. The pen is an active extension (penis) of the male writer; the page is blank, virginal, female. The idea of patriarchal space, language and physicality is challenged by women who write short fiction, interlocking story sequences, the story cycle as "novel". Fictions lend themselves to multiple readings, multiple themes and theses.

Then there are the splits in the modes of perceiving reality through narrative. The argument is that the real is physical and the unreal is metaphysical has been contested since Plato. He regarded our familiar reality as the mere shadow of the perfect idea. Hence, the unreal is true and more real. Surrealists and magic realists have demonstrated that the unreal is perfectly logical, and is super-real or sur-real.

The development of the Canadian short fiction is associated with changing images of the Canadian imagination and psyche. A woman can turn into bees, an astronaut can have sex fantasies, and mangled motorcyclists can be dragged under cars in the new Canadian fiction. Jung discovered that images were the water of the psyche which could be used to understand the psyche's contents.

I have long argued the difference between story and fiction. Story and fiction are divergent creations. This 20th century has led to many profound philosophical and historical crises. Readers have a basic human need for a beginning, middle and end in fiction.

The crisis of the 20th century has led to a different understanding of ending. The destructive weaponry of modern warfare has led, some argue, to a regression in our morals. Lacking faith, we miss a sense of our perfection and we are spiritually hungry. Modern physics demonstrates uncertainty. Many critics have considered that the basic human condition is no longer order, but entropy. The leakage of energy. How to make sense of this in fiction?

The writers in this anthology respond to the meaning of life and short fiction in various ways. A story might be written like Glen Sorestad's "One Last Look in the Mirror". The author pays careful attention to narrative voice, so that "Glen Sorestad" is invisible. The narrating character is psychologically motivated. The story is plotted to uncover its hidden secret. The details are carefully placed. The plot has cause and effect. The woman wants the man's land, so she kills him. There's a security in the telling. The story moves towards a singular ironic perspective.

But a fiction insists on its artifice, as in Brian Fawcett's "The Franz Kafka Memorial Room". It relies on recurrence. We need to know about Kafka, or the title makes no sense at all. A fiction emphasizes that its form is not yet discovered, so the author (who as "Brian Fawcett" is in the story) calls attention to its artifice. A fiction lacks this essential security. "What is *supposed* to happen in a story?" ponders the narrator. A fiction opens up multiple perspectives. What if a story doesn't end? How can a story be constantly re-invented? "Fiction" alters how we read "stories".

Both stories and fictions suggest a view of reality. But what makes short fiction most vital is hidden. In film theory, there's a couple of new ideas I've found interesting. The meaning of a film is how you feel about it. The shots where nothing seems to happen, the master

shots — say, a panorama of Washington, D.C. — contain the most
hidden information, a reinforcement of American might and power,
not the cover shots of two or more characters communicating and
advancing a story line.

Fiction has a basic therapeutic quality: something healing —which
was originally meant to serve the gods — occurs in a good story.
Perhaps, in the deepest images of fiction, we return to the service of
the gods. The gods and spirits we have lost demand re-connection in
a story. Depth psychologist James Hillman titled one of his books
Healing Fictions. Fiction is not only a perspective on life, it is life. A
fiction is a container — a cauldron — for organizing events into
meaningful experience.

Short fiction does not easily lend itself to an historical analysis.
Rooted in the past, in fable, in tales from other lands and in mythol-
ogy, Canadian short fiction has an unclear lineage. Michelle
Gadpaille, in *The Canadian Short Story*, claims the story began in the
19th-century sketch, developed through a period of consolidation in
"realistic" stories, and finally flowered in the 1960s, then moved into
variant directions over the next thirty years.

Anthologist Wayne Grady claims the Canadian story begins in the
telegraph message. And John Metcalf argues persuasively in *What
Is a Canadian Literature?* that the story has no antecedents, except
in its emphasis on style and eloquence. Each writer draws upon
memory of his/her distinctive origins. The story is pulled in a conservative modernist direction or a more radical post-modernist loss
of faith in realism.

Some writers blur the fiction with old contents and new techniques.
Are its roots in the French, Russian or German traditions? Is it part
of the American tradition, fostered by the Iowa Writing School which
in turn inspired several Creative Writing programs in Canada? Or is
Canadian short fiction a mutant, a hybrid of international styles,
regional interest, and writers true to their inner calling? When a story
is rich in the imagery of dream or nightmare, the irrational, the
grotesque, the obscene, the fiction emerges from a place beyond the
rational and reasonable.

Encouraged in part by establishment of writing programs, the small
presses, and the little magazine network, short fiction became

Canada's most distinctive literary genre. Anthologies challenged the idea of canonisation by presenting new groups of writers, new aesthetic or thematic concerns. Books on stories about Mounties, about baseball, about shoes and shit.

The late 20th-century story in Canada challenges the 19th-century scientific and philosophical way of explaining the world. Laws, principles, mapped geographies, explained psychologies, cause and effect, moral dilemma, resolution gave way to fragments, prose poems, parodies, anti-stories, fables, fantasies and metafictions. In these stories are found the basic motifs of psyche.

Short fiction writers challenge or even create our sense of self. Is a self made up of language? Or is a self based on the imagination? Is the self a locus of understanding? The feminist self writes apart from patriarchal structure. Canadian Commonwealth writers and immigrants from many other countries challenge the notion of colonial privilege and change the social face of short fiction.

Leandro Urbina is the displaced Canadian writer. Is his audience to be found in Canada? Or Chile? Yeshim Ternar's story takes place all over the world, emblematic of the wandering refugee. Canada's First Nations peoples, such as Daniel David Moses, have invigorated short fiction with traditional material and highly formal structures.

This anthology has many good stories with recognizable characters, familiar terms. Writers like Sharon Butala, Cynthia Flood, Janice Kulyk Keefer, Glen Sorestad and Carol Shields operate in the realms of realism, lower- and middle-class characters, and social discourse. Other writers approach the avant-garde to challenge our perception of the real, fuse inner and outer space, question the author's role in writing the fiction. Brian Fawcett, Douglas Glover, Bill Gaston, David Arnason, Edna Alford present fiction theory, intertext, fiction about fiction, multilevelled formal structures, elements of parody and metafiction.

Other writers present new scenes, new images in Canadian fiction. Marlene Nourbese Philip documents the psychological trauma in language. The schism between the modern and post-modern is shown in Stephen Guppy's story. Perhaps reality is simply molecules to be rearranged? The power of fiction is its ability to create new forms as does Peter Behrens, capture the prevailing mood of our time as does Cynthia Flood, illuminate human experience with a lightning flash as does Sean Virgo. The challenge to traditional narrative moves beyond naturalism to social, cultural and mythological depths. Dionne Brand in her poetry collection claims: *No language is neutral.*

The best writers in Canada illuminate the hidden sources of their own strength. They give attention to the subconscious within the story, that enormous mythic power. Mary Burns, Dianne Warren, Ernest Hekkanen, Edna Alford, Brian Fawcett and others in this anthology resonate with what I call their alchemical source. The writers of these stories ceased to be themselves at the most intense moments of the writing. Their wisdom is what we once knew, when we were perfect, and forgot. There are the fictions that need to be told. In their dynamics we find our life.

Strip away the layer of event and you'll find an entirely new way to perceive reality. Something in the depths, beyond the rhetoric, tone, sentence structure, rhythm of language. Something that is in the structure of the imagination itself.

Short fiction is a unique, self-contained world. Some 19th-century writers called the short fiction a little laboratory for literary experimentation. I've always liked the small-scale concept, the glimpse into another country. The way a story happens in the images. The way a resolution is an excuse for wisdom.

I like the fast pace of a story. The race against time. Or the fact time is not on the side of the story. It happens in the now. Stops time to make it happen, as my teacher Robert Harlow said. The motorcycle accident is a single stopped event in Lois Braun's "Dream of the Half Man". Time stops around the dolls in Carol Shields's "Dolls, Dolls, Dolls, Dolls". Not the Times demanded of the novel, or the flowing of time demanded of a novella.

The world of the story, and the world within the story, electrically charged. Tense. Time and space in a story are condemned, as Julio Cortázar says, subjected to a spiritual and formal pressure to achieve that wider opening into meaning.

=   =   =

These stories represent the presence of psychic energies attempting to get loose. In this wildness is a necessary terror. Since Aristotle, fiction has been called an imitation of reality. But what, exactly, is the nature of reality? In some mythologies, the basic bio-electrical form is the *kundalini*, the serpent of invisible fire that is the vital energy latent in each of us.

The basic starting point of alchemy is the transformation of the body, soul, and spirit by means of the fire-snake. Is this what happens in fiction, when suddenly, in the body, in the head, in the brain, we feel a luminous fire, which enables us to see through darkness to feel renewed and oddly illuminated?

Morris Berman, in *The Re-enchantment of the World*, notes the sacred activities of alchemy, as both craft and mystery, are related to Genesis and creation: "Metallurgy was intentionally compared to obstetrics: ores were seen to grow in the womb of the earth like embryos. . . In a similar fashion, the alchemical laboratory was seen as an artificial uterus in which ore could complete its gestation in a relatively short time (compared to the activity of the earth)." All metals can become gold, and all men and women are gold *in potentia*. The alchemist is not playing God but, to continue the alchemical metaphor, is a kind of midwife.

A complex statement in Cynthia Flood's "Roses Are Red" alludes to the divine spirit within: "To say virginal of a pregnant woman appears stupid — but I remember it in myself and I have seen it in other women carrying a child for the first time. There is a purity of concentration, a fresh bloom." The bloom is the personification of opposites shining from some place out of time.

These fictions get us back to reality, but it's not quite the same place we started from. If we consider that the Orphic initiates had a vision of the earth itself as a *krater*, the great boiling cauldron of the goddess, then perhaps invisible influences are communicated through the most perceptive of artists, creative writers. *Lumen naturae*, the light of nature, is connected with the goddess Hecate, the light-bringer, who sees all from her cave in the darkness.

=   =   =

In the stories chosen for this collection, I've gone deeper into the depths of the narrative, perhaps to the structure of our human psyche. The invisible connections are stronger than the visible. To find what is subliminal, hidden, and unseen, I've gone down into the darkness of the fiction searching for invariable elements and values. Flickering patterns that are half glimpsed between the lines. A kind of vapour creates a flowing participation between the collective unconscious, alchemical process, the story, and the reader engaged in the fantasy of the moment. Images are the only reality we directly comprehend.

Problems, stereotypes, conflicts, routines: these are the masks of the story. Alchemy is a metaphor that can assist us in understanding the masks. A metaphor is a sign, or group of signs, that names what cannot be named. The images of alchemy, as they appear in these stories, offer a kind of shorthand perception beyond conventional language. We need to go deeper, with intensity, into the depths of these stories to recover the forgotten relationships which the medieval alchemists knew all too well.

Contemporary psychologists consider alchemy an important conjunction of experiences. Dream analysis, for example, is widely used as an imaginal experience between two people, here and now. Robert Bosnak's *A Little Course in Dreams* is based on traditional alchemy. Something dark is the background to consciousness. The imagery that arises out of this dark place is often mysterious, repellent, rotten. The dissolution of elements in the place is the basis of an analysis. The relationship can easily be extended to fiction.

The deepening of experience, the widening of awareness, and the transformation of a personality in a situation is the essence of traditional narrative. As the alchemists knew, the transmutability of elements is the central idea. The elements used in alchemy are considered, at least by Jungians, to be living substances, metaphors for personality. Lead, salt, sulphur, and mercury are seen as archetypal components of the psyche.

In Jungian therapy, an alchemical reaction occurs because the personalities of analyst and patient are combined like chemical elements. The result is a new, third substance, a transformed factor for both analyst and patient.

The transformation is often illustrated by imaginary figures. Alchemical woodcuts show a king and queen, who may symbolize psychological opposites. The soul as a baby or inner child reanimates a dead body. A two-headed king and queen stand on a moon, and

other complex images — sun, moon, virgin, lion, unicorn, blood, eye
of God — indicate the full range of human psychic experience. André
Breton made the connections between alchemy and surrealism in his
Second Manifesto as he continued his exploration of a revolutionary
way of feeling and the subversive essence of Romanticism.

A net of interrelations is alive within these stories; it's not a
communication between readers, but a communication within the
story itself. A story exists on a human level, that interface where life
and its written expression meet across a space of twelve or fifteen
inches. A basic alchemical process, *communitas*, implies three
things: the structure of communion, the structure of a community,
and a kind of physical and psychic substance which is communicated.

Goethe said everything exists in a state of radical interpenetration.
The dark furnace of the cauldron is an active space, full of forces
which can remake us. For the analyst, the cauldron is the enclosure
of the room, and the hour; for the Wiccan, it's the magic circle; for
the lover, the bed; for the painter, the canvas; for the writer, it's the
story which contains the paradoxical combination of physical and
psychic realities. In the cauldron, we rediscover the invisible powers
that created us.

The best stories are more than their storylines, bonded to the very
liquid and unfathomable essence of the human condition. We need
imagination to see again, and with true images we gain
consciousness.

=   =   =

How do we experience the world? We limit and narrow our
experience. Consciousness is an intensity of awareness. We populate
the empty spaces of our knowledge with the imagination of our
memories, the fabrications of our ignorance, projecting our ideal of
the self in fiction. That was also the goal of alchemy and of Jungian
practice.

Carl Jung devoted most of his life to a study of alchemy. He noticed
that many alchemical symbols occurred in the dreams of his patients,
and in mythologies and religions throughout the world. These symbols stemmed from a common source he termed "the collective
unconscious". The archetypes are expressed by means of symbols.
Jung's idea of a "complete self" was one in which all the opposing

forces in human nature, conscious and unconscious, were reconciled.

As Carl Jung proved in his exhaustive and provocative studies, alchemy was a mythopoetic art. In alchemy's bizarre images, Jung maintained, was a precise map of the terrain of consciousness.

Any Canadian community has its New Age centre, its crystal healers, palmists, Tarot card readers, energy massage therapists, fortune tellers, astrologers, empowerment dancers, rebirthers, trance psychics, dream workers and channellers. Alchemy is still real, as Morris Berman calls it, "the last major synthetic iconography of the human unconscious in the west." In the depths of the Canadian short fiction is found the symbolism of alchemical processes which help us to be complete.

The philosophical goal of the alchemists was simple: to create a new man and woman, proud and free, capable of restructuring the world in the service of desire. What was constructed in the alchemist's retort, urn or cauldron, was the homunculus, the perfect person. A fiction.

A full explication of these stories from an archetypal Jungian perspective would take hundreds of pages. Jung's essay "Individual Dream Symbolism in Relation to Alchemy" is a major study of dream images that reproduce alchemical symbols. Edward F. Edinger's *Anatomy of the Psyche: Alchemical Symbolism in Psychotherapy* gave me some pokers to probe the visible alchemical symbols in the stories. Edinger also provided me with a sequence, though in truth no one agrees on the order of the operations or the exact content of them.

An Alchemical Allegory

"In what follows alchemy is the method. A pathology is to be cooked in the imagination until the fluttering fantasies congealed in it bubble and boil and appear on the surface of the retort. . . To the material the hot explosive sulphur of individual fantasy shall be added first. Next comes the dry, briny salt of literature that will prevent the brew from bubbling over by drawing the vapors back down to earth, the bottom of the vessel. The quicksilver of myth will set the vapors rising again to create a *circulatio* as the wildly spinning fantasies begin to move into an orbit around a central theme. More than this cannot be promised since the vessel is no crystal ball. Alchemy is not magic."

James Hillman, *The Puer Papers*

My interest is in the literary, fictive and poetic angle of alchemy. Alchemy is not a hoax nor an antiquated mystic system to turn metal into gold or brew a potion to insure immortality. Alchemy is a philosophy of the world, with the goal of transforming humanity and the world.

Hence, alchemy is condemned by popes, kings, scientists, psychologists and linear scholars who would restrict our desires. Alchemy is a basic principle of Chinese Taoism, surrealism, archetypal Jungian psychology, and witchcraft. Alchemical images, which express the real function of thought, are found in the structure of most Canadian short fictions as the precise "point in the mind" of inspiration, or poetic representation, which precedes the narrative.

Taoists visualized the body as having three important psychic centres, termed cauldrons. These cauldrons store the three main forms of energy. The lowest cauldron is at the base of the spine, where sexual energy, *ching*, is stored, until elevated by the heat of the breath to the second cauldron in the solar plexus, where *chi* is stored. After a lengthy meditation which purifies the energy, it rises to the third cauldron at the top of the head, where *shen* or spiritual energy is stored. The self eventually becomes one with the infinite energies of the universe. Fiction connects us to energies.

As the husband in Carol Shields's story "Dolls, Dolls, Dolls, Dolls" perceptively notes when his wife receives a letter: "Ha, . . . another journey to the heart's interior." We can't escape the images. Magic slips through the most ordinary of vocabulary. We have to alter our attitudes to what is essential within us. Alchemy is revolutionary thought because its aim is to abolish the differences existing between people.

Many of these stories are dark with the repugnant underworld of our commonality. The darkness of depression, the essence of narrative, has a connection to soul. Traditional fiction follows an alchemical pattern. The darkness of the complication, with its depths of decay and change, is similar to what the alchemists call the *nigredo*, or black, or leaden world. The initial process of a fictional transformation has its beginning in rot. Characters find themselves in depression, sluggishness, grief, the sense that the world is falling apart. An old consciousness must be destroyed.

The next stage is the *albedo*, or silver and white world. This moon consciousness, or eye of night, is an adaptation to the darkness. This is a reflective world, the dawn of consciousness, the poetic world of thieves and lunatics. This is where metaphor finds its place in fiction, and fiction is more like poem than prose.

The final stage is *rubedo*, the gold world, the congealed fire of the sun. Fire takes on solid form. The friction of conflicting passions ignites them. The sun brings development to all forms hidden under the earth. The world of the *rubedo* is the world of relationships between sexes, of conflict, clash, confusion and marriage. At the highest point of conflict, the passions melt and fuse together. Inspiration is that moment when the sharp distinction between the inner and outer worlds ceases to be. Contemplation and action are one and the same. The cauldron of fiction is strong enough to contain the heat and friction of the changes taking place within the consciousness of the character, and of the reader. Characters and readers want to escape the failures of the world: they want the gold of their soul. The art of fiction is introspection, the process of imagination, and that leads us to psyche.

Each of the four elements, earth, air, fire and water, has its own alchemical operation. Fire's is *calcinatio*; water's is *solutio*; earth's is *coagulatio*; and air's is *sublimatio*. Any image that contains an element is related to its alchemical operation and the rich area of its symbolism.

Douglas Glover's "The Canadian Travel Notes of Abbé Hughes Pommier, Painter, 1663-1680" begins in darkness and disgrace, the narrator going to France ". . . on the last ship before the river freezes."

Nor can he expect to return to Canada before he dies. The story is solutio, of baptism, of drowning, of ordeal by water. Death of the old life and rebirth. The narrator literally dissolves in his memories, disappears as a priest to be reborn in his new personality as the artist of his own soul.

The dissolution is not a pleasant process — images of mutilation, wounding and sickness permeate the story — because the ego that is dissolved experiences the solutio as an annihilation of itself. Solutio often appears as fragmentation, as notes, which themselves echo the dismemberment of the old self. Solutio is often experienced as an inner drowning, a thirst, in this case for cheap trade brandy, called "darling water" or "spirit helper". Curiously, the narrator's native name is Plenty of Fish. "To souls it is death to become water," wrote Heraclitus.

Edward Edinger remarks that one aspect of the solutio is a Dionysian or orgiastic instinct. The yearning of the lonely alienated ego for containment in a larger whole expresses itself as lust. Within Glover's story, lust suggests the possibility of re-establishing connections with a larger world of humanity. A rejuvenating lust for life beyond boundaries.

The elderly nun described as "an old trout" inspires the artist's greatest painting, *The Mother of the World*, at a time when his personal situation is worst. Beneath the satirical intent of the story (the radiance was merely putrefaction of the gut, itself an alchemical image) is another story: ". . . everyone noticed a radiance emanating from within which could only have been of divine origin."

Fire Beneath the Cauldron has an interplay of premises. Tensions between myths, plots, ideas, stories, symbols, conventions, fabulations and speculations. In the depths of even the most realistic story are ancient motifs. Seven hundred years ago, in the Middle Ages, poetry and alchemical symbolism anticipated the problems of the new age.

These stories are in various stages of all the processes of alchemy — *calcinatio*: to burn; *solutio*: to dissolve; *coagulatio*: to coagulate; *sublimatio*: to become gaseous; *mortificatio*: to die; *separatio*: to separate; and *coniunctio*: to combine.

I. CALCINATIO

The grey Wolf devours the body of the King. Psychologists call this the death of the ruling consciousness, highest structure in the ego. The calcinatio is performed on the primitive shadow side, which harbours instinct. The fire for the process comes from the frustration of the instinctual desires. Frustrated desire is a characteristic of all fictions.

In Zen, fire is the destroyer of illusions. The flame is an arrow of wisdom, enlightnment the flash. Sacred flames burn in Tibetan temples. Buddhists speak of fire without burning, detached in the face of divine enlightenment. God appears in flames and speaks from a burning bush. Fire is the element of the gods. Fire enlightens, provides visions, possibilities. A single flame is a particular ideal; strong flames represent zeal and drive. Fire is self-assertive, all-consuming.

Edna Alford's "The Garden of Eloise Loon" opens with an image of crisis and transition: ". . . she nodded toward the sun as if to say yes. Whatever it wanted to do with her, it could. Melt down the body, even the moving mound in her round belly, render the fat, make soap, dry the withered hide of her and peg it to the ground, stretch it flat and smooth, scrape it free of all the filaments of flesh. Evaporate the water from the blood and scatter the rusted powder of her seed in the fields, wheresoever it should please."

Several alchemical images are combined here: calcinatio as cremation by the sun; the death and blackness of mortificatio; extraction of essence, separatio. The images suggest a personality structure undergoing re-evaluation. The substance to be calcined comes from the shadow side of the personality. The narrative is about the hungry instinct of the devouring worms, which echoes the frustrated instinctual desires of the protagonist. The drama here is both cosmic and spiritual; its conclusion ends in mortificatio, the most negative and dark aspect of alchemy. But darkness turns into meaning, and so becomes light.

Sean Virgo's "White Lies" has many images of calcinatio. Frustrated desire is the chief feature of calcinatio. The Indian boy is in a white Christian man's house. The chained parrot is itself a sublimatio image, a free spirit chained by reality, and set loose as Davie's unconscious literally burns free. The story opens with the mysterious image of "a tree he did not know: with deep grooves like snakes in the corky bark. . ." The tree of life is often associated with the tree of fire.

Most strikingly, during the fire-dance, the young Indian boy David becomes aware: " Davie felt himself there — it was happening to him: his hand hung limply against his thigh and the fingers took on a life of their own, dancing like a little man impelled, fingers taking up the rhythm from the drums which had not stopped once that evening, beating on his thigh like puppet feet in a new dance. For a moment he might have been fainting as the flames and Willie's lolling face floated in the rafters. . . . Then he was back, his limbs shaking under his clammy skin, with the old man's hands across his shoulders now, the smell of him like the beast across Davie's face, and the old voice it seemed whispering something to him across a gulf too far."

Chief Ruben says, "The spirit is strong in you, Davie. You will learn with me until you can be tested alone." The passage concludes: "Across the orchard, fire was wrapping itself around posts and rafters." The story concludes as Davie burns down the doctor's house to find his own freedom.

Bill Gaston's "The Forest Path to Malcolm's" involves the intense heating of a family tale — our accepted story of Malcolm Lowry — until his legend is reduced to powder. The dead father figure is the object of the calcinatio. The story is rich in fire imagery: volcano, lava, beachfire, bonfire, house fire. The story is about a personality undergoing re-evaluation. Calcinatio often takes place on the shadow side of the personality. Frustrated instinctual desires manifest themselves in this story. Furious rage, defecation, nudity, drunkenness are some of Lowry's emotional reactions. The narrator risks being consumed at each encounter. The fire of calcinatio is a purging fire, and this story is rich in the symbolism of purgatory and final fall.

From a simpler perspective, calcinatio is a drying-out process. The narrator concludes, "[H]ot lava is shot blindly out into the world, soon grows cold, and resents having been spewed there." In the closing paragraph, emotional intensity is given full expression as the narrator cries about his mother and rages about his father, beating a fire with a club and sending sparks skyward. The fire of the calcinatio is achieved by expressing attitudes that frustrate, then purge and purify.

Calcinatio brings the ability to see the archetypal aspects of existence. The significance of many stories only becomes clear at the conclusion. Hence, modern Canadian fiction carries with it a high degree of anticipation of a revelatory ending, which will resolve our questions.

II. SOLUTIO

The place of water. To dissolve. To turn solid to liquid. Return for rebirth. Drown. Go into water. Fixed aspects of personality must dissolve. Ego attitudes are questioned. Going down into the unconscious. Love and lust are traditional images of solutio. Problems become unstuck and life flows. Falling for ideas brings about solutio. Bath, shower, sprinkling, baptism, drowning, dew or flood. Death of the old life, rebirth into the new.

Sharon Butala's "Queen of the Headaches" has this beautiful description of the effect of solutio: "She feels like a river, wide, deep, and dark, that flows through the house, that they are all swimming in, turning silently, like dreamers..." The dissolution follows: "... it shines in the hot centre of her forehead. It is sweet now, and bearable. She knows that even Sonia standing down below her, full of hope, feels its gentle, cool flow creeping down her backbone... this is a vision to be borne."

Daniel David Moses's "King of the Raft" has a traditional alchemical image of the king. The swollen ego of the highway boy nearly drowns in the unconscious. Static personalities must be changed, and the archetypal image is of dissolution in water. The boy is held under water until he sees "blue fire".

A Blue Fire was chosen by archetypal psychologist James Hillman as the title of his selected writings with its paeon to the "blue place of metaphor", the highs and lows where dwell the gods, "blue as the prerequisite for all alchemical operations whatever". "The boy who almost drowned found he both feared the king of the raft and missed the waves in his blue-black hair." The descent into the unconscious is always dangerous, always mixed with dense images. One form disappears, the immature youth of the rain boy, and a new one appears, the adult rain boy's desire to search for the city, as noted by Edinger.

The bony teacher — a dismembering figure who works at night under moonlight, a flicker of Artemis in this character — of Cynthia Flood's "Roses Are Red" leads the antagonist, Garth, into a classic alchemical dissolution of libido obstruction. Garth is symbolically returned to the womb, or primal state, and dissolved or dismembered. He's immersed in a creative energy flow, the symbolic birthing. The purification ordeal solves the problems of the main characters, and melts or softens the relationships of all the participants.

Garth could represent the dangerous encounter of the archetypal feminine by an immature ego. This dissolving immersion in the dark lunar side is always unsettling; hence Garth's distress. The men in the class move into their animal natures, watching the birth "the way birds watch snakes". Alchemists considered the rose, one of humanity's most enduring symbols, to be the symbol of regeneration and the scent of the universe.

Glen Sorestad's "One Last Look in the Mirror" has many images of the negative side of solutio. Agnes, who put her cancerous husband out of his misery, describes inner drowning in her beer parlour. Her story is one of dismemberment, from the Church and in part from her marriage. She is also immersed in the creative energy flow of the stories. Solutio always has a double effect: one form disappears and another appears. The use of the mirror as a reflecting symbol suggests Agnes will not take a good look at herself, change and grow. She will remain in her negative aspects. Hence, a solutio may become a mortificatio. The agent of dissolution is Eros, represented by Venus or Aphrodite who was born out of the sea.

The dangerous side of solutio is often represented by mermaids or water nymphs who lure men to death by drowning. Women, water and lust lead to the dissolution of the masculine in male downfall. Jung has a concept of the container and the contained. The "little runt of a man" married by Agnes is swallowed up by his stronger partner who only wants his land. An individual with a stronger consciousness, like Agnes, can bring about solutio. A strong Dionysian principle is associated with solutio. Lust dissolves boundaries: ". . . how we made that bed bounce and rattle!" Alcoholism is often a chronic syndrome when a character is overly identified with Dionysus. Strong thirst and heavy drinking lead to being overwhelmed by water: "'Hope it kills yuh, Pete,' I say, as I hand him another Blue."

Likewise Janice Kulyk Keefer ends her story "Passages", a story rich in water images — blood, seascapes, aquarium, rain, mist and ocean — with a description of solutio. "Under a glimmering sky he watched the freighters sail, orient-bound, their decks pricked out with lights like necklaces. They carried the dead: west to east, from dark to light. Freighters he would ride one day, passage he'd already booked. Not disappearing, but dissolving — round and round the rim of unimaginable worlds." Charles has begun to flow again, he is liquefied. His problems are dissolved.

III. COAGULATIO

Egg white coagulates when heated. Some liquids turn solid as a new compound. Psychic content becomes earth in a particular form. New things are created. As butter is hidden in milk, bliss resides in everything, constantly churned, with the mind as the churning rod, say the Upanishads. Diving, churning, whirling action solidifies the personality. The difference between mercury and lead is the difference between an idea thought and an idea spoken. The power of Saturn appears in images of lead, of depression, heaviness, melancholy, limitations. Saturn with his stone. Prometheus, who stole fire, was punished by coagulatio, chained to a rock of depression. Ego development is associated with evil, criminality and guilt. To be aware of one's own shadow is coagulatio.

Since Edgar Allan Poe first defined the modern short story, writers have used the form to critique the idea of human identity and attack the very idea of the self as stable, discrete and knowable. Since the modern and post-modern short story draws upon orality, parables, fables, myths and fairy tales, insists upon formal experimentation and exploring new subject matter, some aspects of the deep self, which the Jungians see as the anatomy of the psyche, might be expected to emerge. The modern short story has structural affinities with the depths of the imagination.

Dianne Warren's "How I Didn't Kill Wally Even Though He Deserves It" begins with several images of coagulatio, most notably lead, sulphur and magnesia. Magnesia is the impure mix: "I was sick and tired of him being mean and ugly." Next is lead. The narrator is chained to her life: the fourteen-pound sledge hammer mysteriously weighs four hundred pounds. Her free autonomous spirit is virtually grounded. But when the narrator is confronted by her transpersonal spirit, her desire changes. The alchemical agent that follows lead is sulphur, and the transpersonal conscience shows up in a sulphurous yellow jogging suit.

Desire is for power and pleasure. Nothing gives the narrator more satisfaction than contemplating her desires and lusts: hatred, murders, wrath, revellings. Such are the coagulated aspect of the psyche. These images have coagulated for her and provide security, even though they are negative images.

Desire promotes coagulatio. The lure of desire is the sweetness of fulfillment. Cakes, cookies, candy and honey are supreme examples of sweetness. The alchemist Dorn's recipe for joining the spirit with the body required honey. The medicine of immortality is clearly indicated in Stephen Guppy's "Portrait of Helena Leafly, With Bees": "It was as if each of the bees were a thread in some vast Persian carpet... so that you had to see a whole swarm of them working together before the pattern would emerge." Jake and Helena Leafly sell Golden Honey, and keeping bees was for Jake "more of a religion than a business".

But his wife doesn't like the business: "As a schoolgirl, she would creep into her Math class like some lost soul descending into the flames of the inferno, gasping like a beached fish and bugging her eyes out..." A calcinatio aspect introduces her character, and her feeling that "there were times when she thought that her whole life was the working out of some devious pattern, as if she'd been put on this earth for the amusement of some bored, sadistic Fate." Significantly, she was born during a production of *Faustus*. Her life is soul work.

The life of Helena Leafly, fully coagulated, has no further possibility of growth. A consciousness of her ego, and its shadow side, may lead to the coagulation, especially if she remains confined within her personality. Moods toss us about wildly until they coagulate into something visible and tangible.

Stephen Guppy concludes: "In a moment the rest of her hand had dissolved, and her whole body seemed to be pulsing. Perhaps, as her molecules swarmed out the window and vents, she indeed saw the world as a pattern."

IV. SUBLIMATIO

Air. A heated solid becomes gas and ascends to the top of the cauldron. There, it resolidifies. An elevating process. Ladders, stairs, climbing, mountains, flying. The way of spirit. To be high. To get above problems and complications. Where true gold is created. The symbolism of birds, towers, steam, floating, vast heights, funeral pyres and ascensions.

Fiction provides a means of unknowing. As the mystics say, we move through the clouds of unknowing to the clear blue sky of knowledge. The Joycean epiphany, the pivotal Flannery O'Connor moment of grace, the transcendent focus of so much Canadian short fiction leads further into alchemy. The characters in these stories become metaphors as they are caught in their own metaphor making. The alchemical transformations seep into the real world; alchemy becomes myth, myth becomes language, and we act "as if" these are real characters transformed into reality.

Roberta, the woman writing the letter in Carol Shields's story "Dolls, Dolls, Dolls, Dolls", has a connection to the "colour and imagination of childhood". She does not panic when she has the curious mystical experience "that connected her for an instant with an area of original sensation, a rare enough event in our age. She also unwittingly stepped into one of my previously undeclared beliefs. Which is that dolls, dolls of all kinds — those strung-together parcels of wood or plastic or cloth or whatever — possess a measure of energy beyond their simple substance, something half-willed and half-alive."

The feeling of life in the dolls is more than animism; it "seemed. . . to be deliberate and to fulfill some unstated law of necessity." The narrator is profoundly affected by the juxtaposition of ancient, medieval and modern times in her trip to the museum, and by her own protective doll which is "an extension of my hidden self, hidden even from me."

The basis of alchemy is to capture the essence of a world which has no physical existence. Give the invisible world physical identity and individual characteristics in various stages of form.

In David Arnason's witty "Do Astronauts Have Sex Fantasies?", the speculating narrator is truly up in the air of his ideas. His thoughts have turned to gas, and may well be on the way to becoming spirit. As the narrator tries to get above the world and experience the world objectively, he abstracts a general meaning from it. "Doesn't anybody care?" These momentary flights above earthly problems are the way to refine the spirit, and alchemical transformation. "And what of love?

Must that first fierce passion decay into intolerance and mild aversion?" The comic intent of the fiction points to loftier realms, moral categories of good and bad, a spirit that seeks purification by itemizing the contamination that must be separated and overcome.

"The whole history of cultural evolution can be seen as a great *sublimatio* process in which human beings learn how to see themselves and their world separately," notes Edward Edinger (p. 125). The circular motion in the story, up and down, questioning high ideals and false assumptions, is a common psychotherapeutic notion of making the circuit of one's complexes in the course of their transformation. The symbolism of sublimatio is at the core of all human effort for development. A sexually integrated personality is one of the goals of alchemy; hence, astronauts would have "sex fantasies" so they may experience soul.

V. MORTIFICATIO

Blackening, whitening and reddening. Nigredo, albedo, rubedo. To kill. The experience of death. Abstinence or pain. Darkness, defeat, torture, rotting, mutilation, death. To corrode. Become evil. The shadow. To slay the dragon of instinct. Defeat, failure, suffering, frustration: these are the characteristics of mortificatio.

Ernest Hekkanen's "The Mime" is a dramatic account of a meeting with an alchemist. The messages the monk gives, in the form of flies circling his head, are alchemical readings of mortificatio and separatio. Numbers, measurements, weights, geometric lines, the mimes which express parables separate various consciousnesses from the questing reporter. Separatio is closely related to mortificatio.

As the spirit is separated out from the body, the body dies. The imagery of putrefaction, rotting bodies, is an alchemical symbol of incubation prior to resurrection. "The fear of the Lord is the beginning of wisdom." (Proverbs 1:7) The story concludes with images of germination from decay, darkness changing to light, cathedrals, and vaguely comprehended rites.

Leandro Urbina's "The Night of the Dogs" has many strong images of mortificatio. Night, mass killing, a crazy despotic world, mysterious ghostly presences. "They must be dead souls from the orange plantation, come to haunt us, they come down from the mountain top with the fog and go to wash their feet in the river." The central image of the story is dogs with their heads shot off. The political surface of the story, with such dark images, does suggest positive growth, resurrection and rebirth through artistic perception.

A wound to the head of the narrator is also a sign of mortificatio. The wound is the place of transformation, where understanding emerges from the suffering and grief. "I may hear voices, but I don't hear nonsense." The soliloquy with a skull, like Hamlet contemplating Yorick, is an archetypal image of seeking information beyond the ego.

Lois Braun's "Dream of the Half-Man" also has strong connections to mortificatio. The story begins with a heart attack, the dream of the half man, and the car that "did not fly" (so the story is not in separatio). The story describes the effect of a minor car accident on the narrator, whose psyche turns it into a horrific experience too dreadful to contemplate. For her new centre to emerge, she must be tortured. The story has strong images of nightmares, horror films, reptilian imagery (the braided hair of Lou's mother looked like "a bristled chameleon"), mousetraps, the bodies of mice and men cut in half, and a fear of dolls and dreams. The story is in the blackening stage, the dark night of the character's soul.

When Lou lies about setting the mousetraps, the seeds of a new consciousness have sprouted. What is blackest in the story has a stream of associations. The experience of death is alchemically linked with the growth of the psyche's awareness.

VI. SEPARATIO

In the cauldron is the discovery of opposites. To separate earth and sky in a retort or cauldron. The discovery of opposites. The I from Not-I. Immature ego and Self. To separate concrete literal aspects of experience from symbolic. Conflict and ambivalence. The concrete and symbolic. To separate thinking, feeling, sensation, and intuition. Logos-Eros, cutting edge and glue.

The creation of new consciousness requires new contents be carved from the unconscious. Swords, knives, blades, edges: symbols of separatio. The split within the family. Images of death or killing. Death dreams. Death wishes. Separation from relationships. Conflict and antagonism in previously amicable relationships. Sun and moon, husband and wife, earth and spirit. The alchemist as Geometer is a central motif in Ernest Hekkanen's "The Mime", trying to find the centre of a circle that is not for everyone, but for him that knows.

As Yeshim Ternar notes in "Wedding Ninotchka," "There was a time when mother was pure and dreamy and glamorous." The story separates into many countries and many perceptions of the narrator's family. Separation of the parents is part of the basic creation myth. "She was also very beautiful then. She inspired men to write poetry. They elevated her to the ranks of angels."

The archetypal pattern is revealed, and the story is placed in a larger context of international refugees. The son, with his symbolic picture of the hurricane, "was absent from his family in his desire to observe and preserve them. And in the end, he had been expelled from his home for having distanced himself from them."

Separatio is also connected to mortificatio, which means that it may be experienced as a kind of death. "For he had learned in waiting we create our own hell; especially in silence, and in a refuge, the most violent storms explode in our soul." The mood of separatio is mourning, and the image is of orphans, the separated ones.

Marlene Nourbese Philip's "Bad Words" is a remarkable story of creation by separation. Miranda's use of the cutting edge of language — specifically obscenities and curses — sways her world, then shakes it, separates the sacred from the profane. Miranda "sharpened her mouth" around the words. "She felt the sharpness and power" of the obscenities. "They all had edges — hard edges that hurt somehow as she intentionally and deliberately strained her mouth around their shapes, her tongue paying strict attention to their individual shapes. Afterwards she would carefully examine her mouth and tongue for the staining she expected. She was surprised that her mouth did not show the outrage she had just committed."

Philip's story has strong loyalties to opposites. Logos, language and thought, becomes connected to Logos-Eros, both as cutting edge, and glue. "Mother and cunt. In their opposition the two words — one resonant with safety and comfort, the other harsh, defiant, and threatening — were locked together irrevocably. The power of this combination, made greater by the secret nature of it made her feel lightheaded and even faint at times." Miranda's way of thinking is absolutely alchemical. Logos brings her consciousness into power and control over nature. Language dissects, separates, differentiates.

By separating into opposites, language brings clarity. "Miranda felt uninitiated into the world of the forbidden. And her initiation, she felt, had to be a public one — a speaking of at least one of those words in the presence of others." By making the opposites visible, she brings conflict. Separatio is closely related to mortificatio. A beating by her father could be experienced as a kind of death, or individuation crisis, which she recalls "for many months, even years later."

An example of such a separatio appears in the Gospels. "I have come not to bring peace, but a sword. For I have come to set a man against his father, and a daughter against her mother, and a daughter-in-law against her mother-in-law; and a man's woes will be those of his own household." (Matthew 10: 34-36) Separatio is not a final process, but a prerequisite, a cleansing.

As Edinger says, "This corresponds psychologically to the fact that attitudes contaminated by unconscious complexes give one the distinct impression of being soiled or dirty." Miranda's work in her story is to scrutinize her own complexes. The woman she admires, Pomona Adams, "with her shapely breasts and large backside mashing the ground — proudly", could represent the dynamic side of Miranda's Self, which is both the source and goal of the separatio operation.

VII. CONIUNCTIO

Coniunctio is the culmination of the opus. It's the final miracle of alchemy. Things are maimed, killed, fragmented. Transformation occurs here. Death followed by rebirth. Images are fluid, fast changing. The bitterness of experience brings wisdom. Material is reversed and turned into its opposite. What is obscure becomes clear.

Images are the basis of fiction. Cold images, the underworld, on the moon, in outer space. Cold detachment of the critic evaluating images. But the heat is within. The fire of creative fantasy. Reflection is to burn with suphur. Heat comes with imagining. The psyche is scorched. We don't want to blacken the images, burn them with their innate vitality. That's the writing lesson. Be true to the images, and so be true to the soul.

Brian Fawcett's story "The Franz Kafka Memorial Room" contains
complex inner symbolism. It includes all the play of opposites characteristic of coniunctio. Entrapment/space; despair/play;
madness/reason; creativity/creative blocks. The goal of the coniunctio is to experience the opposites at the same time. Love is
fundamental to the coniunctio. A moment of bliss that transcends
sexual attraction and ascends from the profane to the divine.

Fawcett's story moves towards this striking conclusion of the Doctor
and his wife "very much" in love: "But when I think of them together,
and when I see him bumping across the street like the crippled
butterfly he is, the world brightens, and the stinking colossus of
doom that darkens everything these days dissolves, and the walls
that enclose us open up to the story as it might be, whirling around
and around in the air."

Base matter has become noble. Out of the stone a child is born, the
puer eternus, the eternal youth. Something marvellous has happened,
and if we pay attention, it has happened within us at the same time.
A mutual opus has been formed within the story and within our
consciousness.

To be human is to have both body and soul. Images of miraculous
growth, of flowers, birds, or butterflies, often accompany proximity
to the coniunctio. As James Hillman suggests, the soul presents
pathologized images: bizarre, twisted, immoral, painful, sick
fantasies. The special revelations of the soul of the writers. They allow
an entry into life; the soul that cannot be had without them. Splits,
healings, and renewals are the concern of the coniunctio.

Mary Burns's "The Circle" contains this vision of an eternal light:
"The Yukon is a special place on our planet. It borders on the pole
where magnetic forces are concentrated. It shines in the light of the
north star, which all men use to find their way. This planetary belt,
the threshold of the Arctic Circle, is like the antechamber of the great
king." Despite the failure of many people he meets to understand, or
even of himself to understand the foolhardiness of his quest, Donald
is eager to reach the centre of the circle. The best he can hope for is
the lesser coniunctio. The coniunctio leads to the death of the ego.
As Donald chants OM, he identifies with the contents rising from the
unconscious: shadow and anima, inner voices. These are

contaminated and must be purified before he can truly enter the greater coniunctio. But his physical body may die because of his selfish ideals.

For another perspective, Dionne Brand notes in her story of Blossom: "Black people on Vaughan road recognized Blossom as gifted and powerful by she carriage and the fierce look in she eyes. She fill she rooms with compelling powder and reliance smoke, drink rum and spit it in the corners, for the spirits who enter Blossom obeah house in the night. Little by little people begin to find out that Blossom was the priestess of Oya, the Goddess." That knowledge of the Goddess comes to those who have to know. When personalities mix, all are transformed. Reciprocal action is a basic feature of the advanced processes of alchemy.

Paying attention to the imagery generates reciprocal effects. How to read a story: purify yourself. Meditate. Withdraw your attention from material sensations. Then, as Jung says, the imaginative faculty will turn the reader's thoughts to "imagine and picture [mental contents] as if ascended in the higher worlds up the roots of his soul. . ."

You pull back from the world of phenomena out there to land in psyche. To the roots of the soul, the dark place, not the celestial heights of the spirit. The nourishment for fiction comes from the places of darkness. The imagination is the attempt of the alchemist fiction writer to turn the imagery to gold. Not common gold, but living spirit.

Fire Beneath the Cauldron has a simple enough trajectory. I've used some theories from modern psychology, especially Jung and the active imagination, a bit of Breton and surrealism, and alchemical symbolism in psychotherapy. We know the conscious ego is made up from a cluster of associations. Within is the unconscious, simply as it is, without our creation. That's the place of the imagination and imaginal substances. The place of the world soul, where we connect with the cosmos. The place of the archetypes. The alchemical world that has nothing to do with personality development, ego growth, or expansion of consciousness. We then proceed to our destiny.

Peter Behrens's narrator in "Night Driving" describes destiny: "A destiny is something like the stars you see twinkling in midnight sky when you are travelling across Wyoming. A destiny is the place where you will end up, says Daddy, all happy, with problems forgot and sorrows eased. It is a place you lie with all your friends around sipping drinks, with the smell of flowers. . . I feel I'm getting closer to it when I am travelling at night." What is corrupt becomes purified; the turning into opposites occurs.

Alchemy condenses human traits. The principle of combustibility, *magna flamma,* sulphur in all things, the fire beneath the cauldron — metals, herbs, trees, animals, stones are its ore, says the 14th-century Benedictine monk, Kramer. The way surprises appear when an object or an idea is turned around. New colours. Fiction as the art of the soul. The plot of these stories is more or less what happens in the mind of the Canadian reader. The experience of these fictions is the flammable face of the world.

Within the darkness is the alchemical light, the illuminating principle of nature displayed in the truth of fiction. "The almighty God placed in the heart of the world, namely in the earth — as he did in the heart of every other creature — a firelife. . . Over this Archaeus or central fire God hath placed his heaven, the sun, and stars. He hath placed the head and eyes over the heart. For between man and the world there is no small accord, and he that knows not the one cannot know the other," writes 19th-century mystic Thomas Vaughn.

"This was the great discovery of alchemy: that we can take an active part in the ongoing creation of Genesis through the medium of imagination. If the image gives birth to psychic life, and psychic life in turn manufactures the material person-made world from the ideas clustered around the image, then the fullness of life is to be found in an active participation with the image at its own level as well," writes Charles Ponce in *The Archetype of the Unconscious: The Trans-figuration of Therapy.*

Ponce continues: "All of this is another way of saying that the image, and imagination, is life. If one can imagine living a day without the experience of those images that normally pass through one's mind, this seemingly metaphysical statement will take on a different and quite concrete meaning."

Ponce says we need basic mental images — where we parked the car, left our hats, first met someone. We are dead if we don't engage in the imaginal. As Jung said, image and meaning are identical.

The world itself has soul which is presented in images. Without images, we lose our way. *Anima mundi* offers itself through each thing in its visible form. Each is a face with its interior image, in short its availability to imagination. Animals, plants, rocks, the man-made things on the street. *Anima mundi* is the images animated and affecting our imagination. Psychic reality appears in expressive images or fictions, writes James Hillman in *A Blue Fire*.

The real meaning of transformation is not person-centred. It's archetype-centred, it's how we participate in the *anima mundi*. "The gift of the Christian spirit to the alchemical laboratory is a blazing fire that keeps the temperature so incredibly hot — 'He who is near me is near the fire,' says Christ in one of the uncanonical sayings — that images can never solidify into idols; that is, their hermetic qualities are kept alive. If an image is to be a guide of souls, a psychopompos, as Hermes was said to be, then it must be kept moist and fluid. It must be kept on the fire," writes Hillman in *The Puer Papers*.

The poetic and fictive basis of our mind is images. We live in fiction. We swim in the depths of experience. The soul turns events into experience. The difference, of course, is that the soul sees the meaningfulness, value, and full range of experience. Depth, resonance and texture. Imagination perceives the fundamental fantasies that permeate all of life and turn them into fiction. That's how the Canadian soul understands itself.

The Garden of Eloise Loon

Edna Alford

She wasn't one of them. She didn't belong here. She was not what they thought she was nor was she part of any other people. She nodded in the sun on the makeshift step, four large gallon ketchup cans supporting two grey planks, a spike driven through each of them into the tins for good measure. The stoop of the shack faced south and she nodded toward the sun as if to say yes. Whatever it wanted to do with her, it could. Melt down the body, even the moving mound in her round belly, render the fat, make soap, dry the withered hide of her and peg it to the ground, stretch it flat and smooth, scrape it free of all the filaments of flesh. Evaporate the water from the blood and scatter the rusted powder of her seed in the fields, wheresoever it should please. There was nothing left but the beginning of summer.

She hadn't seen Earl since two weeks last Friday. Sometimes he went up to work in the bush, but usually he said if he was going. This time he took his cheque, left without a word, and she hadn't seen him since. Nor had she any idea when she would see him again. She had no way of knowing. She had come to the point of not caring either. To fretting, she preferred moving her feet in small spiralling circles in the dirt in front of her, making smooth furrowed patterns in the grey dust, watching a film of dirt powder slowly accumulate over her feet, her ankles, her shins. She had eaten nothing for two days.

The sun made her dizzy. She leaned her head back and watched the leaves on the poplar trees flutter in the wind. Poplars and spruce surrounded the shack. The leaves were round and green and looked like they were spinning, spinning green, almost lime, they were so new. Her belly was hard now, no longer high. The baby dropped three or four days ago, dropped closer to the hole through which it would make its way, like a worm. She cursed the lump. "Shit," she would say, circling the mound with her arms, laughing and crying at the same time. "Shit, shit, shit." And she rocked back and forth to the rhythm of the curse.

She closed her eyes. The lids flooded orange, then red, like thin hot blood. The red was all over her and warm as if it circled inside her brain and coated every cell with warmth the colour of a red rain. Now there were small black dots beginning to appear scattered over the clear warm red in her head. They expanded and grew, black and grey and elongated, like the worms. Finally they overlaid the red and she shivered and opened her eyes and blinked.

From the stoop she could see two other shacks through the bush. One straight ahead, one off to the right. Both were patched with cardboard and tarpaper. Eloise Loon was hanging out her clothes, grey and dripping, from a tin tub. She was silent and the flies buzzed around her head. There were chickens in her yard, all colours, chickens with ragged heads and one, almost pecked to death late one night, staggered with maggots near the outhouse.

The other house off to the right was grey as a grown-over grave, silent in the heat. Usually there were many children. She didn't know how many; she had never figured that out except she knew there were a lot of them. All ages. Ragged little diapered ones and ones with fine new store-bought clothes and some with running noses, some with faces brown and live and shining round as the round round sun. But today, not one. Someone had driven up in a van a couple of days ago and now there were none.

She stretched her arms out. She wore a checkered blue smock from the Mission rummage, slid the sleeves up for more sun, her skin already a mass of freckles. Her hair was red and thin and she hadn't combed it since the day Earl left. There were freckles on the skin of her face, all over except for the eyelids and the mouth, which was now a round black hole, agape, a yawn.

She felt the first on her foot, looked down, batted off a long black worm with pale yellow ovals along the ridge of its back. But mostly black. The worms were mostly black. They were not really worms, she knew. They were tent caterpillars, by rights, but everybody called them worms.

Last year they layered the bush in a black mass, writhing over the walls of the shack, solid black and moving over the window panes, turning the inside black at the same time as the outside. She stayed outside, batted them off her ankles and her shins. Sometimes they fell from the roof in a clump and landed in her hair, began to move there over her scalp and she would fly from the stoop and scream and run around in circles till Eloise Loon would look up from her garden and laugh. But last year there was food in the house, at least.

And Earl was here. And sometimes he took her down to the lake where she swam. The worms covered the sand but they couldn't really swim. Only once she had seen a fleet, undulating, black, carried over the lake by the wind. Only once had she seen them land and writhe toward the high shore and the bush. They devoured everything in their path. Earl once said they were a lot like people that way. They ate everything in sight and had no natural enemies. But he said they carried their own parasite inside, sooner or later would do themselves in, and the cycle would end. The birds would have nothing to do with them. Even Eloise Loon's starving hens wouldn't eat them. Earl said a man from Chicago had brought a single pair over from Europe years ago. He figured he could make a fortune selling silk.

She remembered the night Earl rode out of the bush wearing a hood and shrouded in the white gauze of the worms, his horse lathered white, the calf a ghost of spun white. But as he drew near, she could see the worms, dropped from trees, black

and writhing over the three, the man, the horse, the calf. When
the worms were finished with the bush, there was nothing left
on the trees but bones, the skeleton branches, like winter
wounds, reached up toward the summer sun which bleached
them clean and thin and white against the sky.

But this year, there wasn't even food for worms much less her.
Much less the baby inside. There wasn't even Earl. There
would be no eating off her this year, she thought, and coughed
a small high-pitched laugh, spat toward the sun.

Last year the worms came into the shack too. There were gaps
in the floors, knotholes in the walls, a ring of sky around the
stovepipe hole. The worms used all of those last year. So let
them come, she thought and shifted on the stoop. And let it
come, the little one.

She wondered if maybe she shouldn't go across to the shack
of Eloise Loon and ask for scraps. But the air was too warm,
too thick, seemed solid between her and the shack of the old
brown woman. And Eloise Loon would laugh. She always
laughed, her fat heaving in round brown wrinkles, her eyes
winking one, then the other, as if she had a tic, these flip-flop
eyes. No, she wouldn't go over for a while yet. Maybe Earl
would come back tonight.

She reached and batted two worms from her legs. One had
climbed as high as her thigh, one only near the ankle bone on
her right foot. She reached over and around the mound of her
bellied child and picked a stick up out of the dirt and began to
hurt the worms, first one and then the other, squashing out
their jelly, green, a kind of green, not lime, but poplar, like the
leaves they had devoured. Like the leaves, she thought and
smiled upsidedown, her thin lips twisted in a small half-circle,
like a pale young branch bent by wet snow.

Earl in winter found her in the snow, half-buried, wearing a
ragged old coat. She had taken the bus from the city where
there were banks and brokers, lights and water, pimps and
grocers, singing in the bars. And other darker things, of

course. But now, as the sun burned low, shattered black by the branches of the spruce, she thought especially of light, the many flickered city light. She could only half remember the rest. Then, the city a ring in her nose, a noose around her neck. She had thought that nothing could ever be worse, cursed the cracks in the sidewalks, broke her mother's back a million times. But she was wrong.

When she got off the bus at Trestle, she began to walk, stopping from time to time to talk to herself, to ask herself where she thought she was going with one cardboard suitcase and open-toed shoes, the snow blowing up her skirt, the cold obscenely creeping into the crotch of her panty hose. The noise, the whining wind, instead of dying, rose and covered her head with the sound of something white, all white and smothering and warm, a swarm of white, like cats in her head, a thousand white and mewling cats. Then howling, bitter ripping cats. Then no cats. Then no white. Then no sound. Only a lying down and a feeling of every round and silent moving thing surrounding her, taking her place, talking with her breath. Oh please. Oh shit, oh shit, and a feeling of rocking. Of rocking herself to sleep in a soft white drift.

Then Earl. In a truck. Earl had stopped and picked her up. Picked her up and put her in the truck and that led to heat and something to eat and bed.

He took her to the reserve. And for a while things worked out all right. She made him supper, peeled potatoes, roasted meat, everything ready every night when he came home from wherever it was that he had been.

She missed no one, none of the other girls who preened in the can at the Queen's every night. None of the Johns, not one. She picked berries all day long, strawberries and dewberries and red currants and black currants and lowbush cranberries and saskatoons, blue. Blue, her fingers blue, dyed blue and red and purple all through the summer into fall when great wedges of geese fell out of the sky and cried for the summer inside the

hope, cried for the sun inside the north, the days the sun was
dying south.

The winter was spent in the mouth of a long black stove. Shove,
shove in the wood, split the wood, carry the wood. Then shove,
shove, the sparks on the floor of the shack, the smoke, the long
black pipe, a ring of winter silver sky around the stovepipe hole.
Then no more wood. Then no more coal. The cold. Everywhere
the cold.

For water she melted snow while Earl was in town running
around wherever he could find a woman white enough. Every
day she hauled her tubs out of the house and into the yard. She
filled them full with a spade, the snow sometimes dry like sand,
sometimes crusted, sometimes so heavy her hands ached for
hours inside the shack where she sat and watched the stove
and waited for the snow to melt in the round tin tub. Sometimes
she saw Eloise Loon in the yard with a tub and a spade, heaving
and hoisting too, laughing and cursing the sun and the moon.

Sometimes she hid from Earl when he came home and the
headlights of the truck shone in through the shack window.
Sometimes she hid under the bed. But he found her and
grabbed her by her thin red hair and banged her head and
banged her head on the cold grey floor, till her nose bled and
her ears rang with the roar of the stove and the white of the
storm. He swore and dragged her all over the shack, backwards until he got tired and fell on the bed and started to snore.

The second summer came the worms, the walls of worms, the
grey floor crawling black. She squashed them and gathered
them all into a potato sack and threw them in the stove. She
laughed. The summer passed and the poplar branches,
stripped clean, began to leaf again, grow green. Earl went up
to the bush. There were no berries because of the worms. She
sat on the stoop and looked over at the shacks across the yard,
watched Eloise Loon hang out her clothes, tend her tattered
garden, weed and hoe and reap in the fall under the sun and

the call of the great wedges falling through the sky around the curve, the round wound of the world.

The white of the following winter, a narrow hole, a silver needle with the dark of a hundred city nights, back to back. The air flecked silver like glitter on glue. She peeled the potatoes and tended the stove, heaped wood in the box till the flue glowed dusty red as powdered blood. In the morning she walked in the bush, clumps of white powdered snow falling from the spruce, sometimes falling on her head, spreading a crown of crystal on her hair, spraying from there down the neck of her coat, down her spine, a thin line of white lumps under white skin, white as the skin of a cutworm in the garden of Eloise Loon.

And the wind blew. Earl returned for two weeks, nailed her to the bed two, three, one day seven times, the long hard line of his own fishing swallowed by her hole, the jigging ungentle, mortal, full of milk, full of resin, full of slime. There was a time in the middle when she could no longer tell the winter day from the winter night. And somewhere in the time of the winter worm, on the bed in the corner of the small dark room, the child began.

Now in the summer sun she sat rocking the round wound, circling the mound with her arms, laughing and crying at the same time, cursing both the sun and the moon. Finally the sun went down and she rose and opened the screen door, flack flack behind, stuttering the present into past, the past into dark future, into the shack. As soon as she was inside she saw the worms begin to move across the floor.

She lay on the bed and regarded the pain from the distance of stars, the moon through the window welding arcs of shimmied light against the wall of the shack, her back a rigid arc, a wall of ache. The hole of the night narrow in her throat, the skin of her bloated belly shiny, white as the face of the moon and tight, too tight, the skin splintered with the silverfish of too much light inside, as if she would explode if ever there were another long hard night of arcing time.

In the morning she sat on the edge of the bed with the bloody child. The sun rose red. In the morning she took a rag out to the rain barrel and dipped it in and pulled it out dripping. She carried it back to the shack and wrung it out over the grey scum in the basin on the washstand. Then she began to clean the child which did not utter a sound. But moved. Moved a little, flinching like an open wound. When she had him clean, she leaned over him and sang a song with no words, a song which found its own articulation deep in her throat, a curve of sound drawing honey from the bush and from the lake and from the wild and cunning throat of Eloise Loon. She wrapped the child and held him to her close.

Most of the morning she sat on the edge of the bed and suckled the child which clung to her breast like the rest of men do to the world. And she thought of the thing that she could do, deliver the child to Eloise Loon and beg for scraps. That was the thing that she could do. Just that. And then she wondered if the van might come and she could talk to the man who drove the van and deliver the baby to him. She smiled, her smile thin and dry, a kindling branch.

Finally she took the child acradle on her arm and she went out of the shack to sit on the stoop where it was warm. With the sun today had come the worms, in swarms, hanging from the eaves in clumps, their gauze in all the branches of the trees. The black of millions lying on the leaves, eating quietly. She saw them moving over the ground, around the stoop, a black mass thick and round on the rain barrel. Over the way, the garden of Eloise Loon, once green and full of bloom, now was black, undulated toward the stoop of her shack, looped over her clothesline, onto her roof.

And still there was no sign of Earl. Earl, if only he would come, could take her to the lake where she could swim in the wide water, a water full of silver and no worms. But by late afternoon,

Earl still had not come and she sat on the stoop, suckling the child and drumming the fingers of her right hand on the grey plank and wondering what she could do.

Watching the worms move, she grew sleepy; the lids of her eyes were low. The clump of worms fallen from the eaves onto her hair began moving now, moving slow across her brow, curling round her ears, up into her nostrils, flowing down her neck, down the white line of lumps marking her spine through the thin white shirt. She looked up at the sun and closed her eyes. For a moment she saw the shadow of Eloise Loon against the lids which flooded orange, then red, like thin hot blood. The red was all over her and warm as if it circled inside her brain and coated every cell with warmth the colour of a red rain.

Now there were small black dots beginning to appear scattered over the clear warm red. They expanded in her head and grew, black and grey, elongated. Finally she brushed them away from her eyes and raised the child in her arms, held him out toward the sun, stood up still holding him high, sighting along him as if he were the barrel of a gun, sighting the poplar and the spruce and the wide water. She left the stoop and began to run toward the garden of Eloise Loon. There she laid him down among the worms. As many as she could gather in her arms, she heaped high in a black and moving mound which began to spin a canopy, a shroud, delivered him to the dark, surrounded by her own laughter and the high arc of the only sky.

Night Driving

Peter Behrens

I like driving at night. I like everything about it. It's the best.

I was a little girl Daddy would say, Hop right up here, 'Face.
And I'd skitter across the front seat and squeeze up into his lap.
He settle back a little into the seat, give me room behind the
wheel, and there I'd be. What cars we had! My favourite was
the last, a '59 Catalina, Wyoming plates, big wide white car with
tail fins. We had the back seat ripped out of her and the wall
cut open to the trunk. Daddy fixes her up with a plyboard laid
down, army mattress, and there we both sleep. Plenty of room.
With little curtains hung on a string 'round all the windows so
what we do is private. Daddy likes it that way. We are asleep in
California six weeks past when "Wham! Bam!" on the doors,
and troopers are there all of a sudden, like out of your dreams,
and arrest Daddy and haul him off to jail. I am in jail too, alone
and so lonesome, but they don't hold me for long, they turn me
loose which is worse until I meet Johnboy at the Church. He
now takes care of me and I take care of him and he tells me
forget Daddy, put that right out of your mind. But I can't. He
says, You are a pore little orphan Vetnamee girl. Pretty little
slanteyes. They send *him* back to Folsom, Johnboy say, for
years. My Daddy.

What I like best was driving at night, me and Daddy both
behind the wheel. On the great black roads out there somewhere empty, Nebraska, Canada.

This past weekend, finally, month and a half after they take
Daddy and stick him in jail, me and Johnboy finally get out on
the road together. We go up to Tahoe in his van. We're getting
married.

Johnboy says, Ah little Vetnamee girl, I love your tiny feet!
'Cause I like to ride at night with my shoes off and my feet
resting up on the dash. I like to steer too, like I done with my
Daddy, but Johnboy won't let me behind the wheel of his van.
Not yet anyways.

After our wedding we spend the weekend up there in the trees
and mountains sleeping at nights in the back of the van.
Johnboy keeps saying he's going to go fishing but doesn't.
Instead he opens up a little chair he bought at Sears in Fresno,
$19.96, and he sits and swallows beer with the tapedeck on
playing Rolling Stones. He says sixties songs all remind him of
his tour. For dinner we have no fish but food storebought I fry
up on the Coleman. At night it is peaceful. But it's not like being
out on the road.

The best of our weekend is the drive home Sunday night. We
come down alongside Merced River and all the lupines are in
bloom. They are my favourite night-driving flower, you can see
'em by moonlight and by headlight, little reflectors out there
in the fields. Such white and spooky little flowers, millions of
them, waxy, glowing. I would like to weave a great big chain of
them and send them to my Daddy back suffering prison time
at Folsom jail.

They say to me, policemen judges social work, what will become of you? and I say I have Johnboy to take care of me now.
And Johnboy is Deacon of the Church, VFW chapter VP,
auxiliary deputy, and has the minister as witness. I am legal
age now after all. I can do what I like.

What I don't tell them is, I will just wait for Daddy. I'll stay here
with Johnboy who takes care of me, and be good. I like to sing
in Church and polish his van, but don't tell me to stop thinking
of Daddy. Daddy is the one planted inside of me.

We sleep near roadside always, in the Pontiac, we drive off into
some little dark corner of a field about two hours before dawn.
Beneath cottonwoods, near riverbanks, is where we like to

park. We get out and swim in the river. Daddy tells me stories. We laugh and have jokes. We go to sleep.

I hate to think of them wrestling Daddy away, Daddy yelling while they're trying to squeeze them in their car, No peace for the wicked!

The trail out of Tahoe with Johnboy Sunday night comes from the mountain in steep canyon walls and gorge, winds down the river for miles and miles until the Valley flattens it out to a road just like any other. Then the lupines disappear and we have the night smells of manure and crops and still water in the irrigation ditches alongside.

I was a little girl we liked the straight highways, my Daddy and me. Daddy says, On a straight road, 'Face, we make *time*.

Johnboy is a much softer person than my Dad. By far. Big and soft and easy which is why I like him so. He's a locksmith. I like the little tufts of beard he has grown all along the line of his chin. His hair to me is the colour of honey. And his cheeks, all pink. His mouth, happy, especially sucking on a beer. My Daddy will drink too but in a different style. Such as one afternoon when we were staying in Montana, Daddy working housepainter up in Flathead Valley, for Swede — I remember Swede well, big floppy moustache and skin speckled with white paint. Next to him, my Daddy looks like brown stick. What happens is, after a couple of weeks Swede owes Daddy money and we want to leave. We go looking for Swede one afternoon. We go to a house to collect but the Swede ain't there. We go to another house, ain't there either. We start in on roadside bars where Swede likes to drink. I wait in the car. At each bar we stop at my Daddy walks inside, madder and madder, and has a drink, looking for the Swede. Then he gets back in the Pontiac and we race down the highway, still looking. Finally Daddy gets fighting with an Indian near Missoula, after almost sixty miles of bars, and brains the Indian with a bottle out there in the parking lot. Jumps into the Pontiac where I'm waiting, scared, and we take off out of there and drive all the way to

Oregon, I think. In Coeur d'Alene Idaho a truck driver tries to
get me up into his cab while Daddy's in the truckstop shower.
"Little Vetnamee girl, Cambojan, suckee suckee," he whispers.
Daddy comes out his hair all slicked back wet and shiny
looking so young and handsome in his fresh white T-shirt and
jeans, you can see the little knife scar inside his forearm he
picked up R&R Sydney Australia. He steps up behind the truck
driver and chops him with his bare hand. We roll him over
then, take his wallet, go on our way.

Now I know my Johnboy ain't like that. He's more gentle, like
a great big soft bear. He's a Deacon in the Church. When we
lie together he pretends to growl. He says he respects me
'cause of all the people in Lettuce Grove I am the one that has
travelled the most and experienced things.

Most of all I am the one that thinks. Thinking is something I
learned from my Daddy, I learned it on my all-night driving.
Daddy says, You see in some ways it is a marvellous and rich
experience for a child, driving.

When Johnboy and me drive home in the van through the
lupine fields and then across the wide flat sweet-smelling
Valley with irrigation water hissing from big spindled pipes
rolled out in the fields and the sound of things out there
growing — why, I am the one most at home, and he is the one
always has a secret little bit of wishing that he was back at "the
place", with beer, hotdogs, tacos, cake, stucco, waterbed,
La-z-boy. We live at a development called the Lettuce Grove.

When I first met Johnboy that night at the Church I think that
he's a richie. He wears a tie and jacket to Church, jacket powder
blue. When he offers me a ride back to the motel I go with him
and we drive around in the van and then instead of the motel
he brings me out to his place at Lettuce Grove. To me, it's a
castle.

My Daddy raised me without religion. On the trunks of our
cars he always paints in big, bright red letters anyone can read,
Fear Not! He would say, We're on the road now Babyface, we

worship wide-open spaces, none of these towns and eyesores is right for us. We get all the Lord Almighty we need driving ourselves into sunset each evening.

This way he'd talk when feeling especial good and roll down the window on his side, stick out his head and yell, Yip yip yippee.

Which was right because things didn't go well for us in the towns. We met in Yuma, where I was working the little Vetnamee store, not even going to school, sweeping up, selling jujubes. Daddy pays 'em just to take me out of there but even so there's a fight.

Once my Daddy got a job on a sewer crew Casper Wyoming. We live there five weeks. He's not the same man in the towns. They start him feeling bad. Itchy-twitchy, he calls it. Sundays he's off work and we drive around looking for something neither of us knows what. We drive to the edge of the town Casper Wyoming, turn around, drive to the end on the other side, turn around again. We go home watch TV. Monday, Daddy goes back off to work. He says no one bother you, tell 'em you're my wife, no one knows the age of Vetnamee girls anyhow. Besides I love you, he says. I take care of you, Babyface. Sugarpie, sweetheart.

He never talked this way except when we were in the towns. At night he would cry. I try to cook him dinners when he comes home but he likes better we go up at the highway eat in one of our truck stops out there on the edge of town. Casper Wyoming. Where we bought the Pontiac.

Driving at night makes me sad with sadness sweet as honey I can't stop eating. Daddy and me have gone through weather in all sorts of places, Dakota snowstorms, midnight 100 degrees in places like Barstow. I tell Johnboy now, sometimes when I'm feeling blue, just what Daddy used to sometimes say — "Baby, let's drive to Texas!" — I said it this morning just before Johnboy leaves for work.

Johnboy gets all hot. He says, Drive to Texas! Ain't you grateful? I have saved you from your Daddy. I have give you room to grow. I have take you to the Lord.

I'm not really serious, but still. And it wouldn't even have to be Texas. Could be anywhere at all.

He just ties on his tool belt and stomps out the door. He loves his job, he's always first in Lettuce Grove to leave for work. I go out through the sliding glass door onto the little porch where the hibachi sits, look down and watch him cross the parking lot. It's early day and the sun throws a long shadow 'cross the cement. Johnboy's the only one out there, no one else in Lettuce Grove leaves this early, there are cars parked all over, vans, Trans Ams, pickups, and bikes and plastic tricycles scattered on the lawns, and flagpoles, and grass that has got to be watered at night by an automatic sprinkler otherwise it gets browned up by noon and curls into prickly little stubs. Sprinkler shuts off a little time before dawn.

Oftentimes me and Daddy roll right through these desert towns, Valley towns, at night and pull up curbside or in some driveway. We tug off our clothes and go out lay there in the thick, sweet, wet lawns and let the mist of water soak right through us. We lay there looking up at the stars while the poor ones like Johnboy are in their houses asleep.

What can I say? I stand there on the porch in the morning sun with a mug of coffee wearing a new nightgown, peekaboo, he bought me J.C. Penney, watching him fiddling with the keys of his van trying to get the door open. He'll look up at me.

You're misfit, that's what you are, he'll yell. You make sure to lock up that porch door when you go inside!

I wave but he just heaves himself into the front seat and drives off.

In towns at night when we were feeling clean and empty, Daddy and me liked to slip into homes on little missions. Roll past a home, and Daddy points and say, That One. Lets me out at the corner, all dark and quiet, and tells me what he wants. Some-times it's something easy, rake from the garden, kitchen knife. Sometimes harder: he'll say, Get me a bar of bathroom soap, Little One.

Or, Fetch me a bedside clock.

I like to slip in the houses, darkness, stay low on the floor. No one ever wakes. I'm good now but Daddy's the best. Once he comes back with a dog collar, big one too, like a Dobie, something mean; says "Rexie" on the collar. Daddy has a way with animals.

Johnboy has lived in this Valley all his life, his mom and pop and sisters live in a deluxe trailer park otherside of the city from us, work in a cannery, we don't see 'em much. They are backsliders. John's born again and the Church, the Pentecostal, now they are his family.

Last night, Sunday night, we drove down twisting alongside the Merced River past little meadows and hillsides of shiny lupine. I get my toes curled on the cool edge of the dash like I like, we stop at the store coming out of Yosemite for Fritos and beer. I am listening to the sounds of the night driving, crackling of the cellophane bag when Johnboy reaches in for another handful, radio noise, wind slipping in through loose corners of shut windows. Johnboy reaches over to pat my feet. I am convinced in these kinds of moments that I have waiting for me a destiny just as my Daddy says when we first met, Yuma Arizona; the way he would tell me and make me believe, over campfires we'd set up in little roadside pullouts in the Rocky Mountains.

Johnboy always trying to get me to tell about life with Daddy. What did he do with you? What did he like? How old was you when you met up with him?

I liked to lean over the fires when they were almost out so I could smell the smoke and get a little of it in my hair and see the last coals glowing. The red embers looked like cities burning and flickering from a plane up high above.

They let me see Daddy just the once while he's still at county jail.

Locksmith, he says. Ha, ha.

I think of our poor Pontiac parked off somewhere in some sheriff lot, getting dusty and hungry for the road. Probably sold by now, Johnboy says, auction, convict goods. Daddy says nonetheless he'll come to fetch me. Nonetheless, Babyface. Just be ready.

A destiny is something like the stars you see twinkling in midnight sky when you are travelling across Wyoming. A destiny is the place where you will end up, says Daddy, all happy, with problems forgot and sorrows eased. It is the place you lie with all your friends around sipping drinks, with the smell of flowers. There'll be a soft little stream and more flowers, floating by.

I feel I am getting closer to it when I am travelling at night. Even with Johnboy. My destiny is a seed that the night and all the trips I've taken with Daddy has planted in me. Even if the destiny dries up and hides whenever we stop, or in the daytime. Even if I can't show it to Johnboy, can't tell him when he asks — he'll never understand, I think sometimes. But I will love him and try to teach him like Daddy taught me. Like when we'd stop at gas stations somewhere after midnight, Spearfish, Moline, Shelby, Farmington, once Duluth, they would wipe the windshield of the Pontiac and say to Daddy as he was about to pay, "Where you going, mister?" and Daddy'd look them straight in the eye and say, "Up and beyond, now, up and beyond is where I'm headed."

The idea is precious seed Daddy has given me and all the night and all the travelling will be sure and land me at the one, the only, place.

At night here in Lettuce Grove when Johnboy rolls over and presses me against the wall, snoring, I crawl out from under and go stand at the window just to check it's off the latch. I can see orange lights out on the highway interchange. I look back at Johnboy's bulk on the bed asleep in pajamas, hear slurp and sloshing of the waterbed when he rolls again, and the sound of trucks out on the road. Sleep, baby, sleep, I whisper him.

A Portrait of Helena Leafly, With Bees

Stephen Guppy

If anyone had asked him what life was all about, Jake Leafly would have told them, without a moment's hesitation, that life was a pattern, an intricate design. It wasn't the things you ran into in this crazy world that mattered, he would probably have added: It was the way things fell together, and the way they fell apart.

Take bees, for example. Look at them one at a time, and you wouldn't think that they were good for much of anything. All they ever seemed to do with themselves, after all, was to fly around buzzing their brains out. But get yourself a couple of dozen hives full of the little buggers, and put them out in a meadow full of fireweed and blossoming clover, and you had yourself a machine for making honey.

It was as if each of the bees were a thread in some vast Persian carpet, like the ones that they sold at that hippie import shop in the Harbourside Mall in Nanaimo, so that you had to see a whole swarm of them working together before the pattern would emerge.

Which was something that Jake Leafly could do any time he liked.

Jake and his wife, Helena, had been keeping bees for twenty-five years, and there wasn't a little corner store from Port Alberni to Victoria that didn't have a jar or two of LEAFLY'S GOLDEN HONEY prominently displayed on its shelves. Tourists would drive fifteen or twenty miles down from the Island highway, just to stop in at their farm and buy a crock or two of their honey in bulk. A fancy health-food magazine that was published in Toronto had mentioned LEAFLY'S GOLDEN in its

"Gourmand of the Backwoods" column. It was a wonder, when you thought of it, that Jake Leafly wasn't rich.

Not that Jake himself ever gave a second thought to making money. Keeping bees, as far as he was concerned, was more of a religion than a business. It was his wife who had to worry about keeping things afloat.

And Helena Leafly had no head for business. The most fundamental principles of day-to-day commerce had always been impenetrable mysteries to her. It wasn't simply that she didn't *like* keeping the accounts or adding up figures: she seemed to have a physical aversion to mathematics. As a schoolgirl, she would creep into her Math class like some lost soul descending into the flames of the inferno, gasping like a beached fish and bugging her eyes out, in terror lest the teacher ask her to attempt some long division. Adding up her change in a supermarket was enough to give her three days of brain-numbing migraines. The mere thought of balancing the books made her nauseous.

God only knows how the business kept going. Every week or so, Helena would tie a cardboard box full of quart jars of honey onto the bockety roofrack of her faithful old VW beetle and make the rounds of all the corner stores up and down the Island, leaving the honey to be sold on consignment. The receipts she was given by the owners of these stores would invariably disappear into the voluminous pockets of her tatty old tartan jacket, where they would remain until they decomposed into fuzzy balls of lint.

If it weren't for the fact that the majority of shopkeepers with whom the Leaflys did business were honest folk who paid up their accounts without having to be prompted, in all probability Jake and Helena would have starved. As it was, there was always a trickle of money coming in from one of their retailers or another, but they were never quite sure just how much they should be making, or where it should be coming from, or when it would arrive.

Under normal circumstances, the precariousness of their income caused the Leaflys surprisingly little worry. Their requirements, after all, were modest to say the least. Jake could rarely stomach anything except Shredded Wheat and honey, while Helena lived on cigarettes, washed down with cups of tea. Neither of them had bought a stitch of clothing since before they were married: old shoes could be sent to the cobbler; old clothes could be mended and patched. And as for entertainment, there was never any problem. Jake rarely did anything of an evening but stand at the window and stare at his beehives, and Helena's weakness for lurid romances could be indulged inexpensively at the Thrift Shop in town.

It was only when they needed a buck or two for something special, like an unforeseen tax bill or a new set of brakes for the vw, that their lack of a steady income became a cause for concern. On these occasions, Helena would toss a case or two of honey into the back seat of the VW and beetle on in to the nearest hotel. Just by lugging the honey into the hotel beer parlour a jar at a time, she had discovered, she could pocket a day's wages in no time at all. It was amazing what a few beer would do to a man's sales resistance. There were men she'd known since childhood, Helena would tell you, card-carrying tightwads who'd skin a flea to save a penny, who would practically knock her over in their haste to buy her honey if she was lucky enough to catch them when they were properly in their cups.

That was the only thing that Helena had learned about doing business: Find yourself a fellow with a beer or two in his belly, and he'll buy the Graf Zeppelin and tow the damn thing home. In all of the years she'd been making the rounds of the pubs around Nanaimo, selling quart jars of LEAFLY'S GOLDEN to the pie-eyed and the plastered, she had only met one genuine exception to this rule.

Bud Posner could have drunk every last drop of beer in the world and stayed sober. Draft beer just ran right through him; he was immune to its effects. He would sit there by himself in the corner of the pub and just pour down one glass of cold draft after another from noon until midnight every day except Sunday, and never bat an eyelash or slur a single word. Helena had long since given up trying to sell her honey to Bud Posner: in all the years she'd known him, he had never bought a solitary atom of the stuff.

It wasn't LEAFLY'S GOLDEN or any other kind of sweet, sickening bee-juice that he wanted, Bud Posner would tell her, pausing briefly to drain another glass or two of beer between phrases; it was the benefit of her wisdom. What he wanted was advice.

Which was nothing out of the ordinary, as far as Helena was concerned. People were always asking her to tell them the meaning of life. Hardly a day would go by without someone or other — Chin Lee the grocer or fat Betty Walmsley or the woman with the blue hair who sat next to her at the Kiwanis bingo or the kid who pumped gas at the garage up on the highway, sidling up to her with a browbeaten, hangdog expression and whining.

"What's life all about, Mrs. Leafly? What the heck are we doing in this crazy old world?"

Now that was just the sort of nonsensical question that her husband would have relished, Helena would often think, when confronted with these querulous neighbours. Ask Jake what he thought about the Meaning of Existence, and he'd stand there jabbering about how everything was a pattern until the sun had burned out like a 40-watt lightbulb and the earth had been sold for scrap to some little green man from Mars.

Him and his goddamn *patterns*. It made you dizzy just to listen to him, mumbling on and on about how the universe was made up of a network of complex patterns, each one of which was just a small part of some other, larger pattern, so that the pattern of the particles revolving in an atom and the pattern of all the stars in all the galaxies in all Creation were really, if you examined them, the very same thing on a different scale. It was all, he would bluster, waving his long, bony fingers at the ceiling as if he were attempting to pull together the strands of his tenuous theory, exactly like the patterns in a swarming hive of bees.

Helena had been listening to Jake's lame-brained theories about patterns for so long that it was starting to make her seasick just to look at a patterned carpet. She couldn't even visit her friend Wildflower McCloskey, who ran the Mandalay Treasure Trove shop in the mall in Nanaimo, without feeling that the huge Persian carpets that covered the Treasure Trove's walls, floor and ceiling were about to dissolve into a swarm of buzzing insects. It was a menace to her sanity, having to spend her life with Jake.

Not that Helena couldn't have told you a thing or two about patterns herself, if she'd wanted to: there were times when she thought that her whole life was the working out of some devious pattern, as if she'd been put on this earth for the amusement of some bored, sadistic Fate.

Take her name, for example. Her maiden name was Palmer, and her father had been the minister at the little church in Lantzville, just up the highway from Nanaimo, and a man whose devotion to the theatre had far exceeded his devotion to God. As his wife had given birth while he was at the church hall performing *Faustus* with Ye Olde Lantzville Players, the local little theatre, it hadn't taken much imagination for him to hit on a Christian name for his newborn daughter. And Helena Palmer was a reasonable name for any girl, as Helena's mother was forced to admit. While conceding to her husband's choice in a first name for her daughter, however, the preacher's wife had stipulated that two middle names be added, names that had been in her family since Methuselah was a runny-nosed boy.

And so, burdened down with this excess baggage, Helena had been doomed to go through life as Helena Eleanor Laurentian Palmer. Or, if you reduced it to her initials, plain old H.E.L.P.

HELP!

It couldn't have been more appropriate if she had dreamed it up herself. All through her girlhood she had been plagued with a sense of impending disaster, as if the sky were about to come crashing down around her ears at any moment, or the earth to open up beneath her feet and let her fall right down to the centre of the world. While her contemporaries strode purposefully through life, bounding like so many antelopes from one triumph to another, Helena had always kept to herself, convinced that any action on her part would be an invitation to disaster, and that the only reasonable solution was to look for a safe place to hide. It was almost as if that name of hers had determined the course of her whole existence, as if the pattern of those four letters was the blueprint of her life.

It was hardly any wonder, then, that she was anxious to get married. It was the only way that she could think of to get rid of those accursed initials. When the neighbour's boy, Jake Leafly, proposed, she practically carried him into the church.

It wasn't until after the wedding was over, and they were standing around in her father's churchyard getting pelted with rice and confetti, that Helena realized she'd made a terrible mistake.

"Congratulations, Mrs. Helena Leafly!" one of the wedding guests shrieked, strafing Helena with another volley of confetti.

As Helena grinned back at the woman, it hit her. Her name, as a married woman, would be Helena Eleanor Laurentian Leafly. And her initials, heaven help her, would be H.E.L.L.

"Oh, *hell!*" she moaned, barely suppressing the urge to run screaming off into the distance, "out of the goddamn frying pan and into the goddamn fire."

Not that her life with Jake had been a hell-on-earth, exactly. It was more like a sort of limbo, a bee-infested purgatory in which every day was like every other, and every year the same year, so that they seemed to be existing in one endlessly-repeated moment, in a succession of days as identical as the cells in an infinite hive. Jake, in his simplicity, saw the whole thing as a marvel, and wandered through life lost in awe at the symphony of shifting shapes and forms that was unfolding all around him, but Helena saw the days of her life as the bars of a cage that contained her, a web of predestination from which no living thing could escape. There were times when she was so unspeakably bored that she could *feel* herself growing older, sitting there puffing a roll-your-own at the tatty kitchen table while her husband clumped through the clovered fields in his clumsy beekeeper's outfit, nodding sagely at the hives with his helmetted head like an astronaut walking on Saturn. There were times when she could have happily cut his throat, and left his carcass for his everlasting bees.

Not that there was much chance of her actually up and murdering her husband. What difference would it make to her life, after all? If she wasn't stuck out on a honey farm with a bee-crazy old duffer who thought he was Aristotle, she would only be mixed up in some even-worse disaster: it was her fate to be unhappy, and there was no escaping fate. The best that she could hope for was that Jake would go on living, because when he finally kicked the bucket she would probably wind up marrying Attila the Hun or Adolph Hitler and have to spend the rest of her life enslaving Asia or goose-stepping all over the lawn.

So instead of trying to change her life, Helena did her best to ignore it. How much longer could it go on for, after all? Another twenty years or so, and she'd be shut of the whole messy business, securely in her cosy grave, without a worry in the world.

In the meantime, however, she had plenty to keep her busy. While Jake looked after the fields and the hives and did the majority of the work collecting honey, she could always amuse herself washing out jars or sticking on the LEAFLY'S GOLDEN labels. And when she wasn't puttering around the place, or out making her endless deliveries, she could beetle on in to the Harbourside Mall and kill some time with Wildflower McCloskey, who was always glad to have someone to chew the fat with in her shop.

Wildflower had been some sort of hippie back in the sixties, and had drifted to the Island with so many others of her generation, in search of a Thoreauesque paradise among the pulp mills and the fog. After idling away a dozen years of thrashing out folk songs on homemade dulcimers and choking down out-of-season oyster stew in a leaky geodesic dome in the backwoods, she had come to Nanaimo and gone into business selling Oriental gee-gaws and books on meditation — at exactly the same time that everyone else in the world had said to hell with the Age of Aquarius and gone into real estate or peddling insurance. Undaunted by the obvious fact that everything she had in the store was at least ten years out of fashion, she sat there resolutely among the silver-plated roach-clips and the Jimi Hendrix posters, gazing in stupefied wonder at the polyestered salesmen and spikey-haired adolescents of the uncongenial eighties, who rarely even *saw* her store as they sauntered through the mall.

It was hardly any wonder, then, that she looked forward to Helena's visits. And besides, there was something so natural, so downright *organic* about old Mrs. Leafly. She would wander in from the shopping mall in her threadbare tartan jacket, peering shyly at Wildflower through her stringy fringe of grey-white hair that looked as if a blind man had cut it with tin-snips, her scrawny hands clutching the quart jar of LEAFLY'S GOLDEN that she inevitably brought along as a present. Then she'd plonk herself down among the lava lamps and the boxes of misshapen pottery, accept the cup of herbal tea that Wildflower inevitably offered, and sit there for hours without saying a word while her hostess babbled on endlessly about life on the Astral Level — which, judging by Wildflower's descriptions, was even more boring than life in the real world.

Helena, for her part, looked on her shopkeeper friend in just about the same way as she looked on her husband. This Wildflower girl, with her Theda Bara wardrobe and her esoteric theories about parallel dimensions and her bearded friends who had given up good-paying jobs to shuck oysters on leaky old fishboats, seemed almost as eccentric as Jake.

But these days nearly everyone seemed to have some harebrained theory about the Meaning of Existence. And it wasn't just the obvious flakes like Jake and Wildflower, either: there were plenty of perfectly respectable folks living right around Nanaimo, people whom Helena herself had known since they were snotty-nosed brats in grade school, who lived in fear of being blown to bits by UFOs from the planet Zargon, or who were waiting for the ghost of Elvis to rise up from his grave and redeem them, ushering in a billion years of peace and love on earth.

Sometimes Helena would drive for hours around the familiar streets of Nanaimo, gazing in absolute bafflement into the windows of nondescript houses, in each one of which, she felt certain, unimaginable lives were unfolding, desperate plans were hatched and irrevocable actions taken, whole families struggled like captured flies in sticky webs of predestination, made sacrifice to nameless gods and appeased imaginary demons, as they frantically tried to free themselves from the patterns of their lives.

It was while she was engaged in one of these endless cruises through the suburbs, weaving up and down the streets and craning her neck out the window, marvelling over the foolishness of humanity in general, that she caught sight of her old friend Bud Posner lying tits-up in the ditch. Posner, of course, was the last man on earth she'd have thought to find drunk in the gutter. While his adult life — and much of his childhood — had been one long attempt to get plastered, he had never, as far as Helena knew, met with anything resembling success. It was enough to break your heart, in fact, to see him sitting there in the corner of the beer parlour sober as a deacon, pouring down gallons of icy draft to no effect whatsoever. It was like watching someone try to hang-glide with an anchor in his pants.

But there was no doubt about it; it was definitely Posner. His awesome belly, the product of years of quaffing beer, protruded from the scurf of weeds in the ditch like a beehive in the centre of a meadow. His drunken snores buzzed loud enough to be audible above the blatt of her VW. He sounded like a swarm of bees on a windless summer evening, Helena thought, as she switched off the ignition and clambered out of her car. Scurrying across the street, she looked down at her friend in the ditch.

Was he *really* drunk? she wondered. Had he finally gotten plastered? One look at the beatific smile on his face as he lay there snoring like a poleaxed hippo was enough to remove any doubt from her mind. How wonderful he must feel, she thought, to have succeeded after all those years. Moses must have felt like that when he reached the Promised Land.

It was obvious, however, that she would have to take him home. God knows how he had found his way to this rather antiseptic suburb in the first place: it was miles from the hotel where he usually did his drinking, and even farther from the shack that he called home. Could she possibly pick him up and drag him over to the door of her VW? Assuming that she managed that Herculean feat, could she then cram him into the car? Impossible as it seemed, she would have to make an effort. She could hardly leave the poor man lying snockered in the ditch.

As she bent down to grasp Bud's beefy arm, a flicker of movement caught her eye — a golden spark that seemed to have emerged from the sleeve of Bud's sweater. It zipped past Helena's startled ear, buzzing like a runaway electron. She was halfway out of the ditch again before she realized what it was that she'd seen.

"Only a goddamn bee. . ." she muttered, sliding back down to Posner. "Goddamn things are everywhere you turn this time of year."

But before she could get to Bud again, another bee rose toward her. In a moment Bud's whole body was a heaving swarm of insects. It levitated slowly from its bed among the crabgrass, shivered into beads of light, a web of graceful motion, and dispersed among the shrubs and trees along the shady street.

Helena stood flummoxed with one foot in the ditch for a moment, gazing up into the canopy of leaves above her with a look of mute incomprehension. Then she dragged herself onto the road again and wobbled across to her vw.

It was that idiot Jake and his patterns, she thought. He had finally driven her crazy. She would wind up making wallets in the Home for the Bewildered, just from listening to him babbling on and on about his theories. From now on everything she looked at would probably dissolve into so many atoms. She'd be walking around in a universe of buzzing, swarming bees.

Her vw, however, seemed solid enough, and the street that it sat on wasn't moving. Wedging herself behind the wheel, she cautiously turned on the engine. Oblivious to metaphysics, the vw thrummed into life. Reassured of her precarious sanity, Helena shifted the car into gear.

It was then that she heard the buzzing. It seemed to come from deep inside her, as if she had swallowed an electric blender. Looking down, she saw that the tip of one of her fingers seemed to be detaching itself from the knuckle. Leaving its perch on the gearshift, it flew up at her, buzzing obscenely. In a moment the rest of her hand had dissolved, and her whole body seemed to be pulsing.

Perhaps, as her molecules swarmed out the windows and vents, she indeed saw the world as a pattern. Or perhaps it was only madness, and what she saw was simply *her* world dissolving. In any case her bulbous car came to rest against a hydrant, its tiny engine buzzing like an angry swarm of bees.

=   =   =

While Helena was away that afternoon, Jake was hard at work gathering honey. The moment she left the house, he put on his beekeeper's outfit. Having donned the wide, bell-shaped hat with its long skirt of netting and insinuated his fingers into stiff leather gauntlets, he stumbled down the rickety stairs and clumped across the yard. Pausing for a moment in the spiky strands of couchgrass at the edge of the meadow, he contemplated the emerald field with its neat rows of conical beehives, each one of which was a microcosm of the universe as a whole. Then, feeling less like a simple farmer than the high priest of some primitive religion, he passed among the buzzing throngs like the Pope among his faithful, waving a benediction with his yellow plastic bucket and stooping occasionally to gather up the molten gold that was the tribute of his flock. Alone among his beehives, Jake felt charged with the power of nature, as if each of the hives were a dynamo and he the lone conductor. His nerve-ends seemed to crackle with a tingling electrical fire.

Normally, Jake would linger a few hours in the cool fields with his beehives, and then, having filled a bucket or two with fresh honey, reluctantly trudge back to the house before Helena came home. Just as he was about to pack up his buckets and head for the farmhouse, however, he slowly began to realize that there was something peculiar going on. There seemed to be fewer and fewer bees in each succeeding hive he came to, and their omnipresent buzzing seemed to be growing fainter with each passing moment. The horrifying thought that there might be something wrong with his precious insects sent Jake scurrying up and down the symmetrical rows of beehives in a panic. It wasn't until he thought to look up that the mystery was solved.

The whole swarm had gathered into a black knot that hovered, pulsating rhythmically, in the crystalline sunlight at the far end of the meadow. Bees swirled out of the long grass toward it like water drawn into a whirlpool. Its buzzing seemed somehow purposeful, charged with inscrutable intention. Jake had never seen anything like it in all of his years on that farm.

Tearing off his veiled hat and shielding his eyes against the dazzling sunlight, Jake peered at the dark, amorphous shape that hung above the meadow, muttering to itself in an unknown, unknowable language, like the mind of an alien god.

And then, as Jake stood there staring in his cumbersome beekeeper's outfit, nervously clenching and unclenching his fists in their clumsy leather gauntlets, the swarm of bees sank slowly to the ground, then congealed and became coherent, forming itself into the mute, accusing figure of his wife.

Bad Words

Marlene Nourbese Philip

How she envied him! this new-found friend of hers. The way
he cursed. Walking before the big mirror in her parents' room,
bony chest — almost as flat as his — puffed up with the trying,
trying hard to imitate him. . . Miranda thought, maybe she
would acquire his knowledge, his way of cursing.

Starting with words like damn and blast, Miranda was slowly
working her way up her list of bad words — from the least to
the most bad. They all shared a common quality — they were
all too heavy for her tongue to lift up — so her mother
pronounced regularly. "Prick! Shit!" Miranda looked at herself
in the mirror; the smile that was reflected there was one of deep
satisfaction. Her mother was wrong — she could, would, and
did lift the weight of these words, these forbidden words with
her child tongue, the secret pleasure all the stronger for being
visible in the mirror as she sharpened her mouth around them
all. "Practice makes perfect," her father had always told her —
practise to be perfect, in control as he was — and her friend —
of words.

When she got to "fuck" she paused, took a deep breath and
mouthed the word silently then out loud. Her heart beat loudly
now as she replaced the "u" with an "o" — "fock". She felt the
sharpness and power of the word — suddenly and involuntarily
she shivered. Was it fear or excitement? She didn't know —
probably both — but didn't care.

Now came the best — the baddest of them all. Whenever
Miranda got to fuck she knew she had crossed a line — as
palpable to her as it was invisible. A different world awaited her
with the next word. A threatening word in many ways. For a
long time she could never say it out loud. As with all the other

words she had begun by mouthing it. The times when she was lucky enough to practise before the mirror as she was now, she thought she looked pretty stupid opening and closing her mouth on the word — like a fish gasping for air. But mouthing this word suggested nothing of its power, and for a long time she remained at this stage, not even being able to whisper it as she had with the others. The taboo against it was absolute — almost.

Hurrying to school one day, late and therefore alone, just so — it came out as she was crossing the bridge over the thin and brown trickle that was the Wapsey River in dry season. "Cunt!" A great wave of relief washed over her as she said the word for the first time. Her surprise at hearing it come from her own mouth brought Miranda to a standstill, and although she knew it was unlikely, she couldn't stop herself from looking behind her both fearing and expecting to see her mother standing there, a silent and stern witness to this new level of her daughter's shameful behaviour. Miranda gave a nervous laugh at seeing no one there, and hurried on saying the word over and over again to herself under her breath.

She had taken a long time to say "the word" — that was how she referred to it — but she had come to like rolling it round and round her mouth, except that you couldn't really roll these words around. They all had edges — hard edges that hurt somehow as she intentionally and deliberately strained her mouth around their shapes, her tongue paying strict attention to their individual shapes. Afterwards she would carefully examine her mouth and tongue for the staining she expected. She was surprised that her mouth did not show the outrage she had just committed.

Why was it that men had words that could excite her? Miranda would often think of this as she travelled the time between the inner and outer boundaries of her life — home and school, school and home. Chaucer, for instance, with all his plumbing the depths of women. Late at night and lying awake in bed, she would ask her older cousin what this meant and the older girl would tell the younger one about men entering women. Miranda would wonder how you could enter another person. *Fanny Hill* and Henry Miller — men's words that she read secretly, her mother not dreaming of the feelings she had, or the wetness between her thin twelve-year-old thighs. Excitement would quickly turn to O.K.-so-what boredom and after the third or fourth time a woman's depth was plumbed, her twelve-year-old mind was bored and wanted something else. So she would go back to her practice make perfect and that most secret of words and most profane when coupled with another. Mother and cunt. In their opposition the two words — one resonant with safety and comfort, the other harsh, defiant and threatening — were locked together irrevocably. The power of this combination, made greater by the secret nature of it made her feel light-headed and even faint at times.

Before moving to the city Miranda had never heard "the word" before. No one told her what it meant. No one had to. From the first day she heard it, felt it sear her ears, spindly-legged and innocent as she was coming fresh from the country, she knew it was bad. Bad bad.

Until then totee was the worst word she had known, but it was child bad. Its badness existed only in the world of children when you could laugh at a boy — only boys had totees — and say, "look, look, I see he totee," and the girls would giggle and scream and laugh and run away leaving the boy shame for having a totee. Except Clarence. He just took his for granted. Clarence was her cousin who played marbles in the hot sun with her and her brothers and sisters for hours on end under the guinep tree and let her play with his balls while they stood waiting their turn.

Every time Clarence stooped to pitch he was facing Miranda — looking back on it that's the way it seemed to her. Her eyes would drop to the crotch of his pants where the stretching, straining cotton threads struggled to hold the seams together, her gaze riveted by what she feared and expected to happen. Suddenly there it was — she let out the breath she hadn't

known she was holding — his little worm, his totee hanging
out. Totee a soft word with none of the edges of these new
words. He let her touch it sometimes, his totee, and the soft
warm snuggly sacs behind it.

She had had no words for them — he just had them. Balls
would come later. In the hot sun, waiting their turn to pitch
their marbles, he would stand patiently while she crept her
hand up his short khaki pants to his totee and then to the cool
yet warm squishy things, her fingers moving and squishing
them around — doing the same things that her tongue now did
with these new words she was learning — exploring the limits
of her world and, therefore, of difference.

Miranda and Clarence had never done anything more than
that. He, in fact, did nothing, a willing subject to her inquiry
and always in public. Her brothers and sisters must have
known what she was doing, but in that sometimes inexplicable
and implacable silence of childhood, no one said anything to
her or to her mother. There had been no secrecy to her
exploration, and they felt no need to swear themselves to
secrecy about something that was no secret. There was consequently nothing to tell.

The words she now explored were, however, adult-bad, big-
people bad and secrecy was the screen behind which she now
travelled into their newness. Secrecy was what she needed to
explore them; and secrecy was the key to why these words
were so bad. She had only to look at her mother's face to know
they were bad — the way she shut down her eyes and her
whole face at the sound of these words, particularly the one
that referred to her — to all mothers.

This word had to do with women, all women. That much
Miranda was sure of. And weren't all women mothers? Maybe
only mothers had cunts because that was the only way she had
ever heard it used. Never your sister's cunt, or your
grandmother's cunt. Only your mother's cunt. And she had
wanted both to cover her ears and stretch them wide to take in
the sound of these words. Would she have a cunt when she

grew up? She didn't dare ask her mother. Did she have one now? Was it something that came with having children? Once left on her own she got a mirror to explore exactly where she knew the word referred to — except she wasn't a mother — not yet anyway. As she explored she said the word soft soft to herself, mouthing it, mashing it between her teeth, tasting it, whispering it — looking to see if she changed as she said it.

In her house there was no word for what Miranda explored with her fingers. Baby girls had pat-a-cakes, or muckunzes or pum pums. As you grew older, the safety of those soft domestic words disappeared leaving behind a thing unnamed, referred to only by the neutral pronoun: "Have you washed IT yet?" Or, sometimes, "Have you washed yourself yet?" She knew full well that the self referred to was not the whole self, but only that tiny part of the self that somehow became your entire self. If you were a woman. Until it became a mother's cunt — harsh, jagged, the words intended to cut to the quick the man at whom it was aimed.

Lips would curl savagely around the words, "Your" shape the words with a blunt and rough-hewn style replacing the "t" and "h" with a double "d", "mudder", only to let fly the deadly missiles that home in and explode — "Yuh mudder cunt", in the man's face, dripping the bitter sweet sticky mess all over him. Miranda had seen grown men grow murderous at this insult. She had seen her brother come home in tears because of this.

It was only men she had heard saying these words. Did women curse it too, or was it only a male curse? And what did women say — "You father's prick"? Somehow it didn't sound as bad as mother's cunt. She knew all the words now and cock or father's cock just didn't count if you really wanted to curse. Put together a bad word like sucker to make cock-sucker the word become really bad, but it didn't, at least in her books, come close in badness to "the word".

The exploration of forbidden words was always always in the practice makes perfect of secret places — at night in bed with

the sheets pulled up tight tight over her head; in the bathroom
under cover of the shower's noise, or if she was home alone,
in front of the big, round mirror in her mother's bedroom. Her
mother and father shared the room but Miranda always
thought of it as her mother's room — it smelt like her, carried
the imprint of her order. The big obzoky bed took up most of
the smallness of the shabby room; in the daytime, with its dark
wood shiny with the high gleam of regular Saturday polishings
it seemed not to belong — did not quite fit — but at nighttime
when hurricane season came round, or during earthquake
time, it was the safest place to curl the body round sister or
brother or mother, its wide expanse like some ballasted haven
among the shaking and the lightning and the thunder and her
mother's voice no longer forbidding but soothing and comfort-
ing at each tremor or flash or roll. Miranda now pranced up
and down the hard mattress feeling boldface and nervous. She
watched herself in the mirror as she formed the words —
excitement balancing risk, like playing with matches under the
house, knowing it was worth the flogging she might get if she
were caught there. To practise make perfect forbidden words
in forbidden spaces. . .

In this new country — for that was how she saw her move to
the city — even the air felt and smelt different. Where before
there were no spaces or places she could not enter, where
before everything was allowed and permitted, now the forbidden was usual: forbidden places, especially for girls, forbidden
books, forbidden people, forbidden words, forbidden thoughts
and yet what was forbidden was all the more clear to her
because it was forbidden. The forbidden had come to life in
new and unusual ways in this new place.

For a while Miranda envied her new friend — nothing was
forbidden him. Miranda's eyes would follow his sure and
insolent swagger, trail each movement of his walk — it was all
the more brutal to her for its casualness and confirmed his
indifference to all that Miranda could not ignore. His ignorance
of the forbidden was absolute. And she could feel her thin body

vibrate with the energy of want — so keen was her desire for this state at times. Then something happened that made her switch her loyalties and allegiances abruptly. Miranda was stubborn in her loyalties once formed, and in making this switch she felt that she had, somehow, betrayed her friend. But it was a war, wasn't it, she told herself as she hurried to school one day arguing with herself, and you had to take sides.

Pomona Adams was a large and beautiful brown-skinned woman. Miranda was impressed. Very impressed with Pomona — with all things about Pomona — her size: she was close to six feet with full shapely breasts — the kind Miranda wanted — wore high heels all the time and had the largest behind Miranda had ever seen. But more than anything else what Miranda was impressed with was Pomona's ability to curse. Miranda was intrigued by how Pomona, her plump arms resting on her window sill, could casually carry on a conversation with her neighbour, pause mid-sentence, calmly tell her son to stop kicking the arse out of his shoes, turn back to her neighbour and continue her conversation as if nothing had happened. Miranda was entranced by the way Pomona could combine words when she cursed — words that she, Miranda, would never have dreamt of putting together, like arse and shoe. Under the pretext of doing homework she would often try to parse the use of certain words she had heard Pomona using — trying hard to understand the context. She was not very successful, for while arse was a noun, shoes did not have arses, yet she knew what Pomona had meant. . . She shrugged her bony shoulders and gave up in frustration after a while. She was young, but she recognised artistry when she heard it and she knew that if ever there was a cursing contest, Pomona would win hands down and she, Miranda, would be there cheering her on.

Pomona, Miranda saw, had powerful words too and she used them as if none were forbidden, as if she had the right to use them all — the good *and* the bad. And something about the way Pomona walked made Miranda suspect that Pomona's

words, especially the bad ones, and the way she used them
were connected with her body. She used her words like she
walked, with a prideful determination that matched her size.
You couldn't even call what Pomona did walking, Miranda
thought as she watched Pomona mashing the ground as if she
owned it and knew that she owned it — each step was merely
intended to confirm that ownership. The proof of this connection between Pomona's body and her words came early one
morning several weeks after Miranda had moved to the city
and while she was struggling to understand this new badness
that was all around her.

Pomona and one of her neighbours hadn't talked for several
months, they just threw words at each other — this Miranda
only found out by listening to her parents' conversations. When
Pomona and Sybil stopped speaking to each other their
children did too. The men, like men, pretended to be above it
all, and would nod to each other. To go out Pomona had to pass
Sybil's house, so almost every day as Pomona passed by,
Pomona and Sybil would be throwing words at each other
under their breath so that the other one wouldn't hear, but
know something was said, or just over their breath so that the
other one did hear. Miranda never found out what Sybil said
to Pomona on this particular morning but Pomona's response
was the reason why she switched allegiances. She saw Pomona
lift one of her solid arms, grab the flesh on the underside of her
upper arm and say, "Look, see here, this is flesh!" She flung
her challenge at Sybil who was by no means a small woman,
but certainly smaller than Pomona. As if this was not enough
Pomona turned her back to her opponent and with two hands
flung her skirt up and up over her behind; down, down and still
further down came Pomona's panties, her hands swift and sure
with the choreography of pride. "Look, you want to see flesh,
this, this is flesh!" And there for all the world who cared to look
and Miranda was Pomona's fat backside exposed to the sweet
morning air as she grabbed a handful of her brown flesh to
demonstrate the proof of its existence. Proud and in her brown
amplitude, unashamed of her size or her words, any of her

words, particularly the bad ones that now, after the unmatched challenge of her flesh, issued forth from her round pretty mouth, Pomona threw her words in her neighbour's face and made a stand for truth — the truth of flesh and bad words. "Come in here now!" Miranda's mother's voice banished her from the forbidden and the desired — to be bad — to use bad words — to make them good perhaps, though she liked the power that badness gave them.

Once again in front of the mirror in her mother's bedroom, the house empty, Miranda throws up her skirt exposing her bony bottom to the mirror. "Yes, yes, this is flesh," gripping her arm, tightly muscled with youth. "Oh, hell!" Disappointed, she flops on the bed. "To have a behind — no, an arse like that," she says out loud — "something you could grab on to." She longed for flesh on her arms or breasts like Pomona. The person she now most wanted to be like was Pomona. In the dark she told herself that she didn't so much want to be like Pomona Adams as to, curse like her. She wasn't sure if there was a difference. Practice makes perfect Miranda reminds herself once again and stand on to the bed now, hoping the mattress would give her the sort of rocking majestic walk of Pomona; she starts to work at her words again, trying hard to get the right inflection, the right sneer. Women curse too — she knew that now. Pomona had taught her that. She had even heard one say "the word", the one that made men cry, the mother's curse. It wasn't only men that used it, but only men cried or got really angry at it. The women didn't carry on like the men did at the mother's curse. Why that was she hadn't figured out. Not yet anyway.

As long as she continued to practise in secret Miranda felt uninitiated into the world of the forbidden. And her initiation, she felt, had to be a public one — a speaking of at least one of these words in the presence of others. She picked one — shit — knowing she was a coward for choosing one of the least bad. Plotting and practising to make perfect in public, she rehearsed all her words, tasting them secretly as you can only words. In the secret spaces of her mouth she spun, unspun and respun

with a loving tongue a new language, the language of badness.
And her testing and retesting of these words became a fuguing
against and with the words of her mother and father.

"But he say massa day done, and that all the children going to
have a free education." Miranda didn't so much listen — these
conversations went on almost every night — as she was aware
of the rising and falling voices drifting in from the front porch
to where she sat preparing for the examination that would give
her a chance to enter yet another forbidden world. Her parents
called it a better education. She heard the voices rise and fall
with the rhythm of passion and excitement which
strengthened the already rhythmic language. "Yes, but he not
going far enough, England and America still going control the
economy." The cadenced voices reflect the trajectory, the rise
and fall of empire. The deep bass of her father's voice, her
mother's higher softer tones throw back and forth between
them words like politics and freedom, pulling a thread here, a
strand there, trying hard to twist and braid these hard words
into dreams for their children — a good job in the civil service
perhaps — they explore the furthest limits of their world —
maybe, even a doctor! As they talked, Miranda felt rather than
heard the urgency behind her parents' words, words which
they had stoked and fired into life and now would not let die,
words which under the lash and caress of their tongues now
transformed themselves — slavery into freedom, nigger into
human. Miranda heard and felt all this, she knew that like her
they were entering forbidden spaces, naming now what they
had only dared to dream of before. In secret. But Miranda also
knew they would never see how her exploration of bad words
was anything else but an expression of vice — proof of her
badness. So she smiled a knowing smile to herself and continued working.

Sunday. That was the day Miranda chose for her initiation. She
had woken up at cock-crow and knew that that was the day, but
when it was to be she couldn't tell. It would just happen when
it was time she thought. After church and the heavy Sunday

lunch, and still dressed in their Sunday best, her mother had taken them all to a neighbour's for a visit. There the two women and the children had all sat stiffly drinking sweet drinks on the front porch before the adults released them to play in the front yard while they talked.

Like her favourite cowboy shoot-out scenes from Saturday matinees where the good guy, usually Roy Rogers or Gene Autry — dressed in white — meets the bad guy dressed all in black and shoots it out, Miranda replayed the scene in her mind for many months, even years after. She was standing close to the top step about to jump all the way down to the bottom — some six or so steps — when someone, she couldn't tell who it was since the push came from behind, pushed her off. She never found out who it was, she never cared enough. Like the morning "the word" had just popped out over the Wapsey River, she didn't will them, the words just came, "Oh shit!" The release was almost too much to bear, and before she knew what she was doing, before she could savour the delight and pride she felt, she heard herself, "Oh fucking, fucking shit!" She saw the shock on everyone's face and felt a rush of excitement. One or two of the other children even had their hands over their mouths as if they themselves had said the words, and that made her want to laugh out loud. Her mother's face was serious — like a bull she remembered thinking. Maybe she added that thought later — as time went on Miranda did have a tendency to embellish the memory. Her mother's full eyes that could, in public, cow them into quiet, now gazed at Miranda commanding her to silence. As if she were rushing toward a cliff in preparation for leaping and flying, Miranda saw it all, and knew she couldn't stop or she would fall and not fly. She saw the licking that her father would give her with the thick leather strap that lay coiled in the bottom of the bureau like some lifeless but still threatening snake — there was a rumour that it had been soaked in pee to make it sting more; she saw the washing out of her mouth that her mother would carry out. But she also saw Pomona Adams with her shapely breasts and large backside mashing the ground — proudly — and thought of her using her words and her body just the way she wanted to, and Miranda smiled and rushed to embrace the unembrace-able, the forbidden: "And your mother's cunt!" She slung her mouth around the words and repeated them all again to no one in particular, but with a bravado and a gauche sureness which was sureness all the same, and an understanding way beyond her years. She had practised to make perfect and she had come close to perfection that Sunday afternoon. She understood badness now and that was what mattered.

The words had not stained her mouth — even in this public uttering. The moist, wet, inner pink space of her mouth had become a tender womb to bad words, any words — mother's cunts, pricks, dicks — the words were embedded deep inside Miranda filling up all the secret places and spaces created by the forbidden. Like Chaucer's male characters the words had plumbed her depths — mother's cunts and all. No one, not even the guardian of space and words, her mother, could take them from her. They're all mine now, Miranda thought as she lay in bed, remembering how she had panted and her forehead had broken out in sweat after she was done swearing. "But see here," her mother's friend had said, "she not even done grow yet and she want to be woman." Miranda's eyes had locked with her mother's — behind the hardness of the glare she could faintly recognise the hurt — she had shamed her in public, and for that she was sorry, but not for saying the words. Her fingers now gently touched the raised weals on her arms and legs from the flogging her father had given her. They were the painful proof of her allegiance with Pomona Adams. And the truth. There was a certain truth in those words, she knew that now; it was that truth that made some people dislike them so — like men crying at the mother's curse. Having uttered them Miranda now felt that she had made the words good, especially the mother's curse, but she now wanted very much to keep the power of their badness. And how was she to do that — make them good yet keep them bad?

On that thought Miranda fell asleep.

White Lies

Sean Virgo

He is very stubborn at meal-times.

The doctor's house was hidden, like the school, from the town's eyes. But not by a wall. There was a high cedar hedge, trimmed neatly, all round the grounds. With a few arching shoots that the shears had missed, pointing to the sky as if they would be trees before the gardener came round again. Miss Danby snicked the iron gate firmly behind them, then made him walk ahead up the curving gravel path to the big house. The lawn was close-cut, in alternating swathes of light and dark green. In the centre of it stood a tree he did not know: with deep groves like snakes in the corky bark and high spreading branches. All round the tree's base was a litter of tiny leaves; even as they were walking the leaves were falling to the grass. Such light and numerous leaves for so solid a tree. The tree was alive, but in early summer it was shedding little leaves all over the immaculate lawn.

The front of the house was a glass room. Things were growing inside — tendrils and vines groping all across the panes of glass. Miss Danby set him aside and rapped on the side door. "You speak up now, David," she said, straightening her shoulders, "and look the doctor straight in the eye." She tugged nervously at her sleeve; he could smell the hospital soap that all the women teachers used. He wondered if upstairs they shared a dormitory too. And if they got their buttocks flicked with a towel when they were too long at the washbasin. "Don't let us down, David," said Miss Danby.

A woman was coming towards the door through the green air of the glass room. Pulling off gardening gloves, a pair of sécateurs gripped in one hand. She was small and moved briskly. Her face at the glass was a dark bird's, but her eyes took you in. Unlike the teachers'. She swung the door towards her. "No need to knock, Miss Danby, you know — it's a wonder I heard you with my face buried in the fuchsias." And laughed, briskly, not to waste any time. "Well, laddie, you're a new face here."

"It is David," said Miss Danby, "he has been with us since Easter but is not settling in as well as we would expect."

"Good morning, David," said the woman. Casting a shrewd look but not intruding.

"David," said Miss Danby.

"Ah he's a mite shy," said the lady, "and no harm in that. I'll go on ahead and see that Ronald is prepared for you."

"That is Miss Macalisdair, the doctor's sister," chided Miss Danby. "And David, you must show respect."

He was left in the room while Miss Danby went through to speak to the doctor. He heard the three voices: one flat, one bright, one hearty. The room was almost empty: leather-bound chairs and a dark heavy table with magazines on it. He clung to the chair he had chosen, swinging his legs. The room smelt of polish, but the wood panels on the wall and the big fireplace gave it a relaxed air. He fingered the knobbed arm of his chair: this town was full of trees he did not know and furniture made of strange wood. The leather seat made the back of his legs sticky. He squirmed. He stuck his hand down between his legs, inside his trousers. To spite Miss Danby whose flat voice he could hear behind the door.

He craned his head round to the window. It looked into the hot glass room full of plants and beyond them he could see the strange tree on the lawn. One of the highest limbs swooped at the end like a swimmer's arm. That would make a good bow. he thought that kind of wood might make the best bow in the world. He could shoot arrows right over the house in the vacations, and his cousins who were free would envy him going

away where there was such wood. He would agree to bring
them back some of the wood though it would not, of course,
be as perfect as his own piece. He would come one day and cut
off that branch. He would peel off that snaky bark and the
sapwood — he could feel it, wet and white, it would smell like
cucumber flesh, and he would make his bow and shoot arrows
over his Chenni's roof.

The door opened and he turned back to the room, slipping his
hand from his trousers though the shirt front came out too. He
put his hands on his knees and shifted onto the edge of the
chair. "Stand up, David," said Miss Danby. "No, no, we'll stay
right in here," the man said, "if you ladies give us leave." Small
like his sister but his hair was a rich sandy colour. The same
briskness. And the eyes that took you in. Pale blue under foxy,
bushy eyebrows. David wondered if the doctor could smell his
fingers. Or if he would mind.

Doctor Macalisdair sat on the edge of the table. "Miss Danby
has been telling me about you, David. The ladies must have
their say first, you see. Oh decidedly." And the wrinkles at his
eyes creased comically. "Now it's your turn, laddie. What do
YOU say?" David decided that he had a friend; "She's a skinny
mean bitch," he said. Energetically. The man looked at him in
amazement. "Oh that's not what I meant at all. Decidedly not.
Oh dear. Well, we'll let it pass now. We'll forget that. I brought
it on myself. Tell me about yourself, lad. You're not eating, you
see."

But you don't get off that easy mister. I don't trust you no more
than the others, and you'll tell on me I know, after your tricks.
Yes and no is all you'll get from me. But the man shrugged it
off and behaved as if they were the best of friends. He was sharp
enough to get all he wanted from yes and no and David almost
enjoyed the sport. And he didn't smell like the school. Later he
caught the boy looking out at the tree. "You'll not have seen
one before, I suppose?" And ignoring the rebuff, "We call it a
locust tree and it's the pride of Miss Macalisdair's heart."

"Would it be good for a bow? The wood?" It was hard not to like the man and this was important.

"A bow?" said the doctor, and looked curiously from the boy to the tree and back. "Well, I wouldna be surprised."

"It has lots of leaves."

"Oh it has, aye, you've noticed that. And most of them on the ground it seems," and he laughed gaily. The lad was easily won. "Come you through here, David, before we join the ladies again." And he pushed open a dark panelled door and held it for the boy. It was a wonderful place. It was full of things. There were spears and shields and a tiger skin on the floor; and paintings on the wall of mountains and cattle and bucks with huge racks staring out at you. And an otter with following eyes. There was a big white bird, bobbing on a perch with a silver chain round its leg. And on one wall a buckskin shirt, with a great bull's head outlined in black and white on the chest. He moved over to look: the design was stitched out of porcupine quills. It was a wonderful place, it smelt good, the air was right. He always was amazed in white men's houses but he did not expect to be impressed.

Then the bird gave a cough and said, "The Lord is my shepherd." David swung round in astonishment and the bird whistled and laughed. Its yellow talons hopped sideways down the perch and it blinked its ugly eyelids. "Karrk," it said, "am I no a bonnie fighter?" And swung itself about on its perch in delight.

"There's a parrot you see, David. We have taught it to speak. Polly is thirty-seven years old, nearly my age, aren't you, Polly?"

"The Lord is my shepherd," said the bird.

"Nae doot, nae doot," murmured the doctor, "oh yes, decidedly. Well we must go, David. You'll come again I hope. Aye, I'll see to it."

"I had hoped to speak to you alone, Doctor," Miss Danby said when they came in.

"Ah no need, Miss Danby. He'll mend, you see. Let him come back to visit me on Thursday."

Miss Danby sighed. "We can't have him spoiled, Doctor."

Macalisdair glanced at his sister. "Ah, I have no criticisms, Miss Danby, but I take an interest in David here. Miss Macalisdair will tell you I'm sure that even a plant takes a while to acclimatize."

Walking back down the gravel path, following the teacher, David looked up into the moulting locust tree and lovingly picked a huge bogey out of his nose.

He would understand a caged thing, Jeannie.

His room at Chenni's house had rough wooden siding, uncovered. It was red cedar except for one plank near his bunk. That was yellow cedar. He had smelt it his first night on the islands and now this was his home. So now he cut a splinter from the plank with his knife every time he came back from the residential school. And chewed the sliver in his sleep, tasting and smelling the sweet peppery oil in the wood.

In his second term at the school he had an essay to write. He had two essays to write every week for homework. At the residential school you did your homework at the same desk you did your classwork in. This was the first essay that he could choose his own subject for. He wrote "In my Chenni's house we mostly sit around in the evenings. My Chenni sometimes cuts faces out of wood. It is alder or yellow cedar. He was a good carver when he was young. Now his fingers is knotted. Mr. Collison bought a rattle from him for twenty dollars and sent it away. We live on the islands in my Chenni's house. When I go there in the vacation he will take me fishing. He used to be a great fisherman, my Nonnie told me so. My cousin Ben is older than me. He doesn't go to residential. Sometimes he sleeps at my Chenni's house. He is a fisherman. No time for more."

"You should call your cousin Benjamin, David, that is his correct name. And you must learn not to use those Indian words, that is not fair to the Reverend Gresham who cared so much to send you here. You will realize when you are older how fortunate you boys are. Not many Indian boys, David, have this chance in life."

Get them away from the sea. It makes them restless.

None of the other boys came from the islands. They came from all over the place, except from the town where the school was. The boys from there were sent to another residential school, somewhere towards Prince Rupert. Near the ocean. When you marched past the houses to church on Sundays, you could see the native people on one of the streets. They watched the crocodile of grey-suited boys in a different way from the white people but they despised you just as much. And you hated them even more. You had to — what else could you do when the little kids yelled at you or threw mud. And at the church there were always a few Indians in stiff clothes, very thick with Monohan and the reverend; always nodding and smiling whatever was said to them. They made you ashamed.

The problem boys at the school would trade stories at night, squatting behind their bedheads against the tin wall. Peter Wilson told stories about Dsonoqua stealing babies from behind the houses and packing them off to the woods in her basket. She was the one with the great hungry kissing mouth. David remembered her from when he was with his father's people and he liked the tales. And about Hamatza the cannibal and his hummingbird.

David would tell about the Gageets, the drowned people's spirit who sits on your roof-beam and drums his heels on the shakes. Waiting for you to stick your head out.

Billy August told them about his uncle who was drowned
fishing and came back again after a year, deaf and dumb and
with the whale-killer's tattoo on his chest.

Jonathan Aretka (though the teachers called him Archer) had
a whale's tooth hidden in his box. It had a raven's face carved
in it. He said he could steal Mr. Monahan's soul away with it
and leave him sickening. If only he could get a bit of his spittle.
They watched carefully in case he ever should spit.

When Mr. Monahan caught them squatting behind the beds
he would beat them. "I know your filthy habits," he said, "why
will you act like savages. Disgusting."

And from the breakfast table Miss Danby and Miss Farel and
Miss Overton would cast virginal and reproachful looks at
them.

But usually it wasn't Mr. Monohan who caught them. Usually
one of the older boys reported them to him. Most of the older
boys at the school kept their starched collars tightly buttoned
all day long.

They did not go outside the school grounds very often except
on Sundays. They did not understand this strange flat land
anyway. If you were to believe some of the older boys, the Devil
was at large out there ready to swarm into the grounds at night
(ignoring the broken bottles cemented to the wall tops) and
wait at the windows for sinners and blanket Indians.

He was exposed to some unfortunate practices when young.

"Ae fond kiss," said the parrot. "Oh decidedly. Amen." "Oh yes,
decidedly," said the doctor, rubbing his hands. "They pick up
things you don't intend, David, they're most aggravating creatures, yes decid—" and the pair of them broke out laughing.
Jeannie Macalisdair called from the conservatory: "Will you
two cackling loons be ready for tea in ten minutes?"

"We will, we will," her brother shouted back, "Yon bird is
getting out of hand, Jeannie. We'll be sending him to school

yet, eh David?" and he cocked his sandy eyebrows ruefully.
"'Twould make a man of him, of a sort. Though for the life of
me I know not if Polly's a he or a she."

"God is good," suggested the bird.

But David had turned away.

"It's always yon buffalo shirt, David. You canna keep your eyes
from it." And for the first time he took it down for the boy to
hold. Try as he would he could not interest David in his
precious collection of stamps, or even in the weapons he had
brought back from Africa. For him the room was built round
those things. But not for the boy. It was this room that David
was most relaxed in but you could see that for him the Black-
foot shirt was the heart of it.

"It's supple yet, you see. Now smell it, Davie, smell the good
woodsmoke on it. That's the secret of good tanning."

David touched the quill pattern. His rather blunt brown fingers
moved as gently as though he fondled a live thing. He held it
folded across his arm and squatted down absorbed on the floor.
The brown boy with close-cropped black hair, squatting in
Christian clothes on the skin of a tiger, holding a buckskin to
him as reverently as if it were the shroud of Christ himself.

And to some, thought Macalisdair, it would make a sad kind of
sense. Indian to Indian. Savage to savage. But he knew better,
knowing something of this uprooted boy, knowing something
too of those people on the plains. He wished he could tell David
the whole story: how the old man had approached him near a
liquor store in Calgary and offered him the shirt for a bottle of
rum. And how he had coveted the shirt and paid the price.

"It belonged to a great hunter, Davie," he said and he squatted
down beside the boy, resting his hand on the tiger's head. "He
had earned the buffalo crest, you see — he had killed so many
and kept his people fed." He fingered one of the stiff locks of
hair along the fringes and sensed in the boy an instinct to pull
it away. To David it was HIS shirt. "D'you ken what these are,"

he asked, avoiding competition. "They're scalp locks, laddie. He was a hunter of men, too." And the boy ran his finger down the sleeve to the last two locks: one blond, one a brighter red than Macalisdair's own. Their eyes met. "Aye," sighed the doctor, "I must put it back now, David." Where was the boy going? What would they make of him in the school? And the devil of it was, what good would it do him? Maybe he and Jeannie were doing the lad more harm than good.

His family were all killed in a fire.

Jeannie Macalisdair came in brightly and lit the lamps. "You'll have no eyes left, you boobies," she said. "Now, isn't that more like it?"

"Kaark," said the bird.

"Oh, now you ungrateful beastie, say something decent."

"The Lord is my shepherd," the bird said lazily.

"Oh decidedly," whispered David in pretty fair imitation.

"Amen," said bird, man and woman as one.

Then they sent him away to his mother's people. It couldn't work.

"Jeannie and I are taking our trip to the East," said the doctor, "and we're leaving in a month. So you'll have two weeks at school before vacations without coming to see us."

"But you'll be fine, won't you David," said the woman.

"When are you coming back?"

"We'll be here before the start of next term."

God sees everything you do. The devil never sleeps.

The man shape blotting out the window; short, massive arms easing the sash free and reaching in for the bed. The four of them awake together in an instant and rigid. Then, in realization, half swallowing back the ball of fear. His brothers and Mary giggling at the adventure, at Davie's own fear, but themselves clutching at the blankets in terror of the grab man. Who at this time of night had no face, like the masked ones. Then roughly enough out into the night, a slap on the back and then the pretence of kidnapping. The silent figure that dwarfed him leading him across the old orchard and around the lagoon to the dance house. Pushed in at the doorway, to the heat and the stink and noise, guided past legs and behind backs that did not notice. Put at a side bench with other young ones where one boy was just forgetting his tears as he looked about him and another, too young, was sleeping.

The strangest thing of all, that it did not seem strange. The raised benches all round the house walls were crowded; not like church; not like a party. People came and went all the time; they laughed and ate and drank and passed remarks, yet their attention was focused somehow, always, upon the scene in the centre.

The biggest men were there: huge figures, stripped to the waist, pounding endlessly like crabs around the fires, stamping their feet, slapping their thighs, grunting, sweating. Younger men and youths in the circle outside mimicked their actions. Along one side sat the old men, nearly all of them small and withered, but dominating. They sat like judges. Every nod and gesture had weight and the great flat faces of the dancers looked anxiously toward them for favour.

A yell came from behind, from the rafters above the door. The old ones raised their hands and the dancers stepped back and threw themselves down, exhausted, by the fires. Women passed down drinks to them. The cannibal pole was out at the end of the floor and two young dancers were writhing like snakes through the tight holes that were its mouths. The head at the pole's top opened and closed its jaws as the flat drumbeats speeded. Sometimes a face peered out from the painted lips, then it would vanish. One of the dancers dived out upon the beaten earth floor and began to go crazy in front of the pole. He buzzed like a hummingbird while the other went on with his snake dance as before. They were in time together despite the frenzy; in time to the drums. And aware of the judgements of the Old.

Then a voice from an empty space of sand by the muted drums. Out of nowhere a command. And from nowhere too, through the smoky flame-shot air came birds winging and diving over the dancers' heads and straight towards the crowd. So they all ducked. They laughed but were afraid. As the birds swooped down and crossed again, the dancer on the pole leapt from the wild man's mouth and somersaulted over the ground towards his companion. Who disappeared — before them all he was clean gone, leaving his pursuer baffled in the smoke.

He looked around for other blood. The old man on the left pointed. The largest of the fire-dancers was attacked, bitten on the shoulder — the wild man danced away in great leaping steps down the length of the house. Now, beside the drums, songs were being chanted softly by the elders and the fire dancers. Almost a muttered singing. Private. The lapsing rhythm picked up again as the wild man swarmed through his pole to the hungry surmounting jaws. Then he, too, disappeared.

The dance house rang with a shout of happy awe, and before the echo could die, the fire dancers were up again.

Davie knew it all — it was not talked of directly among the children: you waited until you witnessed; but now he was there it had its meaning. And the people had meaning too, released in this house from their year-long disguises. From this the old dreamer on his rotting porch, the fat drunk weaving off the highway from the city, got the dignity that defied the White lies. Their privacy.

And when Abe Dundas, a wild youth in grease-back hair and flapping city pants clutching a rum bottle, tried again and again to break yelling into the group of fire dancers, the big man, the cannibal's victim, patiently picked him up and threw him firmly but without rancour into the night. The big man was Raymond Fall, himself drunk four days a week while the money lived, and he did his chucking out with patience, even humour, and left and rejoined the dance without any loss of harmony. And the Old sat impassively, as though all were a part of their purpose.

Later, weariness rolling his eyes up under their lids, Davie himself was standing beside the elders, watching as those the grab man had seized last year performed their dances and songs. Beside him old chief Reuben Fall was poking and pinching at his ribs, kneading the little slack of skin at his waist, stroking dry old fingers down his spine and knuckling each vertebra. Not cruelly or even with much apparent interest — it seemed, as he eyed the young dancers and grunted to the other Old, to be more of physical doodling.

Yet there was point to it. There came the time when Davie ran with sweat; and fear and pain sent the muscles of his stomach knotting and clasping against him. They were watching Willie Martin, just a little older than Davie, having his spirit called. The year since he had been taken to the dance house hadn't worked for him and now the big men were trying to force it. He had been danced until his legs bent crazily under him and his face hung rubbery, swinging from shoulder to chest. He lolled against the men. Now two men held him by the fire and another took out deer hooves from the ashes and pressed them on his chest and belly. Davie felt himself there — it was happening to him: his hand hung limply against his thigh and the fingers took on a life of their own, dancing like a little man impelled, fingers taking up rhythm from the drums which had not stopped once that evening, beating on his thigh like puppet feet in a new dance. For a moment he might have been fainting as the flames and Willie's lolling face turned upside and floated in the rafters. And as if through holes in the shadows he saw other movements — the quick whisk of fur behind salal, little hand paws darted into running water, black mirror eyes in a mask and peeping milk teeth. The sudden smell blew into him too, the subtle individual smell of the beast. Then he was back, his limbs shaking under his clammy skin, with the old man's hands on his shoulders now, the smell of him like the beast's across Davie's face, and the old voice it seemed whispering something to him across a gulf too far.

Chief Reuben was on his feet and turning to the other Old. Then Davie was being pushed outside, leaving Willie to his ordeal, the heartbeat drums and the heat and close togetherness of the firelight leaping round on the mirrors of sweating arms and faces.

So that the night air above Dogfish Bay was like a whip on his cheek. Old Reuben was almost again the little has-been, beside him in the dark, shorter than himself. But he was choosing fathership over him now. "You're going to live in my house, Davie," he said, his voice harsh in the orchard. And pushed the boy off in the direction of his shack with that irritable vehemence that you noticed about him when he wasn't just dozing on his porch.

But his voice softened as they walked, the grass wet to their ankles, and learnt the measure of the night. A looncall from the lagoon threaded itself through the old talking, making a strong rope. "The spirit is strong in you, Davie. You will learn with me until you can be tested alone. I will show you." And from there upon his words to the shelf where the waterfall came dropping down from the plateau, carrying voices in its thunder to the starving, waiting boy...

Across the orchard, fire was wrapping itself around posts and rafters. "That is my house," said Davie; and the old man beside him turned slack and helpless and began moaning softly like a dreamer...

Do not take the doctor for granted, David. Do not depend on other people.

If he was very bad he would be forbidden his walk each Thursday along the outskirts of town to the gate in the cedar hedge. But if he was just bad enough he would be made, now he was thirteen, to clean the staff washrooms. From the window up there, at the end of the corridor, he could see the locust tree, spare and tall beyond the high brick wall and the aspen grove. He would never make that bow now, or feel the cucumber sap of the wood, but the tree mattered and the bow curve of its long arm still stretched like a sign in the sky over the doctor's home.

He was very bad and he forfeited one of his walks. He was dishwasher for a week and he didn't get near the upstairs window. Daring not to show how much this mattered or he would be blackmailed for ever.

He had given his talk to the class about salmon fishing. Told how his Chenni threw salt to the water and spoke to the fish before casting the net. Reverend Rickerts had a thin blue jaw which set nicely around his sarcasms. "David, you are thirteen and you know that it is your GRANDFATHER, not your chinny or whatever barbaric word you say. What is more, it seems to be rather unfair to the old man to air his superstitions in front of complete strangers." A subtle man. A bastard. Everyone laughing, oh chinny boy.

"He catched more fish than you'd ever know of."

The wrong words for this fish. His eyes harden but he knows he will win. "Strange, David Stone, how your English deteriorates so markedly when you forget yourself. It betrays you, you see."

"He IS my Chenni, and she's my Nonnie, and they weren't married by no PREACHER, neither." He feels drunk, he feels the other boys must be rising with him. They are not. He is stranded like a spawned-out fish. "Sit down, David, we will pay a visit to Mr. Monohan after this class." The others are just watching, sniggering, drinking the excitement; hoping with stupid grins that he will not back down. He thinks of the buckskin shirt, the panelled room. He sits, scowling. Chinny boy the dishwasher.

We think he may turn out well. This is always a difficult period.

"Chenni," he said softly. The bird cocked its head and considered him. Its eyes were open. It slowly lifted one of its feet from the perch and began to scratch derisively at the warty grey skin above its eye. The arched claw, scratching, was like an eagle's. "My Chenni," he tried again, whispering. The parrot's tattered crest shot erect in a sulphur curve. It glared at him suspiciously. "God is good," it challenged, "decidedly." "Chenni, my Chenni," the boy began shouting, "My Chenni," he screamed like the bird itself. The parrot made a jungle squawk and hobbled backwards to the far end of its perch. "My Chenni, say it," cursed the boy. The bird fluffed out its wing feathers and ducked its head triumphantly towards the door. Where Doctor Macalisdair coughed discreetly.

"What were you trying to teach Polly?" he asked good-humouredly.

"Nothing," David muttered. Into the silence. "Just trying to see if he'd talk."

"Well don't start teaching that bird to swear, even in a foreign language." The doctor smiled at him. "My sister would have a fit."

"Wasn't swearing. Just trying to see if he'd talk."

"Well that's simple enough," said Macalisdair, who was not deceived. "An easy matter, Polly, eh?"

The parrot hopped to the centre of its perch again. It was in control. "The Lord is my shepherd," it declared. "Will ye no come back again?"

He remains something of a lone wolf.

Ronald Macalisdair and his sister called at the school on their way to the station. David come to them in the hall, marvelling at their debonair hats and coats, their obvious excitement at the journey. In his eyes they belonged only in that house behind the cedar hedge.

"We'll look for you next term, then, Davie, and you might keep an eye on the house for us until the end of your term." Jeannie Macalisdair winked round the corner of her bonnet, where Monahan could not see. All three of them knew the gardener was coming in twice a week. But he could keep his Thursday excursion. Yet David felt loutish here by the school doors, rooted between the principal and his friends in their strange clothes. He hung his head. "Goodbye then," he said. "David must go back to his duties now," said Monahan. "Yes, of course," said the doctor. "Yes, decidedly." And shook David's hand.

Vacations are always a setback for him.

Nonnie gave him a twenty-dollar bill and he went back to Warwick three days early. It was a warm fall, if the Macalisdairs disapproved or had no room, he would sleep in the woods and to hell with the Devil. He walked warily from the station, unable to believe as he passed the wall and the gaunt brick school that he would be inside looking out in just three days. That he'd be having the disinfecting baths and waking the next morning to rows of iron beds.

But when he paused at the doctor's gate he saw that they were not home yet. The blinds on the upper floor were still drawn. They said they would be back before the start of term and they weren't here. He hovered at the gate, wanting guidance. The locust tree was almost bare already: untended drifts of dry leaves had marred the lawn since the gardener's last visit.

He would tidy up. Maybe they would come back today and find him raking their lawn, watering the plants that clawed at the windows, ignorant of the seasons. Maybe the heating was off in the conservatory — he should check that too. And Polly — he imagined the mess of sunflower seeds and droppings that he'd have made. So the buffalo shirt drew his feet across the lawn and past the bow-tree, as it had drawn him back from the islands before his time.

The bird gave its full repertoire, delighted at an audience, and after touching the bull's horns on the shirt, David carefully swept up Polly's debris and brought him fresh water from the kitchen. Polly swung round and round on his perch, hanging upside down with his head almost to the floor and stretching one wing at a time, combing with his long groom-claw. Now the room was David's and he stepped over to face the shirt.

"God is good," said Polly. "Oh yes, decidedly."

David was oblivious. He took down the shirt, stroking out the scalp locks, kneading the fine skin in his hands and waking the tang of woodsmoke. His heart kicked like a snare drum. He put the shirt down on the tiger-skin.

"Braw bricht nicht," said the parrot.

David took off his sweater, unbuttoned his shirt. He threw them down. He slipped the buckskin over his head — it was so much too big for him that his hands were lost and it reached almost to his knees. He was more than the doctor now: he owned the house, the robe invited grand gestures. Only so could he sweep his hands free. To the flat tap tap of the snare drum he began a crab-like dance around the bird's perch, while the parrot shifted, staring dizzily from its crazy eyes, trying to face him. "Decidedly," it squawked. "Oh, decidedly," said David, bowing as he danced and then stepped further and further down the room.

He was sweating against the soft buckskin. The woodsmoke ran into his sweat. The robe grew into him. He stuck out his chest so the bull might charge and his heart began to thunder in the buffalo's skull, urging his feet in long deer-leaps across the fallen tiger, past a fleeting mirror, turning again at the polished desk. He began again, around the walls past the Scottish pictures, while the panelled walls sounded like a camp of drummers. His light breathing skated on the rhythms like a new song growing stronger as he tired. He snatched an African assegai from the wall and jabbed it at the air as he passed.

"The Lord is my shepherd," the bird said nervously, "Kaark."

David broke into panting laughter. He had all day. He rested against the desk, dizzy from the small compass of the room. The shirt moulded him one way, it was strong. The spear had been a strange addition, blending with his dance. But the chair could only mould him into the doctor's self. He felt it steal into him and he was satisfied. Before he danced again he would be the doctor, he would — write a letter; use all this heady apparatus of the desk. The pens lay neatly stacked in a tor-toiseshell tray, but the ink-well had dried up. He had seen, somewhere, a big jar — yes, under the bookshelves. He got up, still breathing hard, leaving the doctor in his chair, and did a scuffle dance towards the bookshelf in the shirt's wide sleeves. Bringing back the jar like a dance partner to the desk.

As he was pouring the black stuff carefully into the narrow mouth of the inkwell the parrot suddenly yelled, "My Chenni, my Chenni, my Chenni," and as he turned with a great beaming grin of triumph the jar caught on a paperweight and flung a charge of ink full on his chest.

He looked down stupidly. The black stain swallowed up the buffalo head as he watched. He dabbed wildly at it and the scalp locks on his sleeve brushed through the ink. The blond lock, the red one, dripping black.

He watched the spoiling hypnotized, and "No" he shouted suddenly, flailing his arms at the air, "No!" The scalp locks swung like tassels lashing his face, daubing stripes across his eyes and brow. "Oh no!"

"Yes decidedly," said the bird.

It was too much; he needed a voice, a guide. Nonnie or Chenni, or even at this moment the firm Miss Danby. How could he wipe this out, go back to the islands, go back to school even, go back to Dogfish Bay?

The spirit is strong in you, Davie.

And there was nothing, he remembered, but the broken stove and the iron bedstead, warped and twisted. No wood, no bone, nothing but the iron left. Wiped clean away around the iron witnesses.

So he did not cry anymore as he unhooked the silver chain from Polly's perch. Even if that might give him away. The bird could fly up to the bow-branch and say its say. But nothing else would stay. Maybe the spearheads, maybe things in the kitchen.

He broke the first kerosene lamp across the doctor's chair.

Dolls, Dolls, Dolls, Dolls

Carol Shields

Dolls. Roberta has written me a long letter about dolls, or more specifically about a doll factory she visited when she and Tom were in Japan.

"Ha," my husband says, reading her letter and pulling a face, "another pilgrimage to the heart's interior." He can hardly bring himself to read Roberta's letters any more, though they come addressed to the two of us; there is a breathlessness about them that makes him squirm, a seeking, suffering openness which I suspect he finds grotesque in a woman of Roberta's age. Forty-eight, an uneasy age. And Roberta has never been what the world calls an easy woman. She is one of my oldest friends, and the heart of her problem, as I see it, is that she is incredulous, still, that the colour and imagination of our childhood should have come to rest in nothing at all but these lengthy monochrome business trips with her husband, a man called Tom O'Brien; but that is neither here nor there.

In this letter from Japan, she describes a curious mystical experience that caused her not exactly panic and not precisely pleasure, but that connected her for an instant with an area of original sensation, a rare enough event at our age. She also unwittingly stepped into one of my previously undeclared beliefs. Which is that dolls, dolls of all kinds — those strung-together parcels of wood or plastic or cloth or whatever — possess a measure of energy beyond their simple substance, something half-willed and half-alive.

Roberta writes that Tokyo was packed with tourists; the weather was hot and humid, and she decided to join a touring party on a day's outing in the countryside — Tom was tied up in meetings, as per usual.

They were taken by air-conditioned bus to a village where ninety percent — the guide vigorously repeated this statistic — where ninety percent of all the dolls in Japan were made. "It's a major industry here," Roberta writes, and some of the dolls still were manufactured almost entirely by hand in a kind of cottage-industry system. One house in the village, for example, made nothing but arms and legs, another the bodies; another dressed the naked doll bodies in stiff kimonos of real silk and attached such objects as fans and birds to the tiny lacquered female fingers.

Roberta's party was brought to a small house in the middle of the village where the heads of geisha dolls were made. Just the heads and nothing else. After leaving their shoes in a small darkened foyer, they were led into a surprisingly wide, matted workroom which was cooled by slow-moving overhead fans. The air was musty from the mingled straw and dust, but the light from a row of latticed windows was softly opalescent, a distinctly mild, non-industry quality of light, clean-focused and just touched with the egg-yellow of sunlight.

Here in the workroom nine or ten Japanese women knelt in a circle on the floor. They nodded quickly and repeatedly in the direction of the tourists, and smiled in a half-shy, half-neighbourly manner; they never stopped working for a second.

The head-making operation was explained by the guide, who was a short and peppy Japanese with soft cheeks and a sharp "arfing" way of speaking English. First, he informed them, the very finest sawdust of a rare Japanese tree was taken and mixed with an equal solution of the purest rice paste. (Roberta writes that he rose up on his toes when he reached the words *finest* and *purest* as though paying tribute to the god of superlatives.) This dough-like material then was pressed into wooden molds of great antiquity (another toe-rising here) and allowed to dry very slowly over a period of days. Then it was removed and painted; ten separate and exquisitely thin coats of enamel were applied, so that the resulting form, with only an elegant nose

101

breaking the white egg surface, arrived at the weight and feel and coolness of porcelain.

The tourists — hulking, Western, flat-footed in their bare feet — watched as the tiny white doll heads were passed around the circle of workers. The first woman, working with tweezers and glue, applied the eyes, pressing them into place with a small wooden stick. A second woman painted in the fine red shape of a mouth, and handed on the head to a woman who applied to the centre of the mouth a set of chaste and tiny teeth. Other women touched the eyes with shadow, the cheeks with bloom, the bones with highlight, so that the flattened oval took on the relief and contours of sculptured form. "Lovely," Roberta writes in her letter, "a miracle of delicacy."

And finally, the hair. Before the war, the guide told them, real hair had been used, human hair. Nowadays a very fine quality of blue-black nylon was employed. The doll's skull was cunningly separated into two sections so that the hair could be firmly, permanently rooted from the inside. Then the head was sealed again, and the hair arranging began. The two women who performed this final step used real combs and brushes, pulling the hair smoothly over their hands so that every strand was in alignment, and then they shaped it, tenderly, deftly, with quick little strokes, into the intricate knots and coils of traditional geisha hair dressing.

Finally, at the end of this circular production line, the guide held up a finished head and briefly propagandized in his sharp, gingery, lordly little voice about the amount of time that went into making a head, the degree of skill, the years of apprenticeship. Notice the perfection of the finished product, he instructed. Observe the delicacy, mark the detailing. And then, because Roberta was standing closest to him, he placed the head in her hands for final inspection.

And that was the moment Roberta was really writing me about. The finished head in her hands, with its staring eyes and its painted veil of composure and its feminine, almost erotic crown of hair, had more than the weight of artifact about it. Instinctively Roberta's hands had cupped the head into a laced cradle, protective and cherishing. There was something *alive* about the head.

An instant later she knew she had overreacted. "Tom always says I make too much of nothing," she apologizes. The head hadn't moved in her hands; there had been no sensation of pulse or breath, no shimmer of aura, no electrical charge, nothing. Her eyes went to the women who had created this little head. They smiled, bowed, whispered, miming a busy humility, but their cool waiting eyes informed her that they knew exactly what she was feeling.

What she *had* felt was a stirring apprehension of possibility. It was more than mere animism; the life, or whatever it was that had been brought into being by those industriously toiling women, seemed to Roberta to be deliberate and to fulfill some unstated law of necessity.

She ends her letter more or less the way she ends all her letters these days: with a statement that is really a question. "I don't suppose," she says, "that you'll understand any of this."

=   =   =

Dolls, dolls, dolls, dolls. Once — I forget why — I wrote those words on a piece of paper, and instantly they swam into incomprehension, becoming meaningless ruffles of ink, squiggles from a comic strip. Was it a Christmas wish list I was making? I doubt it. As a child I would have been shocked had I received more than one doll in a single year; the idea was unworthy, it was *unnatural.* I could not even imagine it.

Every year from the time I was born until the year I was ten I was given a doll. It was one of the certainties of life, a portion of a large, enclosing certainty in which all the jumble of childhood lay. It now seems a long way back to those particular inalterable surfaces: the vast and incomprehensible war; Miss Newbury, with her ivory-coloured teeth, who was principal of

Lord Durham Public School; Euclid Avenue where we lived in
a brown house with a glassed-in front porch; the seasons with
their splendours and terrors curving endlessly around the
middle eye of the world which I shared with my sister and my
mother and father.

Almost Christmas: there they would be, my mother and father
at the kitchen table on a Saturday morning in early December,
drinking drip coffee and making lists. There would come a
succession of dark, chilly pre-Christmas afternoons in which
the air would grow rich with frost and longing, and on one of
those afternoons our mother would take the bus downtown to
buy the Christmas dolls for my sister and me.

She loved buying the Christmas dolls, the annual rite of
choosing. It's the faces, she used to say, that matter, those dear
molded faces. She would be swept away by a pitch of sweetness
in the pouting lips, liveliness and colour in the lashed eyes, or
a line of tenderness in the tinted cheeks — "The minute I laid
eyes on that face," she would say, helplessly shaking her head
in a way she had, "I just went and fell head over heels."

We never, of course, went with her on these shopping trips,
but I can see how it must have been: Mother, in her claret-wine
coat with the black squirrel collar, bending over, peering into
glass cases in the red-carpeted toy department and searching
in the hundreds of stiff smiling faces for a flicker of response,
an indication of some kind that this doll, this particular doll,
was destined for us. Then the pondering over price and value
— she always spent more than she intended — having just one
last look around, and finally, yes, she would make up her mind.

She also must have bought on these late afternoon shopping
excursions Monopoly sets and dominoes and sewing cards,
but these things would have been carried home in a different
spirit, for it seems inconceivable for the dolls, our Christmas
dolls, to be boxed and jammed into shopping bags with ordinary toys; they must have been carefully wrapped — she would
have insisted on double layers of tissue paper — and she would

have held them in her arms, crackling in their wrappings, all the way home, persuaded already, as we would later be persuaded, in the reality of their small beating hearts. What kind of mother was this with her easy belief, her adherence to seasonal ritual? (She also canned peaches the last week in August, fifty quarts, each peach half turned with a fork so that the curve, round as a baby's cheek, gleamed lustrous through the blue glass. Why did she do that — go to all that trouble? I have no idea, not even the seed of an idea.)

The people in our neighbourhood on Euclid Avenue, the real and continuing people, the Browns, the McArthurs, the Sheas, the Callahans, lived as we did, in houses, but at the end of our block was a large yellow brick building, always referred to by us as The Apartments. The Apartments, frilled at the back with iron fire escapes, and the front of the building solid with its waxed brown foyer, its brass mailboxes and nameplates, its important but temporary air. (These people only rent, our father had told us.) The children who lived in The Apartments were always a little alien; it was hard for us to believe in the real existence of children who lacked backyards of their own, children who had no fruit cellars filled with pickles and peaches. Furthermore, these families always seemed to be moving on after a year or so, so that we never got to know them well. But on at least one occasion I remember we were invited there to a birthday party given by a little round-faced girl, an only child named Nanette.

It was a party flowing with new pleasures. Frilled nutcups at each place. A square bakery cake with shells chasing each other around the edges. But the prizes for the games we played — Pin the Tail on the Donkey, Musical Chairs — were manipulated so that every child received one — was that fair? — and these prizes were too expensive, overwhelming completely the boxed handkerchiefs and hair ribbons we'd brought along as gifts. But most shocking of all was the present that Nanette received from her beaming parents.

We sat in the apartment under the light of a bridge lamp, a circle of little girls on the living-room rug, watching while the enormous box was untied. Inside was a doll.

What kind of doll it was I don't recall except that her bronzed hair gleamed with a richness that was more than visual; what I do remember was the affection with which she was lifted from her wrappings of paper and pressed to Nanette's smocked bodice, how she was tipped reverently backward so that her eyes clicked shut, how she was rocked to and fro, murmured over, greeted, kissed, christened. It was as though Nanette had no idea of the inappropriateness of this gift. A doll could only begin her life at Christmas. Was it the rigidities of my family that dictated this belief, or some obscure and unconscious approximation to the facts of gestation? A birthday doll, it seemed to me then, constituted a violation of the order of things, and it went without saying that the worth of all dolls was diminished as a result.

Still, there sat Nanette, rocking back and forth in her spun rayon dress, stroking the doll's stiff wartime curls and never dreaming that she had been swindled. Poor Nanette, there could be no heartbeat in that doll's misplaced body; it was not possible. I felt a twist of pity, probably my first, a novel emotion, a bony hand yanking at my heart, an emotion oddly akin — I see it clearly enough now — to envy.

=   =   =

In the suburbs of Paris is one of the finest archaeological museums in Europe — my husband had talked, ever since I'd known him, about going there. The French, a frugal people, like to make use of their ancient structures, and this particular museum is housed inside a thirteenth-century castle. The castle, if you block out the hundreds of surrounding villas and acacia-lined streets, looks much as it always much have looked, a bulky structure of golden stone with blank, primitive, upswept walls and three round brutish towers whose massiveness might be a metaphor for that rough age which equated masonry with power.

The interior of this crude stone shell has been transformed by the Ministry of Culture into a purring, beige-toned shrine to modernism, hived with climate-controlled rooms and corridors, costly showcases and thousands of artifacts, subtly lit, lovingly identified. The *pièce de résistance* is the ancient banqueting hall where today can be seen a wax reconstruction of pre-Frankish family life. Here in this room a number of small, dark, hairy manikins squat naked around a cleverly simulated fire. The juxtaposition of time—ancient, medieval and modern—affected us powerfully; my husband and young daughter and I stared for some time at this strange tableau, trying to reconcile these ragged eaters of roots with the sleek, meaty, well-clothed Parisians we'd seen earlier that day shopping on the rue Victor Hugo.

We spent most of an afternoon in the museum looking at elegantly mounted pottery fragments and tiny vessels, clumsily formed from cloudy glass. There was something restorative about seeing French art at this untutored level, something innocent and humanizing in the simple requirement for domestic craft. The Louvre had exhausted us to the glitter of high style and finish, and at the castle we felt as though the French had allowed a glimpse of their coarser, more likable selves.

"Look at that," my husband said, pointing to a case that held a number of tiny clay figures, thousands of years old. We looked. Some of them were missing arms, and a few were missing their heads, but the bodily form was unmistakable.

"They're icons," my husband said, translating the display card: "From the pre-Christian era."

"Icons?" our daughter asked, puzzled. She was seven that summer.

"Like little gods. People in those days worshipped gods made of clay or stone."

"How do you know?" she asked him.

"Because it says so," he told her. "*Icone.* That's the French word for icon. It's really the same as our word."

"Maybe they're dolls," she said.

"No. It says right here. Look. In those days people were all pagans and they worshipped idols. Little statues like these. They sort of held them in their hands or carried them with them when they went hunting or when they went to war."

"They could be dolls," she said slowly.

He began to explain again. "All the early cultures —"

She was looking at the figures, her open hand resting lightly on the glass case. "They look like dolls."

For a minute I thought he was going to go on protesting. His lips moved, took the necessary shape. He lifted his hand to point once again at the case. I felt sick with sudden inexplicable anger.

Then he turned to our daughter, shrugged, smiled, put his hands in his pockets. He looked young, twenty-five, or even younger. "Who knows," he said to her. "You might be right. Who knows."

=   =   =

My sister lives 300 miles away in Ohio, and these days I see her only two or three times a year, usually for family gatherings on long weekends. These visits tend to be noisy and clamorous. Between us we have two husbands and six children, and then there is the flurry of cooking and cleaning up after enormous holiday meals. There is never enough time to do what she and I love to do most, which is to sit at the kitchen table — hers or mine, they are interchangeable — with mugs of tea before us and to reconstruct, frame by frame, the scenes of our childhood.

My memory is sharper than hers, so that in these discussions, though I'm two years younger, I tend to lead while she follows. (Sometimes I long for a share of her forgetfulness, her leisured shrugging acceptance of past events. My own recollections, not all happy, are relentlessly present, kept stashed away like ingots, testifying to a peculiar imprisoning muscularity of recall.) The last time she came — early October — we talked about the dolls we had been given every Christmas. Our husbands and children listened, jealously it seemed to me, at the sidelines, the husbands bemused by this ordering of trivia, the children open-mouthed, disbelieving.

I asked my sister if she remembered how our dolls were presented to us, exactly the way real children are presented, the baby dolls asleep in stencilled cradles or wrapped in receiving blankets; and the schoolgirl dolls propped up by the Christmas tree, posed just so, smiling brilliantly and fingering the lower branches with their shapely curved hands. We always loved them on sight.

"Remember Nancy Lynn," my sister said. She was taking the lead this time. Nancy Lynn had been one of mine, one of the early dolls, a large cheerful baby doll with a body of cloth, and arms and legs of painted plaster. Her swirled brown hair was painted on, and at one point in her long life she took a hard knock on the head, carrying forever after a square chip of white at the scalp. To spare her shame we kept her lacy bonnet tied on days and night. (Our children, listening, howled at this delicacy.)

One wartime Christmas we were given our twin dolls, Shirley and Helen. The twins were small and hollow and made of genuine rubber, difficult to come by in those years of shortages, and they actually could be fed water from a little bottle. They were also capable of wetting themselves through tiny holes punched in their rubber buttocks; the vulnerability of this bodily process enormously enlarged our love for them. There was also Barbara the Magic Skin Doll, wonderfully pliable at first, though later her flesh peeled away in strips.

There was a Raggedy Ann, not to our minds a real doll, but a cloth stuffed hybrid of good disposition. There was Brenda, named for her red hair, and Betty with jointed knees and a brave little tartan skirt. There was Susan — her full name was Brown-Eyed Susan — my last doll, only I didn't know it then.

My sister and I committed the usual sins, leaving our dolls in their pajamas for days on end, and then, with a rush of shame and love, scooping them up and trying to make amends by telescoping weeks and even years into a Saturday afternoon. Our fiercely loved dolls were left out in the rain. We always lost their shoes after the first month; their toes broke off almost invariably. We sometimes picked them up by the arm or even the hair, but we never disowned them or gave them away or changed their names, and we never buried them in ghoulish backyard funerals as the children in our English stories seemed to do. We never completely forgot that we loved them.

Our mother loved them too. What was it that stirred her frantic devotion? — some failure of ours? — some insufficiency in our household? She spent hours making elaborate wardrobes for them; both my sister and I can remember the time she made Brenda a velvet cape trimmed with scraps of fur from her old squirrel collar. Sometimes she helped us give them names: Patsy, Gloria, Merry Lu, Olivia.

"And the drawer," my sister said. "Remember the drawer?"

"What drawer?" I asked.

"You remember the drawer. In our dresser. That little drawer on the left-hand side, the second one down."

"What about it?" I asked slowly.

"Well, don't you remember? Sure you do. That's where our dolls used to sleep. Remember how Mother lined it with a doll blanket?"

"No," I said.

"She thumbtacked it all around, so it was completely lined. That's where Shirley and Helen used to sleep."

"Are you sure?"

"Absolutely."

I remind her of the little maple doll cribs we had.

"That was later," she said.

I find it hard to believe that I've forgotten about this, especially this. A drawer lined with a blanket; that was exactly the kind of thing I remembered.

But my sister still has the old dresser in the attic of her house. And she told me that the blanket still is tacked in place: she hasn't been able to bring herself to remove it. "When you come at Christmas," she said, "I'll show it to you."

"What colour is it?" I asked.

"Pink. Pink with white flowers. Of course it's filthy now and falling apart."

I shook my head. A pink blanket with white flowers. I have no memory of such a blanket.

Perhaps at Christmas, when I actually look at the drawer, it all will come flooding back. The sight of it may unlock what I surely have stored away somewhere in my head, part of the collection of images which always has seemed so accessible and true. The fleecy pink drawer, the dark night, Shirley and Helen side by side, good night, good night as we shut them away. Don't let the bedbugs bite. Oh, oh.

=   =   =

It happened that in the city where I grew up a little girl was murdered. She was ten years old, my age.

It was a terrible murder. The killer had entered her bedroom window while she was sleeping. He had stabbed her through the heart; he cut off her head and her arms and her legs. Some of these pieces were never found.

It would have been impossible not to know about this murder; the name of the dead girl was known to everyone, and even today I have only to think the syllables of her name and the whole undertow of terror doubles back on me. This killer was a madman, a maniac who left notes in lipstick on city walls, begging the police to come and find him. He couldn't help himself. He was desperate. He threatened to strike again.

Roberta Callahan and JoAnn Brown and I, all of us ten years old, organized ourselves into a detective club and determined to catch the killer. We never played with dolls anymore. The Christmas before, for the first time, there had been no doll under the tree; instead, I had been given a wristwatch. My mother had sighed, first my sister, now me.

Dolls, which had once formed the centre of my imagination, now seemed part of an exceedingly soft and sissified past, something I used to do before I got big. I had wedged Nancy Lynn and Brown-Eyed Susan and Brenda and Shirley and all the others onto a shelf at the back of my closet, and now my room was filled with pictures of horses and baseball stickers and collections of bird nests. Rough things, rugged things, tough things. For Roberta Callahan and JoAnn Brown and I desired, above all else, to be tough. I don't remember how it started, this longing for toughness. Perhaps it was our approaching but undreamed-of puberty. Or the ebbing of parental supervision and certain possibilities of freedom that went with it.

Roberta was a dreamy girl who loved animals better than human beings; she had seen *Bambi* seven times and always was drawing pictures of spotted fawns. JoAnn Brown was short and wiry and wore glasses, and could stand any amount of pain; the winter before she had been hospitalized with double pneumonia. *Double pneumonia.* "But I had the will to live," she told us solemnly. The three of us were invited to play commandos with the boys on the block, and once the commando leader, Terry Shea, told another boy, in my hearing, that for a girl I was tough as nails. *Tough as nails.* It did not seem wildly improbable to JoAnn and Roberta and me that we should be the capturers of the crazed killer. Nancy Drew stalked criminals. Why not us?

In JoAnn Brown's house there was a spare room, and in the spare room there was a closet. That closet became the secret headquarters for the detective club. We had a desk which was a cardboard carton turned upside down, and there, sitting on the floor with Mr. Brown's flashlight and stacks of saltines, we studied all the newspaper clippings we could find. We discussed and theorized. Where did the killer hide out? When and where would he strike again? Always behind our plotting and planning lay certain thoughts of honour and reward, the astonishment of our parents when they discovered that we had been the ones who led the police to the killer's hideout, that we had supplied the missing clue; how amazed they would be, they who all summer supposed that their daughters were merely playing, believing that we were children, girls, that we were powerless.

We emerged from these dark closet meetings dazed with heat and determination, and then we would take to the streets. All that summer we followed suspicious-looking men. Short men. Swarthy men. Men with facial scars or crossed eyes. One day we sighted a small dark man, a dwarf, in fact, carrying over his shoulder a large cloth sack. A body? Perhaps the body of a child? We followed him for an hour, and when he disappeared into an electrical-supply shop, JoAnn made careful note of the address and the time of entry.

Back in the closet we discussed what we should do. Should we send a letter to the police? Or should we make our way back to the shop and keep watch?

Roberta said she would be too frightened to go back.

"Well, I'll go then," I spoke bravely.

Bravely, yes, I spoke with thrilling courage. But the truth was this: I was for all of that summer desperately ill with fear. The instant I was put to bed at night my second-floor bedroom became a cave of pure sweating terror. Atoms of fear conjoined in a solid wall of darkness, pinning me down as I lay paralyzed in the middle of my bed; even to touch the edges of the mattress would be to invite unspeakable violence. The window, softly curtained with dotted swiss, became the focus of my desperate hour-by-hour attention. If I shut my eyes, even for an instant, he, the killer, the maniac, would seize that moment to enter and stab me through the heart. I could hear the sound of the knife entering my chest, a wet, injurious, cataclysmic plunge.

It was the same every night; leaves playing on the window pane, adumbration, darkness, the swift transition from neighbour-hood heroine, the girl know to be tough as nails, the girl who was on the trail of a murderer, to this, this shallow-breathing, rigidly sleepless coward.

Every night my mother, cheerful, baffled, innocent as she said good night, would remark, "Beats me how you can sleep in a room with the window closed." Proving how removed she was from my state of suffering, how little she perceived my nightly ordeal.

I so easily could have told her that I was afraid. She would have understood; she would have rocked me in her arms, bought me a night light at Woolworth's, explained how groundless my fears really were; she would have poured assurance and com-fort on me and, ironically, I knew her comfort would have brought release.

But it was comfort I couldn't afford. At the risk of my life I had to go on as I was, to confess fear to anyone at all would have been to surrender the tough new self that had begun to grown inside me, the self I had created and now couldn't do without.

Then, almost accidentally, I was rescued. It was not my mother who rescued me, but my old doll, Nancy Lynn. I had a glimpse of her one morning in my closet, a plaster arm poking out at me. I pulled her down. She still wore the lacy bonnet on her chipped head, gray with dirt, the ribbons shredded. She had no clothes, only her soft, soiled, mattressy body and the flattened joints where the arms and legs were attached. After all these years her eyes still opened and shut, and her eyelids were a bright youthful pink in contrast to the darkened skin tone of her face.

That night she slept with me under the sheet and malevolence drained like magic from the darkened room; the night pressed friendly and familiar through the dotted swiss curtains; the Callahan's fox terrier yapped at the streaky moon. I opened the window and could hear a breeze loosened in the elms. In bed, Nancy Lynn's cold plaster toe poked reassuringly at my side. Her cloth body, with its soiled cottony fragrance, lay against my bare arm. The powerful pink eyelids were inexpressibly at rest. All night, while I slept, she kept me alive.

For as long as I needed her — I don't remember whether it was weeks or months before the killer was caught — she guarded me at night. The detective club became over a period of time a Gene Autry Fan Club, then a Perry Como Record Club, and there must have been a day when Nancy Lynn went back to her closet. And probably, though I don't like to think of it, a day when she and the others fell victim to a particularly heavy spree of spring cleaning.

There seems no sense to it. Even on the night I first put her on the pillow beside me, I knew she was lifeless, knew there was no heart fluttering in her soft chest and no bravery in her hollow head. None of it was real, none of it.

Only her power to protect me. Human love, I saw, could not always be relied upon. There would be times when I would have to settle for a kind of parallel love, an extension of my hidden self, hidden even from me. It would have to do, it would be a great deal better than nothing, I saw. It was something to be thankful for.

Passages

Janice Kulyk Keefer

I

At night, he dreamt of mountains: perfectly conical, with tips like ice picks aimed at the soft, grey belly of that sky which had swallowed Belle, swallowed her as a whale might some fat, small fish moving through a mess of plankton. Mountain top pricking open the sky, and riding some cosmic and placental wave. Belle, transformed by death and all the glories promised to the meek and lowly; changed into a rampaging angel come to avenge herself 'on him for all the things she'd never openly accused him of in forty years of marriage, but which she'd stored up inside her like some peculiarly fragile child that couldn't survive outside the womb.

Even though they slept in separate beds, Charles had been able to feel that baby kicking him from deep inside its mother's belly: as Belle put on more and more weight, he couldn't help thinking of that child inside her, growing taller and thicker, developing extra sets of ears and eyes and fingernails. What would have happened had Belle ever opened her mouth and let the child leap out her throat: make its birth scream between them? One monstrous wail — insults, reproaches, accusations? Or would they have heard some answer to their troubles, the child a messenger from Belle's God, telling them all would be well, all manner of things would be well; tears dried and sins confessed as a host of heavenly voices shouted praise from the very mountain tops? Granite breasts swollen with ice, not milk: daggers sheathed in snow.

=   =   =

Dear Vi,

Bad news, I'm afraid. Belle died in her sleep last week — she was buried yesterday morning. Funny, I never heard a thing, even though I'm a light sleeper, as you'll perhaps remember. Doctor said it was her heart — tricky things, you never know when they'll start acting up. I suppose I could have been more careful with her, making sure she took her pills, that sort of thing. But it was her weight that killed her in the end — the doctor said. Still, it was a beautiful day to be buried: river and sky the same clear blue, gulls like little blind angels in the air — noisy angels — do you remember?

I thought you should know, even though you two never met — life doesn't always work out the way we plan, does it? I've sold the Hardware Store — didn't seem much point in keeping it on, or the house, either. I expect I'll find a nice little apartment in town — easy to heat and clean — I won't find another housekeeper like Belle, that's for certain. But there'll be plenty of room should you ever change your mind and come for a visit. You know you're always welcome, as they say.

> *fond regards,*
> *your brother, Charles*

=   =   =

He'd written the first things that had popped into his head: sealed the envelope and mailed it off right before pick-up: he'd even watched it being loaded into the truck and driven down the road, whether to hell or Halifax, it didn't matter — he'd done what he had to and thought no more about it. Once a year he wrote to Vi and she to him: Christmas cards. "Hoping all's well." Forty years of Christmas cards with horses and sleighs, tobogganing children, snow-caked spruce. Three years ago she'd enclosed a note on black-bordered paper:

• *Dear Charles,*

*Harry passed away last month, after a short illness. It's been hard,
but I'm over the worst of it now, and keeping busy with old friends
and new activities. Thank God I still have my health. As ever, Vi.*

He'd written back immediately, asking her to come and stay
with them, though Belle hadn't said a word when he'd told her.
Both of them knew Vi would never come back — didn't need
to: "Thank God I still have my money." Harry would have left
her plenty. It wasn't the price of a ticket from Vancouver that
would keep her away, but Belle. Forty years of Belle in the
house. Now both were gone: he had his apartment over the
lawyer's office, with a view of the river and the low blue hills
beyond. She'd like it were she to come and stay — she should
come back, everyone should come back at least once to the
place they were born. Come home to die — but that was
morbid, there was plenty of time left, plenty of time to sort
things out.

On his way to the Post Office he stopped to lean against the
railing and look out at the basin — there was a park bench
behind the War Memorial: facing the water, not the street.
Miss Jenner had seen to that, she'd published a letter in the
local paper, saying she had no interest in counting the cars that
passed or the number of candy wrappers dropped on the
pavement. No, she wanted to look out at the river and if two
strong men couldn't be found to turn the park bench around,
then what was the world coming to? Two strong men — former
students of Miss Jenner — had been found, the bench turned,
and for the remaining ten years of the old woman's life she'd
enjoyed the view almost as much as her victory. But Charles
could never bring himself to sit down for long on Miss Jenner's
bench. She'd been his English teacher — Vi's, too. If Vi did
come back for a visit she'd have a perfect right to sit there and
count the sailboats gliding by. Vi had done what Miss Jenner
said he should do — leave home, go out into the great world,
make something of yourself. Vi'd ended up as far as possible

from where she'd started out. Vancouver, the West Coast, the Pacific Rim...

It made him think of an enormous circle with boats whirling round and round like a finger inside a wine glass, making the crystal ring. He'd bought Bohemian crystal, decanter and six wine glasses, for their twenty-fifth anniversary, but she'd not allowed him to fill it with anything stronger than soda water. Belle, Belle, Bible Belle, touch a drop and you'll burn in Hell. Not she — he pictured her just as she'd wished to be — in a long white gown floating over, never touching flesh that had been skimmed from her like scum from soup bones simmering. In her heaven Belle would weigh no more than a bird, would sing like a bird, notes true and high and free. *Rock of Ages/Cleft for Me/Touch my dark/Declivities.* No, no that—his mind was fuzzing over, like the lint screen in the dryer: he couldn't get the words right anymore, he couldn't remember.

Miss Jenner had been a great admirer of the early Yeats—had set them "The Rose on the Rood of Time" to memorize for the final exams — "Down by the Salley Gardens" for graduation. He'd recited it to the whole school, his parents in the front row, Vi come home to see him get his diploma. He'd thought it was "Sally", the name of a girl, until Miss Jenner had corrected him. *"It comes from the French word for willow, Charles — your sister could have told you that."* His sister had gone off to Halifax to work as a secretary, earn the money to send him through university, though she could have gone there herself, she was that smart. 100 in Maths and English without hardly cracking a book, while he'd had to sweat blood to manage a 75.

Nice girl behind the counter: the Ameros' girl. "Letter for you, Mr. Spinney." He never got enough mail to warrant having one of the little metal boxes — General Delivery would do for him, and besides, he got to hear the Ameros' girl calling out his name, making him feel—important, alive still. "Thanks, Alice. Give my regards to your folks when next you write. Oh, yes — of course, stupid of me, I'll be forgetting my name next. I was sorry to hear about his passing away — last year, was it? Four years ago? Yes, well, tell your mother hello when next you write." Trying to appear casual, as if he received letters like this every day, on expensive stationery, fountain pen, not ball point ink: "Mr. Charles H. Spinney, Esq./30 George Street,/Annapolis, Nova Scotia." She forgot the postal code — figured she didn't need to use it, Annapolis being somewhat smaller than Vancouver. Mrs. V. Green. 2441 Ocean Drive, West Vancouver.

V. for Violet; H. for Henry: Charles Henry — fine and fitting name to be inscribed on a university diploma: would she have come back for that graduation, too? And for his wedding to Norah Hammond: Dr. and Mrs. Philip Hammond announce the marriage of their daughter Norah Marie to Professor Charles Henry Spinney. It was only Belle who'd called him Charlie, down in the Salley Gardens. But "esquire" — had Alice laughed at that? It was the first time Vi had put that on an envelope — first time she'd ever written him a letter instead of a card. And not at Christmas but closer to Easter. Her Christmas card this year had barely differed from the previous ones: "Hoping you're well" instead of "Hoping all's well." Had she even received his letter about Belle — could her response have been lost in the mail? Vancouver so far away, the end of the earth. . .

Yet here he was with her letter in his hands. He couldn't wait until he got home, he had to open it this minute to find out — On Miss Jenner's bench he sat down, tearing open the stiff envelope but removing the paper as carefully as if it had some rare specimen — a wildflower or butterfly — pressed inside.

Dear Charles,

I would have written before this but I wanted to work out the details quite carefully. You are very kind to ask me to come and stay with you, but of course that is out of the question.

Of course. He looked up, over the river, to the houses on the opposite bank. Counted three white steeples, the gables of the old Hammond house, turned into a bed and breakfast these past fifteen years. Vi had been best friends with Norah

Hammond at high school, even though Norah was two years younger, in his own class. Norah lived in Fredericton now — she'd married a university professor. If Norah had written asking Vi to stay, would Vi have said yes? Had she maybe come and visited Norah, but never told him, never even taken the ferry across to see him — only for a day, an afternoon when Belle was off at the Tabernacle?

My world is on the West Coast now — I simply couldn't imagine myself in the east, even for a visit. One puts one's past behind one and moves out. I've reached, not the end but the very rim, now — and am as content as I shall ever be, with Harry gone. But I'd regret not seeing you again, after all this time: it's unfortunate that circumstances have prevented our meeting.

Two hundred and twenty-three pounds of circumstances, on little snow white feet, the only things about her that had not changed, that had never been other than they'd seemed, that first time.

I have a proposal, then. Why don't you come out to see me? The house is large enough that we wouldn't get in each other's way, and it would make a pleasant change for you. Canada's an enormous country — you really ought to see more of it than your little corner of Nova Scotia, you know. You could take the train out — cross the Rockies, even stop off at Banff or Jasper for a few days. And then spend a week here. I'm afraid any longer would be impossible right now — I have to be away for a couple of months at my daughter's home in Colorado. Let me know as soon as possible if this little plan suits you.

All the Best,
Vi

He put the letter in his jacket pocket. Below him the river ran, still sluggish with broken ice that would not melt away, though it was almost April. Four months from now you'd never know it was the same place — sun like a great warm hand stroking everything; fireweed growing along the riverbank, soft pink cones that would grow anywhere, even in burnt-out rubble.

Walking those long summer evenings, under the swallows' sickle wings, till the church bells rang eleven o'clock, playing the hymn tune to tell her she had to get home. Pink, plumed fireweed, high enough to screen them from everything but sky and swallows and church bells. She'd go first, smoothing her skirts, letting him wipe the smudges from her face and hands, wipe them off with the quivering tip of his tongue. After she'd gone he'd wait till the quarter hour, then head to the house that smelled of his mother's talcum powder, his dead father's tools. His mother who couldn't read more than the labels on the soup tins, his father who wasn't a doctor but a carpenter, though Norah didn't mind: she would wait for him, she said, wait till he got his degree and then marry him. But not go walking in the Salley gardens, not let him do more than shake her hand. "I know you, Charles Spinney, I couldn't trust myself with you."

He'd ask Vi, when he got to Vancouver. "Hear from Norah Hammond at all?" Casual, as if he saw Norah every day of the week, waved to her from across the water. Nice, comfortable kind of river, this — not too wide or deep: coming from some place definite, going on to another just as settled and expected. Not like an ocean, the Pacific ocean — at least England was on the other side of the Atlantic, but where Vi lived, you'd look out and what would there be? Japan and China. . . Why couldn't he remember the other ones — he'd studied them all in geography class. . . Asia. Asia wasn't some place solid and definite like England — they didn't speak any kind of language you could understand there. He couldn't understand Vi having wanted to settle out on the west coast, but she'd explain it all to him when he saw her there. Long way to go, but at the end of it she'd be waiting, she would tell him everything he needed to know. No one could go all that way and not find out something important — it was a scientific fact, what did they call it? A factor of distance, that was it: the distance factor.

=   =   =

If she quizzed him about not taking the train, not taking the train because he was afraid of the mountains, he would tell her the travel agent had advised against it. "There are terrific seat sales on — it would be a shame not to take advantage of them, Mr. Spinney." He could have kissed the girl — she looked too young to be able to make all those complicated arrangements for him, but there it was — signed, sealed — what else? He'd driven in all the way to Bridgetown to collect the tickets, though she could have mailed them to him. But then he'd never have known she was pretty, as well as young. He could have kissed her, young and foolish, and his heart full of — something to rhyme with trees: ease, of course.

He walked along Main Street before driving home. Stopped in at The Elms Cafe for their daily special. Wonderful pastry on the chicken pie — Belle never could make pastry — you had to have cold hands, she'd said. Cold hands, warm heart. Belle's hands small and plump and hot, like turnovers. Belle in the bath, an enormous dumpling in too small a pot: she'd cover herself with washcloths if ever he had to come in while she was soaking on a Sunday. After church, washing off the Blood of the Lamb. Spotless: you had to give her that. Starching his shirts just so, keeping the floors shiny as tin foil, even washing the leaves of her houseplants twice a week. But she wouldn't tolerate pets, that was the only point on which she'd ever crossed him. He'd have liked to get a puppy, train it to bring him his paper, sit by his feet in the evenings while he stroked its long, silky ears. His lease forbade pets in the building — it was too late, anyway, he wouldn't be able to walk a young dog, give it the exercise it needed.

Did Vi have a dog, he wondered? A white poodle, a miniature? Or a watchdog — she'd maybe be nervous in the house with Harry gone. She wouldn't be nervous — she'd gone off across the country just like that, hadn't she? With Harry, it's true, but he wouldn't have had a penny in his pockets after paying train fares and sandwiches and coffee. But things had worked out well for them, most likely he'd died a rich man. *The house is big enough that we wouldn't get in each other's way.* No apartment over a lawyer's office for her. . .

The waitress came with his bill — he took out ten dollars, leaving too big a tip on the linoleum-topped table. This girl wasn't young or pretty: he'd no desire even to shake her hand. That girl in the travel agent's — red hair, green eyes, breasts like new-baked bread under her sweater. . . Even ten years ago he would have been able to strike a smile from her, strike a spark. They'd always tell him, "You're so gentle, so careful, Charlie my darling." Stroking their hair, long and silky, my love and I, my love, till the hymn tune rang and he'd have to get home, Belle would be back from chapel: watching for him, eating a bag of sugar cookies, a whole tub of butterscotch ice cream by the time he finally walked in the door.

Drive Carefully, We Love our Children. No sign like that in Annapolis — silly to put one up — everyone loves their children. Annapolis was full of them, he saw them every day on his walk through the fort — that tall boy walking an Irish setter, the young ones riding on cannons, firing imaginary volleys over the river, into the hills. Would there be a place to go walking in Vancouver — he needed his exercise, the doctor had warned him. If there'd been children, if he could have taken his boys out to play baseball, taken his daughters for walks with the new puppy, round and round the paths threading the green grass at the Fort, over the hills down which children went rolling, faster and faster, shrieking laughter. . . *Make themselves sick,* Belle would say, shaking her head as they walked the paths together on a Sunday afternoon, the only exercise she'd take besides cleaning house every day.

Walk together, but not arm in arm or hand in hand. Single file because Belle was so huge the two of them couldn't squeeze side by side on the path. Huge enough to be pregnant with quints, but you couldn't use that word, you were "expecting" or "that way", what could he do, she was "that way" and we love our children, drive carefully, you'll make yourself sick, rolling fast and faster down the hill, shrieking and laughing. He would fly right over the mountains and never look down. Perfectly conical tips piercing the grey belly of the plane, gutting it like a mackerel, until they all fell laughing and shrieking out of the sky. . .

II

Vi gave him a room from which he could see the bay: draw his curtains in the early morning and watch the freighters glide across water that looked as insubstantial as the mist suspended in the air: dampness that did not fall but insinuated itself into his hair and clothes so that after an hour's walk he felt soaked to the skin. It had rained each of the seven days he'd been in Vancouver — rain that seemed to soften his perceptions, responses, as if they were laundry soaking in a tub till the colours ran and nothing could be sorted out at all.

Vi had been cross about the weather — "this is dreadful, even for Vancouver — I can't remember when we've had such a bad stretch. But it's bound to clear tomorrow, and as soon as it does we'll head off for Squamish and Garibaldi. When I think of how we used to call them 'mountains', back in the Valley — ridiculous, isn't it? Never mind, we'll do the Aquarium today, and there's a concert tonight at the Queen Elizabeth. We'll come back in between — you'll want to rest, and I've got some correspondence I must take care of. But I'll just run out to the shops now — get in some salmon and strawberries for supper. Won't be a minute."

She spoke just the way she wrote — as if his ears were pieces of paper she could inscribe and fold and mail away, just as she chose — as if he'd have nothing to answer back, say to her face. He'd not recognized that face at the airport, though she had known him, straight away. "Well, my handsome brother — you've not changed so very much." But she had — not just her face, her clothes, but her voice, as well. She sounded as if she'd been born Mrs. Harold Green, and not Violet Ethel Spinney: born in a cashmere sweater and pleated skirt, gold bracelets on her wrists. *Our Vi'let's some clever. Mother, you shouldn't say*

"some". Real clever, then. No, mother — Vi had made him repeat
at night, so he'd sound like the son of somebody important
when he went on to university. "Down by the Salley Gar-
dens/My love and I did meet/She met me in the some-
thing/On little snow white feet." How did it go? Feet like
daisies on the grass, he'd told her; elocution: they fall for that.
Fall right back on their round little heels.

He left his room as soon as he heard her car pull out from the
garage. She'd be gone for half an hour at the most: he could
look at the things in her house — he didn't feel right about
looking when she was there. Picking up the little silver-framed
photographs on her writing desk. A boy and a girl: George and
Susan, she'd told him. Plastic cubes filled with pictures of their
children — babies, teenagers — Susan in Colorado, married
to a — doctor? George a civil engineer somewhere in — Africa?
No, couldn't be Africa: what had she told him that first night?
That she'd had the two children — she'd never written that on
her Christmas cards. Imagine having children and not shouting it out across the continent.

His nephews and nieces, goddamnit, he had a right to know
she'd had children. They were his too, even if it was a line of
blood thin as thread between them. These things should be
known. He would ask her for their addresses, write to them,
introduce himself. Your uncle Charles. Your mother's brother,
Charles Henry. *Charlie Spinney, from Royal Hardware* — *can
get you the best deal in town on kiddies' bikes.* The one he'd
bought for the boy was still in the garage when he'd sold the
house: cocooned in plastic, just in case. *These things happen:
better luck next time.*

This portrait on the dining room wall — Harry? It gave him a
peevish sort of satisfaction to look at him at last: wall-eyed,
pencil moustache, snot-grey eyes. A naval rating who hadn't
bothered shipping home after the war: they'd met in Halifax,
she'd said. And that was all she'd tell him — her own brother.
Just the few facts she wanted him to know. And asking him
nothing, as if Belle had been some enormous zero added to his

life, a zero to cancel him out. "Charles? Are you ready? Good.
I'll just put these few things in the fridge and we can be off. I'm
afraid it's raining again — I'd hoped that at least it would stay
mist and we could walk in Stanley Park. It's the mountains, I'm
afraid — they keep in the rain."

Crossing the Lion's Gate Bridge she gestured to what would
have been mountains on a sunny day. He stared intently at the
freighters chugging under the bridge — what would it cost to
hop on board and sail round the world? He'd meant to do that
during summer breaks at university — the big boats were
always looking for crew, and he'd have worked for his keep
alone, just to go off, get out. Those first few months after his
marriage, waiting for the baby to be born, he'd planned it all
out: he'd get a loan from the bank, get in brand-new stock,
enlarge the premises. Save up for a sloop, second-hand — by
the time his kid was old enough to sail with him, he'd have
enough to pick one up. Have their pictures taken on board,
both of them in nautical whites, gold cord, captain's hats: send
it to Vi. *I'm sorry — how unfortunate.*

He was sorry when the traffic unsnarled and they got off the
bridge. Vi spent a long time looking for a parking space — she
didn't want the paintwork scratched. Harry had always been
so careful with his cars — he'd been like a kid when he'd
bought his first BMW. Charles, waiting for her to ask him what
he drove but she didn't — she wouldn't ask him anything.
Embarrassed when he'd told her about Belle, things going
wrong. "She was so strong and healthy-looking before — you'd
have thought she was built for nothing else. The baby was
growing inside her tubes, instead of her —" *I'm sorry. You must
be tired, Charles, why don't* — "Then it turned out there was
scarring of the tubes, something — the doctor didn't explain it
too well. Anyway, she felt it as a judgement —" *How
unfortunate. Well, if you're not exhausted, Charles, I am —
airports are impossible these days.*

Exhausted. Seven days he'd been here: they'd done the Art
Gallery, the Museum, the St. Roche, Gastown, Chinatown, the

UBC campus, seen an opera, a play, a film, gone to lectures —
and now the Aquarium. Sometimes she'd get phone calls, and
she'd always say, "I'm afraid I'm tied up for the present, but
how kind of you to think of me, my dear." Tied up, as if they
were children playing cowboys and Indians, and he'd left her
fastened to the gatepost in the garden. She'd never called him
"my dear", it was always, "Charles", with an invisible exclamation mark, as if she were Miss Jenner rapping him to attention,
correcting his grammar and posture — checking his
fingernails.

All through the aquarium she never stopped talking, telling
him about the dolphins and tropical fish, making sure he read
all the posters, gathering information for which he had no more
use than he did now for Belle's shoe size, her Health Plan
number. They stayed long enough for the whale show, even
though the seats were uncomfortable and the air so wet and
heavy he thought his clothes would melt and leave him naked
there. Naked in front of his sister and the trainer and the
snow-white whales with their dimpled eyes and sleek, vague
flesh, splashing and thumping in the cloudy water, everyone
shrieking and laughing around him, rolling over and over
down the hill. *Make you sick.*

He put his handkerchief up to his brow: it came back drenched
with sweat. His heart lurching like one of the whales; must get
your exercise, the doctor said, must take your medicine. He
hadn't brought his pills, his little vial of pills. Vial, Vi — must
tell her, ask her to take him out, get him away. But her eyes
were fixed on the whales — she was a hundred miles away and
all he could do was grip his knees and bear down against the
pain hard as a fist inside him, little embryo curled up inside the
shadow place where his heart should be.

= = =

The day before his plane was due to leave the rain finally
stopped. Vi explained to him at breakfast how they'd drive up

to Garibaldi — it wasn't the best day in the world, but he couldn't leave B.C. without having seen the mountains. He'd put his cup down so hard and quick the coffee splashed out over the tablecloth. Irish Linen — white: nothing but the best for her little brother. Watching her mop at the stain he remembered the way she'd scrubbed the floors at home, wearing rubber gloves so her hands wouldn't get red and rough. Like Belle's hands, up to the day she died. He'd buried her out of town in the cemetery of the Tabernacle of the Holy Ghost: she'd have wanted to be close to her church, God knew she'd spent enough time inside it. That first year after the baby hadn't been born — she'd not set foot outside the house, and then after the minister had started coming round, she was hardly there at all, except to clean and cook. Snake-oil minister coming round, getting at her, after her — to get him too. *Jesus Christ, Belle, you mean you believe that stuff, you really believe that if I go down on my knees and pray with you, ask forgiveness, we'll get a baby out of it? Didn't you hear what the doctor said?*

"Did you hear me, Charles — we'll have to get moving."

"No." He looked into her eyes, but they weren't violets, they were crystalline, faceted, like the amethyst she wore on her finger. "I don't want to go anywhere."

"Are you all right, Charles — should I call a doctor?"

"Christ, no — why should there be anything wrong with me. I just don't want to go for a drive, I don't want to see mountains, I'm happy just to stay put and — talk."

"Talk about what, Charles?"

"Do you ever hear — I mean have you ever written — Norah Hammond?"

"Pardon? I don't understand."

"Norah. You knew her, she was your best —"

"Oh — oh yes, that prissy little girl who lived over the river. No, of course I don't write to her. Why on earth should I?"

He fiddled with the silver napkin ring, failing to stuff the crumpled napkin back inside.

"Well, if that's all you have to talk about, perhaps we can plan something for the day?"

"It's not all — I need to ask —" Dropping the ring so that it clattered, spinning on the ceramic tile. Watching till it became perfectly still before he spoke again, suddenly passionate: head clearer, words sharper than they'd ever been.

"I have to know, Vi. All kinds of things I want to know, and there's hardly any time left. Why did you ask me here, and then say nothing? Why? Thirty years, and now here we are, just like we used to be — but all that time between? What did I do that was so awful you couldn't forgive me? Marry Belle? Would you rather I'd left her — left her with a baby —"

"She didn't have the baby."

"I couldn't of known that —"

"Couldn't have, Charles — not couldn't of: couldn't have."

"Jesus Christ, Vi, what friggin' difference does it make now? Can't you say anything except what-a-wonderful-place-Vancouver-is — or correct my grammar? I want to know why you never wrote, never told me anything about yourself — your kids, your life. Don't you care? This is your brother speaking, the brother you walked out on for forty years — I needed you then, I had no one. Look, Belle's gone, she can't get in our way again."

Vi bending down, graceful, slender as a sparrow. Retrieving the napkin ring and putting it beside her plate. Then looking up at him, smiling. Pale, powdered face, always a lady's face. Suddenly he wanted to take his hand and slap her, hard; slap till the powder came off in his hands like bits of eggshell, exposing the blood and nerves beneath. His hands, lifting — and falling again as she began to speak: falling into fists clenched in his lap.

"Why are you going on about Belle, Charles? Do you really think it was Belle that made me — what did you say? — walk out on you? Poor lovely, loose, unlucky Belle. She really paid for it, didn't she? Taking advantage of a dumb kid fresh out of high school — don't interrupt. You think you're the only one who took her down to the river on Friday and Saturday nights? You think it was the first time she ever got into trouble? Steady, Charles — you asked me to talk to you, and that's just what I'm doing.

"It was never Belle, dear brother, little brother. It was you, being so stupid. Christ almighty you were that thick. . . You still are — maybe that's why I asked you to come here, just to see if you'd learned anything over the years. Beautiful, stupid Charlie — or maybe I was the really stupid one, believing you could make it to university, get your degree. Letting Miss Jenner, may she rot in her lace and lavender Hell, letting her convince me that you were the one who ought to have the chance. I worked for four years to get you the money to start college, and what did you do? Went rolling in the clover with Belle Beeler, for God's sake. And if that weren't bad enough, marrying her; buying that rundown hardware store no one else would touch —

"I'm sorry, Charles, sorry for both of you about the baby. But have you ever, ever stopped to consider what it was like for me? I could have taken that money and damn well sent myself through college, made something of myself. Instead I had to scrabble round for what I could get. And what I could get was Harry Green. Oh, he wasn't all bad, Harry. And he's dead now — and I've got the children. I have just enough money to live my life exactly as I please — though the possibilities are somewhat diminished, you'll agree?

"You wanted to know why I asked you here? I don't know anymore. I suppose I wanted to prove to myself that I wasn't angry anymore, that I didn't need to hate anybody, resent anything. You said something in your letter about life never working out the way you want, the way you plan. You're right

about that, at least. I've spent the whole week of your visit
terrified I was going to explode at you — why else do you think
I've been nattering away about Beautiful B.C., dragging you off
to every tourist attraction I could find. I wasn't going to confess
anything to you — but maybe it's better this way. It doesn't
even matter, you'll be home tomorrow, and things will be back
to where they were for both of us. Things don't work out. But
we've one day left, and we might as well get through it as best
we can. You don't want to drive up and see the mountains: fine
— why don't I just leave you to your own devices. I have some
people I should see downtown — I can drop you off wherever
you like, Lighthouse Park, Stanley Park, English Bay. Charles
— is that all right?"

She put her hand out to touch his arm, but he brushed her
fingers as if they were flies settling on his sleeve.

"All right, then, Charles. I think it's best if I go out — you can
do what you like here — there's a spare key by the telephone
in the kitchen. I'll be back in time to make supper."

=   =   =

It took him less than an hour to pack, make sure he hadn't left
anything under the bed, in the bathroom. At lunchtime he
opened the refrigerator and stared at the remains of all the
suppers they'd had together this past week. He felt helpless at
the thought of putting them together into some sort of meal for
himself — he'd walk the two blocks down to Marine Drive, and
find a restaurant, instead. He'd spent almost nothing of the
money he'd brought with him — some postcards which he'd
never got round to sending to people back home. *You think
you're the only one who took her down to the river on Friday and
Saturday nights?* He wouldn't think about that now, he wasn't
going to think about any of it, it made him dizzy: fear of heights,
fear of falling —

He was out the door, down the street much too quickly for a
man of his age, a man with his heart. Two blocks down to

Marine Drive, and then along sidewalks filled with lilac-haired
ladies towing pugs and poodles. He jutted out his chin, forced
his shoulders back; tried to catch his reflection in each shop
window. Distinguished: they'd told him he looked distinguished, all the giggling girls, laughing and shrieking, even
though he was too old to run after them, chase them and pull
them down into the fireweed. Handsome — everyone had told
him how handsome he was: his mother, Vi, even Miss Jenner:
*Handsome is as handsome does, Charles — it'll take more than
blue eyes to get you into university, my friend.*

He thought he saw Vi's car heading towards him — he ducked
into the nearest door: Seashell Café. Sat down at a table near
the back: ordered an omelette, toast and fruit salad, none of
which he could eat. Tore the toast into little pellets with which
he encircled his coffee cup. Closed his eyes and thought of the
trees she'd shown him in Lighthouse Park, the day they'd
driven out in the rain. Huge trees, pines were they? Rainforest
like the tropical jungles he'd read about in his geography books
at school. Vi had been able to tell him all the names — arbutus,
he remembered arbutus. . . He opened his eyes, drank the rest
of his coffee: shivered. The lushness, the hugeness of the trees
had repelled him, made his heart lurch, just as had the whales
in the murky aquarium waters. Too big, too high — everything
here was out of scale. Too much space to fill, too huge a silence
to disguise with words.

Vi talking, telling him. . . Cruel, unfair; she made things up just
to hurt him. As if she'd suffered more than he — or Belle. He
tried to stop the sound of her words coming back to him:
clattered his cup on its saucer, drummed his fingers on the
table, began reciting what he'd learned from Miss Jenner,
graduation day in front of the whole auditorium:

"Down by the Salley Gardens
My love and I did meet
She met me in the something
On little snow white feet

> She bade me take love easy
> As the leaves grow on the trees
> But I was young and foolish
> And with her would not —"

He couldn't remember. Elocution lessons, grammar, public
speaking — Miss Jenner had said it was speech that separated
man from the animals. What then of all those silent nights with
Belle? She'd talked to the plants she washed and watered, she
spoke in tongues at the Tabernacle, but with him — had he
ever let her speak? Not just answer his questions but let her
tell him anything. Even when she'd come walking with him
down by the river, even in the waste spaces, screened by
fireweed, pink conical tips like a whole chain of mountains
round them... Laughing and shrieking as he'd chased her,
pulled her down — and then silence. His fingers speaking to
her skin, the darkness into which his body plunged like a car
careening off a mountain ledge: "Belle, listen, hear me, somebody, anybody hear me. Things don't always work out the way
we plan."

"Did you want more coffee, sir?"

"Sure, then, why not? Nice day."

She nodded, moving away to another table, though he seemed
to be the only customer. Japanese — no bigger than a child.
Pretty though — her face made him think of piano keys, the
skin so white, hair like ebony. Fifteen, was she, seventeen?
Belle had been twenty that summer: taller than this girl, but
the same white skin, the same tiny feet. Two years older than
he, though you'd never have knowN it. By the time she was
thirty she'd looked more like those whales in the aquarium
than a woman. When had it been, at what precise moment had
she decided to make herself so monstrous he'd never so much
as rattle the lock on her bedroom door? Silent, tears coursing
down her face those times he'd forced her in the night, young
and foolish but she'd lain like a slab of marble under him, head

turned away, though the salt still stung as he'd tried to wipe her tears. . .

"Will there be anything more, sir?"

"No. Nothing more. Miss?"

Like a bird perched on a branch, wary, rousing itself to fly away —

"Nothing."

Leaving the café, stepping back onto the sidewalk he couldn't account to himself for the fact that he was alone. Where was Vi? What had happened? They'd been having breakfast together, he had dropped the silver napkin ring and it had made a noise like church bells ringing out. She had picked it up for him, and gone off — where? And where was he? Sidewalks crammed with cut flowers in plastic pails. It would still be too cold at home for that — there'd been fresh snow the day before he left. She must be angry at him — there had been words, she had told him — He'd written a letter telling her Belle had gone, Death walking right into her room, standing over her bed, shadow like wings around her, embracing her. Angels are the birds of the soul, Miss Jenner had said, quoting — he couldn't remember who.

He should go home, but instead he took the road to the beach, walking along the concrete path and straining his eyes across the water — where was the river, the narrow, shallow river, Miss Jenner's bench? He couldn't get things into focus — while he was in the restaurant the fog had rolled in, obscuring the edges of things, making it difficult to tell where the ocean began and land ended. He sat down on a log to get his bearings, and looked across the water. On one side an enormous hanging bridge, so far away, so insubstantial in the mist he couldn't believe a car could cross it. The bridge to Granville Ferry had collapsed one day, moments after a busload of school children had got across. God sees the little sparrow, God kills the little sparrow, she had prayed to that God, cursing Charles because he wouldn't: cursing him silently, drifting in her own cloudy seas, battening there like some blind white growth, till he couldn't bear the sight of her, feel of her —

Late afternoon when he woke. Lights had gone on over the bridge — now it looked like a string of children's beads, the ones that snap together, and pull as easily apart. He stumbled to his knees, and then his feet, shaking sand and bits of bark out of his clothes, rubbing his hands over his eyes. And then opened them to see, for the first time, the mountains — soft, low, like a tired animal hunkering down, laying its head on its paws to sleep or die.

This water silent at his feet. Strange how silence makes a sound: slight shock of waves pushing to shore, like a noise heard in the night: vague, muffled, yet loud enough to wake the soundest sleeper. What Belle must have heard as she walked through the door from dreams to death. Is all suffering equal — do we each get the heaven we desire? Would Harry be banished from Vi's? Did Belle's include her Charlie-boy, standing off to the side of that chair in which she sat cradling her baby, their perfect first-born? Would he have in his heaven the Belle who'd walked with him by the river, who'd let him pull her down, silent, into the long grass, green grass, fireweed blazing the sky over their heads?

He sat back down on the log, suddenly, incomprehensibly at ease. It didn't matter what had happened at Vi's, what she'd said, what he could or couldn't remember. Air soft as milk, everything floating: buoyant and free. Under a glimmering sky he watched the freighters sad, orient-bound, their decks pricked out with lights like necklaces. They carried the dead: west to east, from dark to light. Freighters he would ride one day, passage he'd already booked. Not disappearing but dissolving — round and round the rim of unimaginable worlds.

Blossom, Priestess of Oya, Goddess of winds, storms and waterfalls

Dionne Brand

Blossom's was jumping tonight. Oya and Shango and God and spirit and ordinary people was chanting and singing and jumping the place down. Blossom's was a obeah house and speakeasy on Vaughan Road. People didn't come for the cheap liquor Blossom sell, though as night wear on, on any given night, Blossom, in she waters, would tilt the bottle a little in your favour. No, it wasn't the cheap liquor, even if you could drink it all night long till morning. It was the feel of the place. The cheap light revolving over the bar, the red shag covering the wall against which Blossom always sit, a line of beer, along the window-sill behind, as long as she ample arms spread out over the back of a wooden bench. And, the candles glowing bright on the shrine of Oya, Blossom's mother Goddess.

This was Blossom's most successful endeavour since coming to Canada. Every once in a while, under she breath, she curse the day she come to Toronto from Oropuche, Trinidad. But nothing, not even snarky white people, could keep Blossom under. When she first come it was to babysit some snot-nosed children on Oriole Parkway. She did meet a man, in a club on Henry Street in Port-of-Spain, who promise she to take care of she, if she ever was in Toronto. When Blossom reach, the man disappear and through the one other person she know in Toronto she get the work on Oriole.

Well Blossom decide long that she did never mean for this kinda work, steady cleaning up after white people, and that is when she decide to take a course in secretarial at night. Is there she meet Peg and Betty, who she did know from home, and Fancy Girl. And for two good years they all try to type: but their heart wasn't in it. So they switch to carpentry and upholstering. Fancy Girl swear that they could make a good business because she father was a joiner and white people was paying a lot of money for old-looking furniture. They all went along with this until Peg say she need to make some fast money because, where they was going to find white people who like old furniture, and who was going to buy old furniture from Black women anyway. That is when Fancy Girl came up with the pyramid scheme.

They was to put everybody name on a piece of paper, everybody was to find five people to put on the list and that five would find five and so on. Everybody on the list would send the first person one hundred dollars. In the end everybody was to get thousands of dollars in the mail and only invest one hundred, unless the pyramid break. Fancy Girl name was the first and so the pyramid start. Lo and behold, Fancy Girl leave town saying she going to Montreal for a weekend and it was the last they ever see she. The pyramid bust up and they discover that Fancy Girl pick up ten thousand dollars clean. Blossom had to hide for months from people on the pyramid and she swear to Peg that, if she every see Fancy Girl Munroe again, dog eat she supper.

Well now is five years since Blossom in Canada and nothing ain't breaking. She leave the people on Oriole for some others on Balmoral. The white man boss-man was a doctor. Since the day she reach, he eyeing she, eyeing she. Blossom just mark this down in she head and making sure she ain't in no room alone with he. Now one day, it so happen that she in the basement doing the washing and who come down there but he, playing like if he looking for something. She watching him from the corner of she eye and, sure as the day, he make a grab for she. Blossom know a few things, so she grab on to he little finger and start to squeeze it back till he face change all colour from white to black and he had to scream out. Blossom sheself start to scream like all hell, until the wife and children run downstairs too.

It ain't have cuss, Blossom ain't cuss that day. The wife face red and shame and then she start to watch Blossom cut eye. Well look at my cross nah Lord, Blossom think, here this dog trying to abuse me and she watching *me* cut eye! Me! A church-going woman! A craziness fly up in Blossom head and she start to go mad on them in the house. She flinging things left right and centre and cussing big word. Blossom fly right off the handle, until they send for the police for Blossom. She didn't care. They couldn't make she hush. It don't have no dignity in white man feeling you up! So she cuss out the police too, when they come, and tell them to serve and protect she, like they supposed to do and lock up the so-and-so. The doctor keep saying to the police, "Oh this is so embarrassing. She's crazy, she's crazy." And Blossom tell him, "You ain't see crazy yet." She run and dash all the people clothes in the swimming pool and shouting, "Make me a weapon in thine hand, oh Lord!" Blossom grab on to the doctor neck, dragging him, to drown him. It take two police to unlatch Blossom from the man red neck, yes. And how the police get Blossom to leave is a wonder: but she wouldn't leave without she pay, and in cash money too besides, she tell them. Anyhow, the police get Blossom to leave the house; and they must be 'fraid Blossom too, so they let she off down the street and tell she to go home.

The next day Blossom show up on Balmoral with a placard saying the Dr. So-and-So was a white rapist; and Peg and Betty bring a Black Power flag and the three of them parade in front of that man house whole day. Well is now this doctor know that he mess with the wrong woman, because when he reach home that evening, Blossom and Peg and Betty bang on he car, singing, "We Shall Not Be Moved" and chanting, "Doctor So-and-So is a Rapist." They reach into the car and, well, rough up the doctor — grabbing he tie and threatening to cut off he balls. Not a soul ain't come outside, but you never see so much drapes and curtain moving and swaying up and down Balmoral. Police come again, but they tell Doctor So-and-So that the sidewalk is public property and as long as Blossom and them keep moving they wasn't committing no crime. Well, when they hear that, Blossom and them start to laugh and clap and sing, "We Shall Overcome". That night, at Peg house, they laugh and they eat and they drink and dance and laugh more, remembering the doctor face when they was banging on he car. The next day Blossom hear from the Guyanese girl working next door that the whole family on Balmoral, Doctor, wife, children, cat and dog, gone to Florida.

After that, Blossom decide to do day work here and day work there, so that no white man would be over she and she was figuring on a way to save some money to do she own business.

Blossom start up with Victor one night in a dance. It ain't have no reason that she could say why she hook up with him except that in a dance one night, before Fancy Girl take off, when Peg and Betty and Fancy Girl was in they dance days, she suddenly look around and all three was jack up in a corner with some man. They was grinding down the Trinidad Club and there was Blossom, alone at the table, playing she was groovin' to the music.

Alone. Well, keeping up sheself, working, working and keeping the spirits up in this cold place all the time. . . . Is not until all of a sudden one moment, you does see youself. Something tell she to stop and witness the scene. And then Blossom decide to get a man. All she girl pals had one, and Blossom decide to get one too. It sadden she a little to see she riding partners all off to the side so. After all, every weekend they used to fête and insult man when they come to ask them to dance. They would fête all night in the middle of the floor and get tight on southern comfort. Then they would hobble down the steps out of the club on Church or "Room at the Top", high heels squeezing and waist in pain, and hail a taxi home to one house or the other. By the time the taxi reach wherever they was going, shoes would be in hand and stockings off and a lot of

groaning and description of foot pain would hit the door. And
comparing notes on which man look so good and which man
had a hard on, they would cook, bake and salt fish in the
morning and laugh about the night before. If is one thing with
Blossom, Peg and Betty and Fancy Girl, they like to have a
good time. The world didn't mean for sorrow; and suffering
don't suit nobody face, Blossom say.

So when she see girl-days done and everybody else straighten
up and get man, Blossom decide to get a man too. The first,
first man that pass Blossom eyes after deciding was Victor and
Blossom decide on him. It wasn't the first man Blossom had,
but it was the first one she decide to keep. It ain't have no
special reason either; is just when Victor appear, Blossom get
a idea to fall in love. Well, then start a long line of misery the
likes of which Blossom never see before and never intend to
see again. The only reason that the misery last so long is
because Blossom was a stubborn woman and when she decide
something, she decide. It wasn't even that Blossom really like
Victor because whenever she sit down to count he attributes,
the man was really lacking in kindness and had a streak of
meanness when it come to woman. But she figure like and love
not the same thing. So Blossom married to Victor that same
summer, in the Pentecostal Church. Victor wanted to live
together, but Blossom say she wouldn't be able to go to church
no more if she living in sin and if Victor want any honey from
she, it have to be with God blessing.

The wedding night, Victor disappear. He show up in a dance,
in he white wedding suit and Blossom ain't see him till Monday
morning. So Blossom take a sign from this and start to watch
Victor because she wasn't a hasty woman by nature. He come
when he want, he go when he want and vex when she ain't
there. He don't bring much money. Blossom still working day
work and every night of the week Victor have friends over
drinking Blossom liquor. But Blossom love Victor, so she put
up with this type of behaviour for a good few years; because
love supposed to be hard and if it ain't hard, it ain't sweet, they

say. You have to bear with a man, she mother used to say, and besides, Blossom couldn't grudge Victor he good time. Living wasn't just for slaving and it seem that in this society the harder you work, the less you have. Judge not lest ye be judged; this sermon Blossom would give to Peg and Betty anytime they contradict Victor. And anyway, Blossom have she desires and Victor have more than reputation between he legs.

So life go on as it supposed to go on, until Blossom decide not to go to work one day. That time, they was living on Vaughan Road and Blossom wake up feeling like a old woman. Just tired. Something tell she to stay home and figure out she life; because a thirty-six year old woman shouldn't feel so old and tired. She look at she face in the mirror and figure that she look like a old woman too. Ten years she here now, and nothing shaking, just getting older and older, watching white people live. She, sheself living underneath all the time. She didn't even feel like living with Victor anymore. All the sugar gone outa the thing. Victor had one scheme after another, poor thing. Everything gone a little sour.

She was looking out the window, toward the bus stop on Vaughan Road, thinking this. Looking at people going to work like they does do every morning. It make she even more tired to watch them. Today she was supposed to go to a house on Roselawn. Three bathrooms to clean, two living rooms, basement, laundry — God knows what else. Fifty dollars. She look at she short fingers, still water-laden from the day before, then look at the bus stop again. No, no. Not today. Not this woman. In the bedroom, she watch Victor lying in the bed, face peaceful as ever, young like a baby. Passing into the kitchen shaking she head, she think, "Victor you ain't ready for the Lord yet."

Blossom must be was sitting at the kitchen table for a hour or so when Victor get up. She hear him bathe, dress and come out to the kitchen. "Ah, ah, you still here? Is ten o'clock, you know!" She didn't answer. "Girl, you ain't going to work today, or what?" She didn't answer. "You is a happy woman yes, Blossom. Anyway," as he put he coat on, "I have to meet a fella."

Something just fly up in Blossom head and she reach for the bread knife on the table. "Victor, just go and don't come back, you hear me?" waving the knife. "Girl you crazy, or what?" Victor edged toward the door, "What happen to you this morning?"

Next thing Blossom know, she running Victor down Vaughan Road screaming and waving the bread knife. She hear somebody screaming loud, loud. At first she didn't know who it is, and is then she realize that the scream was coming from she and she couldn't stop it. She dress in she nightie alone and screaming in the middle of the road. So it went on and on until it turn into cry and Blossom just cry and cry and cry and then she start to walk. That day Blossom walk. And walk and cry, until she was so exhausted that she find she way home and went to sleep.

She wake up the next morning, feeling shaky and something like spiritual. She was frightened, in case the crying come back again. The apartment was empty. She had the feeling that she was holding she body around she heart, holding sheself together, tight, tight. She get dressed and went to the Pentecostal Church where she get married and sit there till evening.

For two weeks this is all Blossom do. As soon as she feel the crying welling up inside she and turning to a scream, she get dressed and go to the Pentecost. After two weeks, another feeling come; one as if Blossom dip she whole head in water and come up gasping. She heart would pump fast as if she going to die and then the feeling, washed and gasping. During these weeks she could drink nothing but water. When she try to eat bread, something reach inside of she throat and spit it out. Two weeks more and Blossom hair turn white all over. Then she start to speak in tongues that she didn't ever learn, but she understand. At night, in Blossom cry dreams, she feel sheself flying round the earth and raging around the world and then, not just this earth, but earth deep in the blackness beyond sky. There, sky become further than sky and further than dream.

She dream so much farther than she ever go in a dream, that she was awake. Blossom see volcano erupt and mountain fall down two feet away and she ain't get touch. She come to the place where legahoo and lajabless is not even dog and where soucouyant, the fireball, burn up in the bigger fire of an infinite sun, where none of the ordinary spirit Blossom know is nothing. She come to the place where pestilence mount good, good heart and good heart bust for joy. The place bright one minute and dark the next. The place big one minute, so big Blossom standing in a hole and the blackness rising up like long shafts above she and widening out into a yellow and red desert as far as she could see; the place small, next minute, as a pin head and only Blossom heart what shrink small, small, small, could fit in the world of it. Then she feel as if she don't have no hand, no foot and she don't need them. Sometimes, she crawling like mapeepee snake; sometimes she walking tall, tall, like a moco jumbie through desert and darkness, desert and darkness, upside down and sideways.

In the mornings, Blossom feel she body beating up and breaking up on a hard mud ground and she, weeping as if she mourning and as if somebody borning. And talking in tongues, the tongues saying the name, Oya. The name sound through Blossom into every layer of she skin, she flesh — like sugar and seasoning. Blossom body come hard like steel and supple like water, when she say Oya.

One night, Oya hold Blossom and bring she through the most terrifying dream in she life. In the dream, Oya make Blossom look at Black people suffering. The face of Black people suffering was so old and hoary that Blossom nearly dead. And is so she vomit. She skin wither under Suffering look; and she feel hungry and thirsty as nobody ever feel before. Pain dry out Blossom soul, until it turn to nothing. Blossom so 'fraid she dead that she take she last ball of spit, and stone Suffering. Suffering jump up so fast and grab the stone, Blossom shocked, because she did think Suffering was decrepit. Then Suffering head for Blossom with such a speed that Blossom fingernails and hairs fall out. Blossom start to dry away, and melt away, until it only had one grain of she left. And Suffering still descending. Blossom scream for Oya and Oya didn't come and Suffering keep coming. Blossom was never a woman to stop, even before she start to dream. So she roll and dance she grain-self into a hate so hard, she chisel sheself into a sharp hot prickle and fly in Suffering face. Suffering howl like a beast and back back. Blossom spin and chew on that nut of hate, right in Suffering eyeball. The more Blossom spin and dance, the more Suffering back back; the more Suffering back back, the bigger Blossom get, until Blossom was Oya with she warrior knife, advancing. In the cold light of Suffering, with Oya hot and advancing, Suffering slam a door and disappear. Blossom climb into Oya lovely womb of strength and fearlessness. Full of joy when Oya show she the warrior dance where heart and blood burst open. Freeness, Oya call that dance; and the colour of the dance was red and it was a dance to dance high up in the air. In this dance Oya had such a sweet laugh, it make she black skin shake and it full up Blossom and shake she too.

Each night Blossom grow more into Oya. Blossom singing, singing for Oya to come,

"Oya arriwo Oya, Oya arriwo Oya, Oya kauako arriwo, Arripiti O Oya."

Each night Blossom learn a new piece of Oya and finally, it come to she. She had the power to see and the power to fight; she had to the power to feel pain and the power to heal. For life was nothing as it could be taken away any minute; what was earthly was fleeting; what could be done was joy and it have no beauty in suffering.

"Oya O Ologbo O de, Ma yak ba Ma Who! leh, Oya O Ologo O de, Ma yak ba Ma Who! leh, Oya Oh de arriwo, Oya Oh de cumale."

From that day, Blossom dress in yellow and red from head to foot, the colour of joy and the colour of war against suffering. She head wrap in a long yellow cloth; she body wrap in red.

She become a obeah woman, spiritual mother the priestess of Oya, Yuroba Goddess-warrior of winds, storm and waterfalls. It was Oya who run Victor out and it was Oya who plague the doctor and laugh and drink afterwards. It was Oya who well up the tears inside Blossom and who spit the bread out of Blossom mouth.

Quite here, Oya did search for Blossom. Quite here, she find she.

Black people on Vaughan Road recognized Blossom as gifted and powerful by she carriage and the fierce look in she eyes. She fill she rooms with compelling powder and reliance smoke, drink rum and spit it in the corners, for the spirits who would enter Blossom obeah house in the night. Little by little people begin to find out that Blossom was the priestess of Oya, the Goddess. Is through Oya, that Blossom reach prosperity.

"Oya arriwo Oya, Oya arriwo Oya, Oya kauako arriwo, Arripiti O Oya."

Each night Oya would enter Blossom, rumbling and violent like thunder, and chant heroically and dance, slowly and majestically, she warrior dance against suffering. To see Oya dancing on one leg all night, a calabash holding a candle on she head, was to see beauty. She fierce warrior face frighten unbelievers. Then she would drink nothing but good liquor, blowing mouthfuls on the gathering, granting favours to the believers for an offering.

The offerings come fast and plentiful. Where people was desperate, Blossom, as Oya, received food as offering, boxes of candles and sweet oil. Blossom send to Trinidad for calabash gourds and herbs for healing, guided by Oya in the mixing and administering.

When Oya enter Blossom, she talk in old African tongues and she body was part water and part tree. Oya thrash about taking Blossom body up to the ceiling and right through the walls. Oya knife slash the gullets of white men and Oya pitch the world around itself. Some nights, she voice sound as if it was coming from a deep well; and some nights, only if you had the power to hear air, could you listen to Oya.

Blossom fame as obeah woman spread all over, but only among those who had to know. Those who see the hoary face of Suffering and feel the vibrant slap could come to dance with Oya — Oya freeness dance.

"Oya O Ologbo O de, Ma yak ba Ma Who! leh, Oya O Ologo O de, Ma yak ba Ma Who! leh, Oya Oh de arriwo, Oya Oh de cumale."

Since Oya reach, Blossom live peaceful. Is so, Blossom start in the speakeasy business. In the day time, Blossom sleep, exhausted and full of Oya warrior dance and laughing. She would wake up in the afternoon to prepare the shrine for Oya entrance.

On the nights that Oya didn't come, Blossom sell liquor and wait for she, sitting against the window.

One Last Look in the Mirror

Glen Sorestad

People often wondered, I suppose, what I might have seen in that little runt of a man that I married, Ben Kovacz. He wasn't much, that's for sure. But then, looking at the men who come in here and drink themselves into stupid stories and endless arguments, the ones who tell the same story over and over until you get sick to death of the sound of their beery voices, the ones who brag and brag as if to prove they'd really amounted to something, even if they're still stuck in this one-street town like all the rest of us, the ones who sit and drink and don't say much but just pretend they're better than the rest — they're all a pack of fools! Who'd want them? At least when I married that little Pole I knew what I wanted. And I got it too. I made sure of that. His land. That's what I wanted. Land is better than money and he didn't have much of that, for all that he was a bachelor and didn't have a soul to spend it on except himself. And the Church, of course.

There's Pete Wasznuik again. Guess that means the evening run is on now. Only peaceful time a person gets in this smoky dump is over supper when most of them at least have the common sense to go home and eat. Wish they'd just close the place down for an hour or so over supper like they used to and at least give you a chance to get a break from all their crude jokes and their belching and farting. Fart! You never saw a man that could fart like that runt of a man I married! As often, or as rank. When I'd complain about it he'd just grin that stupid grin and say, "Don't you wish you could do as well?" and I'd end up angry and there wasn't a damn thing I could do about it. Imagine having to sleep with a man that farted all night long! One night I called him nothing but a little fart and the little fart hauled off and hit me. In the face. Blackened my eye, he did. The only time though. I fixed him.

"Here's your Blue, Pete. Hope it kills yuh," I say, like I always do to Pete as I put down his Blue and his glass.

"The same," he says, and lifts his glass to me. He always says that, just like I always say the same thing to him. Helps to keep a sense of order to this useless place. Knowing there are certain things that don't change, like Pete's always having a Blue and a glass and always saying the same thing. He's all right, Pete. Drinks too much, but so do a whole lot of others and at least Pete never gets owly or causes trouble for anyone else. Not like others I could name around this place. But having people like Pete who know what to expect of you and who'll always act in a certain way or say the same thing makes the job easier to stomach. And let me tell you, tending bar in the Windsor Hotel is not an easy job to stomach at the best of times.

People like familiar things. Like to do things a certain way. Like old Snoozy. Comes in every day, twice a day, steps through the door and stops, then he stamps each boot down once on the floor before he comes in and sits down. Just like he was shaking the snow off or maybe stamping off the cowshit from the barn. But here in town he does it even when there's no snow and no cowshit! Just something he does from habit, I guess, and now he does it because it makes him feel like it's the right thing to do. Like a ritual in church, I guess.

My Ben was one for church ritual. Catholic Church. I had to join the Catholic Church to marry him. He wouldn't change to my church, not that I ever was one for church, but I was confirmed in the Lutheran Church and Dad said he figured Ben should've at least married me in my own church, even if he wouldn't become a Lutheran. Of course, Dad thought I was crazy to marry Ben in the first place, him being nearly sixty and me hardly twenty. But then he also said I'd never be able to find myself a man to marry because I was so plain and not built dainty like a woman should be. Anytime I'd talk about a young man when I was in my teens he'd laugh and slap his leg and say, "Agnes, you got about as much chance of catching a man as a dog has catching a gopher!" *What the hell did he know?* Men know nothing and it's a damn good thing.

But I was married to Ben in the Catholic Church and I had to see Father Adrian for over a year, once a week, regular, until he thought I was good enough to get married in his church. And all the time I was taking those stupid lessons I was thinking, *I'll get you, you smug, red-faced, whisky-smelling, sonofabitchin priest, just as soon as I get that man signed, sealed and delivered.* Ben was scared shitless by priests, and especially Father Adrian, and so that smiling bastard goddam near furnished the whole inside of his church with the money he squeezed out of Ben Kovacz. If he wanted a new icon, he'd go to Ben. If he wanted fancier vestments, see Ben. If the roof needed repairing, why put another squeeze on Ben. I don't know what he said to that man, but he must have put the fear of eternal damnation into him every time. It wasn't that Ben had a lot of money to give away. It was just that he had no one else to give it to and Father Adrian knew it, just like every other priest before him, I suppose. But once that wedding was over things changed, I can tell you that.

There's old Snoozy. Stamping his goddam boots like it was the middle of January instead of the middle of May and not a cloud in the sky. Might as well get out his Pil. The man probably never drank anything other than a Pil in his whole life and who knows how long that's been. That's one thing about a place like this, you get to know what each of the regulars wants and you don't have to think about it or ask because it never changes. You only order beer once a month and it's always the same order: same number of cases of Blue, same number of Pil, so many Bohemian, so many OV. Snoozy doesn't have to ask for a Pil. He probably hasn't said the word in years.

You gotta take charge of a man and I knew that even before I got married. When I decided I was gonna marry that man I knew what I had to do. I seen the way my father ran our house

and I said to myself, "No man is ever gonna run me that way."
Maybe that's why Dad and me never got along much. That and
the fact that I was not good-looking like the rest of my brothers
and sisters. Six boys and four girls and I have to be the ugly
duckling of the lot! Maybe every time he looked at me he
suspected I wasn't his, or something, but he made fun of me
every chance he could and I stood it only as long as I had to.
On my sixteenth birthday when Mother had made a cake for
me and at least some of us were still at home, I felt pretty good,
but then Dad said, "Agnes, you take a good look at yourself in
the mirror over there. Go ahead, look!" So I did. Then he said,
"Agnes, you're not only gonna be an old maid, but you're gonna
be the *homeliest* old maid in the country." I looked at myself
again in the mirror and I just had to cry. It was the last time I
ever looked at myself in the mirror!

But afterwards, I said to myself, *I'll get even with that man, wait
and see.* And I did. For starters I married Ben before I was
twenty and I didn't ask Dad if I could marry him either. I told
him! And when I told him I was gonna marry Ben no matter
what he said, why then Dad tried to bully me just like he'd been
bullying my mother all those years. But when he saw it wasn't
gonna work, after he was all finished puffing himself up like a
goddam bullfrog with his feeling that only he knew how to run
the world, when he'd finally realized that his Agnes was never
gonna say, "Yes, Papa," any more, why then he changed, just
like that, and all the air went outta him like a flat tire. After that
I had no problem with him at all. But Mother couldn't do that
and so he bullied her right into her grave. *I never forgave him
for that.*

There's the Olafson boys. Carl and Oscar. Haven't been in here
for awhile now. Never see one without the other. That's two
OV's for them. Only ones who drink it. Smallest order of all the
beers when we send in the monthly order. Just the two
brothers and they don't come in no more than once a week or
so. But never one without the other. Lots of brothers like to
drink together, I guess. Even mine sometime. But it seems like

these two Olafsons are scared to come through that door unless there are the two of them. Live on separate farms, yet they're never seen inside this Hotel unless they're together. No two of my brothers are as close as that, I can tell you. Some families grow up close as peas in a pod, but not our family. I don't talk to any of them unless I have to.

I set the beers down for the Olafsons. Carl looks at me and I know what he's gonna say.

"You're looking healthy, Agnes," he says. Seems it's the only thing he can think of to say to me in greeting, so he says it every time he comes in when I'm here. He means I'm as big as ever, maybe bigger. And since he can't say anything about how pretty I look or how nice my clothes fit, he always ends up saying that. I know he don't mean any harm and it's just his way of tryin to be nice. It's just that I wish that for once he might say something that'd make me feel good about being here, or just about being me. I know I'm not much to look at, but bein told you're "looking healthy" doesn't do a hell of a lot to raise the spirits.

When I married Ben I didn't waste any time showing him that I was taking charge. He didn't like it, of course, but he didn't put up much of a fight either. I was bigger and stronger than him and I sure as hell knew what I wanted. He was no match for me. Once when he got angry because I made him turn over his grain to me and I thought maybe he was gonna hit me, I just grabbed him and threw him down and sat on him and pinned his arms until I had him settled down. Once he knew he couldn't beat me and that I was gonna get what I wanted, one way or another, why he gave me no problems at all. He just turned over his cheques to me and that was that. I was in charge.

Mind you, Father Adrian tried his best to turn things around and to make Ben the boss. And Ben would of let him. But I wasn't having any of that shit! At first Ben complained that I wasn't letting him give enough to the Church, but I told him flat out that he'd given a damn sight more than anyone else in the country and that it was time that the others started furnishing the place with all the expensive religious doodads that Father Adrian always wanted. I told him I was giving so much a week and that was that — and not a hell of a lot at that. Plenty for two people on a half-section though. I couldn't see why *I* should now be giving perfectly good money for the never-ending string of doodads that Father Adrian wanted. I think that slippery bugger was pocketing money on the side. When he first seen that Ben and I weren't giving the usual amount, he made a visit to our house and he tried everything short of excommunication to persuade and even threaten me into giving more to the Church. *To his pocket,* I figured. I told him where to go. And he went away, angry as a stirred up wasps' nest, tellin me that God would punish me for my sinfulness. Ben was scared half to death, but I didn't care. The way I figured, it wasn't God that was out to punish me. It was that goddam red-faced Father Adrian!

"Yeah, yeah, I see yuh, Pete! Keep yer shirt on!" Bloody Pete, he's like a goddam blotter. Put down a beer for that man and it's like pourin slop in a pig trough. You turn around and he's squealin for another. Don't know where that man puts it. He's not very big but he's always dry as a desert rat. Might as well get one for Snoozy as well. Looks like he's planning on stayin for another. Probably tellin Pete another of his horse-and-buggy yarns. Old bugger never seems to run outta them. You have to admit though, he knows howta tell a good story, old Snoozy. I've seen him keep a whole table of regulars listenin for three solid hours without repeatin a single story the whole time.

When I married Ben I threw out every mirror in the house. Except for the one little mirror that I let him keep to put above the washstand so he could shave. He thought I was crazy, Ben did, but I just told him that I didn't want any mirrors in my house and that was that. I said that mirrors were for them that had nothin better to do with their time than to admire their own reflections. I told him people who really knew themselves, who knew what they were really like, didn't need mirrors. I don't know if he believed me or not, but he didn't squawk much when I threw them out. As long as he had his own little shaving mirror. I let him keep that. It wasn't that he was admirin himself anyway. He was just tryin to keep from cuttin his throat. And even now, here in town, with Ben dead and me in my own house, there isn't a mirror anywhere. Not one.

When Mother died I grew to hate Dad even more. It was bad enough he bullied her into her grave all the way with his never-ending demands that she do this or that for him. The man couldn't do a damn thing for himself. Just give orders. And after the funeral was over and all the rest of the family had gone their own ways, back to their own places all over the country, there was only Dad and my younger brother Ernie left at home, and that man had the nerve to come to me and say, "Agnes, I figure you should come home for a few weeks and kinda look after things until we get settled in." Imagine that! Me! The ugly duckling! The daughter he said would end up the homeliest old maid in the country. Well, I knew what he had in mind all right, and it sure as hell wasn't just a few weeks, so I told him I had my own man to look after now. And he said that Ben knew how to look after himself, he'd been doin it so long before I married him. But I was havin none of that. Not a chance. I told him that either he or Ernie had better find themselves another woman to look after them, but it sure as hell wasn't gonna be me. He was none too happy about that, I can tell you. He even suggested that him and Ernie would be prepared to move in with Ben and me. *Fat chance,* I told him. He ended up saying that I was no daughter of his and I said, "Funny thing, but I always felt that." He was none too happy about that. Not that I gave a shit.

There they go. Looks like it could be another long evening of stories now with the Olafsons joining Pete and Snoozy. First thing someone'll start in with one of the stories of that crazy old Mrs. Grendall and all the things she says she sees. Pete's got enough of them to keep the Olafsons laughin for an hour and as long as they're happy they'll buy beer. Pete and Snoozy don't have a whole lot of money between the two of them, but their stories usually buy them enough beers to keep them happy. To tell the truth, I wouldn't pay a goddam cent for one of their stories. But then I guess I get to hear them all anyway. Over and over. And I never paid a cent in my life for anything I didn't have to.

Father Adrian wanted me to turn over the handlin of the money to Ben, of course. "Don't you know that what you're doing is against the wishes of God?" he said to me. "God tells us that a man should rule his household, just as He rules Heaven and earth — and that includes the money," he added. I think he really meant, "especially the money."

"Is God a man or a woman?" I asked Father Adrian.

"God is our Father," he replied.

"That's what I figured you'd say. Well, I know more than enough about how fathers run their households and this house is one that He ain't gonna run."

"You are going against God's word, woman," Father Adrian said, and his red face got even redder. The way he said "woman" made it seem like he had a piece of shit in his mouth.

So I said, "If God was a woman then He'd know that a man needs a woman to run things for him. A man's gonna be happiest and live longest when he lets his woman run things for him. Like my man here," and I gave Ben a good squeeze on his arm to let him know I didn't want him openin his mouth at the wrong time, but he was already shrinkin into his chair for fear of what the priest was gonna say or do to me. In the end Father Adrian just got mad and went away like he usually did when he tried to get something outta me that I wasn't about to give him.

When Ben died it was almost six years to the very day from the time we were married. The cancer got him. And I got everything he had. Not that there was so goddam much. But there was the land, two of the best quarters in the country. Maybe he wasn't much of a man in some ways, but one thing he sure as hell was and that was a good farmer. So I knew when I married Ben that when he died I was gonna have the best half-section of land around, and if I couldn't turn that into a little nest egg then there was something wrong with me. After I got Ben shaped up the way I wanted him and after I'd broken Father Adrian's hold on Ben's wallet, I made damn sure that Ben drew up a will and that I got everything, the whole kit and kaboodle. He complained a little, of course. Said he'd promised Father Adrian that the Church would get a generous gift to make sure he didn't spend any more time in Purgatory than he had to. But I just told him he should leave things in my hands and I'd make sure Father Adrian and the Church would be taken care of when he died. He wasn't too happy about it, but I got my way, of course. And when he died, and I had him buried in the Catholic cemetery beside his folks, just like he wanted, I paid the funeral costs and all, but not a penny more. And I told Father Adrian not to bother comin round to see me because I wasn't interested. And that was that. When I sold that land and moved to town and bought my house, Father Adrian never saw a penny of that money, I can tell you that.

I took Ben's shaving mirror and smashed it and threw it out.

There's Fred from the lumberyard. And his wife! Will you look at her, all dolled up and made-up like she was looking for another man. They must be celebratin a special occasion. He don't bring her in here very often. Mostly comes in here before supper, on his way home from work. The lumberyard is just down the street, you see, so it's real handy for Fred. He has one or two Blues and that's all. Sandy, he calls his wife. Sandra Gerbrandt. From all those Gerbrandts north of town. Tries to pretend that she's the cat's ass just because she's married to a goddam Revelstoke lumber jockey. Who does she think she's kidding? Thinks people don't remember. People round here have long memories and she better remember that! Wonder if she ever told Fred about the miscarriage she had in high school? Knocked up by the Phys. Ed. teacher, she was. Ben told me that. Ben's cousin was on the school board that fired the sonofabitch. Lucky thing she lost it though. Not many knew about it. I'll bet a 24 of Blue that Fred don't know a thing about it. Old man Gerbrandt was fit to be tied. He was all for castratin that young teacher, but when she lost the baby I guess he settled for havin him fired. So now she's got a Revelstoke lumber jockey and thinks her shit don't stink. Well, she better not try any airs on me or I'll put her in her place in a hurry.

Like I did to Dad. The goddam nerve of the man! Not one bloody week after I'd buried Ben and he comes around and he says to me that he figures now that Ben's gone I should turn over the farmin of Ben's land to him and Ernie. *The bloody gall!*

"You mean you wanna rent it?" I asked him, pretending I didn't really know what he had in mind.

"Well, no. . ." he said. "We're *family,* Agnes. You got the house. You don't need the land. We'll farm it for you."

"I ain't your daughter, remember?" I reminded him, sticking it into him, cool as an icicle.

He turned all red, then white, and I could see that he was getting madder than a bull in fly-time.

"You're a hard woman, Agnes. You got no feeling for your own family," he said.

"Well, I come by it honestly," I replied. And he just sat across that kitchen table from me and glared. And Ernie just sat there fidgeting and shuffling his feet like the useless turd that he is.

"I'll tell you what I'll do for you," I said. "I'll sell you the half-section for eighty thousand cash and you can have it all — land, buildings, machinery. Everything."

"I ain't got that kinda money, you know that," he said.

"Then what the hell you doing, comin round here and wastin my time? I've only got time for serious offers."

He swallowed hard at that, but I knew he was beat and it felt good.

"Some daughter you turned out to be," he complained.

"Yeah," I said. "Funny how it happens, ain't it? Same daughter that was too homely for you six years ago is suddenly very attractive when she's got the best half-section of land in the country. Well, unless you got eighty thousand dollars with you, don't bother comin round again cause I ain't really interested in seein either of you again."

Wants a *martini* does she? Ordinary bar drink ain't good enough for Sandra Gerbrandt. The hoity-toity bitch. Maybe I'll just spit up a gob and mix it in her martini. Imagine, putting on airs because she's married to a useless tool like Revelstoke Fred. The man's dumber than a bag of hammers. He's worked for Revelstoke for must be fifteen years now and still stuck in the same bloody little lumberyard here where he started. They say it's likely to be closed down if things don't get better round here. I suppose she thinks he'll get transferred to a better position in a bigger place if this one closes down. Fat chance! He'll get canned for sure. Then we'll see how high that bitch carries her nose in the air. Look at her, pretending she's listenin to Fred while she's keepin her eye on Pete Wasznuik. Wonder if there's something there? Wouldn't surprise me a bit. Maybe Fred just isn't givin her enough. Once a slut, always a slut, they say. She's likely lookin at the wrong man though. I doubt that Pete can get it up much with all the drinkin he does. Still, you never know.

Not my Ben though. That man had no trouble gettin it up. Not him! At least not until he got too sick with the cancer. When we got married it seemed like he had sixty years stored up for me. Scared hell outta me at first, I can tell you. I sure wasn't prepared for that. He might have been a runt of a man in some ways, but he was all Pole, that's for sure. Good thing I was such a big, strong woman or he'da screwed me right through the mattress and into the floor. God, how we made that bed bounce and rattle! That wooden headboard would beat on the wall so hard it musta sounded like some giant woodpecker was tryin to eat through the wall. He'd plunge up and down on me like he was diggin a twenty-foot well with a spade. And he was some digger, let me tell you! The sweat would just roll down his forehead and drop down on me and his would get all mixed up with mine and then he'd finally collapse and I'd just hold him there in my arms until we was breathin normal again. I miss the little bugger, though his dyin wasn't an easy time for me.

Jesus, there they go on those crazy Mrs. Grendall stories. That old lady is something else. When her old man died she kinda went off the rocker a bit. Started seein things. Once she told me she'd just had tea with her grandfather, that he'd come all the way over from Sweden to spend the afternoon with her. Her grandfather! Bet he's been dead a hundred years and never did set foot in this country. Old Mrs. Grendall must be eighty-five or ninety herself. I feel sorry for her just the same. She musta had a good man to have missed him so much. At least Ben's death didn't get to me like that.

Ben wouldn't go to a doctor, of course. Said he'd never seen a doctor in his life and hadn't been in a hospital either and there was no way he was gonna start. I knew he was dyin and so did he. It's not easy livin with a man that's dyin of cancer, the moanin and groanin for months at night till you don't get no sleep at all, and then the turnin to cryin out with the pain till I finally had to move downstairs to try to get some sleep on the couch in the livingroom. Still I couldn't get much sleep. Watching him waste away with the cancer eatin him up and him absolutely refusin to let me take him to the hospital, no matter how bad the pain got. I guess I coulda took him if I wanted to, but I figured he deserved to die where he wanted to and I never had much use for doctors, nor hospitals either. But it was hard on both of us. What kept me going was that I knew I had Ben's will and I knew exactly what it said and sometimes when the pain was makin him cry like a baby I would think of that red-faced priest and no matter how bad it got for me I'd just hang on because I figured it would all be worth it just to see the look on his face when I cut that Father Adrian and all his requests off without a goddam cent. And when the pain finally got too bad and I was just about crazy from not sleepin at all, and Ben said he didn't wanna live any longer, I covered his face with the pillow and it was all over in a few minutes. It was the least I could do for him.

"Don't get your shirt inna knot, Pete. There's others need servin besides you." *Bloody men! Have to attend to them like children.*

"Hope it kills yuh, Pete," I say, as I give him another Blue.

"The same," he smiles and raises his glass to me.

The Mime

Ernest Hekkanen

The monk appeared in the morning. There were confirmed and corroborated reports of him having been seen as early as sunrise, but some maintained he had been spotted even earlier, having walked as it were right out of the dark. Dressed in a black robe with a hood tossed back on his shoulders, he seemed to stroll the streets of the town in a rather disoriented manner, twisting and craning his neck as it suited him. Frequently he would fix himself in a pose, his head cocked to one side, seeming to listen with his right ear to what hovered above and slightly to the back of his shoulder. On these occasions his mouth would drop open, he would listen intently for several seconds, sometimes as many as perhaps ten, then he would shake his head vigorously and regain his momentum.

The thing that hovered above his right shoulder seemed to be a moth with human face. Its wings spanned twice its body length, which measured, at the outset, at least a meter. However, this moth was actually composed of numerous flies which, because of a will or an authority that seemed to be in operation, had been forced to assume the shape of the moth, much as cells in the human body have been forced to assume a shape, and activity, that allows the greater mass to move and function as an entity of itself.

On those rare occasions when the monk nodded rather than shook his head, the flies which composed the body of the moth would disperse, fly up into the air, then reassemble in a message with many curlicues reminiscent of medieval script around the edges. Doubtless some sort of communication had taken place between the monk and the moth. There was the "listening" pose that the monk found necessary to adopt, and also the subsequent nodding or shaking of his head, as though he were agreeing or disagreeing with a message that had been transmitted to him. But this was done in total silence and remains largely conjecture, especially in light of what took place later on.

The monk had not previously been seen in Oasis, South Dakota. How he had arrived was a matter of speculation: some said by air, some maintained he had walked in across the desolate and formidable Bad Lands, the dunes and twisted rock formations of which stretch to the horizon, and yet others suggested he had come by somewhat more extraordinary means that verged upon the miraculous. The author of this chronicle prefers the second suggestion, as the monk's feet were wrapped in rags and were bleeding quite profusely. Indeed, his progress through town could be easily plotted by simply following his bloody footprints, and in this manner it became evident that he had no predetermined course. His route through town quite often crossed over itself or retraced the way by which he had come or even went several times in a circle before bearing off tangentially.

Although the monk was approached, and even accosted, on several occasions, he seemed disinclined to speak. This gave rise to the suspicion that he was mute or he had taken a vow of silence. After several hours spent roaming the streets, he had picked up a dozen or so children who dogged his heels persistently. In the beginning it was noticed that these children would try to tease or otherwise provoke him, say with a stick or a missile flung at his person, but under no condition did he speak. Once, on being struck by something quite foul-smelling, he turned to look at the children, who immediately began to deliver a variety of gestures and catcalls. But rather than offering any rebuke, he proceeded to act out a mime. Although what he mimicked was at best ambiguous, his manner seemed to indicate that the intent underlying the mime was of grave importance. The children, viewing his various contortions and gesticulations, scratched their heads or simply looked confused. Two boys responded with further taunts, but the monk remained undisturbed and carried on with the mime until it had reached its natural conclusion, which was construed to have taken place when he turned and walked on, the moth with human face, this unusual swarm of numerous flies, gliding along above his right shoulder.

It was around noon when I was dispatched by the local newspaper to chronicle these extraordinary events. My objective was to find out where the monk had come from and what his purpose might be in coming to Oasis. But my enquiries were met with silence. The look he gave me was quizzical and brought out the foreign aspect of his features. His cheeks were sunken and bore traces of black stubble and his eyes, beneath a pair of extremely arched eyebrows, had a look of fierce concentration. Also, his ears were missing — that is, his outer ears — for there were scarred holes on either side of his head, as though the skin around them had been seared by hot metal.

My attempts to question him were futile and soon the entourage of rowdy children sent up a clamour for me to get out of the way. Their former hostility toward the monk, which I have since confirmed and corroborated, had been forsaken in favour of something closer to that of jovial zealots. The children had picked up sticks and shovels and brooms and were holding them aloft while bantering in a fashion that was quite amiable. Some had tied rags or T-shirts to their implements and were waving them about. One lad, apparently appointing himself a sort of jester, had taken up some chartreuse tennis balls and was juggling them about while balancing a plate on his forehead.

Deciding it was fruitless questioning the monk, I took the opportunity to snap some pictures of him standing in front of the children, with his arms raised in a ballet-like pose, as though ready to pirouette, then, thinking I might document some of his antics, I fell in with the others who were dogging his heels. At that time I did not know that the photographs I had taken, while adequately revealing the children with their sticks and brooms held aloft, had not picked up the monk, not in the shape and aspect I had met him on the street. I was satisfied that I had taken his picture and now, at my station in the middle of the crowd, I was going to follow him around town, hoping to garner enough details to satisfy my editor back at the newspaper. However, one small detail led to another and gradually, like the others, I found myself becoming a follower of the monk.

By now many of the town's more carefree citizens had taken up the march, thus lengthening it by at least a block. The march often became jumbled and disorderly because of the monk's haphazard idea of direction. We pressed up against one another at narrowing junctures or stumbled over each other's feet when reversals in direction took place. But rather than causing ill tempers, it seemed to add to the levity and carnival-like atmosphere. Those who declined to join the march none-theless emerged from stores and establishments and stood on the sidewalk watching us go by. Some waved, some shouted; some decried what they saw, while others looked on in be-wilderment or offered encouragement. We tramped down main streets and alleys, doubled back, eddied, flowed in a seemingly random fashion, and now and then someone stand-ing on the sidelines would be torn away and carried along with us. And every once in a while, the monk would favour us with one of his extraordinary mimes.

There were those who maintained they knew precisely what the mimes were supposed to portray, although I must confess I cannot count myself among them. They maintained if one watched very attentively the meaning would be absorbed by the senses. However, when I asked to have the meaning expanded upon by these individuals, who were quite certain they knew what the monk was saying with his various gestures and locomotions, they gave me interpretations that differed one from another: he is a cloud passing over the ocean; no, no, that circle he just made with his arms, that is the sun; on the contrary, he is a drop of water slackening the thirst of the world. My own feeling is that the monk could best be compared to a flame. A flame is never the same flame, it is constantly dying and being rekindled; however, because this takes place so rapidly, we see only the constant unfurling of one flame.

The monk, as though sensing our confusion, now sought to clarify his mimes by giving the occasional nod to his accomplice, the moth. The moth, on receiving this cue, would disperse into its smaller units, namely the flies, whereupon the flies would take to the air above his head and inscribe a message with many curlicues reminiscent of medieval script around the edges. The first message, as copied down in my notebook, was as follows: *The myth dreamed into flesh has been lost, so deeply has it become buried in the vessel that moves. Aye, but our lowly animation is a vestigial remain.* This first message was greeted in successive stages by: awe, fright, laughter, and finally wild applause. It was considered an admirable trick well worth repeating, although, for the majority of us, there was more than ample reason to be nonplussed. This chronicle is no place to examine the content of each and every message; I will merely offer them as they occurred, to let the reader make of them what he will. For instance, the second message, which was poised with so much rhetorical fervour: *Would this not be a case of the bird flying backwards?* What is one to make of a question such as this? Without knowing the exact meaning underlying the mime the question becomes ludicrous; it has no substance. However, it did produce much laughter when accompanied by the look of surprise on the monk's face, as well as the flapping of his arms, which seemed to propel him backwards. But once again, what was the monk referring to? At best this was ambiguous.

At this point I should say something about the weather. In July the Bad Lands are next to unbearable; the heat is relentless and the wind that frequently comes up will fill the air with choking dust. Towns do not thrive in this terrain, they survive like insects that aren't permitted the right to die. If not for the ore that Oasis fed upon, the dry carcass of the town would have tumbled off across the Bad Lands, driven this way and that by winds funnelling down the many gorges. The relentless heat and dust of summer makes us all a little giddy and perhaps, owing to this, we welcomed the distraction that the monk now provided.

Though in the beginning I had taken up a position roughly in the middle of the crowd, I found with each successive hour that my position was getting closer to the head of the parade as more and more individuals fell into line at the rear. This made for quite a crush whenever the monk came to one of his unannounced stops, as it took several minutes for the marchers at the rear to fully register what had occurred. By the time the march lost momentum to the point where there was no longer any jostling about, the monk would already have thrown himself into his mime. On this occasion the various gestures and locomotions — if one were in a position to observe them — were again unintelligible, although they were enacted with much finesse and conviction. I think by now we were much less inclined to look forward to the monk's rather ritualistic writhings and somewhat more inclined to anticipate the message the flies would inscribe upon the air. This time the message went like so: *Wavelengths, travelling at greater and greater velocity, in effect acquire mass and, therefore, can be seen as particles.* The message had many medieval curlicues around the border and remained in place throughout the mime. During the performance the monk's various gyrations seemed to gather speed and urgency and, toward the end, because my eye could not keep up with them, they seemed to blur or at least to become less distinct.

By now the flies had resumed the convenient shape of the moth; the soft body portion trailed well back over us, almost to the tail-end of the marchers. (Here, I should note that I hoisted a youngster upon my shoulders to confirm this observation.) The wingspread was so enormous the moth had to glide above the tops of the buildings, although nonetheless in back of the monk's right shoulder. As a result, we found ourselves marching in the moth's shadow, and while this did help to mute the direct effects of the sun's rays, particularly for those of us who were balding, it was such a dense shadow it seemed to trap within it a certain amount of heat and humidity.

The next three messages came in quick succession. The first one seemed adamant and chastising and, indeed, there was a certain harshness to the monk's gesticulations. *I say unto you, count the number of gestures you commit in a day. Are not most of them uninspired!* At the end of the mime the monk executed a whiplike movement that suggested an exclamation point. He turned and journeyed on, but only for a few paces. He looked at us with a grand smile and quickly flung himself into another series of ritualistic writhings that the flies interpreted in this fashion: *The Mime is no more than Geometry in Motion, conceptualized in advance of movement.* Again the monk resumed his journey, only to stop a short while later in order to plunge into yet another mime. This time the flies spelled out the following: *I walk now without the flutter of wings. No more does flight design the dream dreamed into flesh.* This was, perhaps, the monk's most depressing mime. He seemed a survivor pitted against the elements, in a terrain devastated by some horrible catastrophe. Everywhere he went he was met by stones and hostile weather. At one point he seemed to be pushing a wheelbarrow; his gestures invited us to look at what was contained in the bucket, but because he was acting out a mime, we could only speculate as to what might be inside.

By now the moth had grown to several blocks in length. It had become thicker and denser and cast a shadow the full breadth of the street. The wing-spread could not be ascertained because the buildings prevented us from seeing out to either wing tip. One would suspect that wings of such monstrous size would create quite a turbulence on being wafted up and down, but on the contrary, the only breeze was the one that normally came up in the afternoon. The head of the moth seemed a mirror image of the monk's, only many times larger. Had I failed to notice this right from the start, or had the faces

become similar over the duration of the crusade? I had continued to take pictures of the monk and the moth and I thought
later that I would assess them to find out if in the beginning
their faces had resembled one another's. Little did I know, at
the time of taking the pictures, that the faces would not, either
one of them, resemble the manifested features of those we had
followed through the streets of Oasis. No, what I would find in
the photographs were areas that resembled heat risers or
shimmering, transparent flames.

I should explain that the breeze which comes up in the afternoon gains intensity until by evening it is of gale force strength.
The air becomes laden with dust that usually sends each and
every inhabitant scurrying indoors. If one must for some
reason go outside during these hours, one does so with a
muffler and goggles. We have become so accustomed to this
we carry goggles and mufflers everywhere we go in case we
find ourselves in the midst of the blow. Now, as the wind and
dust increased in severity, we began to don our protective gear.
Rather than detracting from the ambience of the march our
garb added a certain dash of colour. Our juggler, despite the
wind, had managed to keep his chartreuse tennis balls aloft
while balancing the plate on his forehead; the children were
still waving the implements to which they had tied rags and
T-shirts, but now everyone was wearing mufflers and goggles,
everyone except, of course, the monk, who seemed not at all
disturbed by the hurtling dust.

The next mime was long in coming and consisted almost
entirely of leaps and pirouettes. Throughout this performance
the monk's feet rarely touched the earth; he was in constant
and rapid motion, and sometimes the blurring effect of so much
hectic movement suggested other objects or life forms; now a
candlestick, now a tree, now a horse and rider. Because of the
wind and dust the flies seemed to experience some difficulty
affixing the message above the monk's head. When finally they
did it proved somewhat difficult to read because the script kept
pitching about in such a frenzied manner. We read it in unison,

as though depending on one another not to make a mistake; however, our voices could have been the sawing of the wind.

And thus the Mime will transform your Geometry in Motion.

At the close of this performance the monk fixed himself in a pose suggestive of a bird standing on one leg. His body was thrust forward, his arms were outstretched and his free leg was extended behind him to maintain his balance. Until now the lad who had been juggling the chartreuse tennis balls had not fumbled so much as a single toss, but now he did. One of the balls came down on the brim of the plate, knocking the plate to the ground where it instantly shattered. The ball hit the ground and rolled over to where the monk was frozen in the pose of the bird with unfurled wings. The monk's gaze followed the ball across the ground to where his lone foot was supporting him. He looked at us with a curious expression, then he looked down at the ball, which proceeded to roll up his leg. The ball trekked up his thigh to his hip and looped around to his back and proceeded to roll along his spine — this while the monk shook as though from a chill. When the ball reached his shoulders it began to travel back and forth across them, stopping with a hesitant gesture at the sockets, as though contemplating a journey out onto the monk's arms. Finally the ball stopped directly over the ball joint of his right arm. The monk glanced at it as though offering encouragement, then quite suddenly the ball shot across his shoulders out onto his left arm, barely coming to a halt at his fingertips. The thought that the ball might go hurtling off into space caused us all to gasp. The monk smiled. The ball rolled back and forth between the extremes of his extended fingertips. When it wearied of this it used one of his hands as a springboard and propelled itself in an arc over to the fingertips of the other hand. The ball bounced back and forth in this fashion for several minutes, then it started to bounce on the monk's head. All the while it gathered speed. Indeed, it began to bounce so fast it was impossible to keep up with it and, once again, we saw only a blur of movement. All of a sudden the ball bounced very high up into the air;

it hovered for a moment at the peak of its ascent, then came down on the monk's head where, on impact, it disappeared.

Now, if we had come to regard the monk's mimes with less enthusiasm than we did the messages, this latest performance turned us abruptly around. Our applause was enormous, and also sustained. But no less remarkable was what we now observed: the flies, having reshaped themselves into the figure of the moth with human face, now disgorged the very same tennis ball that had disappeared on contact with the monk's head. It emerged from the moth's mouth and dropped in slow motion onto the monk's skull, without so much as offering a bounce. It then proceeded to roll down his spine to his hips, made a little jog down his leg to his foot and came to rest on his wrapped and bleeding toes. Then the monk, regaining his animation, flipped the ball over to the boy who had appointed himself the monk's jester.

At this point the monk resumed his journey. We took up the crusade with renewed energy, anticipating the next performance and speculating on what it might involve. The next performance was long in coming and we began to wonder if it would ever take place. The crusade had picked up considerable speed. The monk's pace seemed impelled and urgent, as though he must make up for time that had been lost. Many of those who were cripples or youngsters required assistance. We carried them on our backs or strung between us, in relentless pursuit of the monk whose course now seemed more deliberate, if for no other reason than it had gained momentum. I found I had to urge myself and others on. In my ardour to assist I had taken upon my shoulders a young boy who could not keep up. Now there was no longer any frivolity connected with the march. Our jester had ceased his juggling and our banners no longer unfurled with the same foolish glee. We trudged onward like soldiers, hoping the monk would soon reveal to us the impetus behind his mimes.

We pursued him throughout the remainder of the afternoon, through the hottest and grittiest part of the day, our mufflers and goggles clogged with dust. Had the monk lost his way or did he realize the route he took out of town would lead to the vast pit mine several kilometers away? Work in this mine never ceases. The mammoth trucks, which rise to several storeys in height, form an endless chain that conveys ore out of the pit to a processing plant far beyond the hills. The highway spiralling down the sides to the bottom is nearly twenty kilometers in length and allows for two-way traffic. While quite wide by ordinary standards, it is barely wide enough for the mammoth trucks to scrape past one another. We were, to these trucks, like flies and we would have been crushed like flies had the movement of these trucks not ceased. Had someone signalled the drivers to stop? It seemed unlikely, as the drivers remained in their cabs, hands gripping the steering wheels, eyes riveted on the road ahead, as though they were fulfilling their obligations as operators of the mammoth vehicles.

We followed the highway down into the pit, sensing that once we reached the bottom we would discover the intent behind the mimes. I think by now we were all quite exhausted; however, the implied imminence of the end seemed to bolster our spirits. In part because of the downgrade, and in part because our determination had become transfused with expectancy, we strode along with even greater momentum. And it was here, in the middle of the arid Bad Lands, in a pit more desolate than anything that could be concocted by the imagination, that the monk performed his last and greatest mime.

Let me try to prepare the scene. We had come to the very bottom of the mine where dust no longer hurtled through the air. Every type and description of machinery had been frozen in various attitudes of work. To stand down there at the very bottom and to look up at the sky, hemmed in as it was by the rim of the pit, one came to know how very small one really was. And there, giving shade to the pit, was the now monstrous body of the moth. The monk gazed up at his companion. He performed a series of gestures that the moth responded to by fixing itself vertically in the air, with its wings outstretched so

the tips touched the rim. The soft body portion hung down so
the tail end almost touched the monk's head. Then the monk
lay down upon the ground. The moth, seeming to deflate bit
by bit, was sucked down into the abdomen of the monk, a
process that took more than half an hour. The monk's size
remained the same throughout this procedure. When, at last,
the moth had been completely drawn into the belly of the
monk, we saw the monk decompose before our very eyes. His
body became a mound of teeming maggots. These maggots
matured at a fantastic rate and, in turn, became flies that
assumed the shape of a vast cathedral. The cathedral rose up
out of the pit, swelling toward the sky, and soon it blotted out
that once-transparent canopy.

At first there was pandemonium, then resignation.
We searched endlessly for a way out, only to become
completely lost and disoriented in the dark. This state lasted
for what seemed eons. Finally, as though waking from a
troubled sleep, we found ourselves in the light once again,
surrounded by the rough terrain of the Bad Lands. But we had
lost the faculty of speech. The only way we could communicate
was by gesturing, and our gestures seemed to obey a rite we
only vaguely comprehended.

The Circle

Mary Burns

Donald whistled Bach as he packed, oscillating between the four corners of his small room, from bed to basin, window to wardrobe, making a baroque fuss about sorting through the effects he had collected during his few months in Whitehorse. It was four in the morning. He thought he must be the only person conscious in the Stephen's Hotel, but it wasn't so. As he began the first movement of the third piano concerto for the fourth time — he had to keep repeating it because he knew just a few bars — the occupant of the next room threw some heavy object against the wall, causing the crack in the ceiling to smoke with plaster dust. He stopped what he was doing to watch it dissipate in the warm light of his orange plastic shaded bedside lamp.

The nerve of some people, he thought. Yet what did it matter? In two hours he would be on his way. The flotsam who were the guests of the Stephen's Hotel would never again have occasion to remark on who he was or what he did. Even so, he decided to hum under his breath instead.

His next to final selections lay in a pile on his pillow. He sat down on the bed to decide what was essential to him and what he could leave behind. The toothbrush could stay: he tossed it towards the basin. The woolen sock he had found in Theo's cabin was a definite yes, though. This he dropped into the canvas boy scout pack resting against a lump of bedspread at the side of his bed. There were a cheap pair of wooden chopsticks but he couldn't recall why he had saved them. A souvenir from some significant meal? It couldn't have been too significant if he didn't remember it. He flung them over his shoulder. The next item was a sweater Peter had loaned him

one day when he complained of cold. It was blue wool with a
star like a scattering of moth holes near the left shoulder.
Donald brought it to his nose and breathed the subtle trace of
Peter's familiar scent, and Peter's face bloomed like a new lily
in his mind's eyes. Not the face he had seen framed by white
satin earlier in the week, but the one he first saw above the
podium at the front of the Y auditorium. He had gazed on it
many times after that, watching its fine planes shift with the
gentle intonations of Peter's speech as he spoke reassuringly
of arcane things Donald did not understand at the time.

*Don't believe them, Donald. There's nothing wrong with your
ears. You should feel privileged. You have a special gift. Soon the
ringing will stop and you'll hear voices. Don't be frightened.
Listen. Meditate.*

He rolled up the sweater and held it against himself for a
moment, then placed it carefully in the pack with the sock.

There were other mementos of Peter: the Xeroxed pamphlet
on self-healing, a candle stub left on a plate after Peter's single
visit to his room. These things would come with him, and the
three red covered scribblers that were his diary from the day
he left Vancouver. And the speckled rock he dug out of the
snow the day Alice had taken him to the holy place. He rubbed
it on his forehead, directly above his nose, to restore its shini-
ness with skin oil. It soothed him and sent him into a brief
trance in which he had a sudden premonition of Glenn Gould's
death. He saw the pianist's fingers raised in permanent suspension above the keys he had struck with such precision, such
magic — an image of music silenced. The rock tumbled from
his fingers, his fragile core cracked, and faith leaked from him
like the white from a split egg. He slumped onto the green
chenille bedside rug, buried his face in his hands. Each time
he fell he fell deeper, the darkness was colder and emptier than
the time before.

"Peter," he implored, from the bottom of this hole. "Help me."

The northbound bus pulled out of the depot on time, at 6 a.m. Donald sat by a slush spattered window watching the last of night broken at progressively greater intervals by the fluorescent brightness of a locked-up gas station, a porch light burning behind a mesh of bare trees. The man across the aisle, a prospector with long sickle lines on either side of his mouth, wanted to make conversation.

"You goin' all the way to Dawson City?"

"No, I'm getting off before."

"That so?" said the prospector, the sickles deepening in his cheeks. He slapped the cardboard bootbox on his lap and from inside it came the long low yowl of an animal, an eerie noise that made Donald shiver. "Cat," the prospector explained. "He's a mean son of a bitch but he's been with me all the way from Chicken, Alaska to Cassiar, B.C." He slapped the box again. "Settle down in there. You know where I'm goin' now?"

Donald didn't and didn't care to, but the prospector insisted on telling him. He talked the darkness into day and then he slept. Donald looked over and saw that the bootbox was punctured with ventilating holes. Could it really be a cat in there?

He was clear now, breathing easy, but if he should be tested again before reaching his destination he didn't know what he would do. He might not have left the hotel! He reached up to the luggage rack for his pack and took out his diaries to read, to pass the travelling time. Pass the travelling time! A spurt of laughter shot from his mouth before he could cover it. The notion was absolutely hilarious. Hadn't it all been travelling time?

Pasted to the first page of the scribbler labelled Volume One was an article he'd clipped from the *Vancouver Sun*. Marked "Special to the Sun", the story of an Indian holy man's visit to the Yukon. "Monk Consecrates Hot Spot" was the irreverent headline, and the next to last paragraph, which Donald had

underlined with his red ballpoint pen, was a quote from the
holy man:

> "The Yukon is a special place on our planet. It borders on
> the pole where magnetic forces are concentrated. It shines
> in the light of the north star, which all men use to find their
> way. This planetary belt, the threshold of the Arctic Circle,
> is like the antechamber of the great king. All his followers
> gather to concentrate their energies before entering his
> presence and experiencing true unification."

The two pages after that were also covered with red ink:
Goodbye, goodbye, goodbye, goodbye. Two pages of good-
byes to represent every person, every place, every home,
doctor, teacher, school, clinic, street he could remember
having been associated with in the 24 years of his life. He
smiled freely, forgetting the prospector. His mouth opened in
a vertical ellipse and his chin came up like a duck's bill. It was
something congenital, a fault in his jaw that made it impossible
for him to smile sideways.

The bus stopped to let out a passenger at Stewart Crossing.
The prospector blinked awake and his eyes bulged wide at the
sight of Donald, his mouth stretched into a silent scream.

"You okay?" he asked. Donald blushed. "You know I never
seen eyebrows like you got before. Like a caterpillar or something, eh? Like a woolly red caterpillar moving right across
your forehead. They just grow like that?"

Donald feigned concentration, flipping through the accounts
of his trip up the Inside Passage on a ferryliner, the train
journey over the White Pass. At the end of Volume One was a
description of his first day in Whitehorse.

Nov. 15. My first day here I met someone who may be a friend.
Alice. I was standing on the main street and she came right up
to me and said I looked lost. I said I just got here and I didn't
know if I was lost because I didn't know where I was.

She thought that was funny and said why don't you come with me. She took me to this beer parlour. . . .

Alice. He built her face in his mind, the veins in her cheeks, the gap that showed in her teeth when she talked, which was always. The eyes? Brown, as far as he could remember. There was nothing memorable about Alice's eyes. She was a brood hen, needful of someone to take under her wing, someone to cluck over, that's all.

"Do you have a place to stay?" she asked, after they had drunk their first beers. Donald said he didn't. "I know a place. A cabin. It's on the other side of the river, a neat location. Very private. Only. . . " She sighed and began to twirl a strand of long frizzed hair around her index finger. He waited. "Some people think it's haunted. See, last year a guy died there. I knew him. His name was Theo, and he was a painter. He was real tall, you couldn't miss him, and he always wore this big black hat. He painted on everything, buildings, signs, vans, cars. He painted on his own bicycle. He had a far out imagination. Funny. He seemed okay, but one night he went home to his cabin and crawled into his sleeping bag with a rifle he'd picked up some-where, tucked it under his chin and pulled the trigger with his toe. Would you be afraid to live where someone did that?"

Donald wasn't afraid. Theo came to live inside him as Peter did now, and it was Theo, Peter said, who advised him to move. Alice had been skeptical. "That's all right, Donald. I don't blame you. I'd be scared, too." But I wasn't scared, he told her. "Sure, Donald. I know." Alice didn't believe anything, and she didn't believe *in* anything.

He skipped ahead to Volume Two and was still reading when the bus driver geared down and hollered out, "Dempster Highway." He had to hurry to close his pack and get to the front, but the scribblers didn't want to stay in. When he pushed them down they caught on something and pushed back out again. He decided to leave them.

"Hey, you forgot somethin'," the prospector called. Donald ignored him. He'd had enough of that prospector and his curiosity. He didn't even watch when the bus passed him and those sickly imprinted cheeks appeared through the grime of the window glazed bronze by the afternoon sun. No thanks. There was a Satanish quality to that man.

His heart was light, his will strong as he started up the Dempster from the junction. He put one foot down, then the other in a deliberate progression towards his goal. He might ride if a car stopped for him, but he might not, too, for out here the voices would be clearer, he might hear a chorus of them growing in volume and resonance as he came closer. He heard something now, and though he wasn't certain who was speaking, he liked the sound of the words, the rhythm they gave to his steps.

You walk in the footsteps of the man who disappeared in the woods. It was spring and a vernal fire burned in his heart. Flower seeds rose and tickled his soles. Tall trees bowed to him, to the late April wind. It was spring and a vernal fire burned in his heart. The heat coursed through his body. His feet wakened waiting flower seeds. . . .

He could distinguish Peter's voice, and Theo's, but the others he heard as ringing, or crackling static. Peter assured him that they would suddenly come clear, like new stations on a network; that one day he would join them and his voice would rise with theirs in the song of the aurora. This was his simple desire, to be part of the circle of those who had gone before him.

The first vehicle that came along was a camper truck with Alberta yellow licence plates. "You need a ride somewhere?" the driver shouted, through a window rolled half down. He was a cowboy. He wore a sheepskin vest and a cowboy hat and his face was tanned, though it wasn't yet May. A woman peered around the side of his head, younger than him, with some Indian blood showing in her eyes and her long black hair.

"Where are you going?"

"We're goin' all the way, buddy. We're goin' to Inuvik, maybe Tuktoyuktuk. Hell, we're goin' as far as the road goes. That suit you?"

"I'd want to get out just before we get to the Arctic Circle. There should be a sign, Arctic Circle 2 km or something. I want to get off there."

"Okay by me. You wanna ride back there or up here? You want space or heat?" He watched Donald's jaw move as he prepared to answer and figured it had been broken. Odd though it seemed, because of his size, the cowboy decided Donald must be a scrapper, somebody to be avoided. "You better take space, in the back there. You ain't goin' too far."

"What's at the Arctic Circle?" the girl wanted to know. She leaned across the driver's seat to get a better look at Donald as the cowboy got out to open the back of the canopy. "They have any jobs there at the Arctic Circle?"

Donald pretended not to listen. He followed the cowboy to the back of the truck, climbed through a window over the tailgate and made a bunk for himself with a horsy smelling blanket the cowboy gave him.

Except for Johnny Cash's greatest hits, coming from a tape deck in the cab, it was a peaceful ride. He could relax, gaze through the narrow strip of window across the back with no one to stare at him or prod him with useless talking. Fine herringbone clouds made the sky whiter than blue. It was a gauzy day, damp and cold; but with the promise of genuine warmth soon the ground was percolating with growth. The last time he had ridden in a truck like this was the day he and Alice had hitch-hiked to the holy place. It was December and he wasn't dressed for it and she kept insisting they start back to town before they were stranded there, miles from town. He couldn't meditate, he couldn't even think with her stamping around, blowing into her mitts. "You're gonna get frostbite, Donald. I know. Now let's go!"

Alice's words always came to him like a recording more than an actual living voice. The truth was, she was doomed to be a perpetual handmaiden in the antechamber of the king. At the wake arranged by Peter's family and the Catholic priest she had stood talking to Peter's mother, the two of them bent over a flower arrangement by the side of the casket. Peter's mother daubed at her red nose with one hand and twisted chrysanthemum petals with the other. Alice talked in shrill tones that abraded the skin of the gathering. People started shifting from foot to foot, going to use the bathroom. The carpet turned snowy with chrysanthemum petals.

"If the priest thought it was suicide they wouldn't be giving him a Catholic burial would they? I mean it just proves that what he did wasn't intentional. He really thought he could heal himself. He thought he was more powerful than he really was. He didn't die on purpose, he just failed."

Failed. The word had whined like a siren in Donald's brain as he walked from the funeral parlour through town to the riverbank. Alice did not understand. Peter couldn't have failed. He picked his way through brush and mud, stepping over abandoned car parts and bottles left from the previous summer's drinking parties until dogs in the Indian village barked and growled at his approach. Then he turned back.

In the darkness between the village and the town the northern sky rent and the persistent ringing became louder, surrounding as well as possessing him. He stopped walking to watch the lights move, green and pink, opaque as dancers' skirts swirling on a deep stage. Scientists had debated whether or not the northern lights made sound in the atmosphere. That night Donald was certain they did. He heard them as a whirring, the beginning of something. The lights resounded with the same timbre as the garbled voices inside his head, and he knew at that moment the message Peter was attempting to relay to him. He knew what he had to do.

The truck stopped and the cowboy came round to open the back. "You sure this is the right place?" he asked, waving his arm across the empty landscape.

"I'm sure," Donald said, scrambling out. His boy scout pack lay concealed beneath the blanket. The cowboy wouldn't find it until he and his girl reached Inuvik. The girl rolled down her window to look back at Donald as the cowboy drove off. "Bye!" she called. Her black hair flew against the side view mirror; it looked as if a raven had got caught between her and the truck.

When Donald was sure they were gone he checked his bearings and started down the road towards the sign marking the Arctic Circle. He scuffled down the embankment, over gravel and mud, to the tundra where he stood for several minutes breathing deeply and chanting the sacred word OM. As he opened his eyes the white grey land and the cloud-bleached sky were heaving lightly as a blanket over a restless sleeper. At his feet and extending in a soft curving line on both sides of him, the rim of the circle appeared as a quivering blue tube. He ran his cold, brick-textured hands over his burning face. He smiled unashamed. He stepped over the rim of the circle and walked eagerly towards its centre.

The Forest Path to Malcolm's

Bill Gaston

> The cougar was waiting for me
> part way up a maple tree in which
> it was uncomfortably balanced. . .
> Malcolm Lowry,
> "The Forest Path to the Spring"

Unlike the above epigraph, this is not a fiction. I have a distrust, a fear, a hatred of fiction, and I have my reasons. You will find these reasons colourful. I'll give one example now, and it alone should suffice: my middle name is Lava, this name the pathetic result of having had an eccentric and literary lush for a mother.

I have things to say on other subjects, but this has primarily to do with Malcolm Lowry, Deep Cove's most famous man. You'll find I can speak with authority here, my credentials being that I grew up not more than one hundred yards from Cates Park. For those who don't know, Cates Park is the new name for Dollarton Beach, the very place Lowry had his shack, wrote *Under the Volcano*, lived with M—, drank himself cat-eyed, and all the rest. As concerning all famous people, one hears contradictory "facts". What I will supply are the facts indeed.

The first so-called "fact" is this. It is said that Lowry's first shack, containing his only complete draft of *Volcano*, all his possessions, etc., was accidentally consumed by fire. And it is said he was consequently overcome with despair but proceeded, using his vast reserves of memory and imagination, to write an improved draft. None of this is correct.

The true facts are that, one, in a drunken rage, his feet bandaged, Lowry burned his shack on purpose, having cut his feet too many times on the broken glass which glittered all around it. He was in the habit of disposing of his empty gin bottles with but a careless flick of the wrist and, you see, it was time to relocate. (If you want proof, the cost of car fare to Deep Cove will give you proof. The glass is still there, and children still cut their feet.) And, fact two: while a draft of *Volcano* was destroyed, it was a draft which embarrassed him. The three other drafts were scattered around the parlours of Deep Cove's sparse literati. My mother had one.

I will push on with my account now, confident that I need supply no further proof. But I should add that not only do I abstain from alcohol as resolutely as I eschew spinning fictions, I hold no tolerance for those who indulge in either. It amazes me that men like Malcolm Lowry are ever believed, let alone admired, at all. When, head in hands, he announced that morning to the various fishermen, neighbours and squatters, "My god, my home is gone! My book is burned! But at least M— and I are alive," he no doubt looked wretched and despairing. To be fair, how could his audience have known the truth? It was easy for Lowry to look wretched and despairing when he was in fact hungover and ashamed. But I have to ask why anyone would ever believe one whose profession was to weave pained yarns on paper? One who tried to lie and lie well? One whose voice all day was but a dry run for grander lies spawned with purple ink later that night in the name of art? Add to that his drinking. Lowry was incapable to telling the truth. Perhaps I should feel sorry for him. I don't.

While living in Deep Cove, Lowry wrote a story called, "The Forest Path to the Spring." It was published posthumously, by M—. The story is a rather long, rambling affair, and while some of it is a lie, much of it is not, and so I recommend it to those who must read. In fact, it is perhaps the closest Lowry came to not lying, for the mistruths found in it are not so much lies *per se* as they are drunken inaccuracies. I'd like to tell you about them.

The story involves his life in Deep Cove, his life on the beach with the inlet fronting him and the dripping coastal forest pressing on his back. I find it a very nostalgic experience each time I read it, and I have read it many times. (Again, I have my reasons.) Lowry describes the unfurling of sword ferns, the wonderful damp rot of a forest at sunrise. The soft tides of Indian Arm, the greedy, fish-rank croaks of gulls and herons, the smell of shattered cedar, the sacred light in a dewdrop reflecting the sun, the mysterious light in a dewdrop reflecting the moon. He describes creeks and trails I myself know well. He dived off rocks which I and my friends once used for the same purpose. And, more, he mentions in passing the elementary school I attended as a child (where no one knew my middle name); he describes the tiny café where I used to buy greasy lunchtime french fries for a dime after having thrown away one of my mother's inedible eccentric sandwiches.

Again, it is a rambling story, its focus hard to find. Love, perhaps. He tells of his love for midnight walks through the forest, his love for fetching crystal mountain water from the spring, his love of dawn plunges off his porch, his love of M—, his love of live. We know that last one is a bald lie. He hated life, which is why he drank, and why he created a lying life on paper. In any case, the story's climax of sorts occurs one fateful day in the woods when a cougar leaps out of a tree across his path. He is startled, awestruck, petrified. And in what amounts to a none other than cosmic revelation he learns that his Eden, his forest-haven-of-a-life has on its outer edges forces of amorality and destruction. He discovers, it seems for the first time, that a rose has thorns. Critics cluck like sympathetic hens and suggest that what we have here is a classic hidden theme, one which reveals no less than a genius admitting to a suicidal battle with the bottle.

The cougar! What a bitter laugh! All of it!

Before I explain why I am laughing, I want to discuss my mom. Rather, memories of my late mother. Her name was Lucy, and she was unmarried. If there are two kinds of eccentric —

one who doesn't try to be eccentric, and one who does — my mother was the latter. People tend to dislike her kind, withdrawing from their reek of fakery. And since my mother's kind choose their eccentricities, their choices tend to be exaggerations of qualities they admire. Mom, for instance, wanted to be a mad poet. At the start, she was neither, and by the end she was only mad.

In Deep Cove in the forties it was most unattractive to dress up in flour sacks, mauve scarves, bangles and canary-yellow hats. To spout bad poetry in public was abhorrent. This was Mom's choice. Deep Cove was at the time a tight collection of sulking fishermen and poor squatters, and though my mother had a captive audience she had few fans. Perhaps they could smell her self-consciousness; perhaps they noticed her eyes lacked that electrified blankness which marks the true eccentric. And while you may think what you want of her, she was but the tactless extrovert, a wider extension, if you will, of the loud housewife in the turquoise kaftan, and harmless. The harm set in when she began drinking. I see the cause of her drinking to be identical to that of the man who lived one hundred yards down the beach from her: an overactive imagination and no appreciative fans. For Lowry was at that time in no way famous.

I gather these facts from years of researching my personal history. My sources are the aforementioned fishermen and squatters. When they speak of my mother they speak kindly but apologetically. They hadn't much liked her, and I can see in their faces their embarrassment. I keep mum, but am tempted to ease their pain and tell them I not only didn't like her much either, I detested her. And loved her, painfully, in the intense and secret way reserved for only sons. To illustrate: not long after she died I tried to read her poetry, and while I read for only ten minutes, I threw up for twenty. It was dreadful poetry, revealing an embarrassing mind. But only I who loved her so much have the right to hate her so much.

I don't know if Lowry liked my mother or not. In any case I have gathered that it was she who took to him first, if he took to her at all. She must have seen him there on Dollarton Beach, looking slyly Slavic-eyed, yet burping and twitching like a lunatic in the hot noon sun. He would have been as naked as legally possible, for (in the early days) he was proud of his build. Mother would have known he was a struggling writer. She must have thought: At last! Another eccentric, another sparkling mind! I believe she first tried to attract his attention in the local bar, where it's reported she attempted (successfully) to buy him drinks. I don't know what M—, secure in her childlike love for him, must have made of that. And it's said she would sometimes flag him down in the streets, the trails, on the beach. Perhaps she'd borrow a canoe and arrange to accidentally bump bows out on the inlet. I can picture her trying to impress him. My spine creeps as I envision her passing a lime-green scarf seductively over her unblinking Mata Hari gaze. Having caught his eye, my mother now goes for his mind and, with that flaccid flare of spontaneity rehearsed-for-days, she points to the sun and cries laughing, "The moon! The moon!" (I believe my mother was capable of little more than cheap paradox. I also believe she was the last person of this century who held alliteration to be somehow profound. Not long before she died she said to me, in that awesome hoarse whisper of hers, "Meeting Malcolm melted my mind.")

I would suspect that by now you share my embarrassment. But I would also hope that you are coming to understand my loathing for imagination, and writers, and fiction, and drink. If not, keep an open mind — this history will convince you. My sole purpose here is to convince with the facts; to free the steel blade of truth about Lowry from the paste-jewelled scabbard of fable that now hides it. I can assure you I'm not denigrating Mom here for pleasure.

So I doubt that Lowry liked my mother much, unless he was a bigger fool than I imagine. His writing demands that I at least admit he, unlike my mother, possessed subtlety. Perhaps fleeting genius; clarity in bursts (burps). Whatever the case, how my mother got hold of his manuscripts is unclear. It could be that, like an adult relenting at last and giving candy to a brat, Lowry handed over a copy so she would go away. He likely thought it would take a woman like Lucy a full year to sift through such a book as *Volcano*, but he was wrong. No, in Mom's words, she "communed with his mind for twenty-three hours straight," and finished it. And her "communion" with him proved to be the beginning of her end. For my mother, whose mind's sole ambition was to snap colourfully, Lowry's fiction, his obsessive flowery pain-packet verbiage, was the necessary nudge. It was on the day following Mom's twenty-three-hour binge that the Event — and my reason for writing this — took place.

The Event has to do with the story, "The Forest Path to the Spring"; specifically with the cougar Lowry saw. As I mentioned, he was out collecting water from the spring, looked up, and there was the cougar. He describes the encounter this way:

> The cougar was waiting for me part way up a maple tree in which it was uncomfortably balanced... crouched on a branch really too small for him, caught off guard or off balance, and having perhaps already missed his spring, (it) jumped down clumsily, and then, overwhelmed, cat-like, with the indignity of this ungraceful launching, and sobered and humiliated by my calm voice — as I liked to think afterwards — slunk away guiltily into the bushes, disappeared so silently and swiftly that an instant later it was impossible to believe he'd ever been there at all.

There is more, much more. Page upon page about the cougar, Lowry's fear of it, his thoughts about it, his thoughts about his thoughts, his clinging passionately to M— all through the ensuing night, shaking and having tremulous sex together in the knowledge that Danger Lurks.

That cougar made quite an impression on him. However, I'd like to draw your attention to the last eleven words of the quotation I've supplied. Having done so, I'll simply come out with it, here and now. That was not a cougar. That was my mother.

I wonder just how drunk a man can get. I often think about that as I try year by year to understand this man Malcolm Lowry.

Wandering Cates Park again this week, along the path which is now proclaimed by sign to be Malcolm Lowry Walk, I took a good steady look. A sober look. I studied hard this plot of land and sea so described by Lowry to be "everywhere an intimation of Paradise." He found "delicate light and greenness everywhere, the beauty of light on the feminine leaves of vine-leaved maples and the young leaves of the alders shining in sunlight like stars." Oh, he goes on and on and on. Unadulterated opulence, with four adjectives per noun. But here is the one I can't help smiling grimly at: "The wonderful cold clean fresh salt smell of the dawn air, and then the pure gold blare of light from behind the mountain pines, and the two morning herons, then the two blazing eyes of the sun over the foothills." Did you get that? *Two* suns? The words *blaring* and *blazing* to describe light? This is a description not of nature but of a raging dawn hangover. I have lived here on the beach all my life and I have never seen herons travel in pairs.

While walking the identical path I saw beauty too, certainly, but not Lowry's bombastic brand. I too saw rustling dainty foliage of one hundred shades of green. I saw sturdy stoic trees, and mountains with their awesome noble mysterious elan. (It's easy to be Lowry.) Boats on the oh-so-wonderful water, King Neptune's refreshing riplets tickle-slapping the angel-white hulls, etcetera.

But what else did I see? I saw slugs in mid-path, dry pine needles stuck to their dragging guts, their bellies torn open by the sensible shoes of strolling old ladies. I saw dull clouds muffling mountains logged off and scarred for ever; clouds reflected better in the oil slicks than in the odd patch of clear water. I saw rotten stumps, diseased leaves, at least as much death as life. In short, I saw reality. I had no need of hiding from the truth of the visible. I didn't have the need of a man ashamed, the need of a vision hung-over and in constant pain. Lowry donned his rose-coloured glasses and raised the shuffling grey world to the level of an Eden in order to stay sane. Art was his excuse and his tool. He probably believed what he wrote.

But on to my mother, and the Event. I should add that I heard all of this straight from Mom's mouth, and the disturbing mix of anguish and ecstasy in her eyes as she spoke makes me doubt not one word of it. She told me many times, and the story never varied. Her words:

"I just finished reading *Volcano*. In twenty-three hours. Oh, I was in rapture. I was under a spell. He had called out to me, to me alone, and I wanted to answer. I had to answer in a worthy way. I decided to go to him dressed as someone celebrating the Day of the Dead. In the book this was the first thing mentioned — the Day of the Dead, the costumes, the skulls, and all of those things that so horrified poor Geoffrey Firmin. And in the end Death is the last thing Firmin sees. It is the book's heart: Death. It was important that Malcolm knew I understood, as he knew I would. So I made the skeleton costume. The material should have been black, of course, but I had no time, and all I had was a brown one, a rabbit costume left from a Hallowe'en dance. I cut off the ears, and painted on the bones. It wasn't a good job I'm afraid. My word, I had just read *Volcano* and naturally my hands were shaking." I recall as a boy being scared as my mother told me this part, because each time she told me, even though the Event was years past, even though Lowry was years dead and Mother was in her hospital room not really knowing I was there, her hands would begin to shake as she spoke.

"But the idea itself was enough. My first plan was to show up at his door, because I knew M— was back east for three months. She hadn't taken to me, you see. Can't say as I blame her, of course. Malcolm would act positively fidgety around me, a torn man. But anyway I had a better plan. I knew it was important that he *look up* to see me, to see Death, just as Firmin did at the end. So I climbed a tree and waited. I knew he'd be along soon. I spied on poor Malc and I knew his habits. Englishmen, especially Englishmen who drink, have very strict habits." Here Mother would always stare coyly down at her feet, pretending naughtiness, and laugh like a little girl. The final time I heard this story Mom looked very old, her fingers were ochre with tobacco, she was dressed as insanely as always (the staff let her keep her stash of scarves, beads and hats under her bed), and yet she could still giggle as pure and free as a little girl. I felt like crying. I felt like looking up and shouting: You may be dead, Mr. Lowry, but look what you've done.

"So I found a nice tree and waited. And my lord don't you know I fell asleep. All that reading, and no sleep. Also, I confess to having sipped some." That is, had a lot to drink. But I admit I love to picture her up that tree, and love even more Lowry's version, that of a "lion uncomfortably balanced". What a nobly optimistic euphemism for a snoring drooling drunk crazy lady hanging there like a noodle on a chopstick. "But I knew Malcolm would understand. When he gave me the book he said, in that marvellous Oxonian of his, 'This is a tome best read drunk, for so the best bits were thunk.' Ah, Malc, a lad so boyish. A boyish genius, I used to use that as my private tongue twister: boyish genius, boyish genius, boyish genius." Here Mom would drift off. If I felt like hearing more I'd prod her.

"So there I was asleep, eight feet up. The next thing I knew, I heard a scream. Yes, a scream. My lord don't you know I thought it was a woman? I must have started, for I fell. And considering I could have met Death myself right then and there, I wasn't hurt much. A broken rib and a cut on my back — thank the lord for having sipped some. And when I looked up there was Malcolm running with his empty water pails back in the way of his cabin. He was making the most curious noises in his throat. I was concerned. I think he'd been sipping rather heavily that week, what with you-know-who gone."

My mother's story would go on one segment longer. She would gaze off, as if through the walls of years, then seeing what she wanted to see her eyes would close and she'd say, "And I followed Malcolm Lowry home. In I walked, dressed as Death, bleeding from my back, and told him I loved him. He rose slowly from his bed with great big wide eyes and told me he loved me too." Once, and once only, she added: "We... communed." But, perhaps realizing for the first time that her audience was a thirteen-year-old boy, Mom went instantly shy and changed the subject. My mother may have been an extrovert, and insane, but she was exceedingly conservative when it came to certain subjects. ..

I saw Malcolm Lowry only twice that I remember. I was about ten, and it was just before he returned to England for good. The first time, my mother had sent me to his cabin with a letter, sealed in a black envelope and smelling — good god — of an awful perfume. Lowry bellowed "Come!" at my knock, and there he was sitting at his writing table. He had erect posture and a barrel chest, but a big and flabby stomach. A very proud bearing. His eyes looked vaguely Oriental. He just sat there, quite sober I think, and he seemed to know who I was. He didn't look pleased to see me. I gather from my probing that he'd during those years been spending considerable energy avoiding my mother and it seems likely he'd seen us together and knew whose son I was. I gave him the letter and fled.

The second time, two weeks later, I was again a messenger boy. I knocked at the same door and, hearing only the oddest whoops and titters but no invitation to enter, I peered in at a window. There sat the same man, but hardly. This time he was naked. (I have heard he sometimes wrote that way.) He looked dark and somehow Mexican, like a greasy, feline-eyed peasant. His table was littered with papers and books, and crumpled balls of foolscap covered his cabin floor like a layer of giant's popcorn. He was hunched over, and rolls of pale fat lay on his lap. He began to make noises again, noises that are unforgettable but now hard to describe: a high-pitched kind of squealing, but with a deep bass undertone at the same time. As he squealed he swung his head back and forth in great arcs, and while his mouth was clamped open in a toothy grin his scrunched eyes looked on the verge of painful tears. Swinging his head faster and faster, he finally stopped and took several desperate gollups from a bottle he had beneath him on the floor. I recognized the brand: it was the same English gin my mother drank. I stared, fascinated. My gut reeled with the same avid hollowness it gets at car accidents, when there are cars upside down and bodies strewn about, and a cop with a flashlight stands beside a pool of someone's blood. What made me run in the end was this: Lowry finally managed to get a pipe lit after missing the bowl with several matches. He took a long draw and then settled back and sighed as if in satisfaction. But he looked anything but satisfied. Instead he grew dizzy from the smoke. He began to sway in his chair. And suddenly he shot up, threw back his head and howled. At the same instant of howling—I swear this is true—he accidentally shit himself. I *think* it was an accident. In any case it was more like an explosion of diarrhea, all expelled in a one-second burst. Much of it sprayed his buttocks and legs and, screaming now, Lowry began to twirl and slap at the wetness, stumbling as he did so. I ran then.

I realize I am more or less trampling on the reputation of a man a good many readers respect and admire. And I don't mean to rub it in further — no, I only mean to establish thoroughly my reasons for writing this — when I tell you it was that same afternoon I first heard Malcolm Lowry was a famous man. Handing me that latest note, Mother told me, "Be careful with this, dear, you are taking it to a very special person. He is a writer, and his book is in all the bookstores of the world." Well, I had just seen my first writer, my first famous man, and now fame and fiction had a face.

You may have guessed a number of things. First, the reason for my bitterness — namely, that Lowry and my mother had sex after she fell out of the tree. My feelings stem not so much

from the act itself but rather because what meant so much to
my mother meant so little to Lowry. I believe it was his utter
rejection of her after the Event that launched her down
insanity's slide.

Mother never told me about it herself. This I admit. But the
evidence pointing to their carnal union is overwhelming, and I
don't for a moment doubt it took place. The clues are these.
One, she told me she followed him back. Two, M— was away.
Three, as she told me but once, they "communed". And my
research has given me these clues as well: There was a two-
week period during M—'s absence when Lowry was purport-
edly most upset. "Crazy," my sources put it. On a non-stop gin
binge, he was raving to all who'd listen that he'd met Death in
the flesh, that he'd met Death and defeated it. More than one
barfly heard him distinctly say, "I rogered Death all night, from
behind like a dog." (I don't like to picture this.) During that
period of time he would laugh and rave, rave and cry. What
ended his raving was news of a cougar sighting in the area.
Hearing this news seemed to cheer him up. He took to saying
he'd too seen the cat, and so his run-in with Death suddenly
went the way of bad dreams.

It takes no detective to sort out the self-serving machinations
of this drunken man's mind. For sanity's sake, for relief from
devils, he made himself believe he'd seen a cougar, not my
mother, not Death.

I hate but can't help picturing the scene. Lowry, drunk and
whimpering, finds that Death has not only leapt at him from a
tree but has followed him to his door. My mother, ludicrous in
a rabbit's costume with a skeleton etched on it, a broken rib
and bleeding freely from the back, tells him she loves him. She
embraces him and, scared, Lowry can't deny Death its desire.
My mother instigates the unthinkable act. And so two hideous-
ly incongruous dream-worlds unite there in a shack on
Dollarton Beach: my mother believing she has won over her
aloof treasure, her boyish genius, at last. Lowry believing he is
copulating with Death.

In Lowry's behalf, I like to assume that at some point in his passion he reached that minimal level of sobriety where he realized it was in fact a mortal woman in his bed. It appears he at least realized that *something* had happened with *someone*. Someone who was not M—. Though in "The Forest Path to the Spring" he writes that after his brush with the cougar he and M—embraced "all the night long", I should restate that during this time M—was gone for three months, and I doubt whether even a gin-riddled Lowry would be unaware of that. So did he know it was my mother? Or did he make himself believe it was M—? What shape pretzel of tortured logic did he finally construct in order to stay sane? Lowry was by all accounts a loving and monogamous husband, and so perhaps it was his horror at this odd adultery which made him go mad for a while. We'll never know.

For years, my mother assumed he'd known it was her. But when she first learned of his death — she did not read newspapers, and it was me who told her — she said, "But I thought he'd send word. *Some*thing." Then she laughed, and lapsed instantly back into what was now her world, a very advanced state of waking dream. And when "The Forest Path to the Spring" came out in 1960, and after mother read certain parts over and over, she closed the book at last and whispered plaintively, "Oh I thought he *knew.*"

I could go on and on about Lowry's life, Lowry's lies to himself. Indeed, I could water my prose with imagination and assault the man with a decadently flowery language he would have well recognized. It is tempting. For I see now how the taking up of a pen and the posture of writing itself seem to abet some kind of exaggeration. That is, imagination, dream, lie. I can only hope that by now you understand my loathing for fiction is so resolute, it has allowed me during this account to tell you nothing but the accurate truth. But I must admit how much I am tempted to sink into venom, attach the leash of speculation to Lowry's name and drag it through any number of scandalous cesspools. But I won't.

Nor will I go on to describe his final fall, for to do so would be
to ennoble it. His tawdry death. Myth be damned: his death
was nothing but tawdry, as tawdry as my mother's. I'll draw no
cheap conclusion from this, but the equation is there for all to
see: two people, lashed by self-doubt, forced by life's incessant
grinning skull to turn to dreams and poetry and imagination,
poisoned yet further by alcohol — two people die a tawdry
death. My point is made. I give it to you and leave it; I ask only
that you restrain from embellishing either their lives or their
deaths with yet more poetry. I have the right to ask this.

I'll likely never discover whether Lowry knew he was my
father. He may have known, he may only have guessed, as you
might have. Perhaps Mom told him. Perhaps she pestered.
But, not being the kind to ask for money or seek a scandal my
mother would have preferred cherishing me in secret, me her
precious relic of a single sacred meeting.

I'll never know, and not knowing has been hard on me. Harder,
in fact, than having had no taste of fatherhood, save for a
singular image of a naked man squealing, stumbling, slapping
at glistering legs. But it's been hardest of all to admit to myself
that, on the cloudy, booze-blurred afternoon of my conception,
not only was I not planned, not sought for, but was in fact the
result of a man's lust for a woman other than my mother. To
be blunt, Lowry's sperm was meant for M— (or perhaps for
Death!), and was waylaid, like a manuscript, by a lonely woman
in a pathetic bid for a bit of attention. Such was the flavour of
my beginning, and such remains the flavour of my little life.

Proof that I'm his son? It took no wizardry to ascertain the year
and month of the cougar Event, add to it nine months and lo
and behold, arrive at my birthday. My mother had no
boyfriends and was not known to have affairs. Lucy was a
remarkable woman in many ways, not the least of which being
that she knew a man's nakedness but once in her life, and this
while wearing a rabbit costume.

As I mentioned when I began, my middle name is Lava. Throughout "The Forest Path to the Spring", Lowry called Deep Cove "Eridanus". Why did he rename it? No doubt for poetry's lying sake: no doubt Eridanus is someplace mythologically significant. I've never looked it up. My mother's inspiration for "Lava" was equally metaphoric. In this case, though, I know the meaning. In her way of speaking to me as though I weren't there, staring up into space and so talking over my head both literally and figuratively, Mother more than once intoned grandly, "Lava. You are my Lava. My dear little man. You are the emission of a volcano."

She doubtless imagined I'd be as fiery as my father. But, much as I've come to detest poetry I'll travel that road as far as I can stomach and just this once extend her metaphor for her: hot lava is shot blindly out into the world, soon grows cold, and resents having been spewed there. Lava is nothing like the fiery bowels of its father. If lava could feel, it would feel like sloppy effluent, carelessly ejaculated, cold and abandoned — I cannot resist — under the volcano.

As I've been writing this history, I've often stopped and asked myself: whose voice is this? Is it solely the voice of bitterness? Malc and Lucy's bitter bastard boy? If not, why do I smear both a mother and a father? I seek neither notoriety nor a noble name, neither a paternity suit nor a share of his estate, if he left one. So why do I expose? Whose voice is this?

I like to think it is Malcolm Lowry's voice, his voice had he lived, his voice had he learned to stop staring into the roaring guts of himself, had he learned to stop lying, had he learned to lift his head high and breathe for good and all the pure cold energetic air of objectivity. If children inherit one thing from their parents it is the fear, the claustrophobic fear, of their parents' faults. So I can thank mine for helping me, through revulsion, towards clarity. My mind's best food has been the flesh of their faulty, tawdry lives.

I've been drunk but once in my life. I was seventeen. My mother had just died, and I knew who my father was. That it happened to be my high school graduation party didn't matter to me — unlike my friends, this wasn't a celebration but an exorcism. We drank under the stars in — where else? — Cates Park. Dollarton Beach. Eridanus. Paradise. A body had been found there in a burned-out car earlier that week, a suspected murder, so added to the evening was an air of danger lurking. And I drank gin, my parents' brand. I slept with neither cougar, ghost nor woman but still I had a wondrous time. I cried about my mother and raged about my father, pounding a driftwood club into the beachfire, sending showers of glowing amber skyward. None of the other kids noticed me really, for many were on a first drunk as well, and flailing about in their own style and for their own reasons.

The Night of the Dogs

Leandro Urbina

To M.A. Giella

I'm crazy, so you shouldn't pay too much attention to me. This used to be a quiet village, and even though people argued about politics in the bar and in the square, the consequences were never very serious. That's why they brought in people from Santiago; people from around here never would have done what they did. Of course, I'm crazy. The doctor told my family so, not in those exact words, but that's what he meant. Birdy Acuña's mother is missing a few screws too. She told Birdy not to stay out so late drinking, and she asked me to go and look for him when it was almost curfew time. How could I say no, she was my godmother and such a worrywart. So I went to the bar. Birdy and Ramon were there, just the two of them, drinking wine and singing sad tangos. Sure, it was no problem for Ramon, he was the owner of the bar and lived right there, but I had to take Birdy home and he was already blotto and Ramon kept on pouring more wine, so what's the problem, you can always sleep on the pool tables, tomorrow's Sunday, have a drink Miguel, we'll just call the old women on the phone. They don't have a phone? Well, then we'll ask Captain Romero to let them know, he'll be by soon to wet his whistle. I knew what Birdy was like after a few drinks, I'd known him since he was a boy and I knew how stubborn he could be, how he liked to pick a fight. Not that I'm any better, the doctor told my mom that my soul was disordered because of my experiences in life. At least that's what my Mom says he said, but she always gets everything mixed up. My Dad said that meant I was crazy and maybe that was better for me, seeing how things were. That's because I told Captain Romero the guys from Santiago were

going around target shooting and he told me I had a mental
health problem and the Santiago men were almost all students
serving their country and I should keep quiet because after all
there'd been only three victims in the village, not counting the
people at the orange plantation and the cooperative. Captain
Romero is my mother's half-cousin, so as a favour he told her
she should have my head examined as soon as I got out of
hospital; he said I couldn't be sure of anything and the boys
had made a mistake because it was a bit foggy that night. I had
to get Birdy away from the bar because as soon as Ramon told
him the captain would be coming he started saying he was
going to ask him about those rumours that Lieutenant Gatica
had ordered Venegas the teacher shot not because he was a
Socialist but because he was sleeping with his wife. Don't get
mouthy Birdy, you can't say that to Romero, you're just asking
for trouble. He has to defend the honour of his carabineros.
The orders came from Santiago, Birdy. Sure, it's my imagination, right? Doña Esther was putting out through the window,
and you could hear them a block away, they say the lieutenant
is no hell in bed. Don't badmouth authority Birdy, said Ramon.
So I figured I had to get him out of there, in spite of the curfew,
thinking I could always explain to the guys on patrol and they'd
understand. It was a bit foggy and after a few minutes of
walking back and forth we heard the first shot. Get a good hold
on me, said Birdy. Don't let go of the reins. I took the belt in
my free hand and wrapped it more securely around my buddy,
but when we reached the corner we tripped over the first dead
dog and fell on our faces. I felt my heart skip a beat. There was
Birdy on all fours, lifting up the dog by the skin of its neck; it's
a goddam yapper with no head, and it slipped from his hands,
look, they shot its head right off, poor bastard, and the pavement beside the streetlight all slick with blood. Well, it was
enough to drive anyone crazy. Everybody shut up inside their
houses and the village covered in fog with lights on here and
there and a jeep's engine approaching from the direction of the
square and the laughter of the boys in the jeep echoing through
the empty streets, and a block away another dead dog with its

head blown away, a small, woolly dog rolled up in a ball, and my buddy insists he knows the dog, it's got to be Snowflake, from Rojas' store. Better hurry up now, I said. We'll keep quiet and stay away from the light, you never know with these guys. Can you believe the sons of bitches, he was saying. Going around killing poor innocent animals. They probably do it for target practice, I said. Because nothing much happens around here. I hear voices just as he is saying what a bunch of miserable bastards, no wonder they end up like Lieutenant Gatica, with other men screwing their women. Shut up Birdy for god's sake, the walls have ears in this town, and if they hear you you'll be the one who'll get screwed. I'd rather die, my friend. Live honourably or die with glory, that's what I say. Besides, all there is in this town is dogs and incarnations of dogs that go out at curfew time, and fog every goddam night, that milky fog that makes the town drunks lose their way. Don't talk so loud, I said to him, trying to steer him toward a side street behind the church, but just as we left the sidewalk another dead dog turned up and the shots started up again but closer as Birdy bent over to contemplate the third headless body, amazed. Holy Mother, it's man's best friend they're blowing away. I could hear shouted orders and laughter and then a military band imitated by tooting mouths and hands and farts, tootoorooroo, and boots marching over the stones of the square and the echo of triggers being cocked, voices imitating barks that echoed through the empty square and all I wanted to do was get Birdy out of there, trying to figure out where the patrol jeep was, making out the yellow streetlights through the fog, come on Birdy, it's cold, help out a bit, can't you? Those Santiago bastards are killing off all our dogs. I pretend I don't know what's going on, I hear voices. They must be dead souls from the orange plantation, come to haunt us, they come down from the mountain top with the fog and go to wash their feet in the river. They've come to haunt these heartless bastards. Then there is a shot and Birdy screams out. Stop it, goddammit! Then silence, all you can hear is water dripping from the other street and our wet wobbling footsteps and then the dark

engine of the jeep starting up and coming out slowly and we
hear it go around the square and just as we reach the corner
where the drugstore is they stop us. Halt! See Birdy, I told you
to shut up. They were great tall wide-eyed guys wearing a day's
stubble, with big grins on their babyish faces. Look at these
gentlemen, would you please? They forgot there's a curfew on.
Guess they don't know any better, they're just a couple of
country bumpkins. Sorry, Lieutenant, I say, pretending to be
drunk. Then Birdy the loudmouth speaks up, you call yourself
a Lieutenant, why you're nothing but a son of a bitch who kills
dogs for fun, and he mutters at the shapes of the guys who are
getting off the jeep and they shine a searchlight right in his
face. Well, I may be crazy but I'm not stupid. I saw it coming
and it happened all right. I can't talk, though, because I
promised my mother and Captain Romero I wouldn't. So the
next hour that we spent in the street with the fog and the dead
dogs and the guys from Santiago, according to what the doctor
told my mom, was nothing but a disorder of the soul. He must
have meant of the head, because of the huge scar I have on my
head. I think they would have said Birdy had a disorder of the
feathers, seeing how they left him. So why don't you fly away
Birdy, they said. . . But you don't have to believe what I say. I'm
crazy and my mom keeps me at home, sometimes we go out
and I hear people say poor little Miguel, ever since he got shot
in the head he's been kind of strange. And I think, I may be
crazy but I'm not stupid. I may hear voices, but I don't hear
nonsense. And if I am crazy maybe it's because my dad says
it's better that way. I'm getting sick of it, though, seven years
is a long time to hold your tongue. But my mom says I should
keep quiet, and if I have to talk to myself I should do it in my
room and she's sick and tired of hearing the same story over
and over again. What do you expect, I guess I have my reasons
for repeating it, to remind myself that there are people who kill
dogs and birds, and you just have to put up with it, Ma'am, can't
you see I'm crazy.

Do Astronauts Have Sex Fantasies?

David Arnason

Do astronauts have sex fantasies? They must, of course, but has this been taken into account by the planners of space missions? Is any provision made for masturbation during long flights? What would be the effect of gamma rays on a fetus conceived and delivered in space? Is anybody in charge of this kind of investigation? We know these things are too important to be left to chance, but how are we to find out what's going on?

And what about the greenhouse effect? The melting of the polar ice caps will mean the flooding of New York and London, but isn't that a small price to pay for bananas in Manitoba? Who is going to work on the plantations in the Northwest Territories? How many Eskimos are there, and are they willing to pick things? What are we going to do with all those leftover Massey-Harris combines and four-wheel-drive Case tractors?

Are ballet dancers promiscuous? If not, how did all those rumours about them get started? Why do they walk in that funny way, even when they have quit dancing many years ago and now only teach a few of the neighbourhood girls while their husbands, who are lawyers, mix themselves Scotches and watch re-runs on TV? Why do they only marry lawyers? Where do they meet those lawyers? Do the lawyers send dozens of long-stemmed roses backstage after the performances, or are there restaurants frequented only by lawyers and ballet dancers?

Is the French language really in danger? Are English words, like viruses, creeping into French and corrupting whole sentences? Why are crêpes tastier than pancakes? How does one become a member of the French Academy? Is it possible that the president of the French Academy is a mole, an

Englishman who started working in a lycée in Provence after the war, then slowly worked his way up to a teaching job at the Sorbonne, wrote a couple of books on structural linguistics, and was appointed to the French Academy? Does he dream in English?

Is it true that, because of the principles of natural selection, in eighty years all cats will be tabby? Should a cat be allowed one litter before she is spayed? Is there any way of keeping a spayed or neutered cat from growing fat? Do people think less of you if, instead of naming your cat something interesting like Oedipus or Charles, you simply call it White Cat?

What do well drillers do in winter when the ground is frozen? Do they hang around in rural cafés, having coffee with the electricians and plumbers? When the electricians and plumbers go off to work, do the well drillers hang around and tease the waitresses? Or do they take on odd jobs, cleaning a garage here, mending the shingles there? Do they sometimes wonder whether it is all worthwhile? Are their children proud of them?

How do Marxists in the United States stand up to all the contempt they face? Are they, like dentists, inclined to depression and suicide? When they lie in bed at night, thinking about death and fantasizing about all the opportunities to have sex they missed, do they think with words like *proletariat* and *praxis*? Do they become suspicious that all their friends are working for the FBI? Are they sometimes grateful that the FBI sends beautiful female spies to seduce them and learn their secrets, women much more beautiful than they would ever have expected to sleep with? Do they sometimes marry these spies and get jobs teaching political science in small mid-western universities?

Is there any money to be made in lawn furniture? The aluminum lawn furniture with plastic webbing always breaks, and the wooden lawn furniture is always uncomfortable, so you'd think there would be room for someone to create a whole new kind of lawn furniture, wouldn't you? Is any research lab working on this question? Are there secret patents, like the patents for gas-saving carburetors which the oil companies buy up and destroy? Are these patents held by the aluminum, plastic and wood industries, while they go on turning out breakable and uncomfortable lawn furniture?

Why are piano tuners so often blind? Why do strong young men, possibly their sons, take them by the arm and lead them to pianos? Are blindness and an ear for music somehow intertwined? And what of those muscular sons, have they any plans for the future? What will they do when their frail, blind fathers die? Will they find other blind men, or will they weep with joy at their release from their fathers' musical obsessions? Will they, perhaps, holiday in Mexico for a month, then go back to school to retrain themselves as bakers or clerks?

And what of love? Must that first fierce passion decay into tolerance and mild aversion? Can love be kept alive by flowers and meals in fancy French restaurants as the newspapers tell us? Are the wealthy happier in love than we? Does regular sex help, even when neither party much cares? Do outside liaisons, amours and affairs help put the spice back in a fading relationship? Do people in the final stages of debilitating cancer still feel lust? Is anybody looking into this?

Where is Chad? Why are the Chaddians fighting one another? What is the gross national product of Chad, or is it so remote and agricultural that it does not even have a gross national product? What do they drink in Chad when they want to get drunk? Does some importer supply them with Scotch and bourbon, or do they make themselves a lusty native beer from the leaves of some native tree? What is the most popular musical group in Chad? Has any Chaddian ever written a novel of manners that chronicles a young man's rise to power?

Are the underground pipes that bring water to our houses made from asbestos? Are things being added to our water that we do not know about? Is some of our sewage seeping into the river? If things are going wrong, as we all suspect, how much money will it cost to set them right? Can we afford not to be poisoned? Does the city council know all these things but not care? Do the councillors keep bottles of pristine water from deep underground springs in their refrigerators at home?

What has become of Kohoutek's comet? Is somebody still keeping track of it, watching it dwindle into space? Do we sometimes lose discoveries because a scientist is making love to his assistant just at the moment when some life-saving but short-lived compound has precipitated in a beaker or Petri jar? Who actually buys books of poetry and reads them? What happens to all the paintings of failed artists when they die? Why do you keep smoking when you know what it is doing to your lungs? Why can't you resist that extra glass of wine with supper, that extra glass of brandy after dessert, when you know what it is doing to your liver? Why are you so filled with lust and yearning and desire? Why does your weakness threaten to overwhelm everything you do? Doesn't anybody care?

How I Didn't Kill Wally
Even Though He Deserves It

Dianne Warren

What I'm doing right now is tying Wally up, wrapping the rope around and around, and him screaming and kicking and hurling abuses at me something awful. The rope is the one we use to tie the furniture down in the back of the half-ton every time we move. Which is pretty often. Maybe you haven't noticed that someone is helping me. She's so small you have to look two or three times to even notice she's there. Have a close look down by Wally's foot, the left one. She's no more than three and a half inches tall. And you know, it's the funniest thing. You can see for yourself how big and downright mean Wally is. A real bruiser. And you can see I'm nowhere near his size, even if I have put on a few pounds in the last ten years. But with that little slip of a thing down there hanging onto Wally's toe, I don't seem to be having any trouble at all wrapping him up so he can't harm anyone, especially me. And it's going to be a piece of cake getting him into the closet and closing the door. Hard to believe, I know, but it's true. He can fight and holler and curse all he wants, but I'm not letting him out until he learns a thing or two. That's just the way it is and I know I'm doing the right thing. I can feel it.

This whole business started when I decided I was going to kill Wally. I really was. I was sick and tired of him being mean and ugly. A body can only take so much. And I figured I had nothing to lose. The only thing I've got to be thankful for in my life is that we never had any kids, and what kind of a blessing is that?

I thought about how to kill Wally and the only thing I could come up with was a good solid knock on the head. Looking back, that doesn't seem like such a smart idea. Wally's head is like a blacksmith's anvil. I doubt that I could have done much more than make him madder than he is most of the time already. It's a good thing she came along and put a stop to things. Lord knows what he would have done to me.

Anyway, there I was, all set to stand on a chair by the door and knock Wally on the head with his own fourteen-pound post maul. I knew he'd be home any minute and I was going to lift that maul into the air and bring it down on his head. Driven him right into the floor, that's what I'd liked to have done. Driven him right through the basement ceiling and into the cement, never to be heard from again.

I was doing a little practicing, trying to get the maul up over my head, standing on the chair, weaving around, doing a sort of dance to keep my balance, when I heard this voice. A little one, mind you, but a voice all the same.

"And just what, pray tell, is going on here?" the voice said. "A savage killing in the planning stages is what it looks like to me."

What do you do when something like that happens? I can tell you. It crosses your mind that maybe you're going crazy. It occurred to me that Wally and his thirty years of bad treatment had finally driven me over the edge. I lowered the post maul and stood there on the chair shaking like a leaf and sweating. And then it hit me. Conscience, that's what it was. It was my conscience talking.

"Oh no you don't," I said, lifting the maul. "I don't want to hear from you at all. I don't care if what I've got planned here is wrong or right. I don't give a damn one way or the other. I'm going to kill that bastard Wally and then my troubles will be over."

"What about the Ten Commandments?" the voice said. "What about the Golden Rule?"

"I don't care about any of that," I said. "All I care about is that Wally gets what he deserves."

I had managed to lift the maul up over my head and was just about to swing it down to get the feel of it, when all of a sudden the fourteen pounds felt like four hundred pounds. I could feel myself going over backwards and the only thing to do was to let go of the maul and try to get my balance. It landed on the floor and didn't seem to do any damage. I climbed down to pick it up again, thinking that Wally would be home any minute and find me with the post maul in the living room and how would I explain that? By this time I was sick and tired of this conscience business. I had a gruesome job to do and I wanted to be done with it.

I bent over to pick up the maul and there she was, sitting on the end of it, not much bigger than my thumb. She was dressed in a turquoise blue jogging suit and miniature running shoes. Cute as a button, was my first reaction, just what any little girl would like to find under the Christmas tree.

"How do you like them apples, sister?" she said, and I tell you, my blood pressure shot up past the red line in two seconds flat. I forgot all about Christmas and jogging suits and thought, nobody's supposed to be able to *see* their conscience. Not even someone who's about to pound her husband's head down to his kneecaps.

"You can't just up and kill somebody whenever you get the notion," she said, shaking her finger at me.

I thought about Wally and felt myself getting cocky in spite of the situation.

"Why not?" I flashed at her. "The bastard has tried to kill me any number of times. It's time he got some of his own. I can't think of anything else that will smarten him up." I paused, proud of myself. "And just who are you anyway? The good fairy?"

She didn't bat an eyelash (not that I could have seen if it she had), she just sat and swung her legs and beckoned for me to get closer. I squatted down.

"Never mind who I am," she said. "All you need to know is that I'm here to save you from yourself. You're a dangerous woman."

"Oh, am I?" I said. "Is that why I walk around with these bruises?" (I lifted up my dress and showed her a big ugly one on my thigh.) "Is that why I had to get false teeth twenty years ago after Wally knocked out most of my real ones? Is that why my shoulders ache when I lie in bed at night so I have to get up and take a painkiller to get to sleep? Oh yeah," I said, "I'm a dangerous woman all right. Real dangerous. I think that bastard Wally needs someone to protect him from me."

And it was the funniest thing. She stopped swinging her white joggers and her eyes (big green ones) filled with tears.

"It's not Wally I'm worried about," she said. "It's you."

I didn't know what to do. I just squatted there and she cried and finally I said, "Well. There's no sense crying over me. I've been living like this too many years and I quit crying about it a long time ago. Now if you'll kindly move, I'll finish the job and be done with it." I tried to stand up but I'd stayed in the same position too long. I had to unbend myself one leg at a time, like a fold-up card table. It kind of took the wind out of my sails. Still, I was determined. It was too late to turn back and I really didn't give a damn about myself or Wally or anyone else.

After I'd given my back a good stretch I bent over again to pick up the maul, planning to shake the little thing off. She was gone. I'm cracking up, I thought. A few bricks short, as Wally would say. He's driven me to this. He deserves what he's going to get. I gripped the wooden handle of the maul. Wally was coming. I could see him out the front-room window, weaving down the street like a drunken sailor.

"Oh no you don't," the voice said from somewhere behind me. And then I felt something sharp sink into my right ankle. It was her, and she had latched onto me with her teeth. I screamed and she let go.

"Into the closet with you," she said, and darted back and forth between one ankle and the other.

"Stop that," I said, kicking at her. "Stop that right now. He's coming. I have to get ready."

"Into the closet," she said, biting my left ankle like one of those chihuahua dogs that fit into a tea cup. "Get moving. Quickly, quickly." She was so fast I couldn't get at her. I could see now why she wore the running shoes. I was moving toward the closet, trying to avoid her teeth and kicking at her as I went. Before I knew it the doorway was in front of me and then I was inside and something was in my mouth so I couldn't yell. I could feel a rope going around and around me until I couldn't move.

"There," she said, and then I heard Wally coming in the front door. He slammed it behind him.

"What the hell," I heard him say. I pictured him in the living room, drunk and ugly. "Hey," he yelled. "What's this post maul doing here?" Silence. I felt my blood pressure going up again. "It damn well better be gone by the time I'm back down here." I heard him tramping up the stairs to the bathroom. "Do you hear me?" he called from the top of the stairs. Silence. "And you damn well better answer me the next time I ask you a question." I heard him stomp down the hallway and slam the bathroom door.

I don't know what happened to the post maul. It disappeared and I haven't seen it since. I lay scrunched up in the closet for a long time, scared, wondering what Wally would do when I didn't show up.

I must have fallen asleep, and when I woke up it was morning and the ropes were gone. I went to the kitchen and made Wally his breakfast. He came downstairs and fixed himself a tomato juice with four aspirins and a raw egg mixed into it, which is his own special cure for a hangover. I waited for him to ask me where I'd been, but he didn't say anything. When I placed a plate of bacon and eggs in front of him he slapped it across the table. I managed to catch it before it landed on the floor, which is better than some mornings around here. I took it that he was too hung-over to eat so I scraped the eggs into the garbage and headed down into the basement to busy myself with sorting the laundry in order not to be in Wally's road. I felt let down. All my enthusiasm for bashing Wally was gone and I didn't think about killing him again for a long time.

It was the potatoes that did it. I had worked hard, weeding and hoeing, hilling, picking off potato beetles by hand. I figured that maybe we'd been in one place long enough for me to do something homey, build a bin in the basement and keep potatoes all winter like my mother used to. I figured Wally might even like that. So I dug up a space in the back yard, bought seed potatoes with the grocery money, and went to work.

It was early August, just about the time you can start robbing potato hills and have those first meals served up with lots of real butter. The skins on the potatoes are so thin then that you don't even have to peel them. I was feeling good, like maybe I could start calling this little town home. I'd even had a few conversations with Crazy Florence next door, as though we were real neighbours.

I was out in the back yard, digging around in the hills with my bare hands, trying to guess how many potatoes would be in each hill and how big they'd be by the end of September. And what should Wally do but back the half-ton into the yard as close as he could to the back door. I knew what that meant. I'd seen it too many times before. Pretty soon he'd be carrying out dishes and chairs and blankets and loading them all into the back of that truck.

"Wally," I said as he stepped out of the cab. "Just what are you fixing to do? Don't tell me we're off again. Don't tell me you've gone and got yourself fired and we're heading down the road to some other town where I don't know a soul and nobody knows me nor cares to either. Don't tell me that, Wally. I couldn't bear to hear it."

Wally just grunted and slammed the screen door to the house and I knew that was exactly where we were headed. I followed him up the steps and hollered in the door.

"And what about my potatoes, Wally? What do you expect me to do about this patch of perfectly good potatoes? Leave them here for total strangers? Maybe people who don't care about fresh potatoes? Maybe people who will leave them in the ground to freeze and rot? Tell me, Wally, if we leave this place what do you expect me to do about these potatoes?"

I heard him coming and I thought maybe I had gone a little too far. I was not usually inclined to speak to Wally like that. I tended to go along with him, watch him load up the truck and get in beside him without saying much at all. I thought he might hit me, but he just stormed out the door, pushing me out of his way, and leaped into the cab.

"What am I going to do about the potatoes?" he said, starting up the truck. "What am I going to do?" he said, grinding the gears as he slammed it into reverse. And then I knew what he was going to do and there was nothing I could do to stop him. I stood on the step as he drove back and forth over the potato patch and spun the tires and threw dirt and potatoes all over the yard. I watched him and I thought, I'm going to kill him. I sat down on the steps and hatched a plan right then and there. And I wasn't going to let my conscience get the best of me this time either.

I knew a little bit about explosives. And I was pretty sure Wally had some dynamite stored in the garage. I would wire up his truck and when he got in it to drive off, bango, no more Wally.

I needed a few supplies to carry out my plan. I went into the house and got the grocery money from my apron pocket while

Wally was still digging up my potato patch. I headed out the front door and walked to the hardware store.

"Doing a bit of blasting?" Mr. Ferguson asked as he rang up my purchases.

"We've got a terrible big rock right in the middle of my garden," I said.

I stopped at the IGA for bread and milk so Wally wouldn't be suspicious. When I got home the potato patch was ruined. Wally was still sitting in the truck, listening to the radio. I fixed him three fried egg sandwiches and opened two beers and set them on the table.

"Wally," I called out the back door. "I've fixed you a little lunch. Fried egg sandwiches. And beer. Two of them."

He took the bait. He turned off the truck and stomped into the kitchen. He looked me in the eye and I looked him right back, trying not to give anything away.

"So that's what I think of your goddamned potatoes," he said.

"That's fine, Wally dear," I said. "I realize that I can't take them with me and that's all there is to it. You did the right thing. Now just enjoy your lunch and have a nap afterward if you want. I'll start packing up things in the living room."

I saw him eyeing the sandwiches like he was looking for poison and that gave me an idea for next time if the dynamite didn't work.

I took my bag of supplies and quietly went out the front door and around the side of the house to the garage. I found the dynamite hidden under a canvas tarp along with some other stuff Wally had brought home from work.

The truck was parked in the middle of the potato patch and I knew Wally couldn't see me from the kitchen. I crawled in and lay on the seat, figuring I could get the job done easy before Wally came back outside. Three sandwiches and two beers were usually enough to put him out for a couple of hours. I sang as I worked, really enjoying myself.

Oh, what a beautiful mornin'
Oh, what a beautiful day

I was just putting on the finishing touches when I heard the voice, singing along with me.

I've got a beautiful feelin'
Ev'rything's goin' my way

I stopped singing. She hopped up onto the dash.

"I can see you're up to your old tricks again, sister," she said. "I thought you had learned your lesson."

I sat up and stared at her. I reached out my index finger and touched her to see if she was really there. I pinched myself to make sure I was awake and I pulled my hair at the back of my neck, where it really hurts, just to double check. I was awake and she was really there.

"You just stay out of this," I said to her. "I had enough of you last time. This is none of your business."

"Oh, but it is," she said. "Like I said before, I'm here to protect you from yourself." She looked toward the house. "What's he done this time?"

"What's he done this time?" I said. "Can't you see for yourself? Just have a look around. Just have a look at my potato patch and then ask what he's done this time. This is the last straw, I tell you. A body can only take so much and then she has to do something."

She peered through the windshield and checked out the potato patch.

"He really is bad news," she said. "There's no doubt about it."

She paused. I noticed that she was wearing a different jogging suit from the one she had on last time. This one was yellow with bold black stripes. She leaned forward and looked into my eyes.

"Now I want you to think about something," she said.

"Okay," I heard myself say. "I'll think about it."

"You've blown Wally into little pieces," she said. "A million of them. The police come screaming up to your house. Four, five, maybe even six police cars. Men, big bruisers, surround you and they all have their gun barrels pointed at your head. You look for sympathy, but you don't get any because they think you've just blown up one of their own. They take you away and all the neighbours are watching over their fences. They shake their heads and say, 'Well, we won't be seeing her again. She'll be locked up for life, even if he did deserve it.'"

I thought about it. It was like a moving picture in my head. Tut tut, too bad, they were all saying. Mrs. Bidwell across the street. Crazy Florence next door. Even the postman. Their voices were a low hum, getting louder and louder, coming from all around the truck. Tut tut, too bad.

The yellow jogging suit on the dash of the truck joined in. I blinked and she was doing deep knee bends. Tut tut, too bad. Up down, up down. I was going mad; I had to be. A person's conscience never does deep knee bends.

"Stop," I yelled. I opened the door of the truck, jumped out and ran for the house. "I don't want to go to jail," I screamed, covering my ears with my hands.

There was an explosion from behind me. I was thrown onto my knees at the foot of the back steps. When I looked up, the truck was a mass of flames and Wally was gazing through the screen door.

"What the hell happened to my truck?" he said.

I stood up and wiped the dust off my knees, wondering what he would throw at me, wondering if I could make it over Florence's fence in time.

"I hope it's totalled," he said. "It's about time I got a new truck." He went back to the kitchen to finish his beer.

We didn't move. Wally couldn't get insurance for the truck because he had a $500 deductible and the truck wasn't worth that much. He tried to pay a couple of garage owners to say it was worth more, but they wouldn't do it. He managed to get some unemployment insurance by sending me to beg his ex-boss to say he had laid Wally off. But things were worse than ever because Wally was home all the time, calling me names, yelling at me and shoving me around for no reason, leaving empty beer bottles all over, snoring on the couch while I was trying to watch my programs on TV.

I started to forget about jail and think about poison. I figured the hardware store would be a good place to get rat bait.

"How'd the blasting go?" Mr. Ferguson asked me.

"Just fine," I said. "We blasted that rock with no trouble at all."

"So," Mr. Ferguson went on, "I hear Wally's had a little trouble with his truck."

"Funny thing, that was," I said.

"So," he said, busy straightening things on the counter. "Did Wally manage to get any insurance money?"

"None at all," I said, trying to look grave.

Mr. Ferguson shook his head. "Some guys have all the luck," he said.

"Do you have any rat bait?" I asked. "We've got more trouble with rodents than you'd care to think about."

He directed me to the right aisle, and there she was on the shelf right next to the boxes of poison. Just sitting there in her coal black jogging suit with the hood up, looking mournful as you could imagine. A good act, I thought. Well, I wasn't going to let it get to me.

"You again," I said. "Well, you can't talk me out of it this time. My mind's made up. I'm going through with it."

I put my hand on the box, which had a picture of a dead rat with crosses on its eyes. She still didn't say anything, and I got the feeling she wasn't planning to. She looked so defeated I all of a sudden thought I would cry.

"Did you say something?" Mr. Ferguson called from behind the counter. "Finding what you need?"

"Yes, thanks," I called, my voice sounding hoarser than I wanted it to. I looked the woman in the eye. "Aren't you going to try to talk me out of it?" I said.

She shook her head.

"Why not?" I asked.

She didn't say anything, but she looked so miserable that I wondered if she'd buy some poison for herself.

It was the funniest thing. I couldn't bring myself to pick up that box of rat bait. I knew I was feeling low because I had her feeling so low. And I was beginning to figure out that I liked her. I wanted to make her happy. I tried an experiment by moving my hand away from the box. She brightened up as if someone had just lit a candle in her heart. And I felt that way too, as if someone had lit a candle in my heart.

"I guess today's not the day," I said. "I guess I'll go on home and make Wally his pork chops just like I do every Tuesday, and I won't be putting any poison in them either."

"Good for you," she shouted, jumping up. "Now we're getting somewhere."

"You might be getting somewhere," I said, leaving the store empty-handed. "I'm just on my way home to get yelled at and knocked around the house a few times, same old story. If that's getting somewhere, I don't know anything."

"Just don't be so sure," the woman said. "I still have a trick or two up my sleeve."

So. Wally didn't die by rat bait and that brings me to where we are now. Me and this little bit of a thing tying Wally up in the closet. I'm wearing a fuchsia jogging suit just like hers. I found it in the mailbox this morning, wrapped in silver paper.

"So what do you think of them apples?" I say to Wally when we have him tied up good, a sock stuffed in his mouth so he can't yell. "How do you feel now, big boy?" I say. He jerks his feet around a bit. "Things are going to change around this place," I tell him, "and I'll just be leaving you in here for a while to mull things over." I close the closet door, then open it again. "And we're not moving away from here either," I add.

The two of us, in our fuchsia suits, sit on the couch watching *The Lives of Others* on TV and eating popcorn.

"These people are disgusting," I say.

She nods. She's working on a single white puff the size of her head.

"They have no morals," I say, suddenly depressed about the *real* state of things.

She agrees.

"What will we do if it doesn't work?" I ask. "What if he's worse than ever when we let him out?"

"Shhhhhhh," she says. "Just watch this."

On TV, Mandy is blow-drying her hair in front of the bathroom mirror. Lance is singing in the bathtub, scrubbing his back the way people do on TV. Mandy keeps looking at him and moving closer to the bathtub. Suddenly she tosses the dryer into the tub with Lance. He screams. The program cuts to a big yellow box of Sunlight detergent.

"Electrocution?" I ask her, my mouth full of popcorn.

She lowers the white puff of corn to her lap and grins.

Queen of the Headaches

Sharon Butala

Lara drifts in and out of sleep. She hears her daughter's voice calling up the stairs. "Robin, Robin." The pain is behind her eyes now, dull but bearable. She knows she can get up today. She meets seven-year-old Robin on the stairs.

"Hi Mommy," he says. His socks don't match. Wincing as she bends down, she takes one sock off him and sends him down to the kitchen with one foot bare while she goes to his room to find the mate. She leans against the doorframe for just a minute to rest, closing her eyes, but the moment she does she feels herself getting lost in the pain again, so she straightens and glides to the bureau, holding her neck rigid. She looks as if she is on wheels. Her children call it her "headachy walk". When they see it Rosemary always says in her most adult voice, "You'd better lie down, Mother. I'll look after things," and Robin always goes outside to play, or to a place where he can't see her.

In the kitchen Francis is buttering toast and listening to Rosemary, who is twelve, reading a poem she has written.

"What's another word for pain?" Rosemary asks. "A stronger word."

"Anguish," Lara says, before she can stop herself. She smiles with embarrassment. Francis kisses her, she stoops to put Robin's matching sock on, and sits down to breakfast as though she has not been absent for five days.

Before long the children leave for school. Francis decides to stay another hour or so since Lara is up. They both know from long experience that the pain will let up today and tomorrow, and in three days' time at the most, she will be free of it for another two, maybe three weeks. Unless. . .

"Two things," Francis says. Lara waits. After each one of her absences he sits down and tells her everything that has happened at home, at the university, and out in the world while she has been shut away in their bedroom. He can never hide his delight that she is back with them. His concern for her, the care he takes for her, always humbles her. She is grateful to him for loving her. But sometimes she thinks she would not feel so guilty about her suffering if he were not so unfailingly kind and loving. She doesn't allow herself more than an unwilling glimpse of this before she chases it away. "First, the migraine clinic called. Your appointment is set for next Thursday at three. No drugs for thirty-six hours before and so on. They're sending a questionnaire."

Lara's hands, which are resting quietly on her lap under the table, tighten. She feels sweat breaking out on her chest and the back of her neck.

"Good," she says.

"Don't worry about it," Francis says. He always knows what she is thinking if not the reasons. "If you don't like the way they handle it, you don't have to go back." He leans across the corner of the table and kisses her. "How is it now?" he asks. She smiles at him. The pain is welling up in her forehead from her eyes and down the left side of her head. Her ear and cheek feel numb; her neck is stiffening.

"Improving," she assures him. "What's the other thing?" she asks, trying to make her voice sound light. She tilts her head sideways, smiling. It is a girlish gesture from the past which charms Francis because it represents innocence and fragility which he likes to think of as her qualities. She gives this gesture to him as a gift because he is so good to her. She rights her head when the dizziness strikes. She hopes he will leave soon before she throws up.

"Sonia phoned. She's coming over tonight. She sounded very excited, but she wouldn't tell me why. Do you feel up to it?"

"I'll be so glad to see her. I feel as though I've been marooned on a desert island." She is always bitterly lonely during an attack even though she can't bear to have anyone near her. The headache takes all her concentration. She does not like intruders into its kingdom.

"Good," he remarks. Then he frowns and looks at the opposite wall. She wonders why he doesn't get up to go. There must be something else on his mind. "This came yesterday." He takes a letter out of his jacket pocket and hands it to her, watching her face. It is an invitation to be keynote speaker at a prestigious symposium, at a university in Australia. At first all she can think is that he must be very excited to show her this so soon after she gets up. She needs a second to digest it before she can respond.

"That's three things," she says. "Oh, Francis. It's the very top, isn't it? They only ask the best." He doesn't say anything. He is looking at the letter again, pretending to read it, trying to hide his excitement and his pride. "You just go from one triumph to another," she says tenderly. She moves to sit on his lap and kiss him. She wonders how she will ever manage when he is gone, but already she feels relieved at his coming absence. He will ask her to go with him, but she knows she will refuse. She can't leave the children for that long, she will say. If she has a headache — (if?), her mother will come to help.

"Look at the time," he says. He calls to her from the hall. "I'll pick up the kids at school and take them to McDonald's for lunch. You rest today."

When the door closes behind him, she makes it to the bathroom in time, but only retches uselessly since her stomach is empty. She only pretended to eat breakfast, although she thinks wearily that of course she didn't fool Francis. She takes a tranquillizer, bathes and dresses, and begins housecleaning. Francis and the children do only what is absolutely necessary.

She won't allow Francis to hire a housekeeper. It is the one thing she has stood firm on during their entire marriage. She doesn't know why.

She works slowly and deliberately so that she doesn't jar herself. Her expression is steady, her jawline tense. She has no words. Sometimes she stops and, bending over from the waist, rests her forehead on the cool kitchen countertop. Once, while she is vacuuming the living room, she drops to her knees on the rug and then lies carefully full-length on it, face down, while the vacuum whirs beside her body.

"Mommy?" Robin calls tentatively as he comes in the front door after school. He smiles calmly when he finds her in the kitchen making chocolate chip cookies, his favourite. When she hugs him, he looks up at her out of her own dark eyes and she is surprised she is real enough that someone might look like her.

"I've got homework," he announces in a pleased voice. "You can help me. Sit here," he says, pointing to the chair beside him. Meekly, she sits down. For a second, the headache's grip relaxes.

Later, in the evening, when Rosemary has gone to bed and Francis is reading a bedtime story to Robin, she changes into a mauve and purple striped caftan and Indian sandals and puts on the big silver earrings Francis brought her from Morocco before they were married. She twists her thick brown hair into a loose knot on the top of her head, and brings down tendrils to curl on her ears and neck.

"I think a headache becomes you," Francis says. "It gives your eyes a dark, mysterious look. Beautiful. My prairie princess." He is proud of her looks, thinks himself lucky to have married someone beautiful when he was only a skinny, bespectacled graduate student, pale from too much studying and blinking in the light she seemed to shine on him.

"Prairie lily," she says. "Prairie chicken, prairie schooner." It always breaks her heart to recognize his innocence in the face of what she believes is her complexity and deception.

At nine-thirty the doorbell rings. She and Francis go together to answer it. It is her younger sister Sonia, grinning and carrying a bottle of champagne which she holds out to them. Then, before either of them can speak, she says, "Lara, you look gorgeous! Just gorgeous!" She walks around Lara. "Nobody would ever guess you're just a poor peasant girl from Saskatchewan."

"Poor but exquisite," Lara says. Sonia always bring this playful mood with her. Lara always feels better when she is around.

"A rose among thorns," Sonia answers. They giggle.

"Come and sit down and tell us what this is for," Francis says, taking the wine and leading them into the living room. It is a large, comfortable room. It has a temporary air though, as if the decorator were distracted and kept leaving off and coming back unable to remember where she had been. Sonia walks across the room to stand smiling in front of the fireplace that still holds a basket of dusty and out-of-season weeds that Lara keeps meaning to throw away. Francis follows her and sets the bottle on the coffee table. The hem of Lara's caftan catches briefly on the frames of some pictures she has never got around to hanging and which lean against the wall.

"Are you ready?" Sonia asks.

"Yes," they say in unison, smiling.

"Today I signed a contract. My novel is going to be published."

There is a shocked silence while Francis and Lara both absorb this news. Then Francis jumps up, kisses Sonia, and says, "Sonia, that's wonderful! Why didn't you tell us somebody was interested? You must have known!" He is laughing he is so pleased. Lara stands too, tears running down her cheeks, and embraces Sonia.

"I'm so happy for you, Sonia," she says. Part of her is happy for and proud of her sister. But the tears she cannot stop are for herself. They are for the emptiness inside where her enterprise should be. She wishes she were a more generous person, or more honest. But at the same time she feels as if her heart will break. She tries to stop crying. Soon they will both try to comfort her and she knows this will only make her feel worse because she will have stolen Sonia's moment with her neurosis. She wipes her eyes and sits down.

"Open the champagne, Francis," Sonia commands. "We have to celebrate." She tells Lara and Francis all about the details of her contract. "And now I have some money. With what I've saved, I can live for a year — if I'm careful. So I'm going to resign. I'll never mark another English paper as long as I live."

"What will you do?" Lara asks. "Write?"

"I figure I can get another novel well on the way in a year."

"You know if you run low on money you can count on us," Francis says. Lara winces at "us". She has no money, only Francis's. Francis brings in plenty of money. She has never needed to work. Sometimes she thinks she is the luckiest woman in the world, yet often she thinks what a good wife she would be if they were poor. She is sure that she has never heard of poor women getting headaches. She knows she's never seen one in the clinics and doctors' offices she frequents.

She looks at her engagement ring, a large oval amethyst rimmed with small diamonds. The ring embarrasses her, but she never takes it off. When Francis gave it to her and she had gasped with the shame of her own unworthiness for it, Francis, mistaking the gasp for one of pleasure, had blushed and said, "It's the only thing I saw as beautiful as you are." What could she say to that? What could she give in return?

They have finished the champagne. Francis goes to find something else to drink. Some doctors say she shouldn't drink and some say it doesn't matter. Lara thinks it doesn't matter in the least.

"What goes with champagne?" he asks. Without waiting for an answer, he mixes a pitcher of martinis. Sonia is happily self-absorbed. She has earned the right, Lara thinks, watching her fondly.

"You know, writing is so hard that I have to force myself to do it, but it's the only thing that makes me happy. I mean when I'm writing, and it's going well, I feel. . . complete, as if it's what I was made to do." Lara listens but her head hurts terribly. Her vision is blurred by the pain. Sonia seems to float in horizontal slices as though Lara is seeing her through a venetian blind reflected in water. Each word Sonia says falls like a hammer on her head. Vaguely she notices that it is getting worse instead of better, but the conscious level of her mind is occupied with Sonia's words. Has she ever felt complete? Maybe, when the children were born. But she knows she hasn't felt what Sonia is talking about. She knows she mustn't think about it or the pain will drive her mad.

"I can always tell when your head hurts," Francis says, putting his arm around her. "You try to hide it, but I can tell by the way you hold your mouth. Poor girl."

Oh god, not to be so transparent! Not to be married to such a good man. She loathes herself for the thought and smiles at Francis.

"It's letting up," she says. They are all a little drunk. "Now tell her your good news," she says. He tells Sonia about his invitation. Sonia kisses him and tells him how proud she is of him, what a genius he is, what geniuses they both are.

"Apparently several universities are going to share me. I'll be lecturing all over Australia. They want me for two months. It's one of the best things that ever happened to me." Lara notices her own failure with shame: how open he is with Sonia, how he lets his pleasure show as he never does with her. Am I so difficult, she asks herself, that he can't talk to me like that? That he has to tiptoe around me, and feel me out, that he can't just tell me how happy he is? He overdoes it, she thinks. I'm not that delicate, unless he's made me be. She doubts that this is true and feels guilty again remembering how he looks after the children when she is sick, how he suffers for her when her head hurts.

Francis and Sonia are sitting beside each other on one sofa now, while she sits facing them on the other. The one she is sitting on isn't quite right for the first one. She tried to find the perfect mate for the one Sonia and Francis are sitting on, but one of her headaches overwhelmed her and she had to settle for this one. This kind of thing is always happening to her.

She feels isolated, shut out from their world, and thinks how she can never join them. But at the same time she is glad to be left alone for a moment while their attention is focussed else-where. The pain in her head ebbs and flows and she sits and contemplates it, noticing exactly where it reaches and where it doesn't, where its steely fingers probe sharply once and then withdraw, where it lies heavily like a parental hand across the top of her head. She is absorbed in trying to measure its outer parameters when Francis says, "I worry about how you meditate on it." Have they been talking to her?

"Yes," Sonia says. "That's something you've been doing lately that's kind of scary."

Lara blinks, but says nothing.

"She's going to a migraine clinic on Thursday," Francis tells Sonia as though Lara isn't there. "The hormone treatment just doesn't work."

"Neither did the anti-allergy treatment and neither did the heavy tranquillizers. You were like a zombie."

"Yes," Lara says. All three sit and look at one another. Lara notices how drunk Francis is now, and Sonia too. Lara has stopped drinking. Sonia's cheeks are flushed and her black hair and eyes gleam. She vibrates with energy and joy.

"Such distinguished company I keep," Lara says fondly. "Such a pair of successes." For a second the pain blots everything out, she cannot see them.

"Is it worse?" Francis asks. "Can I get you a pill?" He sways a little as he stands up. She laughs nervously, distractedly, blinking and touching her earrings.

"No, no, I think I'll go to bed." She stands and kisses Sonia who has also risen. She puts her hand on Francis's cheek. They look into one another's eyes in the way of married people for a moment before she turns and starts upstairs.

As she makes the turn at the landing just before the second floor blocks her view, she sees Francis and Sonia looking up at her. As she watches, something happens.

She feels like a river, wide, deep and dark, that flows through the house, that they are all swimming in, turning silently, like dreamers. The pain thins, spreads itself out through the rooms, upstairs, downstairs, in the attic and the basement. She feels it cradled in her pelvis, it touches her earlobes like ornaments, it shines in the hot centre of her forehead. It is sweet now, and bearable.

She knows that even Sonia standing down below her, full of hope, feels its gentle, cool flow creeping down her backbone. Above Lara, in her clean, adolescent bed, Rosemary is sighing in her sleep as the pain laps against the smooth, fresh skin of her young girl's body.

Lara stumbles, almost falls. But this is a vision to be borne. She climbs on up the stairs, moving in its certainty.

Dream of the Half-Man

Lois Braun

The night of the heart attack, Lou dreamed again the half-man dream. Sometimes in the dream the jacked-up Bronco soared above the freeway like a Disney incarnation, saving the limbs of the man snagged under its chassis. But most times, when things were going badly for Lou, the Bronco did not fly.

When she was on the brink of puberty, she'd been told the story of the half-man by her great-aunt Laverne, who had moved to Minneapolis to marry an American Lutheran. Laverne and the Lutheran told many horror stories. It was as though Minneapolis was under the tyranny of a sleek wheeled beast that slaughtered citizens at random on their six-lane highways. But the half-man story had disturbed Lou more than any other, for there had been no death. At least, not right away, and when it came, it was at the wrong time.

One hot Minnesota night in July, a man was on his way home from a bar from which he'd been expelled for drunkenness. He was driving a new Bronco with a raised suspension and over-sized tires because he had forgotten he was no longer the hellion he'd been in his youth, riding rough terrain in a high-powered truck with a girl at his side. In truth, he was over fifty and had never taken the Bronco out of the city. In a blurred fury, he tore along the freeways and up and down exit ramps and access roads that would eventually lead him home.

Just past one of the exits, at an intersection, he missed a red light and took the corner at full speed into the path of a motorcycle ridden by a young man and his sweetheart. The sweetheart was thrown to the curb, but the Honda and its driver were entangled in the undercarriage of the Bronco, unnoticed by the drunk. He accelerated and scorched along a segment of straight urban highway heading south. He did not hear the screams of the boy under the truck, or perhaps he thought the screams were inside his own head.

Miles later, he turned onto a gravelled street in the woodsy suburb where he lived. Here the Bronco began to fail. It finally stalled. The drunk was sweating now. He'd begun to feel that something was wrong. Horribly wrong. He abandoned the Bronco and lurched towards his house. He could hear the anguished moans of the half-dead motorcyclist under his truck, but it was too late, he hurried on. Whatever it was, it was too late.

Aunt Laverne's husband's nephew lived next door to the drunk. He was working in his garage, repairing his own car, when the Bronco stopped near his house. He saw his neighbour stumble by and heard the terrible cries. With a socket wrench in his hand, he approached the deserted Bronco. Even from a distance, he could see motorcycle wreckage under the front end of the truck. He ran back to his own house and called an ambulance and a tow truck. The tow truck winched up the Bronco, and a rescue team dislodged the motorcycle and then the mangled half-body.

In a moment of clear thought, the boy said, "I'll kill him."

The story had rested there for many months. Lou often thought about the poetic half-man, without his right arm and leg, appearing in the drunk's doorway. She thought about the drunk man's nightmare of waiting for the half-man to appear with some indescribable weapon, indescribable hatred.

But then Laverne said that the drunk had died of stroke before the half-man was mobile enough to get his revenge. That was when Lou's dream began. In her dreams, she tried to save the boy on the motorcycle, and she tried to kill the drunk. Over and over again. In many different ways.

Last night, Lou's father began to pace and rub the lower part of his left arm, and he began to sweat and mumble. "Open the window," he'd said. But it was ninety degrees outside and no one did. "I'm coming down with something," he said to his wife, Audrey. *I'm coming down with something.* He lay down on the living room sofa and had his heart attack. Audrey called the hospital and the paramedics came and took him away.

Lou had come to her parents' house last night to tell them she was leaving the apartment she'd been sharing with her girlfriend and was moving back home for a while. She'd nursed her roommate through anorexia by convincing her that yogurt wasn't really food, that it had been pre-digested by a pugnacious species of bacteria, and now the roommate had found a boyfriend, and the two of them were edging Lou out of the three-room suite on Osborne Street. But Lou hadn't had a chance to tell her parents before the heart attack. Her mother followed the ambulance to the hospital. "Stay here, Lou," she'd said before she went. "I want someone to be in our house." Lou had gone to sleep in her old room so that her mother would not be alone during the night. Now she simply needed to collect her belongings from Osborne Street. She was home.

Awakening from the half-man dream, and the sounds of screeching metal, Lou heard scraping and clunking from the kitchen. She got out of bed right away and shuffled in old pyjamas to the kitchen. Her mother was on her hands and knees in front of the cupboard beneath the sink. She was surrounded by rusted tins of wax, and jars and bottles of cleaners and window sprays and drain openers. "I thought I heard a mouse," she said.

She needs to kill something, thought Lou. "Did you call the hospital?"

"He's stable."

Stable. The Bronco came to Lou's mind. "It's all that cheesecake. Must've clogged his arteries. You shouldn't have made him eat it."

"You won't find a villain here to bash." Audrey was scattering mothballs in the dark cupboard. Her voice was hollow and bounced with a muffled ping off the metal pipes leading out of the sink. "Anyway, it's you, you know. He thinks Clint is on drugs. He thinks Clint will harm you some day."

On their first date, Clint had taken Lou to see his favourite movie, *The Attack of the Killer Tomatoes*. Then they'd gone to the A & W and he'd asked her to marry him by placing a tiny french-fried onion ring on her finger. Lou loved the little rings from the centre of the onion, so she accepted, and ate it. She told her parents about the movie and the mock engagement. They were uncomfortable. Then one day he came to their house with fresh lobster. He pulled the claws and tails out of a cooler of ice and told Lou's parents that they were a gift from a friend in neurobiology. Clint was wearing oversized overalls with nothing underneath and he had a cold. Lou's father thought he was a dopehead. Lou moved out of the house.

Now Lou said to her mother, "You just said there were no villains."

Audrey put all the tins and jars and bottles back in their places. "None and many." She stood up. Her face was blotchy and her breathing quick and shallow, as though she had worked hard. The braid she wore for sleeping sat on her shoulder like a bristled chameleon. Perhaps she hadn't slept at all.

They talked about breakfast, about the danishes and muffins in the fridge, about eggs. "Too much cholesterol," Lou warned. They finally agreed on toast and grapefruit, but eyed the butter with distrust and used fruit jelly instead.

"We'll go to the hospital right after lunch. Your grandmother's coming. She should be here by noon."

Lou's mother's mother: a cowardly, frail woman who'd had a heart attack once herself. Lou was about to make an unkind comment, but she felt sorry for the cheesecake remark, and answered, "Oh."

"Just what do you mean by that?"

"Nothing. If you want her here, good."

"She'll feel better."

"Should we clean the house or mess it up? What would make her happy?"

Audrey began to laugh. "She's been itching to get at the tiles in your father's shower. Between them, with Q-tips. But he would never let her. Finally she'll have her chance."

Lou laughed too, but Audrey was crying now, though she still made laughing noises and her mouth was compressed in a wide, close-lipped smile. Her breasts and shoulders trembled. Lou reached for her hand among the toast scrapings. "I hardly ever see Clint any more. And we were just friends anyway. We were never going together."

"Let's leave the dishes," said Audrey. "It'll give Mother something to do besides weep and nag when she gets here."

"Yes, let's not even clear them off the table."

=   =   =

A square of light shone on the white rug in the living room. The day would be hot and still, sedated, again.

His magazines were scattered on the coffee table where he'd sat down after supper — *Harper's* folded over at an article about terrorists, *Saturday Night* unopened, a pregnant vertical bulge along it's stapled spine. Two cigarette butts lay in an ashtray beside the remote control for the TV, and next to that a package of Rothman's and a roll of antacid tablets. Packages: the magazines, the television, the cigarettes, the Rolaids. With them Lou's father managed his life, their lives, from the couch in front of the picture window. Whenever Lou came up the driveway, she saw his head above the back of the sofa, framed in the window.

Now she tried to remember her father in some other circumstance, tried to recall some moments of joy they'd shared. The only image that came to her mind was the time he'd found a stray female cat and new-born litter in the garage, had come into the house holding a tiny black kitten on the flat palm of his hand. Lou had been a little girl. Her father had laughed and laughed at the smallness of the kitten whimpering and mewing with its short claws hooked into his palm. Lou had wanted to keep the kitten in the house. But her father had taken it back to its nest behind the garbage cans and the next day the litter and mother were gone. "She moved them to a safer place," he had told her. He hated pets.

Lou sat down on the sofa and looked at the coffee table. She sat there a long time, not touching anything. She did not want to see her father in the hospital. She was afraid.

=　　=　　=

At exactly twelve o'clock, Lou's grandmother, Winnifred, arrived in a taxi, with greasy cabbage borsch and a suitcase and an umbrella. Lou watched her come up the front sidewalk, clutching the wrinkled paper bag to her chest, her glasses around her neck on a black cord. "Borsch and it's ninety," Lou said to herself. She recognized the two-litre shape of the mayonnaise jar outlined by the brown paper.

Winnifred's eyes filled with tears as soon as she had installed the soup in a forward position in the refrigerator, in front of the milk and beer. "Oh my dears," she said as she gave them each a feeble hug. "It's that filthy smoking. Maybe now he'll quit. Well, he'll have to quit. They'll make him. Louise, is your friend still vomiting up her food?"

"Every day," Lou lied. "Hello, Grandma Winnie."

"It smells of mothballs in here. I already have a migraine."

"Mother's trying to kill a mouse. All she'll do is chase it to another part of the house, and then she'll have to put out more mothballs, and pretty soon the whole house will be filled with mothballs and we'll all have to move out."

"I hate rodents."

"But at least there won't be any mice."

"You really should trap it, dear."

"Yes, we'll have to kill it," said Lou.

"Didn't you even wait for me to have lunch?" Winnifred asked, her eyes filling again.

Lou put her arm around her grandmother's waist. "Oh, those are still the breakfast dishes."

"You poor dears. . ."

"I see you brought your suitcase," said Audrey, lifting it to see how heavy it was.

"Yes, I thought I'd stay a few days. Should we have the soup now?"

"It's supposed to be cooler tomorrow."

"You should have closed your blinds hours ago."

Lou went back to the sofa and lay down. Her mother and her grandmother nipped at each other's ankles in the kitchen. The bickering lulled her into a half-sleep, and in her drowsiness she remembered the dream. It was just a flash, as memories of dreams often are — a face, the half-man being pulled with a hard, bright chain from under the Bronco. His face was her father's face.

When she awoke, her grandmother was walking through the living room with Mr. Clean and a box of Q-tips. "We're going as soon as your mother has had a nap." Her mother had never taken a nap in her life. "Oh Lou, you could at least have dumped the ashes. Here, I'll do it. And you can throw out the cigarettes — he won't need those any more. Here, give them to me."

Lou snatched up the Rothman's and took one out of the pack. She put the cigarette in her mouth and gazed loose-lipped and narrow-eyed at her grandmother. With chin a-quiver, Winnifred gathered up the magazines and the ashtray and the Rolaids, somehow making room for them between Q-tips and Mr. Clean, and minced into the hallway in her white Tender Tootsies.

I must set the trap before we leave, thought Lou. She kept the cigarette in her mouth, unlit.

There was a secret room under the basement stairway that had a small door on each side leading to two different rooms. It had been Lou's hideaway while she was growing up, and had provided a handy escape when her boy-cousins had chased her around the ping-pong room, bent on stealing kisses. Now it was the place where her father kept past fancies, like wine-making equipment and fondue pots. It was also where the mousetraps were stored. And it was cool.

The mousetraps were in a shoebox, with dried-up rolls of Scotch tape, old screws, a meat thermometer that didn't work, wine corks, burnt-down candles, a broken pocket-watch, and a bottle-opener shaped like a woman's leg. There were other shoeboxes but the one with the leg-shaped bottle-opener was Lou's favourite. The contents of the box never changed. Nothing was ever added or taken away.

Lou took one of the traps out of the box and, by the glow of a dusty light bulb, read its inscription: *VICTOR, Woodstream Corporation, Lititz, Pennsylvania*. She took out the pocket-watch, too. What significance had it had in her father's life? She held it up to the dim light, looking for an inscription on its back, and ran her fingertips across the metal to feel what might have been engraved there once. It can't be important, she thought. He wouldn't leave it here in this box. But what did she know about her father's past, his souvenirs and his sadnesses? There was so little.

Lou sat down on an overturned laundry tub with the mousetrap in one hand and the watch in the other. The cigarette stuck to her lips and she made it flip up and down with gentle undulations of her lower jaw. Hollow rubbing sounds came from the shower stall off one of the upstairs bedrooms. Audrey must be back in the kitchen, now that it was safe. Lou thought about the dream. She'd never seen the half-man's face before. Her father retreated from her as each minute passed.

Then she heard another sound, a rhythmic gnawing, coming from behind her on the grimy shelves filled with pickle jars and ragbags and shoeboxes. A steady rhythmic grinding of small teeth on wood. Was he trying to get in or out? Lou said, "Hi." The gnawing stopped. He was in there with her. She looked at the mousetrap.

After moments of silence, the chewing began again. Lou pictured the mouse in the trap, tidy metal jaws clamped across the mouse's middle, cutting him in half, snapping his miniature spine.

A voice now, just above her, suddenly loud. "Lou? Are you down there? It's time to go."

The gnawing stopped. Lou was not ready to answer. The space she was in was quite small, but she had started to feel comfortable in it, for its dimensions had grown. She tossed the watch and the mousetrap into the shoebox. Nothing added or taken away.

"Lou?"

The naked doll with the harridan's hair and one arm missing stared glassy-eyed at Lou from the top shelf against the wall. The hand it had was raised above its head, fingers spread. The doll was propped up in a tobacco tin, from the days when Lou's father had smoked a pipe. It was the only doll Lou remembered having. She'd played mostly with toy six-shooters when she was growing up. Dolls had scared her.

She took the nameless, wild-haired child down from the shelf. Its severed arm was in the tin, and showed futile signs of repair. "Susie," said Lou. "I'll call you Susie." But she put the doll back on the shelf. As she was leaving the secret room, she thought she heard a ticking, like a watch. Or was it the sound of little claws scratching on the wood?

Lou met her mother on the stairs. Audrey's hair was on top of her head now, its grey-white-auburn strands tied in a bun in the centre. She'd spent time rubbing cream into her face, and the massaging had evened out her complexion. She smelled of Chanel, but was still in her dressing gown. "You're like your father. He often comes down here to get something from one of those old shoeboxes, and he stays for ages, and comes back up empty-handed." She looked down. "And here you are, empty-handed."

In the car on the way to the hospital, Lou's grandmother told the story of the old man who'd slipped on ice and broken his leg. "I heard it at bingo" she said. "He was an old retired RCMP officer, someone important. He was walking on a street near his house last winter and he fell and broke his leg. And no one driving by stopped to help him, not for a long, long time. I don't know how long. It was terribly cold. I guess people thought he was a derelict of some sort. By the time he was rescued, he was very sick, and a few weeks later he died of a clot in his lung. The family blamed the passers-by for his death, for not stopping to help. But what good does that do? They don't know who to sue."

The hospital was not far away. Its windows stared at them and at the sky above the trees lining the hot streets. Her father would not be watching through one of the windows today, but he might be some other day. How would he look?

"I wish you hadn't told me that just now, Mother," said Audrey. "I had just begun to feel some hope. I wish you hadn't told it."

He should have had a sign, thought Lou. I USED TO BE A MOUNTIE. I AM NOT JUST ANOTHER BUM. HELP ME. She thought about the drunk and the Bronco, the drunk roaring around town, catching sober people under his torture-machine, and about sober people driving by an old man lying on the street, assuming he was just a drunk.

There was construction at the hospital, a new wing. In front of the building, they could see a huge excavation with piers and gridwork. Lou saw the hospital tipping over, dying men tipping out of their chairs and beds and wafting in white muslin to the mass grave beneath their windows.

The three women walked through a long temporary corridor that had been built at the edge of the construction site to join the parking lot to a side entrance. It was a white tube that echoed and rattled with their walking. The people in the corridor were like March hares and lonely Alices trying to get back through the looking-glass.

Winnifred said, "You'll find your father a changed man, if he. . ."

How would he look? Lou was angry at her grandmother for upsetting Audrey, and did not speak as they made their way to the third floor. They passed a gift shop. What could she bring him? A stuffed cat grinned at her from a high glass shelf.

Waiting for the elevator, Lou said, "Grandma Winnie, did Laverne ever tell you about the motorcycle driver that got stuck under this guy's truck?" She would tell her all the gory details. "And had half his body ripped off on the gravel, at eighty miles an hour?"

Audrey said softly, "My god." She walked away.

But Lou's grandmother was unflustered. "Yes, I remember that. Wasn't it just dreadful? Laverne's husband knew the driver of the truck, you know. His name was Teddy. But you're mistaken about the boy's injuries, dear. I remember his picture in the Minneapolis newspaper when I visited Laverne one Christmas. He was suing Teddy's estate for a ridiculous amount of money, considering he only lost an ear and part of his foot. After all, he can walk almost normally."

The elevator door opened. Audrey hurried to it and got on. As they rode up, she stared straight ahead, cold and angry. Winnifred looked at the floor, a pink Kleenex clutched to her throat. Lou felt tears coming and swallowed many times to get rid of them. "You could have tried to make me laugh," said Audrey, and slapped first Lou's, then Winnifred's buttocks with her handbag.

The elevator stopped at the third floor. "It's through that door," said Lou's mother, and they moved towards it.

My father is behind that door. Lou was less afraid now, only half afraid. Here I am, empty-handed. What do you bring a father? What if they only let us in one at a time? Perhaps he'll speak first. He'll say something like, "Who let you in?" Or, "Did you bring me a cigarette?" Or, "It must be a hundred degrees in this place."

Only an ear and part of his foot.

What had become of the half-man? Where was the horrible gun, held in the only hand he had left?

What will I dream?

"Did you set the trap, dear?" whispered Winnifred.

"Yes," Lou lied.

The Franz Kafka Memorial Room

Brian Fawcett

It was a small room at the end of a corridor, rectangular in shape, with a high ceiling — perhaps twelve to fifteen feet. Three walls were made of concrete construction blocks, while the fourth wall, which opened into the corridor, was of steel and glass, and included double doors. Only one thing was in the room: a staircase, opposite the door, led eleven steps up to a blank wall.

The room was discovered one week after the institution it was part of opened, and within a few days, someone with a sense of humour stuck a neatly lettered sign on the door: The Franz Kafka Memorial Room.

The room, you might argue, can be explained. It is part of a "Long Range Plan", which is a device invented by bureaucratic intelligence to create the illusion of competence and control in the face of an economy accelerating more rapidly and massively than at any other time in history. I explained the room to myself that way at first. It was just part of the Long Range Plan, and in the next stage of construction, the blank wall at the top of the staircase was to become a doorway to another corridor.

These days, though, I'm not so sure about things like that. Are you? Can you make the assumption that we are in control with the same self-assurance people could a generation ago? What if I told you that the next stage of construction didn't take place, or was altered in such a way that the extension of that corridor deep into the bowels of the institution was never finished? What if I told you that the corridor, and the blank wall the staircase led to, was meant to be just that? What if I told you that somewhere in that institution the Franz Kafka Memorial

Room still exists, with the sign removed from the door, the glass and steel replaced by more concrete construction blocks and a wooden door with a number painted on it — say, 2062? Inside the room, do the eleven steps of the staircase still end at the blank wall? Or did they jackhammer the staircase away to prevent it from having an invisible existence?

I can't give you the correct answer to those questions. No authority exists that can, and I'm convinced that such a condition of uncertainty is now the true one for me to be in as the writer of the story and for you as the reader.

But this is depressing theoretical stuff, you might be saying to yourself, and why lay it on me here, in what is supposed to be an occasion for fiction. I mean, what is this? A lecture or something?

It's no lecture. I'm trying to tell my story correctly, and I want to set you up to think carefully about what happens to stories when nothing in the world is going anywhere. What is *supposed* to happen in a story? What does narrative involve? How can I believably offer up a beginning, a middle, an end, along with all the usual paraphernalia of fiction — character development, progression of image and idea, cautionary moral, a downer to let you know this isn't propaganda for the Chamber of Commerce or something sweet and sentimental from the Bureau of Sleep?

=　　=　　=

One sunny morning last week I was sitting in the Café Italia trying to think my way through this story. I like the Café Italia. It's large and spacious, and most of the time Tony, the owner, fills it with the kind of music you hear in Fellini movies, the kind of music that makes you believe that life is a cheerful dance that drools significance. But on this particular morning Tony had tuned in an FM rock station, and the place was jammed with synthetic adrenalin instead. I could hear an aerobics/rock number by Olivia Newton-John called "Let's Get

Physical", one that presents life and love as messy distractions
that come up between the hours when the discos close down
and the muscle parlours open up. And the tune was having at
me, despite my attempts to close it out, when I spotted an
elderly man across the street.

He was carrying a manila folder under his arm, and he had a
bad leg that forced him to walk with an awkward hippity-hop.
I watched him make his way across the street, thinking that
the leg must be causing him some pain. Then I noticed that he
had a wide grin on his face, and that he was hop-hobbling in
perfect time to Olivia Newton-John.

I'd seen the old man before, and I began to remember the first
time I'd seen him, twenty years ago when I was in high school.
Tony brought over the cappuccino I'd ordered, noticed that I
was watching the old man, and smiled.

"He's a writer too," he said. "Did you know that?"

I knew but pretended I didn't so I could hear Tony's story. He
likes me hanging around, and in his shy European way he is
proud of my presence, and occasionally even curious about
what it is that I write in his café.

"Yes," Tony went on, "he's writing a book about World Government. He comes here every day, like you, and does some
writing on it."

"I know him a little," I admitted. "A long time ago he came to
my home town to teach in the school. He's an interesting man."

Tony nodded, not interested at all in *my* story. He knows the
old man as a street character in a big-city Italian neighbourhood, and probably thought I was making my story up. The old
man had lived in the neighbourhood for a long time, also
running a coffee bar, where he'd conducted an informal and
almost certainly illegal psychiatric practice. Everyone knew
him, and most knew he'd written books on a variety of subjects.
No one, including Tony, read his books, but that didn't
diminish the offhand kind of respect with which he was treated.

To them, as to me, he was Dr. X, from the University of Rome, subject and nature of doctorial expertise — obscure.

He appeared in my world one autumn to teach Health & Personal Development (a euphemism for social and sexual indoctrination) and drama at the high school. He was in his forties then, short and balding, and he spoke an articulate English under the liquid stutter of a heavy Italian accent. My HPD classes with him were different than any others I'd experienced. They consisted of long monologues concerning Familial Love and Duty and the Attractiveness of Romance as a Way of Living, the latter lessons illustrated frequently by equally long digressions about how much he loved his young and beautiful wife, who'd remained in Italy for reasons the Doctor easily convinced us were well beyond our understanding. I think, in retrospect, that he saw his job as one in which he was to provide us with a vision of how life was supposed to be, leaving the teaching of its detailed workings to the school of hard knocks, which was the one most of us were headed for.

His method of teaching drama was equally novel. In the very first class he announced that we were going to write a play of our own, and then perform it in front of the school. This was unheard of — like asking a teacher questions in Health and Personal Development class. There was to be no memorizing of tedious lines from incomprehensible Shakespeare tragedies, no examinations — in short, none of the conventional signposts by which we normally determined our place in the conservative cosmology of high school.

Nearly everyone, including most of his fellow teachers, quickly decided that the Doctor was crazy. But a few of my friends and I thought he was sensational. He carried around all kinds of exotic information, and he was a compulsive talker. We were his most appreciative audience in that small town, and after a few months, we were just about the only audience he had, aside from the local Women's Art Circle.

But the Doctor was neither nut nor screwball. Not at all. He was a much more unusual sort of human being. He was an expert on all varieties of credulity, and he taught my friends and me something about that limitless storehouse of human credulity, and how it can either be avoided or used to advantage. He taught us to pay attention to the way people chose small parts of reality to sustain themselves, and he taught us to pay equally close attention to the parts of reality those same people suppressed. But mostly he showed us how reality operated by being transparent in how he himself manipulated it. Exclusion, his teaching told us, is the truest trick of a charlatan. And, his teaching implied, exclusion is the most dangerous power of Science, Politics, and Art.

The Doctor never actually admitted that he was a professional charlatan. We recognized it only because he showed us that his identities were as multiple as his abilities. Shortly after he arrived in town he let it be known, for instance, that he was a painter and a psychologist. It was those two identities that brought him to the attention of the Women's Art Circle. Whether he discovered the Circle or the Circle discovered him will remain forever obscure, but he was soon at its centre. The town was short on Psychologists and Artists, just as it was short on everything but trees, trucks and money. The Doctor was from another world, and he played the role of the exotic to the hilt.

Nobody knew enough to be able to evaluate his competence. Only now, and only in the most protected circles, is the competence of Psychology and Psychiatry questioned, and then only in the abstract.

To be sure, a few wealthy loggers with wives in the Art Circle naturally made sure the Doctor's appointment by the school board would not be renewed, but that back-handed critique was predicated on simple jealousy.

Unfortunately, I don't know if the Doctor was a good painter or not. I saw some oil paintings of his that looked like copies of

Salvador Dali's paintings, slithering wristwatches and all, but I couldn't say if they were prints, copies that the Doctor made of the originals, or approximations of the style. Precise data after twenty years isn't available.

What I do remember is the afternoon he showed us the landscape paintings he was selling to the women in the Art Circle in large quantities, and I remember how he painted them: with his fingers. Then I remember him showing us how, when he blocked off a portion of these finger-manufactured landscapes, they *looked* like finger paintings. Then, as we watched, he took another of his paintings — also a landscape, but painted, he said, with brushes — and blocked off a portion of similar size. It looked to us like part of the whole painting.

"That's how you tell a good landscape painting," he said, "or any painting that's good. Any part of it can be recognized sensibly as part of its larger whole."

=   =   =

As an absolute tool for evaluating all painting, the Doctor's principle is faulty. But I still don't know if what he told us about representational painting is true or not. I've tried to find out, but no one seems to be able to confirm it one way or the other. Some of the authorities I've questioned — and there have been a few — just laughed at me, while others, more modestly, have admitted that they just don't know. The questions his casually offered principle raised in my non-painter's head do not, apparently, arise very often in the minds of the professional practitioners of the field. Few of them seem interested in landscape painting, preferring to leave it to the amateur Art Circles, amateur airplane pilots and to whoever (or whatever) paints those paintings that can be seen advertised on late night television, the ones that show up for sale in gas stations or vacant lots whenever the weather is pleasant. "Genuine Original Oil Paintings for under $49.95" say the signs, and lined up next to one another are five or six or fifty identical genuine original oil paintings. And people buy them, not because the paintings are "good" or "bad" but because they're there to buy, they're cheap, and there are more empty walls in the city than Salvador Dali could imagine in his most lascivious nightmare.

The Doctor stayed in my home town for just that one year. My friends and I enjoyed that year of our lives mainly because of him, and so, probably, did the members of the Women's Art Circle. Our drama class wrote an original play for him, which was about a migration of teenagers to the Planet Mars. When we performed it in front of the school, the other students thought it was funny in all the places where we meant it to be serious, and I contributed by forgetting most of my lines. The few teachers who attended the play left after ten minutes and drank coffee in the staff room. I never thought to ask myself if the play was recognizable as a sensible part of the rest of the world, and I'm pretty certain that not very many other people in town asked themselves questions like that. I don't think the Doctor enjoyed his year in my home town.

=   =   =

Twenty years later, here's the now-aged Doctor hobbling across the street with a half-written book on World Government under his arm, and I'm still wondering about his method of detecting bad landscape painting. He enters the Café Italia and sits down at the next table and orders a cappuccino.

He doesn't remember me, and I don't introduce myself. I've always assumed that he wanted to forget the episode in his career that I was part of, and for all my curiosity about people, I'm a reasonably considerate person. But he does look over at my table, sees my manuscript papers and my nearly empty cappuccino, and smiles at me. I grin back, and together, and in our separate ways, we go back to trying to figure out what is really going on, and what to think and say about it.

=   =   =

Let me try another way. Last night I watched the news on television. There was a long and unusually lurid film clip of a car-bombing in Lebanon. The news story contained no unique or even unusual pictorial or analytical content: it offered nothing about who had done the killing and nothing about why people were dying, and it seemed almost smug about not knowing. It was interested in the ever-renewable novelty of blood and gore, and it took delight in recounting statistics about how many people had been killed, particularly the numbers of women and children.

As I watched the film, I saw a man pull a dead infant from the rubble, and then pass the body to another man who carried it aloft through a crowd of onlookers, its small dark head flopping back and forth. Some of the people in the crowd were mourning, but many appeared to cheer at the sight of the dead child. As he reached the thick centre of the crowd, the man the camera was focused on leaped up onto some rubble, still holding the corpse of the child aloft with one arm, and raised his free arm *in a gesture of victory.*

Then the program faded to a commercial for men's cologne: a handsome, bronzed American male lifted a six-foot cologne bottle over his head, turned to the camera and brought the bottle down, exposing the brand name. He did not then give the victory sign. That commercial was followed by another on behalf of the Beef Growers Association, depicting a variety of ways to prepare and eat meat. That in turn was succeeded by a crisp commercial for a franchise restaurant advertising steak and prawns, and implying that if I was really socially competent I would eat their food and participate in their lifestyle. The jingle was catchy, and the people who appeared in the commercial appeared to be extremely pleased about something. Finally, there was the fourth commercial, again advertising perfume, but this time for women.

I clicked off the television set at that point, having seen more than the newscast intended me to see, and realizing instantly that I'd seen the Doctor's recognition principle inside out.

The first conclusion any sane person will draw from the sequence is that television has produced a new and toxic strain of vulgarity. It should be banned. But we already know that, and we watch television anyway, right?

What I would like to draw your attention to is not a moral issue, but a technical one: where does a story begin, what are its responsibilities to material and social existence, and where does the story end?

It *can* end with a bang. Those cold-eyed and fundamentally crazed logicians who run our governments — ours and theirs — *can* push those red buttons many of us have nightmares about. If they do, they'll do it out of sheer terror and frustration, because they don't want to live outside the insular body of professional procedure, and they must certainly be aware, like everyone else, that the body is decaying rapidly all around them. We all look alike these days, sad splendid animals that we are, hobbling up and down the indeterminate corridors of the Institution in perfect time to Olivia Newton-John with our singular memories and our ideas about World Government.

But what if the story *doesn't* end, and what if the present confusion is just signalling to us that we have to reinvent the story? Maybe you recall the Doctor's young and beautiful wife, the one who remained in Italy for reasons that were beyond the ken of me and my teen-aged friends. Did you find yourself wondering if she really existed, or if the Doctor just made her up?

At the time, a lot of people wondered. No one could figure out how such a beautiful young woman could love a short, fat, balding middle-aged charlatan teaching drama, social behaviour and sex educations to loggers' kids in a small town, and mass-producing landscape paintings with his fingers. Even I doubted the existence of the Doctor's beloved wife, although he often showed us a rumpled snapshot of her that he carried in his wallet. But the woman in the snapshot — beautiful and white-blonde-haired — could be, I thought, from anywhere.

And anyway, Italian women don't have blonde hair. I don't know what the women in the Art Circle believed, but I did find out, years later, that he showed the photograph to them too, although for what reasons, and to what effect, I've never discovered. Maybe he turned them all down because he loved her so much, or maybe he used the photo to convince them he was the finest lover in all the world.

I can verify, however, that the young woman in the photograph was the Doctor's wife. About ten years ago I saw them together on this same street, where he now hobbles around with his book on World Government. They were walking arm-in-arm, and she looked ten years older than her photograph, but she was, if anything, more beautiful. And if appearances mean anything, she and the Doctor were very much in love.

I know this isn't much to go on, and I don't even know where the Doctor's wife is now. I haven't seen them together for several years. But when I think of them together, and when I see him bumping across the street like the crippled butterfly he is, the world brightens, and the stinking colossus of doom that darkens everything these days dissolves, and the walls that enclose us open up to the story as it might be, whirling around and around in the air.

Roses Are Red

Cynthia Flood

"Our birth is but a sleep and a forgetting." So wrote Wordsworth; so quoted Queen Elizabeth, admiringly, at the opening of a modern institute for training in obstetrics. Some things I can't forget happened during my labour with our first child, but finally the doctors did more or less say, "Oh let's knock her out and be done with it," and did. When I came up through nausea and confusion I was doubtful about the red wriggling creature they brought to me and said was Colin. Was he mine? Stories of mix-ups in name bracelets. Unlikely in a small hospital in a smallish Maritime city, but I could believe it. Of course Roger was not with me during the birth; this was before such a notion was at all acceptable.

We moved then, to head office in Toronto, and Janet was born in a large urban hospital. Roger was away that time, in England. I was frightened, of course, on my way to the hospital, but felt also that my body was working in a more confident manner than the first time. The contractions came regularly and bearably. However, my labour had begun late at night. I became very tired; they said I could not push effectively and gave me an epidural. In the morning, though, I saw my daughter emerge from me, knew her immediately as mine, and was glad, for she was the last child we planned.

Then we moved again, here to Vancouver. Roger was promoted to responsibility for sales to the Pacific Rim countries, and travels now in the Orient a great deal. Our shared life continues in its I suppose rather peculiar pattern. The children and I are together all the time, and I am happy with them on the whole. I read and read and read. Getting Janet and Colin settled in kindergarten and Grade Two in a new school and city, and fixing up our new house, seem to take most of my energies. So I read, and watch TV, and put up wallpaper. By the time Roger returns from a trip I am spilling over with material I need to express and get reactions to, but that is not so easy for a couple after an extended separation, when there are many other practical and tangible things which cannot be delayed it seems. I think perhaps they could, but I am so warmed and invigorated by his talkative energetic presence, the children enjoy the expeditions we go on so much, and I so relish hearing what he has done and seen that I don't declare myself very strongly. I suppose this is what happens. Then after he has left again I think of all the things I wish I had said.

Recently I found myself pregnant again. I have read enough to know that this does not happen to educated middle-class women in their thirties, whose older children are already in school, for no good reason. At some level then did I will this? Did I deliberately put too little jelly on the diaphragm, insert it carelessly? Not that I remember. Roger is delighted at the prospect of a third child. He loves Colin and Janet extravagantly. I feel remarkably little. Oh, predictably there is fatigue at the thought of the night feedings and the diapers, and joy, and curiosity too — our son and daughter are very different in character, and I wonder what this new child will be like — but none of these feelings is very strong.

The one thing I am clear on is that I want this birth to be different. This will definitely be the last, for I shall have a tubal ligation after the birth. When I enter that world for the last time, I want to know what is happening, and why, and how. I decided to enroll in a series of childbirth classes. I told Roger, and he said, "But darling, why do you want to do this? You've had two already, what could you possibly learn?" He was to leave for a two-month trip for exactly the period that the classes would cover. But I went ahead, and booked a babysitter, and on the first night of class I went out of the house feeling almost excited.

When I entered the room in the church basement, I saw ten heavily-pregnant women lying in a circle on ten pillowed slabs of green foam. Behind them on spindly metal chairs sat ten men. On the floor in the middle of the circle were piled books and pamphlets on childbirth, breast-feeding, nutrition. I found myself a place and lay down. Some of the couples were talking to one another and I felt that the others were looking at me, alone. I wanted to pick up something and read but made myself not. I must not give in so easily. Clearly the women had all dressed themselves with as much care as I had for the occasion. It was strange how the vivid smocks, the shining hair and tinted lips seemed to draw attention to the lump each carried before her. Most of the men wore double-knit leisure suits in pastel colours. Roger did not wear things like that and again I felt out of place. The men sat shifty-eyed, trying to size each other up without being noticed. One had a roll of bristly fat oozing over his collar.

The teacher came in. I was surprised, I think everyone was. I suppose I had expected a childbirth teacher to be soft, maternal, charming? But this was a tall bone of a woman, with a long buck-toothed face, big hands and feet, intelligent grey eyes. I liked her at once. Her stomach under her neat denims seemed positively concave. I saw Boar-Neck's face give a little twitch of distaste, which I think she felt, for she looked nervous as she sat down with us on the floor. I sensed that she was going to begin with a joke, was anxious.

"Well, good evening, everyone," she said too rapidly. "My name's Peg. That's Peg, mind you, not Preg!" A nice clear English voice. People laughed, too readily. She took a deep breath and said more slowly, "Now I imagine that most of you women are happy to be here, and that you're looking forward to learning as much as you can in these nine weeks of classes. And I imagine most of you fellows had to be dragged here and wish to goodness you were someplace else. Right?" She knew exactly what she was talking about, I could tell from her tone.

The couples looked at each other, smiled, looked at their teacher again.

Then a mocking male voice with an English accent said, "Very skillfully done, Peg," and I along with everyone else turned to look at the handsome man who had spoken. How had I missed him in my look-round? He wore a good three-piece suit, like Roger's, and while the other men sat with feet twisted round chair legs he leaned back as if in a La-Z-Boy recliner, displaying his long frame and legs and expensive gleaming shoes. His smile said, "And how are you going to cope with *me*?"

"Thanks," said Peg straightforwardly, and met his stare. After a few seconds he chuckled and broke the eye-contact. Peg looked relieved. She asked us to introduce ourselves.

The man who had spoken leaned down and whispered to his wife, a pale young woman with long floating hair who wore a plain blue linen dress. She looked a lot younger than he, and then I realized another reason why I felt so out of place — I was the oldest woman there by years. No wonder some of them had looked at me so oddly. The young woman's face did not change when her husband spoke to her and took her hand. When he sat upright again she removed her hand from his and placed it protectively over the enormous hump of her stomach.

The voices continued quietly round the circle. I'm Eleanor. I'm Don. This is our first child. This is our second, I'm Shelly, he's Martin. We have an adopted little boy and I'm so happy to be pregnant. (Smiles of empathy.) I had a hard time with our first, the doctors were terrible (puzzled frowns, Peg's among them), and I'm hoping this one will be easier if I can really learn from this course. Sandra, Wayne. The doctor thinks I may have trouble carrying to term. Now me.

"I'm Linda. My husband's away on a long business trip, so that's why I'm here alone." But would he have come with me anyway? Would he have stayed, after seeing these people who were not our kind?

"Don't worry," said Peg comfortably, "you'll learn it all and then teach him when he comes home. Is this your first?"

"Oh no, my third. I didn't — well, the first two experiences weren't that good."

"That's what we're here for, to make it better."

The lovely young woman now.

"I'm Grace."

"I'm Garth," rather loudly. "This is our first. Not for want of trying, though!" And he gave a big wink at the man next him. Boar-Neck and several others recoiled. We all looked at the floor, at the walls, at Peg. She looked intently at the next couple in the circle.

"I'm Jane," said the woman nervously. Peg smiled at her, Jane's voice picked up strength, and the process continued till all the couples had introduced themselves. I looked at Grace. The stillness of her face had not altered. She gazed down at her hands on the baby-lump. Some of the other women were also looking at her, puzzled.

Then Peg began her introductory talk. As her clear friendly voice traced the history of natural childbirth practices from Dick-Read to Lamaze, Kitzinger to Leboyer, I felt myself relax and become absorbed. This was what I had come for. The attention of the class was total. Some people asked questions. Peg encouraged women who had had babies before to explain or comment by describing their own labours. They were not very articulate, but I knew what they were talking about, for the power came clearly through their words, the immense taking-over power of that experience. Grace listened and listened, her hands rubbing back and forth slowly over her baby. I did not speak, though Peg's glance invited me to. Garth stared continually at Peg and she avoided looking at him.

Then we had a juice-or-coffee break, and the smokers were sent out into a little ante-room. Grace reached for a book and began reading attentively. I lay and watched the class. Garth joined the smokers. At first the group looked sideways at him and did not move. He began to talk to one of the couples. I could see him turning on the charm, I've Roger do the same thing at parties, and saw the woman laugh. A moment later there was a sort of ripple in the group, and there was Garth in the admiring middle. One of the men looked curiously at Grace, who was turning a page. What would Roger make of this? I had a letter half-written to him at home; how would I describe this class to him? Peg was checking through some file-cards. Once when there was a big laugh at something Garth had said she looked up. She seemed nonplussed and returned to her work.

After the break Peg began teaching us how to do the first level of special breathing, for use at the beginning of contractions. A-level: in nose, out mouth, in nose, out mouth, very gentle blow-out, barely bend a candle-flame. All of us women lay flat, eyes focused on chosen points of gaze, breathing quietly, absorbed. At first I felt silly but that passed very quickly. The men were doing it too, and the ones I could see didn't even look embarrassed any more. There was such a good feeling of learning in the room. Peg came round to check that each of us was doing the breathing properly. She came last to Grace and Garth. Grace was staring at the coatrack as though seeing a vision. Her hands still moved rhythmically over her stomach and I could hear her smooth regular breaths.

I could hear Garth doing the breathing too, with a kind of satiric perfection, as if saying, "Dearie, this is just *too* easy for someone as clever as I am." Peg sat back on her heels and gave him that straightforward grey gaze again. He snorted with laughter and stopped. Peg said, "That's fine," as if to a serious student, as if trying to convert this sarcasm to honest effort. Nothing on Grace's face. Peg got up; she was ungainly, I saw contempt flicker in Garth's expression, I saw her flush.

He said, looking up at her body, "Tell me, is this all just theory for you? Or do you have experience in the field?"

"Yes," she said simply, looking down at him. "All instructors for this course have borne children. My husband and I have two." He began to smile and she turned to the class as a whole. "Any questions about what we've done tonight? Okay then, practise the pelvic rock and the A-level breathing, and I'll see you next week." She began picking up the books from the floor. Garth glanced around and several of the men grinned at him. The women looked blank. Then they heaved themselves up from the pads and the men sorted out coats in a jovial bustling way. There was a lot of cheerful talking in the parking lot.

On the way home I realized that the thing between Garth and Peg had to do — partly anyway — with language. I have learned from Roger about the gradations of accent in England, and I knew enough to recognize that Garth's manner of speech was higher-level than Peg's. His and Roger's were alike. I looked a long time at the blank half-page of my letter to him. Finally I wrote, "The first class in the childbirth course was very interesting. I'll tell you more about it next time. Love, Linda."

In a subsequent class Peg said, "Do you know what happens to women's pelvic bones during a pregnancy? They soften. That's to facilitate passage of the baby's head. Then after the birth they harden up again."

And she said, "Colostrum. That's not been understood generally until recently. People thought it was just gunk that had to be sucked out of the breasts before the milk could come through. A sort of plug. But you know, our bodies don't do wasteful things like that. Colostrum. Full of protection for your baby, protection against disease. No medical lab could make it better." Roger never liked the sound of a baby breast-feeding, the eager squelchy sucking. Both of ours had gone on the bottle at three months.

And she said, "I'll teach you all I can about second stage. How to push. But really you already know. When the time comes, it'll seem so obvious you'll think, 'Why did she bother? Of course this is how I do it.'" Several women laughed, not in ridicule. I hoped with all my heart that this would be so for me, this last time.

And she said, "Pregnant women have really amazing endurance. Courage. Not only physical, but mental and emotional too. Women have coped with all sorts of awful situations for the sake of the unborn child, and borne it strong and healthy at the end too." She looked down at her notes and went on to the next point. I did not move my own eyes, but could feel a couple of glances going past me to Grace.

And she said, "Everyone always wants to know, Will it hurt? The answer is Yes. There's no point saying otherwise. For some of you a lot and for some of you a little. But you'll know why. And you'll know what to do, or have done, about it." It was very good that she said this so matter-of-factly. I think that those of us who had already had children felt pardoned, in a way, and those who were pregnant for the first time felt relieved.

Roger wrote, "Tell me more about this course you're taking. Does the teacher treat you like a graduate student?"

I wrote, "Our teacher is English, I think from the north — Huddersfield? The exercises she is teaching us are based on the theory of psycho-prophylaxis. Some of them are quite hard to do. You'll have to learn quickly when you come home."

He wrote, "Are you really sure you want me to be there? I bet it'll just pop out, this time."

I could not visualize Roger in the class at all.

As I was leaving for class three or four weeks later, I realized that I had not changed my clothes. I was wearing jeans and the old shirt of Roger's that I'd had on all day. That night I saw that many of us were less dressed up, made up, than we had been at the beginning. I thought of dancers practising, the stripped-down look, hair bound back, total absorption in the movement of the body, in the discipline and understanding of the flesh. Also I liked the words, the terms, that we were learning, and found that several of the women shared my pleasure. We enjoyed using this gynaecological and obstetrical tongue with each other. Pride, really, it was. I tried to express this to Roger, giving him examples — dilation, effleurage, presentation. He wrote, "My goodness, this all sounds terribly technical," and I could see him sitting in the Tokyo hotel room, filling the crisp blue airletter before him on the desk.

I felt that Peg was preparing us, we were preparing, to give birth honourably, no matter how our labours turned out.

Yet one thing about the class distressed me, nibbled at the edges of autonomy.

The men. Why were they there?

Peg said, "You fellows now. You've got to understand that there's two of you having this baby. You're a team. It's all teamwork."

She also said, "You have to know all that I'm teaching as well as your wives do. Better, in fact. You've got to know the signs of transition, so you can tell her when to change to the special breathing if she doesn't do it herself. You have to notice if she's hyperventilating. Or if she's getting leg cramps. Or if she's becoming exhausted. The doctors will rely on you."

And she also said, "Remember, you're the coaches." She said this many times.

A lot of us found the C-level breathing hard to learn. It requires high control. As always, Grace had no difficulty learning it. She seemed to do everything perfectly, and she always had that disquieting passionate look, as if she saw something no one else could. Not something pleasant; occasionally her expression was close to horror, revulsion, strange looks on the pretty young face. She looked so young to me. She was very much alone. By now the rest of us women chatted in groups, before class and during the break. I tried, several of us tried, to include Grace, but she did not respond and we stopped. The only person to whom she related was Peg.

Garth — of course — also breathed C-level like a master on the first try. He watched the struggles of the class for a bit and then said, "Oh come on girls, you can do it. Can't they, fellow-coaches? Look, we'll show you," and he began loud C-level breathing, gesturing to the other men to copy him. Many did. Many of the wives looked at them anxiously, humbly, and tried again. I could feel exactly how I would have looked to Roger if he had been there. I looked to Peg for help but she was working intensively with one couple — deliberately? — and did not see what was happening. I could sense us women retreating into our separate selves, and I swear I could almost see bonds forming between Garth and the other men.

Then when we had to lie on our sides to practise breathing for transition, Garth gave Grace a heave over, saying, "OK fatty, here you go!" Grace did not react. But a lot of the men chuckled. Some of the women looked hurt, puzzled, and one had tears in her eyes as her husband exasperatedly "helped" her to turn over. I was glad that I had to make the move myself.

Then, in the sixth class, the childbirth film was shown. At the moment when the baby's head began to emerge from the mother's body there was a close-up. The silence in the classroom was complete. People held their breaths. Then Garth's voice broke in, saying chattily, "Bit of a butcher-shop look to the whole thing, isn't there?" And indeed there was a lot of blood about, but I am sure that most of us, women and men alike, had been seeing new life. It was a near thing. There was some relieved male laughter, but then Peg said, "Look, there's the shoulder turning," and it was, and there was a great rush and the child was born and the class fully caught up once more. Of course Garth's words still stayed in the mind.

Now here is the part that I don't know how to try to communicate to Roger. I can feel so exactly what his response will be: "But Linda, why didn't you do something about this man, if he was as nasty as you say?" Why indeed? Why didn't *we*? Particularly, why didn't I? I had age and experience on my side. I suppose I am a coward. I could imagine so easily how Garth

would turn aside, turn around, anything I might say and transform it into emotionalism or prudery. And I did not know if the
other women would support me, with their husbands there.
And I could not think of what to say. It was hard, because
Garth's manoeuvres were so quick. Seconds after he'd spoken
and the class had reacted, he and his followers would be back
in their serious student roles, breathing or counting or singing
their D-level songs. A few times Peg said, "Garth, please.
Attend to your own practising," or, "Garth, I think the class is
doing just fine on their own." And he would say, "But Peg, I
was only trying to help," and look aggrieved; and some of the
men — and one or two of the women — would give little
snickers, and then Peg's reaction would seem like a silly fuss.
She stopped. I did not want that to happen to me.

I believe that most of the other women, and a few of the men,
felt as I did, but none of us spoke up. It was something like this:
These classes are about preparation for the birth of a loved
child. That's *all*. They are not about confrontation, or rudeness,
or mockery, or hatred. So even if there is someone introducing
these things, we will not grant them validity by countering. I
did not even speak to Peg, though I knew she would have
welcomed my approach, welcomed an ally. That's perhaps
what I feel worst about, that I didn't move towards her. But I
did not want to be in that ruling role. And I suppose we all
thought — I know I did — the usual things like, There are only
a few classes left anyway, and We don't want to waste precious
time with this stuff. But still what it amounts to is that we, I, did
nothing. Not then. And therefore, I believe, other things had
to happen. After a certain point they had to, as after a certain
point abortion cannot happen and a birth must.

Garth went on making his nasty interventions.

Grace looked at Peg with grateful love and otherwise behaved
as though she were alone in the room.

We, the women, began to look angrily at Grace.

"She should do something."

"He's her husband, after all."

"She should speak to him." I myself said that.

"I think she's crazy."

"So do I."

And so we went further than stopping our attempts to include her. We avoided her.

Now we were at the seventh class. One of the couples in the group was Japanese, and neither wife nor husband spoke fluent English. Peg had got into the habit of spending the ten-minute break with them, going over the material just presented to make sure they had understood. At first the class smiled on her for doing this. Then I heard Garth in the smokers' circle say, "Seems a bit unfair to me. I mean why should the Japs, sorry, Mr. and Mrs. Nakamura, get all her attention? They should have special classes for these people. Of course this is the first class Peg's handled all on her own" — how had he found that out? was it true, even? — "so perhaps she's just not able to deal with this sort of problem yet. Pity." That was the first time he had moved openly against Peg herself, and the excellence of her teaching was armour against his words; yet when people came back into the classroom there was a murmur all round the circle as the non-smokers heard what Garth had said. He looked smug. Mr. and Mrs. Nakamura had that awful look of people who know they are being talked about but don't know what is being said, except that it's negative.

Here again, you see, I think of Roger. How by this time in the class he would have known the Nakamuras — I didn't even know that was their name till I heard Garth say it, I had stayed at the friendly-to-foreigners smile level — in fact he would have known everybody's name. And instead of lying on my mat during the breaks, I would have been up with him, socializing in the anteroom, even though neither of us smokes. And how he would have said to Garth, robust and direct, "That won't do. Peg's meeting her responsibilities to *all* the people in the class, best as she can." And he would have gotten friendly with Peg and chatted with her about England; almost certainly he would have found a friend of a friend, or a place, or an occasion, that they had in common from their lives in Britain, and Peg would have warmed to him and felt some support. At least I think, I hope, that's what he would have done.

In the second half of the class that seventh evening the topic was baby needs — clothing, furniture, toys. Discussion showed that some new parents were buying as if there were no tomorrow — I remember doing that for Colin — and others were relying on borrowings and hand-me-downs. Garth's eyes glittered, and then somehow the issue became whether each set of parents was buying a new crib or using a second-hand one. It was dreadful, the ugliness, judging each other on the criterion of money. Boar-Neck's wife was almost in tears and so was I; I have rarely felt so helpless. Peg finally spoke, angry and nervous.

"Really, Garth, you make it sound as though people like us who don't have much money can't really love our children."

"But I said nothing of the kind!" he expostulated. "Did I?" and of course he himself had not. But on this matter even some of his most ardent followers were on the other side, and so he lost ground. Temporarily.

"Lot of silly extravagance, I'd say."

"Just for show."

"As long as the baby's warm and cosy, what does he care, eh?"

"Right dear," said Boar-Neck.

Peg then firmly moved the class back into session, and said we would take a few minutes for any questions, on any subject. Episiotomy was mentioned. Was this really necessary? Always? Evidently in the Scandinavian countries obstetrical staff were trained to ease the baby's head out slowly, gently, so that there was no tearing. Peg frowned, and then some of the women who had already borne children began to speak up.

And I myself said, "Those damn stitches were so sore afterwards. That was almost the worst part, hardly able to sit down for days." And others were starting to tell similar stories, when Peg interrupted, speaking sharply as she had never done before.

"Well then? You want not to have an episiotomy, and risk tearing right from the vagina back to the anus, massive repairs, your body ruined, semi-incontinent perhaps? Well then go ahead. But if you take my advice you'll listen to your doctor and if he wants to do an episiotomy he should do it." She looked down at her lap and we saw her shaking. We were all quiet and afraid.

Garth said, "Trust your doctor, eh? Doctor knows best?" There was joy in his voice. "You'd agree with that, Peg?"

She took a deep breath. "I'm sorry I spoke as I did. But I still think what I said is right. Now please, just before we leave, let's have some breathing practice. For transition, please. Husbands, give your wives the count."

Garth smiled broadly as we women all obediently turned over, wanting to do our best for Peg — at least that's what I felt as I tapped the rhythm on my leg. We lay there, all us women, going, "One-two, one-two, hah!" And for a few moments everything began to feel right again, the learning was taking over. Then Garth began to parody our breathing, making sounds like the heavy gasps given just before orgasm. Boar-Neck snorted, a few men completely broke up in laughter, several women turned red, I could feel heat erupting on my own face. But again he stopped so fast and got his own people back into real practising so fast that some of the class didn't even grasp what was happening. The atmosphere was terrible, anger and discord and humiliation jittering and jagging as we got ready to go home. I could hardly wait to get out of the room. Peg did what she could, spoke to each couple in her best friendly-teacher manner, but I could see that although they were grateful many felt that the thing was simply too much for her.

Damn Garth, what he'd said about this being her first class
series. The cars pulling out of the parking lot were noisy with
argument and tears. I was grateful to be home, so glad to be
away from the shame of not having spoken. I drove home and
reread Roger's most recent letter. "I don't care for the way most
of the men here seem to treat their wives. They are extremely
courteous but I think that is only on the surface. There doesn't
seem to be the companionship you and I have."

All that next week I said to myself that I was not going to go to
the next class and all the time I knew surely that I would. I
thought about Grace. There must be some ruling reason why
she had to stay with Garth till the baby was born. Money? She
had none although obviously he did? Once I'd heard Garth say,
"Since we've been in Vancouver," so perhaps she was
friendless? (Who, after all, could I turn to if I were in the same
boat?) I felt dreadful for the way I had behaved to her, and yet
it did not seem as though it was wholly me, us, the other
women, who made and kept up the barriers. Was it that she
felt she had only strength to cope alone and could not handle
any new connections, attentions? As if she had drawn a circle
around herself and the baby. There was a quality in her which
I found very moving. To say virginal of a pregnant woman
appears stupid — but I remember it in myself and I have seen
it in other women carrying a child for the first time. There is a
purity of concentration, a fresh bloom. These meet their end
in the birth and do not come again in subsequent pregnancies.

I wrote to Roger on the morning of the eighth class. "I'll be so
glad to see you next Tuesday. My last class ends just an hour
before your plane gets in, so I'll have good time to get out to
the airport. Roger, when you are home we must talk about
ourselves." Then I thought I should have written, "I want to
talk to you about myself," but I did not want to cross out what
I had written nor to recopy the whole letter, so I sealed and
mailed it as it was.

The first part of the eighth class was low-key, after all my, our,
agitation. The class was smaller, though; one or two couples

were not there, and Peg did not make any happy
announcements. We had visitors, two sets of parents from a
previous class series and their extremely small babies. The
sight of those two wrinkled snuffling infants was very satisfy-
ing, especially to the first-time parents. They were real, they
had really come, after all the muscle relaxations and counting
and breathing and exercising. Grace hardly blinked as she
gazed at them. Peg seemed pleased at the happy attentive class
before her, and then towards the end of the hour I saw her
glance at her watch and run her tongue nervously over her big
teeth.

When we gathered again after the break, Peg did not sit down
with us in the circle. Standing at the edge, she cleared her
throat.

"Tonight," she said, "we're having a dress rehearsal. We're
going to start towards the end of first stage. Go through
transition. Second stage. Pushing practice. Special breathing
for crowning. Delivery. And to make it as real as possible I've
brought some props." She went swiftly to a standing partition
at the end of the room and emerged pushing a tall narrow
stretcher with a thin green leathery mattress. At one end, metal
stirrups clanked and wobbled. The delivery table was piled
with masks, green gowns, draping cloths, gloves, packets of
instruments. Everyone gasped, there was excited Oh look
chatter. Peg smiled. Her lips were tight over her teeth.

"Now we need a mother. No girls, not you. I don't want one of
you pushing too hard and suddenly doing the real thing. We
need one of the fellows to play mother. I think we need Garth,"
and her long bony finger pointed straight at him.

There was a great Aaah sound as we all took breath. And
looked at Garth. He was completely taken aback and for a
second did nothing and then it was too late, I was getting up,
we were going at him, and we were all around him, he was
surrounded by enormous bellies.

"A good plan." That was Mr. Nakamura.

"I like it, I like it!" That was Boar-Neck.

"Sorry, dear fellow-students," said Garth in his snottiest and most sarcastic tone, looking up at us, "but it's no go."

"Oh yes it is," said Peg, and we women moved in more closely around him and then he was up. We moved him en bloc, nudging him along to the table. He stumbled and I shoved him upright. I could hardly believe what I was doing. I turned to see Grace. She gave one long intent look at the procession on its way to the caseroom. Then she picked up a book.

Garth stood by the delivery table. His face was fish-belly white. The atmosphere of the room was terrific, silence pounding. I don't know if he got on the table by himself or if we pushed him, but there he was, flat on his back. We all got round the table and shared out gowns and masks and put them on. The gowns looked like giant bibs.

We got a gown and a pair of long green floppy socks on to Garth. I myself took his beautifully-polished shoes and threw them on the floor. Roger would have had a fit. One woman shoved a pillow under his head. One took his pulse. One listened to the fetal heartbeat. Peg said, "Contraction starting now," and we ran him right up through the breathing levels from A to D and down again.

"You didn't sing anything for D," I heard my voice saying sharply.

"Transition's just about over," said one of the women.

"Up then," said Peg, and two of us took Garth's feet and put them into the stirrups. He looked awkward, helpless, legs in the air and genital area wide open. Several women smiled, and I felt my lips opening.

"Contraction now," said one.

"He's not breathing properly," said another.

"They get confused in transition," said a third, "here, give him the rhythm." And we all chanted, "One-two, one-two, hah!" We stopped.

"Next time you can push, dear," said one of the women kindly.

The men watched the birth the way birds watch snakes. A couple of them were dragging on unlit cigarettes. The woman next me happened to glance their way in search of a syringe, and they flinched as if a searchlight had fallen on them.

Grace had laid down her book.

"Contraction now. Head back, deep breath, head down, *down*. And push. Push!"

"Down and forward and out. Down and forward and out."

"He's a rotten pusher."

"They all expect to have it done for them, these days."

"Shall we put him out?"

"No, make him push some more, he's just lazy."

"Come on now mother, we've got work to do, we can't do it all for you, you know."

"Here we go again. Deep breath, head down, *down*. And push. Push!"

"He's not getting anywhere with this."

"Epidural and forceps."

"OK."

"Now dear we're going to give you a little shot."

"Turn him over."

"No, wait till he's in the middle of a contraction, it hurts them more then."

"Over."

"Back down now."

"Now dear, you can't tell when a contraction's starting any more, 'cause you're frozen. *We'll* tell you when it's happening."

"Push now. Push." That was Peg.

Roger's face, Garth's face, I mean, very white now, a few tears on the cheeks even.

"No point in snivelling, mama, you're almost there."

"What're you crying for? You can't feel anyway."

"There's the head."

"No more pushing. Gently next time, be crowning now."

"He doesn't know what that means. Listen dear, just don't push so hard now, OK?"

"Shallow breathing, lightly lightly, that's right."

"Soon your beautiful baby will be born."

The whole class was now stiff with excitement waiting for ? to be born. Birth, birth, new life, the excitement, the fear, will it be all right? Oh please let it be all right, let it come, be born now, oh be born now, now, new life be born.

"Head's all out. Gently now."

"Next time'll be it."

"Shoulder's turning."

"There!"

We all moved back from the delivery table a bit, and the woman who had been bending down close to Garth's crotch stood up, triumphant, cradling in her arms — nothing, of course. The emotional temperature in the room fell about thirty degrees. She turned uncertainly to Grace.

"Did you want a boy or a girl?"

Our fantasy disintegrated before Grace's expression of nauseated loathing.

The doctor uncradled her arms and took off her medical accoutrements, and the rest of us did the same. Garth got his feet awkwardly out of the stirrups. His hair was messed, his Pierre Cardin shirt rumpled. Silence. Hatred. Rage. Some of the men went to get coats. Garth walked over to Grace and sat down by her to tie his shoelaces. She looked at him.

What a look.

With gravid dignity she rose and walked out of the room. The child went before her. Peg took a step after her and then stood still, concerned.

We women were still red-faced and panting.

Garth got his coat and buttoned it up. There were twin threads of saliva at the corners of his mouth. He went shakily out.

"Does he ever look crazy," said Boar-Neck. People blinked.

Today I got a letter from Roger. It seems he unexpectedly spent the last two days of his trip out of Tokyo, so he won't have got my last letter.

Tonight was the last class. Grace and Garth weren't there. Peg didn't say why. The group was low-key and attentive. People smiled at each other gently, carefully, and some of the couples held hands. When the lesson was over, Boar-Neck thanked Peg on behalf of the class, and we all clapped. Peg blushed.

Then came the surprise. The men had arranged for flowers to be delivered to the classroom, and so there were red roses for each mother-to-be. Some of the women cried.

The road to the airport is busy as usual. I have to think hard about my driving, for I'm awkward behind the wheel now that I'm so big. But I can feel the roses crimson on the seat beside me, and soon Roger will see them, and I shall have to try to explain.

Wedding Ninotchka

Yeshim Ternar

Part I

There was a time when mother was pure and dreamy and glamorous. Mother insisted that I know her as she was at that time. As a result, I knew mother best in that time period before I existed. She was at the height of all her accomplishments then. She spoke languages; guided not just her own family, but a group of other generals and their families across India. It was during the same trip that she was sixteen and one night alone at Taj Mahal, under a full moon, she was so moved by the power of love that she cried. She was very pure and innocent then. Everyone marvelled at her command of languages and her knowledge of the history of the different cities they visited, her ease with court etiquette, and her ability with mathematics. She was also very beautiful then. She inspired men to write poetry. They elevated her to the ranks of angels. They told her she looked like Ava Gardner. Those years her sister still looked like Shirley Temple.

To a party at the British Embassy in Kabul shortly before the second world war one night, she wore a dress of pastel green tulle. She had copied its design from an American carte-postale that had found its way to a variety store where the diplomats shopped. In that carte-postale, Greta Garbo posed sideways. She was the heroine of a movie mother does not remember seeing either at the British Embassy or the German Embassy. But no matter. She had not bought the postcard to remind herself of the movie. On the contrary, she knew that she had a duty to perform and that was to represent her country at those balls. Of course she wanted to leave the best impressions with diplomats and generals and Khans.

Grandmother remembers the dress as her creation. The original idea was hers; Greta Garbo only confirmed it and added a few embellishments. It was a strange coincidence that Greta Garbo had chosen to wear that same dress to have her picture taken for the international carte-postale. But of course, that also confirmed mother's and grandmother's conviction that this was indeed the dress mother should wear to the British Embassy party.

"Was it a garden party, mother?"

"This one wasn't. This party was to honour the birthday of the ambassador's wife. She was quite an ugly woman with the standard bony British look. She used to wear the strangest of satin hats perched sideways on her ridiculous hair-do. She never lost her dignity at a party, though. When I was younger, I used to wonder if women like her ever laughed aloud."

"Maybe they did mother, if they ran into their bedrooms, and locked the door. Maybe they laughed a lot when they were alone. Then when they go all their laughs out, they went down the stairs into the Empire Ballroom."

"Yes, and this party was in the Empire Ballroom. The crystal chandeliers and the crystal mirrors sparkled with the colours of the guest's gowns. All the blues, pinks, oranges, and greens: the organdie, satin, chintz, and taffeta struck you in flashes reflecting from the glass that was everywhere and over-whelmed you."

"Were you allowed to drink at those parties, mother?"

"I remember drinking my first glass of wine when I was sixteen. It was at the same party. The German Ambassador, Herr Bundel he was, a rare representative of the Germans at this British party, offered me my first glass of champagne. It was clear Rhine champagne. I still don't understand how they imported those wines and cheeses from Europe into Afghanistan. We had plenty of the best of everything at those parties. Herr Bundel had twinkling blue eyes, a trifle sad.

Like the Baltic Sea in the winter wind. He said to me, bending
down a little, for he was a tall slender man, 'Leila, you are a
delightful young woman. I would like to offer you our best
champagne.' He filled a crystal glass and presented it to me.
Then he filled a glass for himself and lightly touched mine. I
still remember the ring of those two glasses. There is nothing
like pure crystal if you want echoes.

"I sipped it slowly, looking at his eyes. He watched my hair. My
hair was beautiful then. It was a natural deep black. In those
years, it was fashionable to have discreet waves in your hair.
How I used to try to get it just right with every wave in place
except one loose one falling in the middle of the forehead as if
it was accidentally freed by the wind.

"I was a little tipsy after my first glass. I tried to suppress my
laughter, so I looked down at the folds of my dress; the green
tulle one that we had sewn for the party. The bodice was taffeta
of the same colour. So was the inner skirt. It was the outer skirt
that was tulle. We had appliqued hundreds of small taffeta
leaves on the tulle. My skirt looked like a shower of leaves
flowing from my waist. When I bent my head down to hide my
laughter, I felt that I laughed through the rustle and rush of
leaves."

Grandmother remembers the hours of patient, meticulous
stitching that went into the making of that dress: "We worked
for hours, weeks before the party. Imagine, each leaf had to be
cut identically. Then we pinned each one to the skirt to create
the feeling of a leaf shower. Leila would put on the dress and I
would ask her to turn slowly, rotating slightly with miniature
dance steps. She had big feet even then and she always took
big steps however hard she tried. As a result, it took hours for
us to get those leaves just right on the skirt."

"Did you sew the whole dress yourself, grandmother?"

"Oh, that's another story," said grandmother. "The British
Embassy recommended an Afghan tailor whom we located in
downtown Kabul in a run-down building. His name was Zahir.

He used to wear a turban and carry fabrics in the basket of his bicycle from one diplomatic residence to another."

In that basket under folds of rough linen, to protect the finer goods from the dust and mud of Kabul streets, Zahir carried red velvet fabrics with fashionable designs. He carried a supply of green and blue ones as well. Zahir was more than a tailor; he was also a salesman. Most of his goods came from the black markets of Russia and China via the Khyber pass. He had contacts with reliable smugglers who delivered the goods on time. These men knew exactly what appealed to the tastes of the diplomatic community. Very ornate Chinese needlework sold well, for example. So did Chinese silk robes-de-chambre. From Russia, pure wool shawls with subtle designs woven into the texture of the fabric with a slightly lighter shade of thread were quite popular. Bukhara rugs coming from Russia were a classic item as well. Every diplomat lined his ante-room and study with the smaller samples of Russian rugs. In dining rooms, Persian rugs, preferably Azerbaijani, were spread. For living rooms, Chinese rugs were the standard maintained by the best informed and the most respectable.

Zahir did not carry these items in the basket of his bicycle, of course. During his regular visits to take orders for robes or shirts at a diplomatic residence, he would pass the word that such and such a shipment of goods had arrived downtown and could be located through the tea house operated by Tarik Bayjani. Zahir left it to the diplomat's wife to arrange the rest. Soon after Zahir left, Mrs. Edwards or Madame Roquin would call the domestic orderly and send him downtown to locate the contraband goods. Thereupon, she would set a date to inspect the new shipment and send the orderly downtown once again. The next week at tea time, Madame Roquin's visitors talked about the profound blues at the edges of the new carpet. Perhaps Mademoiselle Roquin wrote in her letters to her cousins in Lyon a description of the colours and designs of that new carpet to explain the Orient to less fortunate Frenchmen.

=   =   =

I came to inherit that exquisite taste for Russian, Indian, and Chinese textures through the traces of my mother's memory of Afghanistan. For tactile evidence, there was a bundle of fabrics, some unsewn, some that had been sewn and then taken apart, stacked in the back of my grandmother's closet in Istanbul. I begged her to give me some of that fabric when I was a teenager. I wanted to make fairy-tale skirts for myself and wear glass bead necklaces and pretend that I came from abroad. Grandmother was relentless. She hung on to those remnants of Afghanistan like a dispossessed princess hoarding the last of the royal jewels. Even when she aged and lay sick in bed for days demanding and getting attention, she did not repay any favours with those fabrics. Once, only once, when my mother was away, my aunt was given a piece for no apparent reason. When she went home and unfolded the embroidered tablecloth, she noticed that the border design was missing on one side.

"Did Zahir sew that green tulle dress at all, mother?"

"Oh, he was a terrible tailor. He was so used to sewing those loose robes and pants they wear in Afghanistan that everything he cut came out loose and shabby. He did the first cut and put it together, but after the first fitting, we had to salvage the dress and restore it to the original design. When we finished with it, it was a dream. A true dream," mother said with a sigh.

=   =   =

"Tell me, mother; did you personally meet any royal men? If you were so beautiful, how come you never married any one of them? Then we could have had a different life! Imagine me a princess! We could have lived in a villa with roses in the front garden and a Chinese garden gate shaped like a pagoda like I always imagined it to be in Kabul. I could have had a maid to pick up after me. Then you could have dressed up every night for balls. We wouldn't have had a single worry. I think you would have been a happy woman, mother, if you had remained in high society. You are the kind of woman who would have been happiest in the company of refined people. People who did things right at the right time. You could have continued singing and reading. Wasn't there anyone at all you could have married there?"

Mother's eyes lit up, for this was the favourite part of her story. Perhaps she would tell me certain parts of the story she hadn't told me before. I wanted it all; like the sound of slippered feet on carpets, like the chirping of birds in the May of Kabul; like the smell of rice pilaf from the kitchen downstairs. I wanted it all. Even the open sewers. "How did you jump over them, mother? Oh, how terrible for a city that had Khans and roses to have open sewers."

We were alone in the room now. Grandmother had left. She had hastily cleared away the lunch dishes and retired to the back room for her customary nap. This was a rare spring afternoon with mother for she had been away for a long period working at a sanatorium in Bursa.

"Didn't I ever tell you about Farouk Khan? Strange that you don't remember."

"You never told me the whole story, mother; and I do forget."

"Farouk Khan used to visit our house often. He didn't visit me, of course. He came to converse and discuss military matters with your grandfather. Farouk Khan had great respect for him. They would talk for hours in the study. Everyone knew Farouk Khan would be a leader some day. They must have discussed military strategy together. We would leave them alone. In those days it was not proper for women to bother men when they discussed important matters. We would serve them tea or coffee, or if it was summer, sherbet; but we would leave them alone. Sometimes I would serve the refreshments. That's how Farouk Khan could see me. But your grandfather was very meticulous about social etiquette. You could say he was timid about things other people would have considered normal. He feared gossip like the plague. If he weren't that timid, I could have married Farouk Khan. You couldn't say that he was not interested. A woman can always tell when a man is interested in her. It is instinctive. You know it. It is as simple as that."

"Really? Will I be able to know some day? Could you teach me how to tell?"

"It is not something I could teach you. Every woman knows how to tell when a man cares about her. Strange, I was your age when I could sense everything."

"So what was he like, Farouk Khan?"

"Oh, he was so handsome. He looked like Rudolph Valentino. He had sharp black eyes shaped like an almond. He had a glistening black moustache. He had an agile, lean body; a perfect gentleman.

"Once when your grandfather and Farouk Khan were talking in the study and your grandmother was napping, I tiptoed to the door of the study and watched them through the keyhole for hours."

"Why didn't you just open the door and go in? Couldn't you have told grandfather that you forgot something in the room? Once they saw you, maybe they would have invited you to join them."

"You didn't do things like that in those years."

"So you never got close to him. Perhaps if grandmother could have called him over with his mother for afternoon tea. . ."

"They were royalty. It was Farouk Khan's respect for your grandfather that brought him to our house. Otherwise it would not have been proper. There was some talk, nevertheless, that he was interested in me. But nothing ever came out of it. Perhaps Farouk Khan feared your grandfather would say no. As a member of the Afghan royalty, I don't think he could have risked refusal. Also maybe his family would have objected to a Turkish bride. I don't see why, of course. Turkish women have always been prized. And I was just the right age for a royal wedding. But then, I would never have studied as much as I did. I would never have become a doctor. I would have been happy, though. As you say, I am made for a diplomatic life. And I would have continued singing."

= = =

Until 1978, I thought it was a pity that mother had not married Farouk Khan. But when the coup took place in 1978, the prince who looked like Rudolph Valentino was shot along with some other royalty. Mother and I could have died in 1978 had we chosen to live in Afghanistan.

Part II

In southern Hessen is a small farming village called Güllerhausen. It was close to this village at a spa that my mother was practicing medicine under the terms of a *Gastarbeiter*. I was doing my Master's in Ottoman history at Columbia University in 1981. That's when I visited my mother in Germany for a summer.

Güllerhausen was typical of the farming villages in the Hessen province. The visible inhabitants were all middle-aged. When they tended their fields, pruned the plants in their front yards, and took their late afternoon walks after coffee and *kuchen*, they left the impression on a stranger that all their questions had already been asked. Whatever unanswered questions there might have been seemed to be tucked away in the storage chest of a life that did not accommodate contradictions. Consistency was achieved with the help of timetables, at the small expense of passion. Voices were never raised, gossip never elicited any laughter. Sex was doomed to a single final groan. The women took pride in wearing their starched white shirts devoid of a crease. The men hardly ever soiled the colourful socks they wore in their orthopaedic sandals. Each resident suffered resignedly from his fair share of a chronic ailment: arthritis in the knees, shortage of breath caused by asthma, a persistent dizziness dispelled only in the summer or a benign tumor that constantly grows and is promptly removed after the recommendation of a physician.

Mother went off to the hospital at eight in the morning, leaving me to quiet periods of reading and daydreaming interrupted by a familiar American song broadcast from the American base radio station or an occasional trip to the small supermarket in town where I shopped in my broken German saying things like, "Lean meat, half kilo please; where the carrots?", or "No more wheat bread?"

On sunny days, for these were rare even in the summer, I took walks in the dark woods where I was reminded the whole time of Hansel and Gretel and other grim German tales. Sometimes I would sit in some clearing and look down at the village in the valley where the residents quietly minded their business and dutifully said "Gutentag!" whenever they encountered each other. I felt like the fool on the hill in the Beatles song.

Mother didn't have many friends in Germany. She always complained about the distance of Germans, their lack of humor, and their methodical civility. There was one woman whom she felt close to though. Frau Tante was different from the others, she said. She could have sworn Frau Tante had some Turkish blood. If not that, perhaps some Hungarian or Gypsy blood. Whatever it was, it made the difference, for Frau Tante was warm-hearted. She had run away from Eastern Germany during the war. "So, that's why!" mother had said when she learned this fact about Frau Tante. "That's why she is different." Frau Tante swore to her true German origins, but of a clearer and less tumultuous line than those found in West Germany. She had run away from Eastern Germany about forty years ago with an illustrated bible, an ancient notebook on herbal remedies and an antique telescope inlaid with silver. Frau Tante had enjoyed a stable life in the West, and had made full use of what she had brought along. She attended the Evangelische Kirche every Sunday morning and recited her prayers light-heartedly. Her only daughter had grown up to be a specialist in natural and herbal healing methods. As for the silver telescope, it was her best companion. When her husband was away visiting their daughter, starting at dusk, Frau Tante directed her gaze at the sky. She often focused on Venus and the moon. She had some interest in new cosmic phenomena which often turned out to be weather balloons. As soon as her vigilant left eye sadly registered this fact, Frau Tante would retreat from the window to her white-tiled kitchen where she knitted in acrylic oranges. This was the woman mother trusted.

Among her medical cohorts, mother had befriended a Rumanian woman of Turkish origin, more out of necessity to speak Turkish than her respect for Fatima's character. Ironically, Fatima believed she was smarter and a better survivor than mother. It was evident in the way she always tried to show mother the more expedient solutions for the daily problems they encountered at work. For the philosophical ones as well, Fatima felt entitled to advise mother. "Look, Leila, you don't have to tell anyone you're divorced," she would say. "A divorced woman is always questioned even in the most modern society. Tell them he is dead. He is dead for you, isn't he? He is finished for you. You don't want him, you don't talk to him, he is no good for you. What's the difference from having a dead husband? Tell them he is dead."

Mother would shake her head at this blasphemous suggestion, but smile all the same, with thoughts of childish vengeance.

When Fatima was gone, mother imitated her drawling Rumanian accent with high pitched sentence endings, and said she was cuckoo, poor woman. Well, all that Marxist education in Rumania, the sly escape into Turkey, and the world's best-planned capitalist system in Germany was a hard mixture to take. Fatima was confused. Here she was, working like a horse to make more and more money, but did she give any of it to her children? No, it all went into her various bank accounts. Then she would worry about how she was going to reduce the tax on the interest. She hardly served meat to her children. It was all macaroni.

But every time mother felt confused and needed to take a decision, she dialled Fatima's number and talked to her.

I don't really know who it was that summer of 1981 that reminded mother I had better hurry up and find a husband. Perhaps it was a casual remark by Frau Tante in the street. "Your daughter, does she have an American boyfriend in America?" Or Fatima's fat pathologist husband, "She has a special kind of beauty; she should find someone before it fades away." Or Fatima maybe, "She is too much into books. I know someone who went crazy like that in Bucharesti and had to take hormone pills."

In the middle of the summer, mother got anxious and suggested that I come visit her at the hospital more often. But I had never been interested in doctors. Their frantic rush across hospital corridors with their white coattails flying behind them has always left me unsettled. I have always been contemptuous of their self-righteousness. I had absolutely no desire to marry a doctor and yawn across the dinner table for lack of subjects to talk about. Doctors always have some excuse for not reading the paper, or good literature; not seeing art shows, or going to plays and concerts. Why should I marry a doctor? I certainly did not want to marry a patient either.

"Leave me alone, mother," I told her. "I am having a perfectly good time, let me relax. I am always rushing around in New York. So, let me enjoy the quiet here for a while."

When I visited mother in the hospital a couple of days later at lunch break (we had planned to go downtown to look at some walking shoes I had been wanting to buy for a while), we ran into Fatima in the hallway by chance. She told us that she was going downtown, too, and would give us a lift if we waited for her to change and pick up some things from her office. Mother and I were pacing in the corridor, waiting for Fatima, when a tall red-haired man asked mother where the floor director's office was.

Mother told him to turn to the right at the end of the corridor, then knock on the second door on the left. He thanked her in some strange accent. Pursing his lips, he had said *"Danke schön"*, and was about to walk away when Fatima appeared in the hallway and yelled after him. "Herr Daoud!" she said in her shrill voice. "Herr Daoud, this is the Turkish doctor and her daughter I was telling you about." So he turned back and with that same odd accent of his, almost grimacing with politeness, he said, "I am very pleased to meet you;" and extended his hand to mother. Then he shook my hand, looking directly into my eyes.

Fatima hastily introduced us. "Herr Daoud, this is Pinar; she is studying in New York." And then to me, "Pinar, you should talk to Daoud. He is very interested in learning about America. I am sure you can tell him a lot about life in the States." Then she said to mother, "Herr Daoud is from Afghanistan. He is new in the orthopaedics clinic."

Mother was immediately interested. She asked him about Kabul. Daoud had done his medical training in Kabul, though he was from Herat. They talked about the countryside, the Hindukush mountains, and the incredible sunsets in the north. They talked about the unfortunate turn of history, and the gentleness of Afghan people despite all their misfortunes. They talked about how different Afghanistan is from neighbouring Iran and Pakistan and India. Mother was exhilarated. After so many years, she had found someone to authenticate that part of her past that her children had treated somewhat as a fantasy. She seemed to have forgotten about our plans for lunchtime. When I gently reminded her about them, she seemed a little hurt that I wasn't sharing her enthusiasm. "We must get together again," she said to Herr Daoud. "Oh, certainly," said Herr Daoud, again pursing his lips.

As we were leaving, Fatima looked at him with a coquettish insistence and said, "You could invite them over for an Afghan dinner at the Afghan house." "Oh, yes, that would be nice," said Herr Daoud a little coldly. "Did you ever taste Afghan food?" Fatima asked me. "It is so tasty. You should taste their rice pilaf especially. Isn't it so, Herr Daoud?" she said, turning to him, eager to elicit his approval.

Mother and Herr Daoud exchanged home phone numbers with some tentative plans to talk some more during the weekend. We hurried away for not much was left of the lunch break of this punctual country.

Daoud was washing his car in the driveway on Saturday morning. There he was, pursing his lips again, obviously preoccupied with something; holding the hose over the roof of the car and watching the water run in rivulets down the edges of the side windows and doors.

I saw him as I was going down the street where we lived to the bakery to buy some strawberry cheesecake for a mid-morning treat. I had told mother to make some fresh coffee; that I would be back in a second.

I hadn't realized that Daoud was living this close to our house. He recognized me immediately. "Hello, Pinar, how are you?" he said in an awkward English accent. *"Sehr gut, bitte,"* I said. (I had conversed in broken English and German with him at the hospital. It seemed like we always answered each other in the language other than what the question was asked in.) "How is your mother?" he asked. "Would you like to come to the swimming pool, today?" he said, articulating each word slowly. *"Schwimmen? Ja, sehr schön,"* I said like an idiot.

"Um zwei uhr, hier," he said; which I took to mean that we would meet at the spot at two o'clock. "Okay, fine," I said, "See you then."

Daoud was not alone at the spot. I was introduced to Farhad, another Afghan, and Monica, a mousy German girl clinging to Daoud's arm.

Monica drove the car. It was obvious that she owned it. Daoud sat in the front; Farhad and I in the back. Monica drove nervously, taking turns like a maniac, heaving us from side to side at each bend of the road. She dropped us all off at the pool. "Isn't she coming with us?" I asked Daoud. "No," he said, "She will go back to the house." He arranged with Monica to pick us all up at 6 o'clock.

We swam with arthritic patients, the town residents, and two travelling gypsy musicians who later invited us to play pool under fake sunshine in the upper level reserved for relaxation under simulated tropical conditions. To my surprise some more Afghans joined us. From strained and carefully worded questions, I learned that they were all refugees, including Farhad, who were given passes by the German government to use the health facilities for leisure. Other than those passes, they received minimal subsistence aid and their movements were severely curtailed.

Daoud was the only one who had found a job, being a doctor and in possession of his true documents. Daoud had left Afghanistan for a medical conference in Libya. But instead of leaving Libya for Afghanistan at the end of the conference, he had left for Turkey. In Istanbul, he purchased a round trip ticket to London with a stopover in Frankfurt. At Frankfurt airport, when the plane stopped to pick up some new passengers, Daoud left the plane with the rest of the passengers who were continuing the flight to wait in the small waiting room. There he hid in the toilet crouched on the seat until the plane left. When the same plane had gone to London, back to Frankfurt, and taken off again, Daoud turned himself in to the police and asked for asylum.

Monica had prepared tea and cake for us at Daoud's apartment. It was a small, one-room apartment with a bed, a round table, a bureau with a mirror on its door, and a desk. We sat in the old chairs around the table, sipping tea from glasses. Farhad had ground some cloves and put them into the brew. The pungent taste of the tea reminded me of the Asia depicted in National Geographic articles illustrated with photos of wind-darkened men intently conversing in a tea house. Windows glazed by ice. An orange glow in the room. The caption reads: "Old friends exchange stories by the skirts of the Hindukush range."

I was awakened from my reverie by a cassette Monica had put on the tape recorder. It was distinctly an American voice who said:

"Hello, Monica; I thought you might like to hear some of the hit songs of the summer here. Do they play any of these on the radio there? Let me know... I am doing fine. I go swimming every day after work. I look forward to my vacation in August. I am going to laze around in the backyard and work on my tan. Is it sunny there? Well here are the songs:"

To the accompaniment of Olivia Newton John, Monica explained to me that was her penpal from Gary, Indiana.

America can be an afternoon's diversion in Germany.

We concluded the Saturday with a trip to the nearby Wundersee to watch fireworks. We climbed up to the old forest where, in the ancient courtyard, Germans were eating sausages and drinking beer while the carnival cannons fired from battlements volleys of red and purple light across the lake. At times, the parabolic trajectory of one red volley intersected with a yellow one fired straight into the sky from a cruise boat on the lake. As the two streams of light met, they erupted in joined colors, revealing the night sky in flashes of deep blue.

The Germans screamed with pleasure at these explosions and gulped down mugs of beer. Monica hugged Daoud like a child enjoying a spectacle with a parent. Farhad and Daoud were expressionless; watching what was there to be watched.

The next week, sitting in Farhad's room in the small refugee camp, a former country school, I asked him to tell me his story. We had finished eating the lavish rice and vegetable stew he had prepared despite his limited income.

Daoud and Monica were downstairs in the yard playing table tennis with two refugees.

Farhad brought out an album of photographs from his metal closet. On the first page was an intricate carnation he had drawn with colouring pencils. On the second page, he had placed a photograph of his family in the front yard of their house. Modest rug merchants from Kandahar: his three sisters, four brothers, grandfather, and parents. On the second page was a photograph of his fiancée, a hardy girl in army fatigues, holding the reins of a horse. Farhad said she was with his family in Peshawar now. I asked him when they would be able to see each other again. Farhad wasn't sure. "Do you want to stay in Germany?" I asked him in my limited German.

Farhad smiled. He said he wanted to go to America or Canada. But how? He knew it was hard. He needed, like all of those refugees everywhere in the world, whose faces we see in fleeting frames of occasional TV news, someone to bring him somewhere. He needed a paternal hand without the face; a hand that activates an auxiliary mechanism in some bureaucracy in the west. He needed the life in the west in his recovery from immolation. Farhad now asked not simply for life, but the magical life of the oppressors he had fought against.

On his wall, above his bed, Farhad had placed a centrefold photograph from *Stern*. It was the photograph of an island in the Caribbean, the few palm trees on it bent in the hurricane, everything in shades of violent blue, forms almost indistinguishable in the torrent. In white block letters in the lower right corner of the photograph, the caption read: "Karibik, Paradis mit Problemen."

I asked Farhad why he had put that photograph on his wall. "Is it because that's how you feel here?" I asked. He smiled. For he had learned that in waiting we create our own hell; especially in silence, and in a refuge, the most violent storms explode in our soul.

Farhad had spent two years in the infamous Puli-Charki prison in Kabul. The police had arrested him in a demonstration he had taken part in in front of the university during his first year as an engineering student. He had been arrested for opposing the Soviet takeover; for not accepting an imposition. He had been questioned and tortured for questioning an intervention in his home country. He had made the mistake like so many of us in believing that we have the right to question those who act in our behalf. The price he had paid was the recognition of his vulnerability, of his fallibility as an individual. He had escaped from a prison cell in Afghanistan to a spotless prison cell in Germany.

Farhad was living out an omen contained in his family photograph. He was the one who had taken the picture; he had stood behind the camera to record those he belonged to. In that photograph, he was absent from his family in his desire to observe and preserve them. And in the end, he had been expelled from his home for having distanced himself from them.

I proposed to go outside to feel the sun and the sky. It was a naïve attempt on my part to reconstitute what we had lost in that room in our ponderings about our stories.

For down in the yard, there were more refugees, all contained within a space loosely enclosed by wire fences; and more concretely enclosed by German bureaucracy, international law, and the Geneva convention.

The women and children were quietly grouped together on one bare mattress laid out at the side of the driveway; some of the men were sitting in a similar fashion on another mattress nearby. Their turbans shielded their eyes from me. Another man was doing pushups to improve his already developed muscles. What is he getting ready for, I asked myself. Life in Germany as a worker on the mass production line? Another life in Canada or the States in search of another refugee claim? Perhaps he would be returned back to Afghanistan where he would have to fight once again.

Daoud and Monica were still playing table tennis, returning each other's strokes. Daoud would stay in Germany, with Monica. He had made the right moves. He would stay where he was.

King of the Raft

Daniel David Moses

There was a raft in the river that year, put there, anchored with an anvil, just below a bend, by the one of the fathers who worked away in Buffalo, who could spend only every other weekend, if that, at home. The one of the mothers whose husband worked the land and came in from the fields for every meal muttered as she set the table that that raft was the only way the father who worked in the city was able to pretend he cared about his sons. Her husband, also one of the fathers, who had once when young gone across the border to work and then, unhappy there, returned, could not answer, soaking the dust of soil from his hands.

Most of the sons used the raft that was there just that one summer in the usually slow-moving water during the long evenings after supper, after the days of the fieldwork of haying and then combining were done. A few of them, the ones whose fathers and mothers practised Christianity, also used it in the afternoons on sunny Sundays after the sitting through church and family luncheons. And the one of the sons who had only a father who came and went following the work — that son appeared whenever his rare duties or lonely freedom became too much for him.

The sons would come to the raft in Indian file along a footpath the half mile from the road and change their overalls or jeans for swimsuits among the goldenrod and milkweed on the bank, quickly, to preserve modesty and their blood from mosquitoes, the only females around. Then one of the sons would run down the clay slope and stumble in with splashing and a cry of shock or joy for the water's current temperature. The other sons would follow, and, by the time they all climbed out onto the raft out in the stream, through laughter would become boys again.

The boys used that raft in the murky green water to catch the sun or their breaths on or to dive from when they tried to touch the mud bottom. One of the younger ones also used to stand looking across the current to the other side, trying to see through that field of corn there, the last bit of land that belonged to the Reserve. Beyond it the highway ran, a border patrolled by a few cars flashing chrome in the sun or headlights through the evening blue like messages from the city. Every one of the boys used the raft several times that summer to get across the river and back, the accomplishment proof of their new masculinity. And once the younger one who spent time looking at that other land, crossed and climbed up the bank there and explored the shadows between the rows of corn, the leaves like dry tongues along his naked arms as he came to the field's far edge where the asphalt of that highway stood empty.

Toward the cool end of the evenings, any boy left out on the raft in the lapping black water would be too far from shore to hear the conversations. They went on against a background noise of the fire the boys always built against the river's grey mist and mosquito lust, that they sometimes built for roasting corn, hot dogs, marshmallows. The conversations went on along with or over games of chess. Years later, one of the older boys, watching his own son play the game with a friend in silence, wondered if perhaps that was why their conversations that year of the raft about cars, guitars, and girls — especially each other's sisters — about school and beer, always ended up in stalemate or check. Most of the boys ended up winning only their own solitariness from the conversations by the river. But the one who had only a father never even learned the rules of play.

One sunny Sunday after church late in the summer, the one who had only a father already sat on the raft in the river as the rest of the boys undressed. He smiled at the boy who had gone across through the corn, who made it into the water first.

Then he stood up and the raft made waves as gentle as those in his blue-black hair — I'm the king of the raft, he yelled, challenging the boy who had seen the highway to win that wet wooden square. And a battle was joined, and the day was wet and fair, until the king of the raft, to show his strength to the rest of the boys still on shore, took a hank of the highway boy's straight hair in hand and held the highway boy underwater till the highway boy saw blue fire and almost drowned. The story went around among the mothers and the fathers and soon that son who had only a father found himself unwelcome. Other stories came around, rumours about his getting into fights or failing grades or how his father's latest girlfriend had dyed her Indian hair blond. And the boy who almost had drowned found he both feared the king of the raft and missed the waves in his blue-black hair.

One muggy evening when pale thunderheads growled in from the west, the boy who had almost drowned, who had the farthest to go to get home, left the raft and the rest by the river early. On the dark road he met the king, who had something to say. They hid together with a case of beer in a cool culvert under the road. The king of the raft was going away with his father to live in Buffalo in the United States and thought the boy who had almost drowned could use what was left of this beer the king's father would never miss. The boy who had almost drowned sipped from his bottle of sour beer and heard the rain beginning to hiss at the end of the culvert. He crawled and looked out in time to see the blue fire of lightning hit a tree. In the flash he saw again the waves in the king's blue-black hair, the grin that offered another beer. The boy who had almost drowned felt he was going down again, and, muttering some excuse, ran out into the rain. The king yelled after him that old insult boys use about your mother wanting you home.

The boy who had almost drowned found he could cross through the rain, anchored by his old running shoes to the ground, though the water came down like another river, cold and clear and wide as the horizon. He made it home and stood on the porch, waiting for the other side of the storm, hearing hail hitting the roof and water through the eaves filling up the cistern. Later, out of the storm, he could still hear far off a gurgling in the gully and a quiet roar as the distant river tore between its banks. The storm still growled somewhere beyond the eastern horizon.

The raft was gone the next evening when the boys came to the bank and the current was still too cold and quick to swim in. No one crossed the river for the rest of the summer. The king of the raft never appeared again anywhere. In the fall, a rumour came around about his going to work in the city and in the winter another one claimed he had died. The boy who had crossed through the rain thought about going down even quicker in winter river water. Then a newspaper confirmed the death. In a traffic accident, the rain boy read. None of the boys had even met that impaired driver, that one of the fathers, surviving and charged without a license. One of the mothers muttered as she set another mother's hair about people not able to care even about their kids. The rain boy let the king of the raft sink into the river, washing him away in his mind, and decided he would someday cross over and follow the highway through that land and find the city.

The Canadian Travel Notes of Abbé Hughes Pommier, Painter, 1663-1680

Douglas Glover

Bertrand de Latour describes Pommier as an artist whose paintings were all bad, although he considered himself a neglected genius.
(Harper, *Painting in Canada*)

Envoi

Tomorrow I embark for France on the last ship before the river freezes.

In disgrace.

The Bishop has ordered it, though he was happy enough to embrace me sixteen years ago in Vendôme when, inspired by the Jesuit martyrs and an unfortunate incident with Mme de A——'s girl Alice, which was bound to get out, I begged him to send me among the savages so as to perish in a State of Grace.

I have with me two satchels of sketches, woodcuts and water-colours, as well as three larger works on ship's canvas in a roll which His Lordship has said I might keep.

Besides these, nothing but my cassock, torn and muddy at the hem, and a broad-brimmed hat much eaten by rats.

For shoes the last nine years I have made do with the wooden sandals of the Recollets. And I am much heartened at the thought of a new pair of leather ones my sister Adèle has written she will buy for me the moment I reach Paris.

I hear the Watch passing the Seminary gate, tracing his path along the ramparts, reluctant to be away from his fire this cool autumn night. I pull the worn trade blanket tighter around my shoulders and crouch towards the candle. Someone shouts in his sleep.

I am forty-three and, in the nature of things, cannot expect to return to Canada before I die.

The Voyage Out

Bishop Laval and the new Governor Mézy were my shipmates on the voyage out, both treating me with exemplary kindness and piety.

Laval was but forty-two or -three, thin-lipped, balding, with a forehead like a dome, and much given to mystical excesses which he encouraged me to practise. These consisted of fasting and squatting in uncomfortable positions on the open deck in all weathers.

Mézy, a bluff, soldierly fellow, an old friend of the bishop's, often humbled himself as well by picking up sailors and carrying them about the ship on his shoulders, whether they wanted him to or not (one or two were nearly lost overboard when the governor missed his grip during high seas).

I followed Laval's instruction until my stomach felt like a prune, my legs burned and my head split; after which I discovered that he often became quite unconscious during his meditations so that I could go off and gnaw a piece of leathery pork while I sketched an old tar repairing sail of splicing sheets. (The bishop discouraged the drawing of sailors, sea-birds, etc., on the grounds that my time would be better spent making copies of religious scenes for the edification of savages and children when we reached Canada.)

As we approached landfall, an incident occurred which surprised me and made me doubt my vocation.

A large herring-gull, having lit upon a spar above the bishop, who was deep in ecstasy or faint from lack of food, did drop a load of dung on the holy man's sleeve.

Laval awoke with a start and licked up the slime with relish, exclaiming to me that it was the best thing he had tasted in weeks.

I was afterward violently sea-sick for upwards of an hour.

First Holy Work

They put me off shortly after at a fishing station called Sheep Death on an island at the mouth of the St. Lawrence where the *curé* had recently met his end at the hands of the local savages.

I rowed ashore in the ship's boat with a little pack containing my portable altar, wine, wafers, holy water and extra stockings, a sword at my waist and a travelling paint kit up my sleeve where the bishop failed to notice it. I had a little paper for writing my annual letter to the Minister and the Papal Legate and I thought tree bark or animal skin would do for canvas till I reached civilization again.

The village consisted of five families far gone in debauchery but full of good humour nevertheless. Every female in the place above the age of twelve was pregnant, with a voice like a bull having its stones cut off. The men were small, bearded, coated with fish oil and carbon from the rendering fires, and addicted to brandy.

One and all greeted me with enthusiasm and then seemed to forget my presence.

I kept my hand on my sword the first two weeks, not knowing precisely what fate had befallen my predecessor.

A fellow named Fanton, whom I suspected of being a Huguenot though he denied it, took me to the place where the *curé* had died; there was nothing left but six charred ribs and a bit of jaw. We gave him a Christian burial, and I said what I could for the sake of his soul.

I did eight sketches of Fanton's wife as the Virgin in a shawl made from an old sail with the latest of her fourteen children at her tent-like breast for the Christ-child.

For the first month I swam in the ocean to keep clean, but as the weather closed I abandoned myself to the filth of the place and became a haven for eight varieties of insect life.

There being no church or manse I bedded in a shack with the Fantons, usually with five or six children draped over my body for warmth, the husband and wife groaning disgustingly a yard or two away.

I drew up plans for a little chapel on a piece of birchbark and got Fanton to organize the men for the building, a project which was greeted with much public enthusiasm, but nothing came of it.

I married two couples, one with five children, one with three.

A third couple with six children said they were married though I knew they were not. When I taxed the wife with her sin in the confessional (at other times used as a toilet in foul weather), she admitted to being married already to a man in France whom she thought might be dead. Her Canadian lover refused to marry her on the grounds that it might force her into bigamy, a sin, he thought, as much frowned upon in the Bible as murder or eating meat on Friday.

I became depressed listening to her babble and gave her five Hail Marys and one Act of Contrition as penance which earned me a reputation for being overly lenient.

During the idle winter months, the men traded brandy for furs with the savages, a practice strictly forbidden by the Church on pain of excommunication and by the King on pain of death.

When the Indians were drunk, they traded their weapons, their clothes, their wives and their children for more liquor. The men of my parish being given to venery, there were many half-breed children in the Indian camp. Some wandered back and forth half-naked between their white and red families.

Indeed, it was not uncommon for me to wake in the morning to find some lice-ridden Savage child with its arms wrapped tightly around my neck and snot dribbling into my cassock.

The savages painted themselves with red ochre and then pranced around naked as though they were dressed in court finery. It was a repellent sight but I made many an interesting sketch of it.

In order to cleanse my mind and render myself worthy of the death I was certain awaited me the next summer at Québec, I tried to fast and meditate as the bishop had taught me, but my bowels seized up and gave me the most painful hemorrhoids which Mistress Fanton soothed with the application of a Savage remedy and some incantation in the native tongue.

In the spring, I was relieved by the first ship from France (five ship's officers contracted fleas from the circumstance of my sharing their cabin) and left the place, I failed not to believe, far better than I found it.

Québec

Québec, the capital of the country, was a hamlet of seventy mean houses and about 400 Christian souls with as many savages sleeping in the streets. On the rock above, Laval had built his seminary, the Ursulines their convent, the governor his palace and a small fort, and Jean Boisdon his tavern.

The bishop met me at the pier but soon went off with eight Jesuits new from France and also on the same ship.

Later he saw me in the Seminary library and greeted me as Pierre. He said he had heard great things of my mission in Sheep Death (this seemed strange as I thought myself the only person to come out of that place in a year).

He noticed me scratching an armpit and smiled. Drawing up his robe, he showed me a veritable hive of insect activity on his privy parts.

He then strongly urged me not to turn or change the straw on my pallet as this might accustom my body to unwonted ease.

I asked the good bishop if I might paint his likeness for the Hôtel Dieu wherein it would serve as an inspiration to the sisters, the sick and the poor.

The bishop said no.

Notwithstanding His Worship's instructions, I hired the bath-tub at the rear of Jean Boisdon's establishment and took there a fine dinner of turnips, salt pork and dried crab-apples while his wife boiled my clothes.

I became drunk on cheap trade brandy and said a Requiem Mass for the poor dead mites which floated about me in their hundreds. (Later Bishop Laval heard of this by some spy and it was marked down as one of the reasons for my exile to Boucherville.)

I also sketched Boisdon's servant girl as Mary Magdalene with her bodice uncovered and half a dozen angels looking on.

The town was in a mood of religious exaltation with half the populace expecting martyrdom at the hands of the Iroquois every night and the other half drunk with terror. War parties haunted the woods and byways and crept into the town under cover of darkness to murder and kidnap. Every cabin had a small cannon and a statue of the Virgin.

I carried my sword again though the bishop disapproved. I explained to him it was not so much to protect myself as 1) to make the savages bethink themselves before they brought upon their heads the terrible sin of priest-killing, and 2) to give myself an opportunity to escape should they happen to fall upon me whilst I was not in a fit spiritual state.

(I recall one alarum when we took refuge in Notre Dame — there were five men in the rood loft before the Holy Sacrament preparing to die and Arlette Boisvert at the door with an iron fry pan — but this is getting ahead of my story.)

I went to visit Governor Mézy whom I found alone in his apartments suffering from the grippe and in a chaotic state of mind.

He and the bishop had disagreed. Mézy was under threat of excommunication for having discharged Bishop Laval's friends from the governing council, which he claimed was made up of frauds, profiteers, and illegal traffickers in beaver hides. The bishop had accused Mézy of being a Huguenot, a Jansenist, and an illegal trafficker in beaver hides.

Upon investigation, Mézy had discovered that Bishop Laval and the Jesuits were also involved in trafficking in beaver hides. For a man who had been wont to carry sailors about the deck to humble himself before God, it was a bitter draught.

Hearing of my visit, the bishop ordered me to preach a sermon against Mézy in the pulpit the following Sunday as a test of my loyalty. The look on the governor's face as I listed his sins and described the precise torments he would suffer in Hell as a result has haunted me ever after. He does not know it, but I continue to pray for the old soldier to this day.

I was assigned to teach Latin and Logic at the Seminary. The students were mostly boys from the local seigneuries, rude, stupid and overfed. Farting during the recitation of declensions was considered by many to be the height of wit.

Though these were boys especially selected by the parish authorities for their religious aptitude, I never observed any but the most grudging respect for Our Lady and her Holy Son. Most left school before they were fifteen to marry girls in advanced states of pregnancy. The rest ran away to the forests to trade in beaver hides.

One boy, Boisvert, could draw somewhat and became a favourite of mine. (The Boisvert were an old Québec family having been there upwards of eight years.) In my spare time I taught him the rudiments of figures, composition, Christian and heroic symbolism, etc.

Shortly thereafter he was expelled from the Seminary and sentenced to the stocks for making a series of sketches of an Ursuline nun named Thérèse de la Sainte Assomption being ravished by the Flemish Bastard, a noted Iroquois chieftain. Boisvert rendered the sketches on birchbark scrolls which he then sold at five *sous* apiece to his classmates.

Though my role in this affair was concealed from the general public by the good offices of the bishop, I was enjoined to refrain from practising my art and given a severe penance which consisted of two hundred Hail Marys to be said while standing up to my thighs in an ox midden.

His Worship further ordered me not to bathe, which occasioned much surreptitious delight amongst my remaining students.

Martyre des Pères Jésuites chez les Hurons

Notwithstanding the bishop's command (he no longer spoke to me, or recognized me in public, though I would see him nearly every day in the street), I soon received my first major commission from the Hôtel Dieu sisters who had heard through gossip that I was the artist responsible for the Ursuline scrolls.

The sisters wanted a large canvas for the chapel wall depicting, in a suitably inspirational manner, the deaths of the Jesuit brothers at the hands of the savages.

I set to work immediately on a piece of sail cloth, mixing my own paints as best I could and using the back room of Jean Boisdon's establishment as a studio.

A Huguenot hog-gelder named René Pettit had taken up residence in the back room while he plied his trade in the farms round about. A muscular fellow, with a Roman nose and cruel eyes, he modelled for me as an Indian brave.

Jean Boisdon's chambermaid, Paulette, stripped to the waist, with her skirts tucked up between her legs, did nicely for Indian maidens in the background.

For the martyrs, I painted myself as Brébeuf using a small glass mirror Boisdon kept by the bathtub. Boisdon himself became Lalement, showing, after consuming half a flagon of arak I was forced to purchase for the company, a remarkable talent for rolling his eyes and heaving out his chest in a counterfeit of agony.

Later he told me arak gave him gas.

Thrown constantly together thus as they worked with me, René and Paulette conceived a sudden, immoderate passion for one another, which ended in the latter becoming pregnant and demanding to be married. With the painting only half done, René ran away to live with the savages.

Meanwhile, the studio was still in use as a bathroom, so that customers were always coming in and out to wash, often while I was painting. (Boisdon charged ten *sous* for clean hot water, eight for moderately warm water used only once, and so on.)

Word got abroad about my work in progress, and I became a sort of entertainment for the local drunks, bawds, critics, and trappers come to town to sell beaver hides.

The latter were often vociferously abusive, making fun of my savages, the horrific poses of my martyrs, etc. Sometimes I could tell that their advice was well-intended, thus several well-meaning inaccuracies were avoided, including classical Grecian elements — amphorae, Macedonian lances, a lyre, Ionic columns in front of the longhouses, etc. — which I had unwittingly imported into my representation of native life.

It was in this way that many of Québec's unsavoury element made their way into my painting of the Holy Martyrs.

And, though I believe they enhanced the liveliness of the scene, the result was that the Hôtel Dieu sisters recognized the two prostitutes, the Huguenot hog-gelder, and a man under sentence of death for killing his wife and running away to the forest to trade in beaver hides. This man, who modelled for the wise old Sachem in the top right corner, was arrested, tried, hanged, cut down before he died and castrated, then burned to death in the Lower Town.

The whole of Québec society turned out for the occasion with a festive air. Two young ladies fainted straight away at the sight of the condemned man's mutilated body, and afterwards made a show of needing to be carried thence by several gallants who made a sort of invalid's litter with their arms.

The sisters refused to pay for my work, which was confiscated by the bishop. Later, they begged it of him at no charge and had gowns and pantaloons painted over the naked members by one Michel Lemelin, a plasterer who owed them money for medical care.

I never saw the painting again.

Mistress Arlette, a Shameful Episode

I was bitterly disappointed, as you may guess, having found Canada a poor place for an artist to make his way.

I began a period of spiritual decline and excessive drinking. Turning my face from God, I often borrowed money from my students or robbed the poor box to buy the cheap, watered trade brandy which the Jesuits exchanged with the up-country savages for beaver hides.

Several times the Night Watch discovered me asleep in the gutter, curled up between a couple of snoring braves, with my robe up over my face, and it was only their affection for me and the belief, happily common in the town, that I was an artistic genius, that kept them from reporting me to His Worship.

That fall Governor Mézy, ever more scattered in mind and suffering a theological distress, went on a pilgrimage to Sainte Anne de Beaupré, crawling much of the way in his soldier's armour upon his knees, then died the following spring and was buried in a pauper's grave.

His former friend, the bishop, took no notice.

The Iroquois sent a mission to Québec to sue for peace, then killed a farmer named De Lorimier in broad daylight. Three soldiers were tried for murdering an Indian and hanged from the wall by the city gate. The Indians were appalled at such barbaric punishment, saying they would just as soon have had an apology and some brandy.

A comet appeared in the sky in the shape of a blazing canoe. Everyone agreed it was a difficult sign to interpret.

My former student Boisvert, now aged sixteen, unemployed, and the father of two, picked my pocket during the procession on the day of the Fête Dieu.

At my request he was whipped in the Upper Town, then marched to the Lower Town and set up again.

When it was over, I was so horrified I fell on my knees before him and begged his forgiveness. Later I lent him my cloak to hide his wounds; I never saw it again afterward, Boisvert having disappeared into the forest to live with the savages.

(It was difficult to blame the young men for thus liberating themselves from the yoke of wage work in the company warehouses, the drudgery of clearing the land, or the hectoring of their young wives. In the forest, they lived the lives of nobles in Old France, hunting large animals for their food, not to mention debauching young Indian maidens, who are, I was told, nubile and complaisant.)

I took to visiting Arlette, the young man's abandoned wife, to offer her the consolation of my ministry, not to mention taking the price of the cloak out in hot meals served close to the fire.

She was a fat, depressed woman with a nose like a knuckle — but her desire to serve the Lord was ardent and she told me she volunteered without a second thought to come to the New World when the religious nature of the settlement was first demonstrated to her (though I have heard certain malicious tongues say it was because of the prospect of a forced marriage.)

There was but one other artist in the colony at this time, a Jesuit missionary to the Iroquois called Father Pierron, a favourite of the bishop's. Mother Marie de l'Incarnation (a pious woman, a letter-writer, and a wonderful lace-maker, a skill not often found in these rude parts, with a wen the size of a duck's egg on her chin) was wont to go around saying, "He preaches all day and paints all night." Which made me ill to hear.

Pierron specialized in miniature scenes mostly, genre pieces illustrating the vices and the virtues, Heaven and Hell, the Temptation of Eve, etc., which he used for Bible classes among the savages who were apparently much illuminated on this account.

My triumph came upon the death of Sister Marie-Catherine de Saint Augustin in the Hôtel Dieu (a nun famous for the production of miracles: On February 4, 1663 while working in the hospital, she had seen four demons shaking Québec like a quilt with the Lord Jesus restraining them; a year later, she converted a recidivist Huguenot with Brother Brébeuf's charred thigh bone.)

Apparently, she had admired my *Martyre des Pères Jésuites* which reminded her of the great paintings (Georges de la Tour, Guido Reni, etc.) that hung in her father's house in Rennes. (Also Father Pierron was out of town.)

I was at this time undergoing treatment — a decoction of sassafras being a sovereign specific, according to the savages — from an old Christianized Tobacco Indian named Nickbis Agsonbare for an ailment I had contracted from Jean Boisdon's servant girl.

The Hôtel Dieu concierge found me asleep on a pile of young Boisvert's illegal beaver hides in a corner of Arlette's kitchen, though it was midday and hot as Hades with the weather outside and the brick-faced mistress sweating over her baking bread inside (the hides stank atrociously).

I had not painted for upwards of a year, my classes had fallen off, I had said Mass but five times. Indeed, the sole positive result of my labours since the *Martyre* set-back was that the Boisverts were soon to be blessed with a third child, an event which delighted everyone since the government had embarked on a system of Royal grants for the fathers of large families.

The Sister had been dead a week when I was summoned. She was dry as a nut and a sickening shade of grey-green, with her old white hair hanging in ribbons. I had to work quickly for the smell, and used my imagination liberally.

For once I had the best brushes and paints to be had in the colony, the concierge kept me supplied with cognac (I was once nearly caught napping with my feet upon the coffin lid), and I finished in two days, with only an hour or two for sleep.

After the funeral, I stayed on at the Hôtel Dieu to add some finishing touches, a flight of cherubim, some corner scenes illustrating life among the savages left over from the *Martyre*, a halo with rays and such.

Her eyes proved the most difficult test of my art (because they had been closed in death), and I painted them upward of twenty-nine times till I had the concierge sit for me in an attitude of prayer and gave her his eyes, one brown, one hazel, slightly squint, with yellow sclerae, gazing heavenward.

Mother Marie said she had never seen such a likeness, that she had first thought my picture nothing short of a vision, a proof of corporeal incarnation, with the real Marie-Catherine about to step out of the frame and address her (they used to call each other "little cabbage").

The *Marie-Catherine* hung in the public room at the Hôtel Dieu where the bishop chanced to see it. I thought this would soften his heart toward me, but it did not.

Instead, I was summoned before the Master of the Seminary in his office where Houssart, the bishop's valet, read a list of offences (including indolence, idolatry, blasphemy — that Requiem Mass in the bathtub — drunkenness and excessive personal vanity). I lost my job at the Seminary and was exiled to Boucherville, near Montréal, where it was hoped curatorial duties would mend my soul or I would find a martyr's end.

Among the Anderhoronerons

Boucherville was a one-year-old village of eight log hovels, a two-room, half-timbered manse for the seigneur, and a makeshift dock with the pitch still dripping from the timbers (which fell down when the ice went out in the spring), where the pigs outnumbered the human inhabitants by five to one.

There were but three hundred English yards of muddy street in all, and the narrow fields running down to the river were studded with stumps as tall as a man's shoulders between which a few meagre spikes of Indian corn struggled for life.

I was much torn up leaving Arlette behind, but my good friend and medical consultant Nickbis Agsonbare eased the pain of my departure by agreeing to remove with me.

I was also somewhat relieved to be temporarily out of the bishop's eye, whence I had heretofore received nothing but censure and contempt, despite my good efforts to win favour.

Unfortunately, the ignorant villagers took me for the bishop's man, there being considerable jealousy between the Jesuits of Québec and the Sulpician monks of Montréal (including disputes over who could produce the best miracles).

They gave me a former hog barn ("former" only in the sense that they moved some hogs out that I might have the space) for accommodation and refused to entertain construction of a parish church until their crops were in, after which they decided it was too cold to commence extensive outside work. (I was blamed for this delay when the bishop moved me to Sorel two years later.)

Meanwhile, I discovered that Nickbis Agsonbare was trafficking in illegal beaver hides (after seven years in the colony, I had yet to see a live beaver — something like a large, flat-tailed rat, I supposed) and was using his friendship with me to conceal this activity from the authorities.

He assured me that this was not the case, but I could not forbear remonstrating with him about the piles of beaver pelts which reached the ceiling on all sides, and I did not afterward trust him in quite the same old way.

I took to wearing an old shirt done up around my head like a turban and calling myself a priest of the prophet Mahound, but no one paid any attention.

I heard by the express canoe foreman that in my absence a fresh new face had appeared in the Québec art scene, a Recollet brother called Frère Luc, styled Painter to the King. In two months, Frère Luc had surpassed my total output since arriving in Canada, having already completed a portrait of the Intendant and three large religious scenes for the Church of Our Lady.

All at once, painting and sketching, which had heretofore been a great joy to me, seemed suddenly tedious, nothing but daubs of colour and stark lines without any meaning.

Nickbis, seeing my melancholy, suggested a trip to visit his in-laws hard by the Lac des Chats, or Lake of the Erie Nation, far inland.

At this time it was a capital crime to spend more than twenty-four hours in the forest — a measure meant to stem the traffic in illegal beaver hides and keep young men from running away to the savages. Nevertheless, I agreed, neither caring if I were hanged or not.

We set off in June, without a word to the congregation, in an elm bark craft that would have sunk except for constant bailing with an alms bowl. For paddlers, we had Nickbis and his nephew Henderebenks, a simple-minded boy with a snapping turtle tattooed on his left shoulder and two fingers missing from his hand.

We cleared Montréal in a day and carried the canoe past the rapids at La Chine at night. Thence we threaded our way upriver through a myriad of rocky islands infested with black flies and mosquitoes. We saw no other human for a week, which made my heart lighten.

It is customary for explorers' accounts to include lists of wonders encountered and lands claimed for the King. I saw eight dragons that breathed a mixture of fire and smoke, a tribe of elves who shot arrows at us the size of knitting needles, a giant bustard as big as a house with a beak as hard as stone, two man-like creatures that bounced rapidly over the ground on a single leg, and a mermaid (possibly a large pike).

I claimed the following lands for King Louis: Pommierland, Pommier Island, the River Pommier, Lac Pommier, Baie Pommier, Painter's Reach, etc. (our journey being delayed continually on account of my insistence that we get out of the boat and put up birchbark signs to mark these geographical features).

On the eighth day, about five leagues from La Salle's trading fort at Cataraqui, we were captured by a roving band of Anderhoronerons who fell upon us in our sleep (we generally took a nap after lunch). There were nine of them, two old men without teeth, six boys in their early teens, and a younger one about seven, all stripped naked, covered with grease and red war-paint against the flies, and nearly starved.

We spent two more days in camp while the Anderhoronerons ate what was left of our provisions.

On the third morning, we set out for their village but had only gone a league or two when the little boy began to weep petulantly, saying it was his first war and he wanted to kill one of the enemies.

The old men of the party consulted and agreed to let him kill Henderebenks who immediately fell on his knees and began to sing his death song which consisted of the words,

"Woe! Henderebenks, the dancing turtle, is no more. Woe! Woe! Woe! The dancing turtle is no more."

I gave him the sacrament of Extreme Unction, after which he and Nickbis Agsonbare got into a theological argument as to whether the sacrament was "any good" without wine and wafer (these having been eaten by the Anderhoronerons).

The little boy struck Henderebenks with a stone club, knocked him to the ground, and then proceeded to scalp him with a flint knife which was barely sharp enough to cut the skin. Henderebenks woke up part-way through the operation and began to sing, "Woe! The dancing turtle is no more!" until one of the older boys clubbed him with Nickbis's arquebus.

Nickbis said he was sorry I had had to see this, that he hoped I wouldn't hold it against him, that really he had taken all the precautions he could, and that these Anderhoronerons were nothing but filthy savages to whom his People would never have given the time of day.

After two weeks of forced marches, we reached the main Anderhoroneron village or "castle" (a pleasant little town of thirteen bark-covered sheds or longhouses with a sort of picket fence all around) where I was adopted by a young widow, named Sitole, of the wolf clan.

Sitole took my tattered cassock and presented me with her dead husband's beaded moccasins, his breechclout, a five-point trade blanket, a bear lance, two bows and a dozen iron-tipped arrows, and a complete set of polished stone woodworking tools.

The next day I was made a civil chief, or royaneur, of the tribe and given the name (which had also previously belonged to Sitole's husband) Plenty of Fish.

Nickbis admired my moccasins and said to watch out that I didn't get my paint brush caught in the honey pot, a turn of phrase I did not at once comprehend. Nickbis had also been adopted but by an old man whose wife had died in childbirth, leaving him with twin girls to bring up.

Indeed, as I began to get about and observe things, I came to realize that more than half the Anderhoroneron population consisted of prisoners taken in war: Passamaquoddy, Mississaugua, Nanticoke, Mahican, Winnebago, Tutelo, Delaware, Sioux, Chippewa, Maqua, Cree, Arapaho, etc., and enough French, English and Dutch to make a small inter-denominational congregation for Sunday service. The rag-tag war party we had encountered at our camp on the St. Lawrence River was the entire military strike force remaining to this once thronging nation.

To tell the truth, I have never felt so welcome as I did living with Sitole among the Anderhoronerons.

I took my duties as a tribal chief seriously from the beginning, sitting up many a night before the fire, smoking tobacco and sipping trade brandy (called "darling water" or "spirit helper" by the savages), discussing local political issues with the other head men (and warrant I would have had a notable impact on their history had it not been for the language barrier which made it difficult for all but one or two of us to understand each other).

Sitole's cornfields were ripening beyond the stockade and required little attention. We lolled together day after day, naked under the summer sun, in a nearby creek, and I even began to sketch and paint a little, taking classical subjects such as Leda and the swan (for which I substituted a wild goose Sitole was raising for the pot), the judgement of Paris, Venus at her bath, that sort of thing.

Within a month, she was with child. (Nickbis, who was called Mother Nickbis by the Anderhoronerons, scowled at the news and said we ought to be thinking harder about escape.)

Instead, I learned to hunt, finding myself adept at tracking deer and bear in the nearby forests, though I hardly needed to as the savages were more than happy to trade me supplies of meat for portraits which I rendered on stretched doeskin with paints Sitole helped me manufacture from herbs and minerals. In short, by first frost, there wasn't a longhouse in the village without an original Pommier hanging in the place of glory.

At midwinter, I helped the Anderhoronerons kill the white dog and myself ate of its heart. I joined the Little Water Medicine Society and participated in the ancient dream-guessing rites and laughed uproariously at the antics of the False Face dancers.

But as the winter wore on food became scarce, the deer no longer rushed to impale themselves upon my arrow points. Sitole was forced to cut my beloved paintings into strips and boil them with tree roots to make a soup. One by one, the old people began to die. Nickbis Agsonbare's husband was the first to go despite my old friend's valiant efforts to keep him alive.

The last day of February, our son (Adelbert Pommier Adaqua'at) was born. I baptized him and said Mass and we ate the last of the pictures (Venus-Sitole admiring herself in a hand-mirror) in celebration of his name-day, inviting as many of the neighbours as could fit into our home to join us.

That night a stranger stumbled into the village, a half-starved white man, burning with fever and covered with festering boils. He had come, he said, because he had heard there was a Black Robe, or priest, among the Anderhoronerons, and he wished to receive absolution before dying. As I made the sign of the cross on his forehead, I recognized the face of young Boisvert, my former student, Arlette's husband, now aged and deformed beyond belief.

The next day Boisvert died. Within a week, half the Anderhoronerons followed him. The other half fled into the forest where most of these starved or froze to death. Sitole went mad with the fever and drowned herself in the icy creek where the summer before we had been wont to dally. Adelbert expired in my arms one or two days later. I don't know when exactly, for I carried him about for a week without noticing while I nursed the sick.

Nickbis Agsonbare and I were spared, God alone knows why.

We knelt in the centre of the village, surrounded by corpses, for two days and nights, singing our death songs to no avail. Then we set fire to the place and started off together on foot, heading west, away from New France, toward the Anderhoroneron Land of the Dead.

The Mother of the World

The epoch of martyrs and apostles was passing. My own great works were behind me. Many of the best people I called friend were in the grave. My hemorrhoids were chronic and most of my teeth had broken off as a consequence of gravel in the native cornmeal.

Nickbis and I wandered among the Far Indians for a year (indeed, I saw my first beaver that winter near Fond du Lac, a small juvenile afflicted with mange which was immediately clubbed to death by a local hunter and sold for a cup of inferior brandy), then made our desolate return to Boucherville.

In my absence, the village had swelled to a dozen log hovels all sinking into the spring mud at a great rate. A horde of infants, barely toddlers, the hope and future of Canada, raced shrieking up and down the street, tormenting the hogs and fighting with them for scraps of food. Raw-cheeked housewives screamed at each other over their laundry tubs.

There was a letter from the bishop waiting for me at my pig-barn manse.

Once more, His Worship complained (in that pious tone he affected), I had proved lazy and inattentive to my priestly duties. I had failed to begin construction of a church, had performed no marriages, baptisms, burials, sick-bed visitations, etc., in the past year, and had neglected to send my annual letters to the Minister and the Papal Legate. I was to remove immediately to Sorel, a problem parish downriver, where I would surely learn the necessary lessons of discipline and humility.

At Sorel, I built an Indian house and sweat lodge at the edge of the village, a hermitage where I passed my days in solitude, ignoring my parishioners who I felt certain would find something to complain about no matter what I did. The bishop heard of it and had me moved again.

This happened more times than I care to remember. The years were trammelled with uprootings, forced marches, and fresh failures.

It was in Sorel that I began work on a definitive French-Anderhoroneron dictionary and an illustrated treatise on native customs, with my memoirs to follow. These documents, along with my notes and sketches, were lost when a bateau loaded with my belongings foundered off the Beauport shore during a subsequent transfer.

At Île d'Orléans, Nickbis caught a head cold and went off in a day, without a whimper.

At Lévis, I drank myself into stupors between weddings and confessions, until my health broke from too much adulterated brandy. Since then, I have lived on a diet of water and sagamite, a sort of Indian porridge.

(They say that God tempers the souls of His artists with suffering that their works might speak to the ages. I think it more likely He means to muffle them.)

A month ago I was recalled from domestic exile to paint another saintly corpse, that of Mother Marie de l'Incarnation of the Ursulines, my last full-scale portrait in oils while in Canada.

The mourners had just lowered the old trout into her grave and were about to nail down the coffin lid when everyone noticed a radiance emanating from within which could only have been of divine origin. Eager to record this miracle for posterity and against the Sulpicians, the bishop ordered the body exhumed and sent his man Houssart to fetch me and my paint box (they had to consult their records to discover what distant pulpit they had last assigned to me).

But Mother Marie had died suddenly of a gastric blockage, and I could see well enough that the illusion of radiance resulted more from putrefaction of the gut than saintliness of spirit. Nevertheless, I put onions up my nose and stretched the job out as long as possible since His Worship rarely allowed me to visit the capital.

Working from memory, I painted Sitole naked, with her hands upraised in the centre of the Anderhoroneron village, with the sun shining down and a garland of lilies and marigolds in her hair. I put Adelbert at her knee and myself next to them in my Indian clothes, my face painted half-red, half-black, the sign of the Whirlwind from which the Anderhoroneron say we are descended.

I called it *The Mother of the World* and signed it H. Pommier-Plenty of Fish.

Then I painted Mother Marie over top of Sitole, in the grand manner just the way Frère Luc would have done, with a halo like a China plate behind her wimple, a great wen on her chin, a pious squint, a bit of needlepoint in her hand, and that mysterious radiance which was nothing more than Sitole and the Anderhoroneron sun coming through.

I blacked the background and put in a narrow cruciform window such as the sisters had in their cells, a Sacred Heart, and a Bible on a lectern with little beaver tails for bookmarks.

It was a third-rate portrait (I didn't bother to sign it) much admired in the colony, though the bishop noticed the beaver tails which he chose to regard as a satirical interpolation and evidence of my spiritual incorrigibility.

It was on account of the beaver tails that His Worship finally lost patience with me and ordered me back to France.

One evening, while I was still engaged on the *Mother Marie*, I paid a call on Mistress Arlette Boisvert and we wept an hour together for our youth (she with eight children and a ne'er-do-well shipwright she called Bo-Bo for a husband).

She had a boy, she said, who took much after me and could draw like an angel. She had apprenticed him to a stone mason so he could learn to make his living carving religious images.

The next day I went to see the boy in the stone-yard next to Our Lady. He had my eyes and the long arm- and leg-bones that gave me my awkward grasshopper look. I asked to see his work, and he showed me a gargoyle he was doing for the transept roof. Then I asked to see the work he loved.

He gazed at me thoughtfully for a moment then swept the marble dust from a sheaf of drawings.

There were eight Mary Magdalenes in crayon, five or six Annunciations, a Holy Family, an Adam and Eve in a Garden populated with moose and beaver, and a copy of my *Martyre* which he said he had seen while working inside the Hôtel Dieu basement with his master. All the female subjects were from the same model, a girl just past puberty, half-Indian by the look of her cheekbones and hair, with breasts like brown hen's eggs and large pale nipples.

He himself had posed for the Adam.

Notes

EDNA ALFORD was born in Turtleford, Saskatchewan in 1947, and now resides in Livelong. In 1974 she was co-founder of *Dandelion* magazine in Calgary. Her story collections include *A Sleep Full of Dreams* and *The Garden of Eloise Loon*. She has received the Gerald Lampert Memorial Award (League of Canadian Poets, 1981) and the Marian Engel Award (Writers Development Trust, 1988).

DAVID ARNASON is an editor, freelance writer, critic and professor of Canadian literature and creative writing at St. John's College in Winnipeg. He is the author of *Marsh Burning, The Icelander, 50 Stories and a Piece of Advice, The Circus Performers Bar* and *The Happiest Man in the World*.

PETER BEHRENS was born in 1954 in Montreal where he attended Concordia and McGill. In 1985-86 he held the Wallace Stegner Fellowship in Creative Writing at Stanford University. His stories have been published widely in literary journals and in *Saturday Night* and *Atlantic Monthly*. His first collection of stories was *Night Driving*.

DIONNE BRAND is a Toronto writer who was born in the Caribbean. She has published five books of poetry: *'Fore Day Morning, Earth Magic, Winter Epigrams and Epigrams to Ernesto Cardenal in Defense of Claudia, Primitive Offensive,* and *Chronicles of the Hostile Sun*. Her non-fiction includes *Rivers Have Sources Trees Have Roots — Speaking of Racism,* and *Lives of Black Working Women in Ontario — An Oral History*. Her first story collection is *Sans Souci*; her latest title is *No Language Is Neutral*.

LOIS BRAUN was born in Winkler, Manitoba in 1949. She now lives in Altona, Manitoba, where she teaches elementary school. Her first collection of short stories, *A Stone Watermelon*, was nominated for the 1986 Governor-General's Award for fiction. A second collection titled *The Pumpkin-Eaters* was published in 1990. Lois Braun is fiction editor of *Dateline: Arts*. Her story "The Pumpkin Eaters" was nominated for the Journey Prize in 1989.

MARY BURNS lives in Vancouver. Her stories have been published widely in the literary magazines and collected as *Suburbs of the Arctic Circle*, published by Penumbra Press.

SHARON BUTALA was born in Nipawin, Saskatchewan. She has written two volumes of a trilogy of novels, *Gates of the Sun* and *Luna*; the third volume, titled *The Fourth Archangel*, is in progress. Her first collection of stories, *Queen of the Headaches*, was nominated for a Governor-General's Award. *Fever*, a collection of short stories, was released in the fall of 1990.

BRIAN FAWCETT is the author of four books of short fiction, *Capital Tales, My Career With the Leafs, The Secret Journal of Alexander Mackenzie*, and *Cambodia: A Book for People Who Find Television Too Slow*. His most recent work is *Public Eye*.

CYNTHIA FLOOD lives in Vancouver where she teaches English at a community college. Since 1970 she has been active in the women's movement and left-wing politics. Her stories have been published in numerous periodicals and anthologies. Her first collection of stories was *The Animals in Their Elements*. She was the 1990 winner of the Journey Prize.

BILL GASTON grew up in Winnipeg, Toronto and Vancouver. In 1989 he published his first short story collection, *Deep Cove Stories*, and in 1990 a novel, *Tall Lives*.

DOUGLAS GLOVER was born and raised on a tobacco farm in southwestern Ontario. He has published two story collections, *The Mad River* and *Dog Attempts to Drown Man in Saskatoon*, and two novels, *Precious* and *The South Will Rise at Noon*. His stories have been reprinted in *Best Canadian Stories* (1985, 1987, 1988) and *Best American Short Stories* (1989). His story "Story Carved in Stone" won a 1990 National Magazine Award.

STEPHEN GUPPY was born in Nanaimo on Vancouver Island. He has published a book of poems, *Ghostcatcher*, and co-edited, with Ron Smith, *Rainshadow: Stories from Vancouver Island*. His first story collection was *Another Sad Day at the Edge of the Empire*.

ERNEST HEKKANEN lives in Vancouver. He has published two collections of stories, *Medieval Hour in the Author's Mind* and *The Violent Lavender Beast*.

JANICE KULYK KEEFER lives in Eden Mills, Ontario. Her writings include a novel, *Constellations*, as well as two books of criticism, *Reading Mavis Gallant* and *Under Eastern Eyes: A Critical Reading of Maritime Fiction*, and three collections of short fiction, *The Paris-Napoli Express, Transfigurations*, and *Travelling Ladies*. Her first poetry collection was *White of the Lesser Angels*.

DANIEL DAVID MOSES is a Delaware Indian from near Brantford, Ontario. He has an MFA in Creative Writing. His most recent publications are a play, *Coyote City* (Williams-Wallace), and *The White Line*, poems (Fifth House).

MARLENE NOURBESE PHILIP, a poet, writer and lawyer who lives in Toronto, was born in Trinidad and Tobago. She has published three books of poetry; the manuscript collection, *She Tries Her Tongue; Her Silence Softly Breaks*, was awarded the 1988 Casa de las Americas Prize. Her first novel, *Harriet's Daughter* (1988), was short-listed for the 1989 Toronto Book Awards. In 1990 she was made a Guggenheim Fellow in Poetry.

CAROL SHIELDS was born and raised in Chicago and now lives in Winnipeg. Her novels include *Small Ceremonies, The Box Garden, Swann*, and *A Fairly Conventional Woman*, as well as stories collected as *Various Miracles* and *The Orange Fish*. *Swann* won the Arthur Ellis Award for the best mystery in 1988.

GLEN SORESTAD is a Saskatoon writer, publisher and editor. His work includes short fiction pieces, many of which have been broadcast, and a number of poetry collections, notably *Ancestral Dances* (1979) and *Hold the Rain in Your Hands* (1985). *Air Canada Owls* (Nightwood Editions) appeared in 1990 and *West Into Night* is slated for publication in 1991 by Thistledown Press.

YESHIM TERNAR was born in Istanbul, Turkey in 1956. Her fiction and poetry have been published widely in the United States, Canada and Europe. Her Ph.D. thesis, *The Book and the Veil*, is a critique of orientalism from a feminist perspective using a combination of fact and fiction. Her first collection of short stories, *Orphaned by Halley's Comet*, was published by Williams-Wallace in 1990.

LEANDRO URBINA came to Canada with the wave of refugees fleeing the brutal military regime in Chile. He studied at Carleton and completed his MA at Ottawa University. He is the editor of a volume of Chilean-Canadian fiction and author of the recent story collection, *Lost Causes*.

SEAN VIRGO lives in rural Ontario. He is a prize-winning poet; his fiction includes two collections of short stories, *White Lies* and *Wormwood*, and a novel, *Selahki*. A new story collection, *Waking in Eden*, appeared at the end of 1990.

DIANNE WARREN is a Regina fiction writer and playwright. Her first story collection is *The Wednesday Flower Man*, and her play, *Serpent in the Night Sky*, will premiere in Saskatoon in the spring of 1991.

Acknowledgements

Edna Alford. "The Garden of Eloise Loon" reprinted from the collection *The Garden of Eloise Loon* by permission of the publisher, Oolichan Books.

David Arnason. "Do Astronauts Have Sex Fantasies?" © David Arnason, from: *The Circus Performers' Bar*, Talon Books Ltd., Vancouver, Canada.

Peter Behrens. "Night Driving" from the collection *Night Driving* reprinted by permission of Macmillan of Canada, A Division of Canada Publishing Corporation.

Dionne Brand. "Blossom, Priestess of Oya, Goddess of winds, storms and waterfalls" published with the permission of Williams-Wallace Publishers. © Dionne Brand.

Lois Braun. "Dream of the Half-Man" from *A Stone Watermelon*, © Lois Braun, Turnstone Press, 1986. Reprinted by permission.

Mary Burns. "The Circle" originally published in *Suburbs of the Arctic Circle*, Penumbra Press, 1986.

Sharon Butala. "Queen of the Headaches" © Sharon Butala, from *Queen of the Headaches*, Coteau Press, 1985, 1986 and 1990.

Brian Fawcett. "The Franz Kafka Memorial Room", © 1986, Brian Fawcett, from *Cambodia: A Book for People Who Find Television Too Slow*, Talon Books Ltd., Vancouver, Canada.

Cynthia Flood. "Roses Are Red", © 1987, Cynthia Flood, from *The Animals in Their Elements*, Talon Books Ltd., Vancouver, Canada.

Bill Gaston. "The Forest Path to Malcolm's" reprinted from *Deep Cove Stories* by permission of the publisher, Oolichan Books.

Douglas Glover. "The Canadian Travel Notes of Abbé Hughes Pommier, Painter, 1663-1680" © Douglas Glover, reprinted by permission of the author.

Stephen Guppy. "Portrait of Helena Leafly, With Bees" reprinted from *Another Sad Day at the Edge of the Empire* by permission of the publisher, Oolichan Books.

Ernest Hekkanen. "The Mime" reprinted from *Medieval Hour in the Author's Mind* by permission of the publisher, Thistledown Press Ltd.

Janice Kulyk Keefer. "Passages" from *Transfigurations*, published by Ragweed Press, Charlottetown, PEI. © Janice Kulyk Keefer.

Daniel David Moses. "King of the Raft" © Daniel David Moses, 1990, reprinted by permission of the author.

Marlene Nourbese Philip. "Bad Words" first appeared in *border/lines*, Spring 1990. Copyright © Marlene Nourbese Philip, reprinted by permission of the author.

Glen Sorestad. "One Last Look in the Mirror" from *The Windsor Hotel Stories* is used with the author's permission.

Carol Shields. "Dolls, Dolls, Dolls, Dolls" from *Various Miracles*, is reprinted with the permission of the publisher, Stoddart Publishing, 34 Lesmill Rd., Don Mills, Ontario, Canada. The story first appeared in *Aurora* and was broadcast on CBC's "Anthology".

Yeshim Ternar. "Wedding Ninotchka" first appeared in *Canadian Fiction Magazine* and is reprinted by permission of the author. © Yeshim Ternar.

Leandro Urbina. "The Night of the Dogs" from *Lost Causes* published by Cormorant Books is reprinted by permission of the publisher.

Sean Virgo. "White Lies" © Sean Virgo, reprinted by permission of the author.

Dianne Warren. "How I Didn't Kill Wally Even Though He Deserves It" © Dianne Warren, from *The Wednesday Flower Man*, Coteau Books, 1987.

About the Editor

Geoff Hancock is an eminent Canadian scholar of the short story. He became the editor of *Canadian Fiction Magazine* in 1974, and since then has evaluated over 20,000 manuscripts and worked with Canada's most renowned authors. His special knowledge of the form and his feel for current movements and trends make him an ideal commentator. He has extensive experience as a workshop leader and speaker and has provided guidance from a writer's as well as an editor's perspective to a large variety of creative writing groups.

He is the author of *Canadian Writers at Work: Interviews with Geoff Hancock* (Oxford, 1987), and a forthcoming history of small presses in Canada, *Published in Canada*, from Black Moss Press. Geoff is also a contributor to *The Canadian Encyclopedia* and *The Oxford Companion to Canadian Literature*.

His critically-acclaimed anthologies include *Magic Realism* (Aya Press, 1980); *Illusions: fables, fantasies and metafictions* (Aya, 1983); *Metavisions* (Quadrant, 1983); *Shoes and Shit: Stories for Pedestrians* (Aya, 1984); *Moving off the Map* (Black Moss, 1986); and *Invisible Fictions: Contemporary Stories of Quebec* (Anansi, 1987).

Geoff Hancock was born in New Westminster, B.C., in 1946. He earned a BFA and MFA in Creative Writing at the University of British Columbia in the 1970s. He now lives in Stratford, Ontario.